BLADE BEARER

BOOK 2 IN THE RISEN AGE ARCHIVE

REBECCA P. MINOR

REALM MAKERS

For permissions, please send your request to contact@rebeccapminor.com

Printed in the United States of America

Realm Makers Media

939 N Washington St

Pottstown, PA 19464

Cover art by Kirk DouPonce, DogEared Design

www.dogeareddesign.com

For the ladies of Spec Haven, who have always had words of encouragement ready when I repeatedly hit the point where I doubted I could write this book.

PROLOGUE

No one threw a High Priest of Queldurik into his own fires of sacrifice and lived to boast of it. Not an Elgadrim knight. Not even an elf warrior. Least of all, a witless girl. And yet, Ba-al Zechmaat, fiend overlord of the Garashean temple, struggled to his feet amidst flame, ash, and bone. He roared in wordless indignation. His fury echoed from the three-story stone walls of the sacrifice pit that towered above him.

The flames that raged along the pit's floor licked over his flesh, familiar, but comfortless. Zechmaat disentangled himself from the last loop of chain around his foot. Despite his broken wing's searing protests, he slammed his talons into the wall and sent chips of obsidian flying in a pelting spray. He hauled his weight, one shuddering arm length at a time, away from the bottom of the moat of flame that ringed the altar platform. The strain of the climb threatened to unravel what remained of his composure.

Plagues upon the weaknesses I endure while I linger on this mortal plane.

A temple guard wearing a steel skull mask peered over the edge of the pit. "Your Eminence, can I assist you?"

Even from a full story below, Ba-al Zechmaat detected the tremor that ran through the guard's body. "Assist me, you simp? How about this? Find them!"

"With all due respect, my liege . . . find who?"

Idiot humans and their ceaseless questions. What did the almighty Queldurik see in them?

"Imbecile. The Elgadrim dog and his little decoys." Zechmaat snarled. "Catch the insolent thieves. Drag them back to me. Then strap them to these pitted idols and slow roast them until their flesh falls from their bones."

A red-robed priest joined the first guard at the pit's edge. He extended a length of rope and made ready to toss it to Ba-al Zechmaat.

"Don't bother." Zechmaat heaved his way up the final two fathoms of the wall.

At the far end of the chamber, a cluster of three gaping acolytes huddled at the main exit. They parted when another ebony-skinned fiend, akin to Zechmaat in gnashing visage but smaller in stature, shouldered through the group and into the chamber.

Stretching to his nine-foot height before the guard, Zechmaat snatched a fistful of the petrified servant's tunic, then lifted the man to address him nose-to-nose. "How is it you did not see, you steaming pile of dung? Was it you who admitted a Knight of the Phoenix to the temple?"

"He . . . the knight . . . Your Eminence—he was disguised." The salty tang of fear emanated from the guard's flesh. His breath echoed against his mask in erratic gasps. He glanced down to the priest. "It was a powerful deception, was it not?"

The priest stood mute, holding the rope in white knuckles.

The lesser fiend stomped to Zechmaat's side. "And it was your duty to notice such disguises! You're not even worth the fuel it will take to burn you."

Zechmaat wheeled a scathing glare on the second fiend.

"And just where have *you* been, Hilekar? Or did you dismiss the clash of weapons as no cause for concern?"

Hilekar lifted his chin. "The doors were subject to a fixing spell. It took me until moments ago to break it."

The guard clutched at Zechmaat's wrist. "Your Dark Eminence, the infidels did nothing to diminish Queldurik's majesty. No need to get—"

"No need?" In a single thrust, Zechmaat flung the guard into the pit behind him.

The man's scream ended in a fleshy *thud*. Acolytes in the doorway stood wide-eyed as the welcome aroma of charring flesh reached Zechmaat's nose. The fool of a guard had met his rightful end.

"Are you blind to what's happened?" Zechmaat ripped the empty scabbard from his back and dashed it to the floor. *Blind to what* will *happen when Almighty Queldurik learns of this failure?*

The priest shifted his attention from the edge of the fiery moat and turned a frown on the scabbard. His jaw tightened.

Zechmaat drew a breath, ran a hand over the curvature of his left horn, and quieted his rage. He extended his awareness until the priest's thoughts echoed in his own mind.

The sword you shouldn't have been wearing in the first place, you swaggering . . . ?

Zechmaat belted the priest with a balled fist before the man had time to blink. He crumpled to the black stone floor with a misshapen cheekbone, a blank stare, and blood flowing from his ear.

"Hilekar." Zechmaat spoke softly. "If this fool regains consciousness, flay him." He paced and rubbed his tense brow for a few strides. "Deploy hounds. Perform Incantations of Seeing on the falcons—we will learn which way they've run."

"Shall I report their location and heading to you, O Great One?" Hilekar asked.

"No," Zechmaat grumbled. "I dare not leave the Almighty's

temple in the hands of such incompetent men as these. As soon as we have a notion of the thieves' location, you will lead the group to capture them. Haste!" He thrust a clawed forefinger toward the door.

Zechmaat turned and marched for his chambers, and though every stride sent shocks of pain through his weary body, he poured great effort into masking his limp. He fumed. Hissing breaths streamed through his gritted teeth.

The heady Radromirian girl would soon discover the bitter price of her mission. Save her precious Papa? Pfah! At Zechmaat's hand, she would learn the true meaning of suffering.

1

Not Fast Enough

$\mathcal{D}$anae Baledric heaved for breath, her palms pressed against her knees. The Tebalese tundra offered too little air for her laboring lungs. Her glance swept the barren expanse. The deepening twilight was treacherous, slowly stealing any hope her untrained eye had of spotting horsemen who might be in pursuit.

Might be. Danae scoffed. Of course they were scouring every league between herself and the temple in Garash. The Sword would draw them like vultures to carrion.

Danae hitched the Sword of Creo's Patron higher on her shoulder, but the improvised scabbard her friends had fashioned from a woolen blanket and some rope made the five-foot blade unwieldy cargo at best. The rope shoulder strap ground against her collarbone, and Danae found no spot she could bear the Sword's weight that was not already rubbed raw. She winced and straightened her aching spine. Wisps of hair that had worked free of her braid stuck to the slick of sweat that ran down her cheeks. At least that eliminated their tickling nuisance as they fluttered in the tundra wind.

"Danae! Are you unwell?" Culduin called to her from at least three dozen strides away. His light footfalls approached from the rear, followed by the heavier jangling Praesidio made as he ran.

Danae sucked a few more breaths. No matter that she and her companions had been running all day, they would run into the night as well. The elf and the old knight of the Elgadrim slowed to a stop at her side. Neither seemed particularly winded.

Danae had come to accept Culduin's seemingly inexhaustible physical resources, assuming them to be part of what made elves live so extraordinarily long. As for the pace Praesidio kept, running like a man a quarter his age, it just seemed unfair.

Culduin intercepted her glance. "Are you in need?" He examined her face and furrowed his brow.

"I'm fine," she said. "Don't I look it?" The corner of her lip pulled crooked in a tired smirk.

Culduin tucked his copper waves of hair back over his ear points and bound a leather lace around them. "It is insensitive of me to expect elven endurance of you." He placed a light palm on Danae's back. "My mind is bent too much upon haste."

She flinched. Could he tell how disgustingly sweaty she was under the cloak and tunic she wore?

"You've been plenty sensitive in allowing me to set the pace." Danae met Culduin's clear, blue-eyed glance. Just behind him, a cool glow caught her attention and drew her focus over his shoulder.

Culduin turned.

In the failing light, luminescent fronds of a plant clung to a jutting rock behind the elf. The alchemist's apprentice within her sparked to life, eclipsing her fatigue. Surely she had never labeled any jar in Papa's shop that held an herb like this. She stepped around Culduin for a closer look.

Between breaths that steamed in frosty clouds, Danae pulled a dagger from her bandolier, then applied it to the roots of the fronds, reverent of their snowflake intricacy.

"What have you found?" Culduin asked.

"I'm only guessing." She sawed gently at her specimen and detached it from the stone. "But I think it's a lichen that's specific to tundra. I read about something like it in one of Papa's books about antidotes."

Praesidio mopped his brow and laughed. "Your father's inquisitive thirst for herb and ore has taken quite a root in you."

A dart of worry pricked Danae's heart. For all of their collective inquisitiveness, Papa's peril had not diminished. In fact, it increased with every moment she dared linger. Neither had her brother Tristan's situation likely improved. She sawed faster.

Once Danae detached the specimen from the rock, its glow faded away. She frowned but tucked it into her smallest belt pouch anyway.

"Are you able to press on?" Culduin asked.

"We really should travel another two hours, at minimum," Praesidio added.

The thought of another two hours of running made Danae want to cry, but she swallowed the protest. "Well, if *you* can keep going like this, I certainly had better be able to." She wriggled her parched tongue against the roof of her mouth.

Praesidio rubbed the white stubble on his chin. "Are you calling me old?"

"Mostly I'm calling myself pathetic, given the difference in our ages."

Culduin smoothed a lock of hair back from her cheek. "The

count of our years does not fully define us." He pulled a water-skin from his belt and uncorked it. "Since I cannot offer rest just yet, at least take a drink while we have stopped. You need not suffer in silence."

"Silence?" She chuckled. "I'm puffing so loud that Ba-al Zechmaat's underlings could track us by my panting alone." Danae gathered another handful of the glowing plant, less delicately, now that she knew careful removal still extinguished the light.

The shrill cry of a bird of prey caught Danae's ear, and she tipped her chin skyward to seek it against a backdrop of stars.

"Speaking of tracking . . ." Praesidio glared into the blackness overhead.

"That clinches it in my mind," Culduin said.

"Clinches what?" Danae resheathed her dagger. The sudden tension in both Culduin and Praesidio's faces filled her limbs with jitters.

Praesidio drew back his hood. "That's the third hawk I've heard tonight."

"The fourth for me," Culduin said.

Danae's attention volleyed between her companions. "And that means something?"

"There is no species of wild night hawk native to Tebal." Culduin pursed his lips. "We have lingered longer than we can afford."

Danae readjusted the five-foot Sword again. How the blade seemed to have tripled in weight since she had taken on its burden just a few short hours ago. She grimaced.

"I can bear the Sword if you would like." Culduin reached out a hand. "And you have not yet taken a drink."

She accepted the skin and poured a small mouthful from it. "You've carried the Sword more than both Praesidio and me . . . combined." Danae returned Culduin's water. Did he hear the hint of protest that had crept into her voice?

"Please, allow me to serve you in this way," Culduin said softly. "My height makes it a lesser burden."

Plausible, since he stood more than a head taller than Danae. She contemplated his offer for a moment. The weapon dragged on her like a prisoner's weights.

The raptor's cry echoed in the distance.

Danae squeezed her eyes shut against a dull pressure that swelled behind them. Embers of dread flared in her stomach. She pulled the Sword from her back and handed it to Culduin. "We'll be faster if you carry it, I suppose."

Once Culduin settled the Sword's bundle across his shoulders, he stretched just a fraction taller, and a resolute look settled into his eyes and jaw. "This is best. Off we go." He turned to once again run a southerly course.

Praesidio tightened the straps on his pack over his gray cloak and heavy robes, his gaze fixed on Culduin all the while.

"What?" Danae pondered the tightness around Praesidio's eyes.

With a slight shake of his head, he replied, "Now is not the time for words. Keep up as best you can."

Just minutes into the next leg of running, Danae's heart resumed a dizzying rhythm. The landscape transformed from one of seemingly endless flatness to a region of rises and falls, with islands of rock jutting at irregular intervals. Every ascent up the rocky slopes left Danae panting for air.

The moon rode higher in the sky and bathed the landscape in shades of blue, with harsh black shadows beneath the tufts of diamond-leaf, caribou moss, and bearberry. Danae struggled to lift her heavy feet clear of the low flora. Her eyelids drooped.

In a confused moment where the world suddenly whirled on a shifting axis, Danae crashed to the frozen ground with a rattle of teeth and a clatter of equipment. A fiery sting radiated from her left hand. Bright spots danced across her vision.

"Stupid slate. I must have tripped," she grumbled. She tugged her glove off the hand that had landed first. A scrape on the heel of her palm wept red. She put the wounded skin in her mouth.

In the moment of quiet, devoid of her tramping feet and jingling pack, a low throb reached her ears. Its quality was reminiscent of twenty distant drums, beating at odds with one another.

Praesidio turned back first, who then grabbed Culduin's sleeve. They both rushed to Danae's side.

"What's that sound?" Danae blinked away the motes in her vision.

Culduin paused, then snapped his attention to the northeast, back the way they had come. "Look!"

"Maybe if I had an elf's eyesight," Danae said. "What do you—"

"Hush!" Praesidio squinted the same direction as the elf. "I hear . . ." His face blanched. "Hoofbeats."

Dread filled Danae's stomach. Not even Culduin could outrun hunters on horseback.

"A score of horses!" Culduin said. He put out a hand to Danae. "Are you hurt?"

The revelation swept away Danae's weariness in a surge of panic. She clasped Culduin's hand and accepted his offer of help to her feet. "Hardly. What do we do?"

"Once they found our heading, we knew it wouldn't be long before they caught up to us," Praesidio said.

"Right. So what's our plan?" Danae swallowed against the tightness in her throat.

Praesidio and Culduin exchanged uneasy glances.

"You mean we've been running for two days with no idea what we'd do when Queldurik's lunatics closed in?" Danae shrilled.

"We had hoped to make the cover of the canyon to prevent anyone from sighting us," Culduin said.

Praesidio blew out a heavy breath. "If we can be clever, we may yet lose them. Come, one more burst of fleetness." He waved them onward and broke into a long-striding run. "The canyon is still our best hope in this wasteland."

Danae and Culduin followed. "But . . . giant scorpions . . ." Danae blurted between searing breaths. "And who knows what else after dark!" She gritted her teeth against the manic quality of her voice.

"Better the worst of creatures than the swords of men," Culduin said.

Praesidio added, "Or the Curses of priests or Inquisitors."

The occasional rock formations and rolling hills worsened to a broken and tumbled maze of treacherous footing, compounded by the darkness. The terrain forced them to a slow jog, and still Culduin labored to choose a path free of hazards. Danae perked her ears for hoofbeats, fully expecting their low throb to grow to a thunderous pounding, but the sound never swelled. Instead, it diffused. The sudden walls of rock and uneven ground, coupled with poor light, cut off any hope Danae had of glimpsing their pursuers.

Danae staggered after her companions, up the steep face of a rise. As they crested the rocky hill, the lip of the great chasm—the canyon of Quel Mahaar—drew into sight, cut into shards of black and silver by the moonlight. A rough slope stretched before them, the last half-mile before they reached the canyon's edge.

Culduin slowed to a stop and flashed a smile back to Danae. "Here we are. The depths are nearly ours—"

"If we can get to them." Praesidio pointed to the southward stretch of the landscape between them and the canyon.

Danae stared the direction Praesidio indicated. There was no denying pursuit now. Eight horsemen closed upon their position from the southeast, and eight more thundered in from the southwest. Behind the southwestern group, three pony-sized canines loped. One of them bayed. The riders slowed their horses and advanced toward Danae's party, shrinking the gap between predator and prey.

2

Crumbling Cover

"They must have galloped to our flanks to cut us off from the canyon. *Cha-thrath!*" Culduin said.

"No need for incivility." Praesidio scowled.

Was he joking? The exact meaning of Culduin's words aside, this felt like a perfectly reasonable time to curse. Danae wrung her cloak and took stock of the riders.

Most of the Tebalese horsemen wore the shaggy cloaks and banded leather armor of soldiers. Boiled hide skullcap helms, edged in iron, covered most of their dreadlocked heads. All carried swords and quivers. Three wore the red-and-black robes of temple priests, and one came clad in both armor and robes. Despite the bright moonlight, the distance obscured any further details.

The rearmost figure of the group, the cowl of his sable robe shadowing his face, sent a prickling heat across Danae's skin.

That prickling can't be good.

A hawk's cry screeched above the hissing wind, and a great

falcon dropped from the sky. It perched on the sable-robed pursuer's shoulder.

"I think he's a huntsman," Danae said.

"The hawk and the hounds support your guess," Praesidio said.

She took a faltering step backward, then searched the landscape behind them. No place to hide that way. Taking a stand was suicide.

The riders reined their shaggy, dun-colored horses and assembled in two lines, leaving a fifteen-pace break between them, as if to dare the travelers to try a dash through.

"His hood's not deep enough to hide the maw of a dragonkin." Culduin eyed the falconer.

Praesidio's voice came in a low rumble. "There are worse creatures in Queldurik's service."

Even from the full quarter mile that stood between the horsemen and Danae, a palpable sense of malicious evil emanated from them like a foul stench. Yes, something about this huntsman was different from the reptilian beast who had pursued her before.

"Follow me!" Culduin darted back down the rise and to the west.

Danae fumbled after Culduin, but the stone-littered path and the silty footing slowed her pace. Whoops from the Tebalese horsemen and the hounds' barking echoed off the rocks like the brash notes of horns.

"Where are we going?" Danae yelled.

"Something I saw on the way up. A small chance." At the bottom of the rise, Culduin turned to follow a long-dry streambed.

The course of the streambed deepened as it wandered onward, until the simple gully grew to a narrow gorge. The farther they followed the streambed, the darker it became, until the world around Danae fell into shadow upon deeper shadow.

Culduin slowed to a stop, then scanned behind them with narrowed eyes.

"Through here." Culduin pointed into the blackness ahead. "Their horses have no hope of navigating this crack."

"But hounds will, and what if it's a dead end?" Danae's stomach threatened a revolt against overexertion.

Hoofbeats drummed, closing in.

Culduin grasped her shoulder. "We must deal with troubles as they come. I cannot know, but the likelihood of a watercourse running to a dead end is small."

An arrow whistled through the air and stuck in the ground by Praesidio's scraggly boot.

"If naught else, it'll provide cover." Praesidio plunged past Culduin, pulling Danae after him.

The defile's absolute darkness obliterated what little remained of Danae's vision. She groped her free hand in front of her. Praesidio's shuffling pace implied he, too, saw little or nothing. Danae barked her knee on a jutting rock, and she bit back a cry.

"Here," Culduin whispered in the darkness. He took Danae by the elbow. "I can lead you both. Just a bit deeper in."

The pursuing hoofbeats thundered somewhere behind Danae. Culduin guided her on a winding course she could only assume steered her around obstacles. The strength of Culduin's grasp steadied Danae's careening panic, until overhead, the raptor shrieked again. Her chest constricted.

"Blast that bird," Praesidio muttered.

Culduin stopped and released Danae's arm. His bow creaked, close by, and the hiss of an arrow sped off.

The falcon's next cry ended in a squawk.

"A shame, really," Culduin said. "Such a fine bird put to ill use." He slipped his arm around Danae's once again. "On we go."

They inched their way through the narrow cleft in the rock for a dozen paces more. Above, voices called to one another.

"Keep the hounds up here," someone bawled in Tebalese. "No use hitting them too."

The distinctive *whoosh* of arrows descended upon them, and Culduin shoved Danae to the side.

"Stay down!" he said.

Lights flared in the gorge. Danae blinked her dazzled eyes. A half-dozen flaming arrows stuck at intervals along the cleft floor. Culduin covered his eyes and grimaced.

"Culduin!" Praesidio yelled. "Take cover."

A series of mechanical twangs chattered from above, and more missiles rained down. Culduin twisted out of the path of one of the incoming bolts, but a second sank into his shoulder. He grunted and spun around the rock Danae used for cover. The barb stuck too deep to pluck from the wound in a hurry.

Danae craned to see the edge of the cleft, but she could glimpse little more than shifting shadows against the night sky. Certainly not enough to take any kind of aim. No use sacrificing her few daggers to wasted shots. What she could not see, however, she could feel. A thorny onslaught that raked over her skin warned her that the slavering and snarling beasts above were indeed Hounds of Queldurik. Three hounds dashed along the lip of the gorge. Their cursed presence tormented her. Her flesh teemed with it.

Culduin fitted another arrow to his string. He pulled back with his wounded arm and growled through his teeth. Sweat streamed down his forehead. The moment after he sent the arrow skyward, a cry of pain rang out from the higher ground, confirming his aim.

Danae pressed her palm against her temple. Was there a Virtus she could employ in time to be of some use? How well could she target an enemy she could not truly see? Would the phrases she knew from her father's notes still work, or were they really Curses? So much of how Creo's Virtusen worked remained outside her knowledge.

The clacking of gears announced the Tebalese had reset their crossbows, and after a single shout, another volley of ammunition streamed down. Many of the bolts either stuck in the dirt or skittered off rocks. One grazed a rip in Danae's sleeve. She huddled tighter to the boulder in front of her. A quick glance assured Danae she remained unwounded, but the edges of the tear bore an oily green stain. An acrid scent tainted the air.

A thousand miles from home, and here she was, cornered by Queldurik's zealots just like she had been in her father's apothecary. The sting of helpless fury blew away Danae's fear. She checked on Culduin, whose face had shifted from its usual warm glow to an ashen pallor. He grimaced with every move of his wounded arm. Something about this bolt challenged even his measure of toughness.

Danae took a quick sniff of her own sleeve. The acrid odor from before originated here, strong enough to sting her nose. *Poison.* It did not take an alchemist's apprentice to venture that guess.

The first flaming arrows to plunge into the defile burned low, so the Tebalese sent another wave. In that moment, Praesidio burst out in a loud chant. An updraft of wind ripped through the gorge and sent the arrows back toward their shooters, and astonished outbursts broke out amidst them. The arrows landed in the brush above, kindling some to flame.

"Work your way deeper in," Culduin said between shots. "We're still too exposed here."

A little light to work by. Danae smirked. On the run to the next hiding spot, she readied a dagger, now that she could target a few of their attackers. But another volley of crossbow bolts sent her for full cover before she could take aim.

"Leave the fighting to us," Praesidio said. "You must get *certain things* farther from these enemies. *Albetrechne, sule tintaerna!*"

A flare of light swelled around the knight, and from it

streaked a column of blue-white energy. The column slammed into the frontmost Tebalese warrior, enveloped him, and broke into spokes of light that collided with the pursuers around him. Their mouths gaped, but any screams they might have uttered produced only silence. The first opponent erupted in a cloud of ash that crumbled to the ground and left no recognizable trace of him. The others around the ash heap collapsed, pale flames licking their hair and clothes.

Danae sheathed her dagger. *Right. I guess Praesidio and Culduin have this under control.*

In the momentary pause that followed Praesidio's assault, Culduin flung the Sword bundle Danae's direction. She scooped it up and ducked to the next outcropping of rock in the defile. Slipping the burden back over her shoulder, she eased backward around the bulge of stone.

Culduin let another arrow fly, which caught a robed enemy in the chest. The man fell forward, tipped over the edge of the chasm, and landed with an ugly crunch on the floor of the gully. Danae took another step back. The victim's spiked steel gauntlet on his right hand marked him as an Inquisitor, a warrior priest of Queldurik, and even with an arrow in his ribs, Danae preferred not to risk a confrontation with him.

Her foot slipped backward when she put it down, as the silt gave way beneath her heel. She scrambled to recover her balance, but the footing continued to drain from beneath her. Before she could muster anything more than a gasp, the ground around her collapsed with a gritty crunch, and down she plummeted, into blind darkness.

3

Darkness and Lights

*D*anae rediscovered her voice when she bounced from a jagged obstacle. Her right shoulder collided with something unyielding as stone, and it knocked her into a spinning fall. Her hip smashed against more rock. No amount of flailing or searching with arms or legs slowed the descent. Had she stepped over the lip of the canyon? No, there would at least be moonlight. Here, there was only blackness and descent.

Her back crashed into another painful barrier, and this time, her head knocked against it in a secondary jolt. Flashes of brilliant color broke across her sightlessness, and a piercing tone filled her ears. She flipped forward. A fraction of a moment later, her whole body hit, chest first.

And kept falling. Slower, but breathless, black, and freezing.

No, she had not crashed onto a surface, but water. A wilder sense of panic seized Danae. Which way was up? The weight of her gear stymied any attempts at swimming, her buoyancy compromised. Her near-drowning in the Nuruhain had been terrifying enough. Here, without light, without river flotsam to grab, not only her traveling gear dragged her downward, but the cumbersome bulk of the Sword.

The wailing in her ears persisted, and the frigid water made her limbs sluggish in mere moments. She thrashed and fought the instinct to scream. For all her kicking and paddling, her sightless, watery nightmare dragged on.

If nothing else, her sinking slowed. But a crushing demand for air gripped her lungs. To come all this way and lose the Sword on the floor of some underground lake? To drown with it hauling her into unseen depths? Danae reached her arms toward what she hoped was up and pulled against the water. And again. Still, she did not breach the surface. The erratic throb of her heart joined the shrill tone in her ears.

Would Praesidio and Culduin be able to find her drowned body wherever she had fallen? Or would the hope of destroying the false god Queldurik wash away with her? Would anyone else figure out the truth of Papa's ailment? She tried to reach again, but numbness held her flesh captive. A flurry of bubbles poured from her mouth. *I'm sorry Creo, I can't . . .*

Sharp pain crushed her bicep, and another swirl of confusion hauled at her. Pale pinpricks of light rushed above her. The rumbling, indistinct drone of immersion shattered in violent splashes. Cold air swept over Danae's face.

She swiped at the streams of water running down her cheeks, fighting to clear her eyes. But still, she could see only a hazy cloud of blue motes nearby. She fought for a gasp of air, but her chest constricted, as though a giant wrung her out like a sodden rag.

Someone—or some*thing*—dragged her by her arm across pebbly ground. Again, her lungs convulsed for want of air, but this time, they erupted. Danae lay on her side. Shallow, frigid water lapped over her legs, and spasmodic coughing forced the rest of the liquid from her stomach and chest. The pitch in her ears receded to a persistent ringing. Her head, her shoulder, her hip throbbed, and the rest of her was soaked and freezing. Shivers more like a fit overcame her.

Where did the lights go? Were her eyes even open? She blinked and stretched them wide, but all that remained was unbroken darkness. Maybe she had gone blind. *Please, no.*

A series of shifting vocal pitches, punctuated by what sounded like tongue clucks and clicking came from Danae's left. The grate of small stones underscored the reality that she was not alone on the beach. Danae's scream snagged on a burst of hacking that seared her throat.

"Stay away!" she croaked through her distress. She scrambled to sit and flailed an arm toward the sound, clumsy and lethargic. With a fumbling grasp, she sought her bandolier for a dagger.

The gravel chattered again. A hundred tiny flares of bluish light swelled to life but blurred as they darted, in unison, to the side. Faint illumination danced over the watery tumult of a splash.

Danae wrenched a dagger free of its sheath and swung. The weapon cut only through air. Darkness overtook her once again as the points of light dissolved away, somewhere beneath the water's surface. She cringed, waiting.

Only deep quiet and a gentle trickling of water followed the splash. The sounds might have been soothing, were it not for the utter darkness, cold, and pain. Danae's pounding heart marked the passing time. The air smelled cold but green . . . of algae and wet stone.

She bent her knees and pulled her legs the rest of the way from the water. Her joints ached and fog clouded her mind. *Light. Warm up. Am I bleeding?*

She wriggled stiff fingers under the rope strap holding the Sword to her back. As she pulled the wet hemp over her head, it brushed her cheek, and she winced. Her skin burned. Even the lightest touch to her cheekbone proved the area already swelled. Danae pulled the strap as far from her face as possible to lift it over her head, and once she was free of the weight, she put the bundle partway under her seat where she could still feel its position.

She then shrugged off her pack and cloak. What a relief to drop the weight of sodden wool.

Still, her wet tunic and pants ushered the cool cavern air straight to her core. Her useless shivers demanded she shed the sopping fabric. One danger exchanged for another—with clothing, she would likely freeze. Without it, she was that much more vulnerable to monster bites or weapon blades.

At least the still cavern air carried less edge than the open tundra. She dropped her heavy cloak and peeled her tunic away. Tugged and twisted and fought the boots from her feet, then wriggled painfully from her trousers. The effort brought on a bout of vertigo that plunked her once again on her rear. Once her sense of pitch and yaw steadied, she cupped her hands over her mouth and exhaled warm breath.

She sat in the dark and rubbed her bare arms. What was that odd series of clicks she had heard before? No creature in Radromir made such sounds, at least not that she had ever heard. And what about the tiny lights? Were those just some phantom effect of hard knocks to her head? Or would some awful cave predator return with friends to share her in a quick meal?

A glimmer caught Danae's notice—or perhaps it was just a grasping hope of something other than directionless blackness. She focused where she thought she spied it. Yes, a faint and wobbling glow, but how far was it? It grew until it illuminated the walls of a rough stone tunnel. The light—no, lights, and not hundreds, but thousands, moved toward her in a cloud, just below the surface of the water. Danae scuttled back but soon bumped against a rock face.

The collective light of the underwater galaxies revealed a figure under the water. A woman swam toward Danae, and the tiny motes speckled the swimmer's cheekbones, forehead, and tips of flowing hair. The swimmer held some kind of illuminated orb before it, but the shifting reflections on the water's surface confused any details.

The orb broke the water's surface in a slender, pale hand. Soon after, the woman lifted her head and shoulders from the water.

Danae gaped. The swimmer who brought the orb had smooth skin, slicker in appearance than her own, and though the bluish light that radiated from a fascinating pattern on her face made other colors nondescript, Danae suspected the girl's complexion was whiter-than-human. Lavender hair hung in long, wet sheets, far down the swimmer's back. Each strand ended in a miniscule light, making the woman's hair appear scattered with stars.

She wore a woven garment, no wider than a scarf, that hung around her neck, crossed below her throat, then split to cover her pale breasts. Barely. She remained submerged up to her muscular belly.

I guess she won't care that I'm only in undergarments. Danae hunched. The swimmer's scant attire did not make her any more comfortable in her own half-naked state.

The girl opened her mouth and uttered a rapid series of sounds, some musical, others percussive. She held the lit stone out to Danae and blinked her extraordinarily large, tilted eyes. The irises shone in a silvery, iridescent dance, cold and bright like fish eyes.

Danae hesitated.

The swimmer frowned, clicked some more, and thrust the stone forward. *"Lumienne?"*

Lumienne. Light-stone. Danae gasped. In the Delsin dialect, she said, "You speak Elvish? Praise the Maker!"

The girl frowned again and looked at Danae sidelong.

"You do speak more than one word of Elvish, right?" Danae asked.

A few clicks and a long, mournful tone provided the visitor's response.

"Pox," Danae grumbled. Better a light from a stranger she could not understand than total darkness, for the time being. She eased forward and accepted the stone.

The swimmer drew her hand back, and folds of webbing creased between her fingers. Danae sucked in an inadvertent gasp.

The visitor flinched back. All the lights on her face, as well as the lines of luminescence that appeared on her arms, flared bright.

"No, please. I'm sorry." Danae squinted at the shimmering surface of the water that obscured her companion's lower half. "Thank you." Her voice came out hoarse. The stone, however, was pleasantly warm in her palm. "Remarkable. I've never seen anything like it."

The girl tipped her chin higher and returned Danae's smile. Her lights undulated, bright-dim-bright.

The stone's illumination revealed that Danae stood on a shore of worn pebbles in a huge cavern whose opposite wall she could hardly glimpse. Rough rock walls ran higher than the orb's glow would reveal to her, and an underground lake filled the expanse. From a tunnel at one end of the cavern flowed a current of water, and the lake dove through another natural archway on the opposite side.

Danae turned, and behind her, the light glinted in a multi-colored gleam. The Sword lay partially unwrapped. Her throat tightened.

She kicked the loose flap of blanket back over it.

Hiss.

What was that? Danae's glance pinged around the cavern. She listened. No other sounds reached her.

After a long breath, Danae returned her attention to the girl. She pointed to herself. "I'm called Danae." She then held out a hand to her new companion.

The swimmer, whose attention lingered at Danae's feet, startled.

Danae lifted her palm. "No, it's all right." She slowly touched her fingertips to her chest again. "Danae."

The girl uttered a few cooing sounds, her brow furrowed. She began again, and wrestled with the sounds for a moment until she made a pitched rendition that could have passed for Danae's name. The swimmer's speech reminded Danae of something between a throaty bird call and a singing child.

"Right, Danae. And you?" Danae kept her gesture small this time, but still pointed to the newcomer.

A pitch, a click, and a quick, higher scoop of sound came from the swimmer's mouth, though she hardly moved her jaw to utter them.

"That sort of sounded like . . . um . . . Ikirra," Danae said. She laid a hand on her chest. "Danae." Pointed to the visitor. "Ikirra?"

The girl in the water shrugged and repeated the tone, click, and scooped pitch. Her lights fluttered in sequence, as if chasing each other over her cheeks, forehead, and arms.

Danae's rendering of the name was as close as she was going to get, so it would have to do. She clutched the *lumienne* closer to her middle, though the stone did little to warm her. Her bent arms shook with deepening cold.

A scraping chatter echoed from above Danae, and she looked up, just in time to catch a face full of sand as it rained down from overhead. Scuffling joined the scraping, and indistinct voices echoed from above.

Ikirra's metallic eyes stretched wide, and she vanished beneath the water's surface. Her glow extinguished.

Danae spun on the shore. Should she grab her daggers? Her panic landed on the Sword. She had already grown too relaxed about leaving it on the ground, but then, multiple knocks to the head did breed muddled thinking. She scooped it up, as well as one of her daggers. How ridiculous. *Shivering in my skivvies, trying to protect a weapon that's as tall as I am with a knife.* Danae's breaths sped, and her head pounded.

Words echoed from above. "She must be down here."

Culduin! Danae lifted the *lumienne*. "Culduin, I'm down here!" Maker's mercy. She crouched and grabbed her sodden cloak, hauled it up to her shoulders, and wrapped it around her body, worsening her shivers. She waved her light back and forth.

More chatter bounced from the cavern walls. Some of it, probably Praesidio's responses, came to Danae's ears too muffled to comprehend, but Culduin's clarion tenor rang in the rocky cavern. "Wait! There!"

Danae squealed. "Where are you? I can't see you."

"Patrons be praised, you're all right!" Culduin said.

"The Tebalese are . . . gone?"

"News should wait," Culduin said. "We will find our way down to you, worry not."

"Be careful. It's a long fall," Danae said.

"Indeed. Longer than our ropes. One moment." Culduin's words came with the tightness of exertion.

The wait for him to speak again seemed interminable. Danae squinted into the impenetrable blackness above her, but the elf's shape did not emerge.

"Have you found any way out, besides the way you got in?" Culduin asked.

"I'm still recovering from the way I got in," Danae said. "Haven't gotten to exploring." She turned and shone the light from the *lumienne* over the water. She whispered, "Ikirra? Are you still here?"

On the very edge of the *lumienne's* circle of illumination, Ikirra emerged partially from the water, leaving everything from her cheekbones down below the surface.

"My companions," Danae said. "It's all right." She beckoned Ikirra to come toward her.

Ikirra eased about a pace closer but remained mostly submerged. And dark.

"Will you help us?" Danae asked. *This is pointless. She doesn't know what I'm saying.*

"Danae, are you talking to someone?" Culduin called. "And where in creation did you get a *lumienne?*"

Ikirra glanced toward the ceiling.

An apologetic shrug was the best answer Danae could offer Culduin. "Yes, someone's here, but we haven't really gotten acquainted."

Ikirra eased above the surface, head and shoulders, and pointed to the cavern heights, the direction of Culduin's voice. She then gestured to the beach.

Danae called to Culduin. "I think she wants you to come down, but I don't know if she can help us. She doesn't speak. Well, not like us, anyway."

"Caving is not my area of expertise, but neither of our routes onward are ideal," Culduin said.

Ikirra eased back into Danae's circle of light, her gaze fixed upward. A smile blossomed on her full lips, and a sparkle lit in her eyes. She toyed with her long hair, pulling it over one shoulder and smoothing it.

The impish look on Ikirra's face tightened Danae's jaw. "Are you *sure* I shouldn't try to find a way up to you, Culduin?" The girl may have saved Danae from drowning, but why?

"A pair of enemies fled on their horses, so it is only a matter of time before they return with reinforcements," the elf replied.

"The odds of finding a hiding place down here are better than on the surface. We need to regroup."

Danae swallowed. The odds of dying in either place looked stacked against them.

"I am going to throw our gear to your landing. Then I will drop and swim to you. Without more rope, that seems the only solution."

A moment later, an overstuffed pack came hurtling out of the gloom and skidded across the stones. "My bow is coming next. Please try to catch it," Culduin said.

"I'll do my best." Danae braced herself for the next arrival.

She managed to catch the white haft of the bow and prevented it from hitting the landing or dropping into the lake. The quiver came so quickly after, she could only dodge it. Culduin's aim seemed to be deteriorating with each throw. His longsword plunked into the shallows, but Danae managed to retrieve it. A heavy splash announced his plunge into the lake.

Danae scuttled to the shore's edge and extended the *lumienne*.

Culduin breached the lake's surface and took a noisy breath. "Really cold!" He swam toward Danae and pulled himself ashore, mostly using his left arm.

Danae wrapped her wet cloak closer, but her teeth still chattered.

He stood, and streams of water ran from his clothing onto the beach pebbles. After a quick survey of the shore and cavern, he tipped his head. "You are certain you saw someone else down here?" He reached toward her throbbing cheek but did not touch her skin. "This fall was not without collision, it would seem."

Danae searched the areas the *lumienne* revealed in soft, shifting light. "Well, somebody was here. I'm pretty sure I'd be at the bottom of the lake otherwise."

Culduin clucked his tongue. "A mystery to unravel later.

Your lips are blue, dear one. You need something dry. I thought I taught you better."

Danae folded her arms. "If I had anything dry, I'd be wearing it. But since you were joining me, I figured I'd better not be standing here in my undergarments."

A smile pulled at Culduin's lip. "As your surgeon, I have seen you in less."

All Danae could manage was a sputter, but at least her chills lessened for a moment while everything from her shoulders up flamed with a sudden flush. Perhaps it had been a product of her amnesia that prevented her from contemplating just how Culduin had once assessed and treated her broken ribs—or maybe it was pure avoidance.

He brushed past her and grabbed his pack. "I have an extra tunic and a blanket. I shall keep the pants for myself."

The prospect of changing clothes on such a small beach made her stomach flip and her mouth dry up. Did he mean to march around shirtless while she wore his spare tunic? The thought drew her attention to Culduin's ripped sleeve, where a new, round wound still wept blood.

She pursed her lips. "I forgot you had been hit. Is your arm all right?"

"If I could feel it, it might seem worse," Culduin said. "Everything around the wound is numb, and my lower arm is tingling. I am fortunate to have made the climb down."

"We need to see to that," Danae said.

"Not before I see to your hurts and your warmth."

Stubborn elf. Danae prepared a rebuttal, but Praesidio's echoing voice cut her short.

"Culduin!" Praesidio called from the heights. "Are you ready?"

"Oh, right." Culduin handed his satchel to Danae. "Ready. Heave it hard, Praesidio. It is farther than it looks."

While Danae pulled the dry clothes from Culduin's pack,

Praesidio lobbed his gear to Culduin, who caught it one-handed and set it on the beach.

Danae put her back to the elf, dropped the wet cloak, and shoved her arms into the tunic's sleeves. She yanked it over her head and down in an unreliable grasp. The garment hung nearly to her knees. The smooth, thick weave of the fabric slid over her skin, its touch far more luxurious than her own clothes. Rather than spoil the tunic's potential to warm her, she also unlaced her sopping stays and slipped them from beneath the shirt.

The old sage soon joined them, drenched from his quick swim to shore. He wore only a long, linen garment that reminded Danae of a nightshirt, and its lower hem ran rivulets of water down Praesidio's shins and over his bare feet.

"I'm glad we find you only bruised," Praesidio said. "When we saw the drop, I won't hide that we feared much worse."

Culduin lifted an eyebrow. He glanced at the *lumienne* Danae had set on the ground. "Where did you get that?"

"From the person who found me. Very strange! She had glowing spots on her face, arms, hair—"

"Is that so?" Praesidio's expression darkened.

"She's clearly skittish, because she keeps coming and going." Danae stroked her upper arms, as much caressing the silken sleeves as warming her skin. "Her name is something like Ikir-ra." Danae glanced about, then raised her voice. "Well, this is all of us. Can you help now?" The dripping quiet of the cavern answered with melancholy emptiness.

Culduin stripped off his wet tunic and dropped it on the ground. He hopped lightly on the balls of his feet and rubbed the gooseflesh that sprang up across his arms. "Still cold enough down here to cause trouble."

Clearly, a lifestyle of swordsmanship and traveling had chiseled Culduin's physique into a state of statuesque definition. Culduin's glance intersected with Danae's stare. He smiled.

Her cheeks warmed. Forcing her eyes away from the elf and

squinting into the dark heights, she strained her vision for any signs of pursuit. "Have we cornered ourselves down here?"

"No more than we were already cornered, and at least here, no one is shooting at us." Praesidio wrung out his garment and shuddered.

Danae lifted her sodden pack, and a steady stream of lake water ran from it. "But wandering caves—Papa always stressed that unmapped caverns are no place to try your luck." A wave of melancholy bubbled up in her chest. Had her family given up on her returning with any help by now?

A noisy splash erupted behind Culduin. The elf snatched his sword from the ground in his off hand, spun, and leveled it at the commotion.

Ikirra emerged, upper body only, from the settling froth, about eight strides from shore. She uttered a long, low tone.

Praesidio froze mid-motion, the fabric of his clothing clutched in white knuckles. His glance snapped to Culduin.

Culduin's eyes rounded, but as the newcomer and the water stilled, he relaxed his stance. "Well, greetings. Are you the one Danae has called Ikirra?"

Praesidio leaned close to the elf. "*Caudi prenemiten*, Culduin," he whispered.

Proceed with caution. A nervous quiver skittered through Danae's gut.

A quick, baffled glance passed from Culduin to Praesidio. In the moment the men spoke, Danae studied Ikirra, whose probing glance crawled over Culduin from head to toe and back again.

Ikirra adopted a cross between pout and smile, then closed the distance between herself and the shore. When she reached the shallows, she pushed up on her arms and lifted a silver-gray, sleekly muscled tail from the water. A thin, translucent dorsal fin ran from her lower back and along about a third of the tail's length, and matching flukes flared from its end. The edges of the fin and flukes brightened with cold, blue light, as did the patterns Danae saw before.

Danae's jaw fell slack. *Impossible . . . a woman with fins? Underground?* But then, the journey had so far been a string of one impossible encounter after another.

Ikirra tilted her head and blinked slowly, her attention still fixed on Culduin. She cooed and clicked.

Praesidio muttered in his own tongue under his breath. He then raised his volume to more audible speech. "If this has any hope of success, at the very least, we'll need to understand one another." He stepped between Danae and Culduin, then set a chilled hand on each of their shoulders.

The chant he uttered had a soothing quality, despite his touch awakening sharp pain that radiated down Danae's arm.

"You are a finless soothsayer," the fish-girl said.

Danae sputtered. "You can talk? Why all the games till now?"

Praesidio shook his head. "It is by Creo's might we shall seem to share a language."

"Oh . . . of course." Danae's posture collapsed into a sheepish slouch. "The Virtus in the Account of the Sojourners, right?"

The old sage nodded. "Excellent, young learner." He then regarded Ikirra with a hard expression. "We call my talent Thaumaturgy. I am a servant of the Maker."

Ikirra blinked. "At least the sounds you are making are much better now." She returned intense scrutiny to Culduin. "You must be what my people call an elf? Unless there are other finless with such *very* interesting ears."

I guess it isn't rude to stare when you're a fish-girl. Danae bit her cheek. In that moment, it struck her why Ikirra's facial appearance had seemed odd. Her wet hair did not part around or curve over any external ears. Her closer examination determined the girl had slits behind her cheekbones.

Culduin's cheeks flushed. He rubbed the back of his neck. "Well . . . yes. I am elfkind. How do you know of us?"

"The males of my people sometimes trade with overlanders. They have described beautiful ones like you who give us the brightstones like the one I brought Danae."

"That explains why we see one down here," Culduin said.

Ikirra twirled a lock of her hair. "It seems to me, my people have under-described—"

Praesidio stepped forward. "Too much chatter. What is your price to help us? Our chances of evading our pursuers using a surface route dwindle with each passing moment."

Ikirra flinched. "Who said I had a price?"

"Other overlanders." Praesidio's posture was rigid.

"Well, I don't believe I've met your kind before." Ikirra reared onto her tail and folded her arms. "Are you all so snappish?"

Danae gaped. If she knew anything about Praesidio, snappish behavior only came after long provocation. Whatever he had heard of Ikirra's ilk must have been memorable. In the worst possible way.

"You have not answered my question," Praesidio said.

Culduin moved to Praesidio's side. "I see no reason to start on such unyielding footing." He bowed to Ikirra. "I am Culduin Caranedhel, and it is my pleasure to meet you, as it is my companions'." He flicked a brief glance of reproach to Praesidio. "We are in dire need of your help. Is it possible to navigate these tunnels for many leagues south, and then return to the surface?"

Danae's shoulders tensed at the unspoken conflict roiling between Culduin and Praesidio.

Ikirra smiled again. "It's possible. But only if you have a guide. The only other finless I've met down here are the skeletons of those who must have tried our tunnels without one."

"As Praesidio indicated, we do not presume upon your help uncompensated." Culduin crouched to meet her eye level. "Is there a price you would name? I do not know the currency of your kind."

"I think the company should be reward enough."

Danae's chest tightened. Her brows furrowed reflexively. She shook the tension loose. *What am I getting all in a knot about? I mean, she is quite lovely in her own way. And barely dressed. Oh, please, you insecure fool. There's no reason for any of this to bother me, unless it's for Praesidio's reason—jawing instead of escaping.*

Ikirra gestured to Culduin's blade. "You are the warrior of the group?"

Culduin shrugged. "I do my part."

"Your friends look like they're in good hands," Ikirra replied, her voice stretching into a croon.

The rumble of irritation rolled through Danae's middle. "And I need a place to tend Culduin's wound. I think he's been poisoned." She gathered up her wet clothes and bundled them for carrying.

"Another reason we should move now," Praesidio said. "Which way? Will we have to swim?"

Ikirra narrowed her eyes at him. Her lights flared and dimmed. "Not to start, if you're not a fumble-fins . . . I mean, foot." She turned to the tunnel the lake flowed into. "There's a narrow ledge on this side of the outlet."

Culduin squinted that direction. "I wish we had a raft or boat. It would be much quicker."

"What you might get depends on who's doing the wishing." Ikirra shrugged one shoulder higher.

A fall of small stones chattered in the cavern. Ikirra's glance snapped to the ceiling. "It sounds like we're running out of time. This way." She glided through the water toward the tunnel she had come from.

Praesidio huffed. He took the *lumienne* and held it high.

Danae wriggled as quickly as she could back into her wet boots. The group gathered their gear and scuttled for the tunnel. Somehow, Danae could not shake the feeling they were fleeing known enemies simply to discover new ones.

4

Frostbalm

With Ikirra swimming in the channel, Culduin leading the way along the narrow, slick ledge on one side, and Danae between the elf and her mentor, they plunged as quickly as they dared into the depths of a subterranean maze.

The *lumienne* cast its dancing light on the jagged edges of the rocks, giving unnerving life to shifting shadows that often made Danae second-guess where to place her feet. She strained her ears for any sound that might filter from behind, besides her own short breaths and her companions' shuffling feet and clinking gear.

The air was damp and close. The sense of entrapment whispered with nagging insistence in the back of Danae's mind. Throbbing aches from her long fall made every tenuous step painful, but she fixed a brave face over her woe.

They made so many turns into one black tunnel after another that Danae lost any hope of retracing her steps to the cavern that led to the surface. Why were they following this coy creature if Praesidio clearly had reservations about her, or at least about her species? But then, her encounter with Shamir had shown her even Tebalese could defy assumptions, so who was she to weigh Praesidio's impression of Ikirra over her experience of rescue? If only they had the luxury of more time to discuss it.

Culduin's quiver slipped from his shoulder and clattered to the floor, and only Danae's quick grab saved it from spilling all his arrows into the river.

"Thank you." Culduin cast the quiver a beleaguered glance and reached for it with his left hand. His brow and upper lip glistened in the scant light, even though the tunnels were raw and cold. Chill bumps covered his arms and shoulders.

Danae clenched her teeth. "The arm is bad, isn't it?"

"I can keep going," Culduin replied.

"Maybe your legs can, but what if you need your right arm for balance?"

Culduin sighed. "It has grown completely numb, shoulder to fingertips."

"Ikirra," Danae called. "We need you to take us to another chamber where we can stop. If I don't try to do something about the poison in Culduin's system, who knows? It could work its way into his chest and stop his heart."

"But are we deep enough into the caverns that the Tebalese will not simply catch up?" Culduin panted for breath.

Praesidio glanced back. "We must hope so."

Ikirra swam back to Culduin and peered up at him with wide eyes, filled with either genuine concern or a great show of it. "Just a little farther. Then you can rest."

After mincing their way along a path that grew so narrow they needed to leap the river to continue on its opposite side, they reached a chamber that offered a strip of beach, comprised of huge chunks of sloping slate. The footing threatened to turn

Danae's ankles, but at least they could sit. Culduin lowered his equipment to the ground and plunked down with uncharacteristic weariness.

Danae eased into a stiff crouch beside him and inspected the wound. His plunge into the river had washed away any traces of poison from the crossbow bolt that might have remained on his skin.

Praesidio produced a leather folding case from his pack. "I took this from the Inquisitor who fell into the gully just before you, well, left us. I thought it might be informative."

Danae received the case from Praesidio and unfolded it. Inside, she found three hollow-tipped crossbow bolts, a vial of pale green sand, a vial of emerald-green liquid, and a little pouch, though it was flat enough that it was likely empty. A quick sniff of the liquid vial confirmed it was putrid like the substance that had stained her sleeve. The sand had no scent. Danae rubbed her forehead. *Papa, do you know how much I need you right now?*

She dipped a fingertip in the sand and rolled a few grains between her fingers. The act caused some tingling. A quick brush on her tunic removed the debris. "Well, there's a good chance this is the base for the poison."

Ikirra hauled herself out of the water entirely and sidled with a serpentine motion toward Culduin. "I have heard our warriors say the horseriders often shoot with something that freezes the muscles, and then they carry the victims away."

"And then what?" Praesidio asked. "Does it wear off?"

Ikirra shrugged. "Might depend on how much they use."

"Have they ever mentioned a cure?" Danae asked.

"There is something called glowlace that comes from the overlands, which we've mixed with a mineral paste, and that has helped our kind. But we rarely have glowlace."

Glowlace. Danae pulled her journal from her pack, but when she felt how heavy it was with water, she dared not open it.

"The pages will just rip," she mumbled. Her copy of *The Tree* was certainly in similar shape. In search of it, she pushed aside her belt and a small pouch at the bottom of the sack, and realization struck her.

Danae wrenched the pouch from her satchel and yanked the drawstrings loose. She fished in the pouch for the lichen she had harvested outside the gully. When it was dry, it looked lacey. And when it was attached to the rock . . .

"I remember! Papa's book called it Frostbalm!" She thrust a handful of the lichen toward Ikirra. "Like this? Is this what you're talking about?"

Ikirra cringed. "I don't know. I have only heard, not seen."

"Do you know what they do with it? Make the patient eat it? Make tea? A poultice? What's the mineral?"

Culduin closed his eyes and leaned his head back against the cavern wall. "Fair warning," he said. "I feel as though I may retch."

"We need to move here," Danae said. "He's getting worse. My left arm for a lab. Both arms for more time!"

Praesidio placed a steadying hand on Danae's back. "Seek calm. You are wise in the way of herb and ore. Trust that gift and Creo's guiding hand."

Danae offered Praesidio a momentary grin. "You're right." She turned to Ikirra. "Do you have any idea where to get the mineral?" Danae asked. "And Praesidio, can you find a way to heat some water? I can try an infusion first."

Ikirra glanced down the next tunnel. "If I find some, you can help Culduin?"

If I say I'm mostly guessing, does that mean she won't get the material her people use? Danae nodded. "Right."

"I'll try." Ikirra slipped under the water and swam downstream.

By burning a stack of parchment and a pair of wool socks, which created smoke of a particularly putrid funk, Praesidio was able to heat a small copper cup of water. Danae took it and steeped half of her lichen in it. The result was a peppery-scented infusion.

"Do you think the mineral is an active component in the treatment?" Danae asked Praesidio. "Or is it just a way to thicken a poultice?"

"I'm not the healer or the chemist in our midst." Praesidio shrugged.

Danae's stomach fluttered. She took the cup to where Culduin lay.

"Culduin," she whispered. "Have you been listening to the discussion?"

He grunted with a slight nod. "We are all guessing."

Ugh. With no idea how long it would take Ikirra to return, Danae despaired of doing nothing until then. Better to try something in the meantime. She lifted the copper cup to Culduin's chin.

"You'll need to sip at this."

He wrinkled his nose without opening his eyes. "Smells delicious."

Danae chuckled. "I'm a chemist, not a confectioner. Now come on." She tipped the infusion until it wet his lip.

The first sip came spraying back in a mist.

"Sorry," Culduin said. He tried again and managed to swallow a couple mouthfuls, but not without a lot of coughing and grimacing. "It is worse than I imagined."

Danae glanced into the cup. "Let's just stop at half for now." She set the infusion aside.

Danae found a hollow in the rock floor and filled it with the remaining Frostbalm, then mashed it with another stone. She stared at the pulverized fibers. *Any time, Ikirra.*

Culduin still sweated and rolled his head back and forth on the stone embankment, but maybe he looked less pale? Praesidio stood aside, leaning on his staff, face downcast, eyes closed. Probably in prayer. The solemn *drip, drip, drip* of the caverns, the claustrophobic darkness, and the inescapable complexity all weighed on Danae's shoulders. Time ground by. Danae paced on the shore.

A ripple in the water caught her ear, and apparently Praesidio's too, because he looked up. Flickers of light beneath the surface winked into sight. Ikirra broke the surface close to where Culduin lay. She blinked her oversized eyes and pursed her lips, then reached with webbed fingers and placed them on his forearm. She gasped.

"So fevered." She extended a small cone of pale stone to Danae.

Danae scuttled across the rough bank to Ikirra and took the stone, then paused to place her own hand on Culduin's brow. Indeed, he was still fevered, but maybe not any worse than before.

She squinted at the crumbly stone. "Mix this with the Frostbalm—er, glowlace?"

Ikirra nodded.

Danae returned to her makeshift mortar and pushed the pulverized lichen aside. She crumbled an equal amount of the stone into the hollow and crushed it to sand with little force. A few bits of the stone spread to touch the Frostbalm, and where the two met, the fronds emitted a pale glow. Her heart quickened. When she combined the full portions of sand and lichen, the whole hollow emitted muted light.

It's too powdery. Danae chewed her cheek. She added a touch of water and a few drops of the honey Culduin carried to make a paste. *Better.*

When she packed a gob of her creation against the elf's wound, his eyes shot open, and he hissed through his teeth.

"Ay! That stings." After he blew out a breath, he added, "Though in this surgeon's opinion, that is probably an improvement." He closed his eyes again.

Ikirra rocked on her hands and furrowed her brow. "Do be careful!"

Danae scowled. What did it really matter to the fish-girl how careful she was?

"Now what do we do?" Ikirra glanced down the tunnel.

Danae tucked a blanket around her patient. "We wait."

After perhaps a half-hour of nervous pacing, Danae assessed Culduin's arm, with Ikirra paying close attention from the water's edge. The swelling at the site of the bolt wound had lessened, and Culduin had dropped into a placid slumber. His clamminess had subsided. She blew out a stream of air, releasing the tension that had been mounting.

"He's looking better," Ikirra said.

"More comfortable, at the very least." Danae smoothed her bedraggled hair.

"Get some rest, Danae," Praesidio said from where he sat reading *The Tree*. "I can keep watch."

"Are you sure?" The suggestion of rest had a glorious ring.

Ikirra stretched taller, propped on straight arms. "I can help keep an eye out for trouble too."

Praesidio nodded to Danae. "Absolutely. Just give me the bundle before you close your eyes."

"Bundle?" Danae tilted her head. "Oh, that one." She shuffled to the pile of gear and hauled the Sword over to Praesidio.

"What's that?" Ikirra asked.

"Just an old temple artifact," Praesidio replied. "Academically meaningful to me."

Danae passed the wet burden over to Praesidio, then shuffled to the farthest edge of their beach from him. Putting some distance between herself and the Sword carried an inexplicable sense of relief. She curled her legs inside her long tunic, propped her head on a backpack, and within a few breaths, slipped away from the waking world.

The next she knew, Culduin's groggy voice—slurred even, murmured in the background.

"You really should not," he said, though his tone carried a smile.

Danae pried heavy eyes open, but in no way could she drag her body into motion. From the corner of her vision, she found Ikirra beside Culduin. The confounded fish-girl held a reed flute to her lips with one hand, and with the other, she traced a pale finger around the edge of his ear point, then ran her fingernails along his jaw.

Culduin chuckled, but at the same time he waved his hand in front of him. Sloppy. Sluggish. Like the gestures of a drunk man. His eyes remained closed. Could it be an effect of the infusion?

Ikirra removed the flute from her lips. "Not to your liking?" She pouted. Her skin and hair glow waxed and waned in a sleepy cycle.

"I said no such thing, dear one," Culduin slurred. "Just not propo . . . aro . . . appropriate."

A surge of indignation heated Danae's face. *Dear one?* She bolted upright. A bout of dizziness kept her on her rear, though.

Ikirra glanced over her shoulder with a scowl, but upon meeting Danae's wakeful gaze, a smile chased away her dark expression. She slipped the flute behind her and tucked it under the back strap of her garment. The length of her lavender hair fell over the instrument.

Danae hauled herself to her feet and moaned. Everything hurt, but her hip, shoulder, and face most of all. Where was Praesidio in all this? It seemed unlike him to stand by if something Culduin deemed inappropriate—even while laughing— was going on. The old sage, unfortunately, sat in the shadows at the edge of the landing with his head dropped back, his eyes closed, and his mouth wide in a snore.

Danae tromped toward the elf and fish-girl. "You shouldn't be bothering him. He needs to recover."

"*He* does?" Ikirra scoffed. All of her illumination winked out. "You should look in a still pool sometime. And besides, I wasn't bothering him." She smiled at Culduin. "Was I?"

Culduin opened heavy eyes. The glazed expression of confusion dominated his face at first, and he blinked several times. After taking stock of Danae's position and Ikirra's, he cleared his throat and put the heel of his hand to his temple. "I—I am not myself," he said. "I am awake now. And it is true, Danae needs tending. I neglect my duties by leaving her battered while I drowse."

"What do you need to aid your recovery, Culduin?" Ikirra traced a little circle on Culduin's arm with her fingertip, and a sprinkling of sparkle arose in her lavender locks. "I'm sure I could find you whatever comforts you lack."

He glanced down at her hand and let out an awkward chuckle.

Danae shouldered her way past Ikirra and crouched at Culduin's side. She placed a palm on his forehead, which was dry and cool. "How's your arm?"

The fish-girl inched back from Culduin's personal space.

Flexing his fingers, then bending his elbow, Culduin nodded. "Good. A little stiff, perhaps, but usable for sure. All I'm noticing is a little residual head fog, but that is clearing. Congratulations, apothecary."

Ikirra snaked across the rocks and slipped into the water. "We'd better keep moving, then. Once the old one wakes."

Loath as Danae was to wake him from an earned sleep, she eased over to Praesidio, and the closer she drew to him, the greater a sense of unease swelled in her mind. *Hissing. Chittering.*

She squeezed her eyes shut as she whispered his name.

His gray eyes snapped open.

"Heavens, did I doze?" He sat up straighter and stretched. "I had no intention of drifting. How's the patient?"

"Almost like new." Culduin pulled on his armor padding and chain shirt from his pack. "Thanks to Danae's handiwork."

Danae could feel Ikirra's scowl burning into her back. "Please, Culduin. Compliments make me queasy." She willfully fought the inclination to glance the fish-girl's way.

"That is probably just the head injury." The elf stepped to her side and rubbed a palm over her back. "With all you have managed of late, you had best get accustomed to the accolades."

The sensation of his touch might have soothed Danae if it did not also bring on a surge of nervous belly flutter.

Praesidio rose and picked up the Sword from where he had been leaning against it. He weighed it in his hands and regarded it with a sober frown. "Either of you feeling you have the fortitude to carry this?"

Culduin shot out his hand. "I forbid Danae to volunteer. At least until that rub on her shoulder improves."

Danae shifted the wide neck of Culduin's tunic to cover the patch of raw skin that had peeked from beneath the collar.

Ikirra swam back and forth in the water and glanced fretfully into the farthest tunnel. "We really would not be wise to stay in the same place for much longer."

"You think the Tebalese might be in pursuit?" Praesidio asked.

"They aren't your only problem," Ikirra replied.

Praesidio's wild gray brows drew into a knot. "Care to elaborate?"

"Well," Ikirra said. "It's not customary for merfolk of my station to have contact with overlanders. The war matrons—my mother being one of them—are fairly protective of us."

A cold skitter of suspicion ran down Danae's spine. "Then why are you helping us?"

"Not that we are anything but grateful," Culduin hurried to

add. He rummaged through his belongings to produce a small jar of salve and a bundle of bandages.

Ikirra's impish grin returned. "Because safety is dull. You never meet anyone interesting or see anything new."

The faceted glint in Ikirra's expression jabbed at Danae's nerves.

"I would gladly accept a heaping dose of dullness," Culduin said. He scooped a little salve, likely yarrow, onto a folded strip of bandage.

She's a liar. Danae winced at Culduin's careful ministrations to her cheek wound. *Well, if these "overlanders" end up running into merfolk war matrons, we'll just have to prove that Ikirra brought them more of a fight than she bargained for.*

5

Festering Thoughts

*A*fter wrapping the worst of Danae's abrasions and dressing his own crossbow wound, Culduin hefted the weight of the Sword of the Patron. A prickle ran through his palm, and for a moment, he scorned the wool that shrouded the magnificent blade within. He fingered the edge of the poor cloth.

"Ready, Master Caranedhel?" Praesidio said. The Elgadrim knight's gray eyes searched Culduin's face.

"Quite." Culduin shouldered the Sword and followed Ikirra into the next tunnel.

The mermaid slipped above and below the surface of the water, her sleek, marine physique sweeping along with the current. The way her living light accentuated her delicate features tugged on Culduin's fascination. Was he staring? He focused on his boots. No need to invite more flirtation. Although being noticed was nice in its own way.

His gut twisted—how much had he murmured aloud? How much of the dream that churned in his depths had come to light? How muddy and confused his rest had been, full of reedy music and the light tingling the Sword brought on. It was all probably a result of the poison working its way out of his system. That, and his scant acquaintance with true sleep. Most often, the elven practice of meditative repose was enough to refresh him. Collective sleep was a luxury he, Danae, and Praesidio could ill afford.

His glance flitted to Danae, but she focused only on placing her feet between the loose obstacles along their path. His tunic draped crooked on her petite frame, exposing most of her shoulder and collarbone. Strands of her strawberry locks framed her bruised and scraped face in disarray, and her long plait hung well down her back in a scraggly tangle. Still, the bright green of her keen eyes, the fairness of her complexion, and her compact, lean build, suffered no diminished loveliness. Oh, for a respite from her striving, where heavy cares did not distract her. Culduin's heart ached.

"This way," Ikirra whispered, her tone low and songlike. She turned to a right-branching tunnel. Though the passage was utterly dark, her luminescence kept her in easy sight.

The last of the strange effects of the lichen infusion had worn off, thankfully. Culduin forced the lingering impressions of his groggy encounter with the mermaid behind thoughts of survival. How many rations remained, unspoiled by river water? Since Danae's fall into the lake had ruined her provisions, they would have to travel with tight belts, at least until Culduin found a way to supplement their food.

The need troubled him as he worked it over in his mind. The possibility of decent foraging in the tunnels seemed remote. He had noted a few varieties of fungus, but if they were not outright poisonous, their nutritional value would not be dense. The types he saw only reminded him of above-ground mushrooms he knew, and that was not good enough, in his mind, to risk eating them.

"Ikirra," Culduin said as they followed her along the new channel. "I am curious. What do your folk eat?"

"Some of the lake chambers have fish we can spear." Ikirra turned back to them and floated upright. She maintained the posture with slow sweeping motions with her arms and tail. "Sometimes the hunters can corner and take down one of the great eels, and then there's quite a feast." Her facial lights brightened with a shimmer. "I bet you'd be a great hunter, since you're so strong."

Mermaid forthrightness is jarring. Culduin laughed. "What sense do you have of my strength?"

"Well, look at you," Ikirra said. "Muscle is muscle, whether you live above ground or below."

Culduin stretched a little straighter as he walked. How was it this bubbly mermaid was so immediately bold about her impressions of his appearance, while Danae seemed blind to him?

Danae's stomach rumbled audibly. "Any chance we might be able to try our hand at a little fishing?"

Ikirra shook her head. "Oh, no. There are always merfolk in the fishing chambers. They'd spot you for sure, and then I'd be in trouble. They'd drag you in front of the council, and, well, I haven't seen that work out in any overlander's favor yet."

"How long are we planning on traveling underground?" Danae asked.

Culduin drew in a deep breath. "If we can't bolster our supplies down here, it's my guess we'll need to return to the surface in three days at the most. Although game on the steppes will not be abundant."

Danae chewed her lip. "That's worse than I thought. We might even have to go through Cray, or some village, or something crazy like that."

"We would do better to risk starvation than set foot in any civilized place on this side of the Tebalese border," Praesidio said. "Ikirra, do you know if your cave network passes into Kelmirith?"

The mermaid pursed her lips. "I don't know much about the overlanders' tribes and territories. But I can take you far to the south. Once I figure out an excuse for being gone so long, so mother doesn't send anyone looking for me."

Danae's posture collapsed, if only slightly. "So you're not supposed to be helping us. What happens if your people discover you are?"

Culduin dropped back beside her. "It will be all right. Any ground we can cover out of sight of unfriendly eyes will give us a better chance of reaching Bilearne with fewer entanglements."

Praesidio's breath hissed through his teeth.

Culduin turned and lifted a brow.

"Let us try to keep the specifics to a minimum," Praesidio whispered. "We cannot be certain what dangers lurk in these tunnels."

The challenge of food remained, then. Coupled with the growing mix of agitation and defeatism in his companions, the time ahead threatened to be trying indeed. Culduin hitched the Sword higher on his shoulder and pressed on.

After traveling an unmeasurable time, over which Danae's strides grew increasingly sluggish, Ikirra halted at an intersection of tunnels. She pointed to the outlet to Culduin's left.

"That passage climbs up to a chamber, and even has a narrow slit to the surface," Ikirra said. "It's not big enough to fit through, but perhaps it would be a comfort to you to glimpse light from the overlands?"

"That sounds great!" Danae said. She turned for the passage.

"One moment, Danae." Culduin grasped her arm with a gentle grip. "You are weary. Let me go first to be sure it is safe."

"Ikirra, how long do you deem it's safe we stay in this place?" Praesidio said.

"None of my folk come here," she replied. "We don't climb well."

Culduin glanced across Ikirra's lower half. "Understandable —it's not what you're made for. Just like those of us with legs are horribly inefficient swimmers. So, as Praesidio asked, how long? We have gear we should dry out, and we all need real rest."

"It is time for my first sleep, I believe, so I will return to my pod, rest, and then come back to you after the second sleep. Don't wander off in the meantime," she replied. "I would feel just awful if something befell you." Ikirra smiled and dove under the water.

"Good fortune to have her as a guide," Culduin said.

The silent, skeptical frowns of his companions gave him a start.

"We can talk more about it once we've ensured the cavern she's offered is indeed secure." Praesidio pulled himself up the slope with his walking stick.

The ascent through the passage proved rough, making the choice of footing and handholds numerous, but treacherous nonetheless. Culduin climbed ahead of Praesidio and Danae. The farther they climbed, the more the darkness waned, and at the summit of the climb, the passage opened into a conical chamber. Filtered daylight illuminated the cave. Even Culduin, for whom darkness presented no compromise in vision, gladdened at the sight of real sunlight.

Along the ceiling of the chamber ran a jagged slit, but as Ikirra had indicated, it was far too narrow to provide an exit without a great deal of toil with a pickax.

Danae gasped and clapped her hands over her mouth.

"What is it?" Culduin whirled.

She faced the right side of the chamber, where tucked back

in the shadows, two skeletons, draped in rotting tatters of furs and leather, leaned against one another. But behind them . . .

Culduin's heart leapt. A dugout canoe? How had the deceased labored it to this place? "What fortune!" he cried. "If we can ride the current instead of walk, we will make much better time toward Kelmirith."

"About that," Praesidio said. "Please refrain from speaking any more details about our plans."

"If Ikirra knows nothing about surface geography or politics, I imagine most of our intentions would seem unintelligible."

"Am I the only person concerned that there are *skeletons* in this cave?" Danae shivered.

Culduin winced. Perhaps his excitement over the canoe had been a touch callous. "Forgive my bout of pragmatism."

"I would still feel better if no one, not even someone completely disconnected with the surface world, knew anything." Praesidio set his pack down. "I happen to know that the merfolk have surface dealings on the Kelmiri side of the border, and they are seldom without hidden entanglements. Merfolk have little love for those who go on two legs. Remember that."

"The same doesn't seem to be true of young mermaids." Danae opened her gear as well and pulled out her journal in one hand and her copy of *The Tree* in the other. "Do you think we can salvage them?" Her face was drawn.

Culduin rode the current of her shift in thought, inwardly content to dodge the subject of Ikirra's attention. Still, a glimmer of satisfaction surfaced at the chance Danae was at least a little jealous . . .

He reached over and brushed a wisp of her strawberry hair from her eyes. "A little air certainly cannot hurt." He scanned the chamber, which was more earthen than the lower passages, with occasional woody ends of roots protruding from the walls. In the center of the expanse, a pile of ash sat. More blessed still, they found a haphazard stack of what must have been sections of roots, hacked from the walls, judging by the splintered ends.

Culduin moved to the pile, lifted one of the sticks, and found it to be dry . . . almost brittle. He could probably keep such dry fuel from smoking much, which would limit how much snaked out the cleft in the ceiling and alluded to their presence. Finally, dry boots! The last trouble Danae needed added to her list was foot rot.

"I shall get a fire going, and we can focus on getting your clothes and shoes dry right away."

Praesidio took the books from Danae. "To touch on your point, Danae, mermaids do regard those they call 'finless' differently than the males of their species."

Culduin's shoulders tightened. He set to hooking Danae's damp garments on root ends. Upon the ash pile, he arrayed a portion of dry wood.

"Merfolk do not hold to the same mores you were raised with. Affections are like a game." Praesidio's face soured. "No, more of a competition. There is no marriage in their culture. No covenantal bond or long-term expectations."

"I fail to see why this matters at all to us," Culduin said. Heat crept up his neck.

"I suppose you think it was innocent curiosity that brought her to your side when none of us was aware enough to take exception?"

"Inadvertent or calculated, it was equally embarrassing." Culduin dropped his pack and then pulled the Sword off as well, but he hesitated to set it down. He weighed the weapon in both hands. Again, it tingled against his palms, even with the blanket bundled around it. Without thought, he loosened the rope that bound the bundle. The wet wool slipped free of the crystalline blade, and the play of light across it captivated his senses. He knew he ought to push the thing aside, yet he could not.

Seductive curves of illumination in blue, purple, and white slipped along the contours of the Sword's blade in a tantalizing dance as Culduin turned the Sword in the filtered light. There was song in its beauty, the rich aroma of summer branches heavy with fruit in the blade's strength. The world around the chamber receded into mundane obscurity, and Culduin ran one reverent thumb along an impeccable, notchless edge and gem-studded quillons. What warrior could fall short of greatness with such a weapon in hand? He licked his lips. A pulse of nameless desire swelled through him.

Praesidio's voice cut through the moment. "And perhaps most importantly, Ikirra is never, ever to catch so much as a glimpse of the Sword. Who knows what it would speak into her soul? Whether she would succumb to fell deeds at its prompting."

Culduin lowered his eyelids to keep from rolling his eyes. When had Praesidio become such a lecturing bore? He focused on the weapon again and took one last draught of the Sword's majesty. "Do you not trust that I, of all people, would ensure I do not repeat my brother's errors?"

Danae's back straightened. "Thalius? What has he done to earn such a sneer?" She cast the Sword a sidelong glance and wrapped her arms around her middle.

"Oh, nothing, if you ask him," Culduin said. "Just neglected his post at Formenos so elves of lesser rank and judgment could fall prey to the schemes of Tebal."

Danae's glance hopped between Praesidio and Culduin. "I don't understand."

Praesidio took on a measured tone. "My understanding is that Sir Thalius was left in command of the keep Formenos in Lord Kaylonos's absence, and while Sir Thalius was abroad in the countryside, agents of Queldurik stole the Sword."

"*Sir* Thalius," Culduin snapped. "His knighthood dictated he observe his duty over his preference, so if he wanted to remain a scout, he should never have accepted the appointment to captain of Lord Kaylonos's guard. *He* approved the admission of supposed emissaries to the keep, and then went gallivanting in the woods. Can you imagine what grief the world—your country, Danae—might have been spared, had Thalius not decided to go browsing the laurel instead of watching the gate?"

"Are you basically blaming Thalius for the war?" Danae gaped.

Praesidio stepped up to Culduin. "It's a foolhardy leap, friend. Am I not also correct that your people did not know what they had in hand until it was lost to them?"

Culduin clenched the Sword's grip. A surge of heat ran through his body. "Another act of shortsighted neglect. A child's inquisitiveness might have ascertained the truth, and Queldurik would be little but an irritating memory by now." *What a relief to air festering thoughts!*

"Your usual temperance and good sense seem to be in short supply," Praesidio said. "I think, perhaps, you should rewrap the Sword and take some rest on the opposite side of the cavern from wherever you lay it."

Culduin drew a slow breath. His anger cooled, and if he allowed honesty to prevail, a section of his heart chastised him for his loose and scornful tongue, even if the greater part longed to rail. Something about the Sword was both seductive and repellent all at once. Freeing and frightening.

"Perhaps." Culduin pulled his roll of binding cloths from his gear. "We should also dry this blanket, so these will have to serve as wrappings for the time being."

Once Culduin had mummified the weapon, set it down, and returned to the task of the fire, a wash of regret coursed over him. Had he just indulged such baleful words against his brother? Regarded Praesidio with such disdain? Enemies in pursuit seemed a pale concern if such villains lurked within.

6

Unsavory Influence

$\mathcal{E}$ven though exhaustion pulled at Danae's weary body, no matter what position she lay in, sleep eluded her. The rough cavern floor prodded her every bruise and scrape as she tossed and turned. Worse, however, were the proddings within her thoughts. Culduin's harsh words, the mocking cast of his crooked smirk, and his hard eyes planted a seed of fear in her chest. The journey had of course been wearing on them all, but the Culduin who spoke of Thalius's culpability was not the Culduin who shared a tearful goodbye with that same brother just weeks ago.

Something suspicious was happening to him.

Why was he so drawn to the weapon she wished she could flee? Did he suffer no ill impression of it, while she fought a sensation of slimy, crawling worms every time she made contact with it? Her sensing ability, at times such as that, felt more a curse than a gift—another unwieldy trouble she must learn to manage.

She sat up and scooted closer to the fire, which crackled low but heedlessly merry in the dismal place they camped. It was good to be warm. She glanced toward the ceiling, where she found only darkness now, so night must have fallen. At least in the surface world, where night and day had meaning.

A sigh, unnaturally loud in the stillness, made Danae jump.

She scanned the dim edges of the cavern, and her attention came to rest on Praesidio. He sat on a ledge of rock, his banded knuckles gripped around the hilt of the Sword of the Patron, though the blade remained covered in its wrappings. Praesidio hunched over the weapon with his forehead pressed to the pommel. His eyes, squeezed shut, and his frown, almost a grimace, deepened his usual wrinkles and creases. He shuddered. Although the cavern was by no means hot, a bead of sweat dripped from the tip of Praesidio's nose.

Danae hesitated. She forced her glance everywhere but Praesidio's direction, but his shivering, sighing struggle wore on.

"Are you all right?" Danae whispered.

Praesidio's only response came as a throaty groan.

"Protector?" she ventured, a little louder. A tremor of fear chattered through Danae's limbs. Should she intervene?

The old knight leapt to his feet and thrust the Sword away with a clatter.

"Begone, vile foe!" he yelled. His wild eyes lacked focus.

Danae scrabbled backward.

Praesidio lifted his shaking hands and stared at them, his face a mix of bewilderment and disgust. He took a staggering step to the side.

Danae dashed to him and caught his arm, just as the old man's left knee buckled.

Culduin sprang into the chamber from his watch post closer to the water. He carried his blade drawn. "Enemies?"

Praesidio's haunted glance met Danae's. He blinked. His face relaxed, and he regained his balance. "My apologies. I must have woken you." Praesidio reached a hand, steadier now, to smooth his straight silver hair away from his face.

"No, it wasn't you," Danae said. "I woke up on my own."

"No need to fear," Praesidio said. "We are safe here."

Culduin inclined his chin. Though his narrow eyes rumored worry, he descended the cavern approach to his watch post once again.

Danae studied the old man. The ridge of bone around his eyes cast stark shadows in the shifting firelight, but more than a trick of the light, his haggard look worsened by the hour. It was unpleasantly reminiscent of how her father had begun to look before she left home.

Danae pursed her lips. "Forgive me for saying so, Praesidio, but I'm worried you're unwell."

Praesidio eased back to his seat and cast the Sword a scornful glare. "I grow weary of its voice, but alas, it seems I do not have the strength to silence it. At least not until Ba-al Zechmaat's hold on it weakens."

"How long will that take?" Danae picked at the edge of her ring finger's nail.

"Too long." Praesidio cracked a weak smile. He took her hands. "There's no scrap of nail left to break, Danae."

She ducked her head.

"A servant of my strength does not undo this kind of corruption in the time we have. High Lord Ecleriast may have the might to do so, but his help is still a distant hope. One obstacle at a time."

Danae nodded. "With Ikirra as a guide, I can't help but worry the obstacles might multiply." She craned to catch a glimpse of Culduin, who reclined near the cavern entrance. In a whisper, Danae added, "I don't trust her, Praesidio."

"I fear I share your skepticism. But without her, the chances of our blundering into dead ends, of getting hopelessly lost, or otherwise ending up like those fellows"—he nodded to the skeletons by the canoe—"are real indeed."

Danae clenched her jaw. Nothing galled her quite like being at the mercy of an untrustworthy ally. Especially one who seemed inordinately interested in one member of their group.

"She's said outright we're not welcome down here and that her people are hostile to humans. There's something underneath her willingness to guide us."

"Vigilance is all we have until a safe route to the surface becomes evident," Praesidio said.

Danae huffed. "And why does Culduin insist on playing advocate?"

Praesidio shrugged. "My hope is that he is just trying to make the best of a bad situation and promote harmony. My fear is that he's falling prey to the mermaid's wiles."

7

To Save Twelve Days

*P*raesidio, Culduin, and Danae's watches all passed, they ate the sparest portion of dried meat and hard tack and sipped tea Praesidio shared, but still, Ikirra did not return. Sunlight filtered through the cavern ceiling again, their fire burned to low coals, and no trip to the water's edge revealed a waiting mermaid. Danae's stomach churned.

"We need to stop wasting time," she said. "Do you think we could make a way back to the surface from here?"

Culduin frowned. "Not without the proper tools."

"Well, I think we've given Ikirra more than enough time. Something must have happened. Should we backtrack?"

Praesidio cinched his pack shut and buckled the flap. "We have made many turns to get this far. I am not confident we could find our way back, even if that didn't seem a foolhardy choice. The Tebalese will likely still be watching that area."

"I'd rather skip starving down here, and I'd also prefer not to fritter away my papa's . . ." Her voice caught, and the sting of tears blurred her vision.

Culduin eased to her side and put a hand on her shoulder. "We know, Danae. If moving on alone was less perilous, we would have done so hours ago. It matters—"

"Culduin!" Ikirra's voice echoed from below the cavern entry passage. "Culduin, you're still here, I hope?"

Funny she had not called for the rest of them. Danae gritted her teeth.

The elf brightened. "There we are. You see? No need to worry." He raised his voice. "We will be right down."

Praesidio doused the fire while Danae hurried to her pack. She sighed before she picked up the Sword, but she added it to her load.

"I said I would carry it until your abrasion is better." Culduin held out his hand.

"You, master elf, need to help me carry the boat," Praesidio said. "Chivalry has its place, but we will need to distribute the rest of our burdens for now."

Danae forced a smile over a stronger desire to wince at the grinding hemp on her shoulder, then stepped to the cavern outlet. If nothing else, at least the long delay had served to dry her clothes, except the very toes of her boots. She led the way through the exit. Her companions then hefted the canoe, though no amount of careful jockeying prevented them from toppling the skeletons. Shoulder joints separated, a skull rolled to the floor, and the forgotten remains chattered to the cavern's stone footing. Danae shivered at the grate of dry bones.

"Creo gather you in." Praesidio winced.

After a ruckus of shuffling and grunting, the men managed to drag the canoe down the slope behind Danae. In the water at the slope's foot waited Ikirra.

"What's that?" She tilted her head and frowned.

Culduin craned around his end of the cumbersome craft and smiled. "We found a canoe."

Ikirra's expression remained quizzical. "A . . . canoe?"

"A boat," Praesidio said. "The type of thing we finless use to navigate the water without having to swim." He set his end at the water's edge and stretched his shoulders and neck.

Ikirra peered inside. "Oh, so you get inside it, and it floats. I've heard of boats but have never seen one up close. I pictured them bigger."

"There are different types." Culduin lowered the stern. "This is a very small craft. One moment, and I will return with the paddles."

As Ikirra studied the canoe, she rolled her lips inward and descended into silence. "This changes things a bit—opens passages to you that you might not have otherwise taken."

"So the route south will be faster, right?" Danae said.

"It should be." Ikirra provided the answer without meeting Danae's gaze.

A taut silence fell over the group. Danae cleared her throat. "Will you have to be gone so long every time you report back to your people?"

"No," Ikirra said. "I've made some excuses to be gone a few days, so that should help move things along."

Culduin returned with the paddles, rough-hewn as they were. Patches of crumbling bark clung to the handles, and a long split ran up the blade of one. "Praesidio, you get in first, and Danae, you sit in the middle. I will shove the craft into the water and take up the position of steerage."

Danae followed Praesidio into the boat, and when she stepped forward, the vessel rocked and threw her off balance. A staggering step steadied her.

"Try to stay low if you have to move about," Praesidio said. "I've rowed better craft in my time."

The canoe scraped and lurched, but once in the water, it

glided quietly. Even better, the trip into the river revealed no hidden leaks. Yet.

"This way." Ikirra dove forward and led them into the dark, the *lumienne* Praesidio now carried their sole source of light in the long, hungry throat of the tunnel ahead.

. Why the mermaid did or did not use her glow, Danae could not puzzle out. Was she even in control of it?

Borne by the current of the subterranean river, the stony walls of the caverns slipped by, and now that Danae did not need to spend so much energy minding where she stepped, she took in more of the underground network around them. In some places, the rock piled in jagged stacks; in others, the tunnels opened into vast, lake-filled caverns. Were these lakes deep and empty? Or did hungry horrors patrol their unseen depths? Danae swallowed against a tight throat.

Drip formations, stretched by long years of trickling moisture and minerals, hung from the ceilings, and one cavern required deft paddle handling as Praesidio and Culduin wove between stalactites that extended nearly to the water's surface. Danae dodged one formation only to knock her shoulder against another. The canoe rocked.

Good heavens, I'm going to dump us all into the water. She curled into a ball, hugging her knees.

Some tunnels glittered against the light of their illuminating stone. Some wore a mantle of shaggy, brown growths. Moments wore into hours.

Ikirra glided onward before them, the undulating motion of her sleek silver body carrying her to the water's surface, then back under in a sighing rhythm. She used her arms in only the strongest currents to work her way around rocks that jutted from the river floor.

Their paddling and splashing seemed so cloddish by comparison. Noisy enough to draw the attention of anyone who disliked intruders.

In a tunnel that branched left and right, Ikirra came to a stop. She turned and faced the canoe. "We have a choice to make, so maybe you can grab the edge and keep the current from picking for you?"

Culduin and Praesidio eased the craft to the right side of the cavern, and Culduin wedged his paddle between rocks. Praesidio reached up and gripped an overhead outcropping.

"Both routes serve our purpose?" Culduin said.

Ikirra nodded. "The left way is much swifter. Tricky to navigate, even for swimmers. But it cuts more directly south and would save much time." She made eye contact with Danae. "The right tunnel is easier, but arcs around before we can connect with passages that journey southward again."

"How dangerous?" Praesidio asked.

At the same moment, Danae said, "How much faster?"

A smirk tugged at Ikirra's cheek. "We don't really measure time in the same way you overlanders do. But I believe you would save many—perhaps a dozen—of what you call 'days.'"

Danae gulped. "Then there's really no question. With little food and no way to get more, we can't waste nearly a fortnight."

Praesidio twisted back toward her. "One or more of us drowning would cause a bit of a delay, don't you think, young learner?" He lanced Ikirra with a pointed gaze. "Again, I ask. How dangerous?"

"There are two stretches of whitewater between lake caverns," Ikirra said. "The rocks are tall and sharp. But I can swim it. Not all my people can, though. Most don't try."

Culduin pursed his lips. "I can see, better without the *lumienne*, in fact. If the current is as strong as you say, I would not likely need you to paddle, Praesidio, except in cases of extreme correction. Twelve days is a worthy savings."

Danae pried at the stubborn set of Praesidio's jaw with a plaintive pout. "There are so many steps to go in the journey, the first of which is getting out of here as quickly as we can, with still two destinations remaining..."

The old sage softened and patted Danae's shoulder. "I know you are anxious. And I know Deklan needs you. Because this is formally your quest, Danae, I will allow you to choose. But please consider. Wild water. In the dark."

Danae drew a long breath, closed her eyes, and reached out with her mind. *Creo, I'm supposed to seek your guidance in all things, right? Which way?* She looked again at both tunnels. A sense of impending tribulation in the whitewater tunnel warred against the crushing words, "too late," that seemed to echo along the smoother way. The Sword hung especially heavy, and pressure built behind her eyes with throbbing insistence. She pinched the bridge of her nose. The headache grew, and so did the threat of fleeing time.

"The whitewater," she whispered.

Praesidio's face fell. He opened his cloak, tucked the *lumienne* into an inner pocket, and folded the fabric closed. In the moment utter darkness fell, the chatter of currents unseen grew to a mocking whisper, one that eroded Danae's conviction. The canoe eased into motion. Once they had chosen their course, the canoe surged forward with speed that left Danae's heart somewhere behind.

8

Deep Water Denizens

"Try to stay curled low in the boat," Culduin said. "It will lessen the chance of us flipping."

Flipping. Wonderful. Danae clenched her hands together. Cool cave air breezed past her cheeks, much faster than any previous part of the journey through the caverns. In still water, she had nearly drowned. Only Ikirra's help had saved her.

The blinding dark of the tunnel stole her sense of direction. The canoe slipped along in a smooth, gentle rock at first, but the chatter of water against stone soon amplified. The boat lurched left, then right. She pressed her face to her knees and hugged her legs, but still the erratic dance of the boat threw her side to side.

Thunk.

"What was that?" she cried.

"Not to worry," Culduin replied. "Just a little bump . . . no hurt to the boat."

Icy water sprayed Danae's cheeks. The canoe seemed to spin beneath her.

"You're all right?" Praesidio called. "Any help?"

Culduin grunted. "Still fine. Focusing, thank you."

The tumbling roar of the current filled Danae's ears. Another knock. A surge of motion. Danae gripped the side of the canoe with one hand to brace against the shifting momentum her body always seemed one instant behind. *Maybe this wasn't such a good choice.*

The front end of the boat pitched downward. A splash soaked Danae's back. Praesidio yelped.

"No fear," Culduin said. "We still float. Sorry for how I hit the boil in that reversal."

"The what?" Danae said.

"We can talk terms later." Culduin laughed. "Whoa!"

The boat jammed to a stop, and the back end angled to the left. Danae's seat tilted right.

"Lean! Lean!" Culduin yelled.

This is where we die. Dizzying fear twisted Danae's insides.

Danae thrust her weight left with the hope that was the direction Culduin meant. A thunderous churning of water broke out, coupled with grunts of exertion. Everything rotated again, the canoe eased upright, and forward motion resumed.

After a swift continuation forward, Culduin blew a long breath. "That was a little close."

The current continued to bear them on for minutes Danae could not measure, but she also received no further frantic instructions or dousing. The current quieted to rippling. Only after a long stretch of placid gliding did Danae's thundering heart settle to a normal rate. Metallic aromas of wet stone hung in the still air.

"Praesidio, if you would prefer, you can produce the light again," Culduin said.

Danae lifted her head when cool light filtered through her

eyelids. The tunnel around them widened until it opened into another chamber. This cavern had no beach or landing. At first glance, she discovered no outlet either.

Ikirra sat about six feet up, on a narrow ledge, scarcely wide enough to hold the bulk of her slick body. The flukes of her tail hung toward the water.

"Wasn't that fun?" she said. "You're a skilled pilot indeed, Culduin." Her glow pulsed, especially the patterns across her collarbones and throat.

The elf grinned, laid his paddle across his knees, and cracked his knuckles. "Not the worst job I have done, by any stretch."

The boat lurched sideways and rocked. Danae yelped. Culduin fumbled for his paddle and scarcely saved it from falling into the water.

"What was that?" Praesidio said.

Danae scanned the water, but only blue shimmers reflected back. She lanced Ikirra with a narrow-eyed glare. The mermaid shrugged.

"Right," Danae mumbled. She raised her voice. "What just happened?"

Crack! The boat rocked right, harder this time.

"There's something in the water!" Danae gripped both sides. "No wonder our little guide isn't in with us. Why else would she get out?"

Ikirra scowled. "Human gratitude. Hmph."

"Well, if I'm wrong, why don't you jump back in?"

Culduin gasped. "Danae, really. Need you—"

"I'm tired." Ikirra pointed her nose in the air. "Unlike some people who just curled up for a ride, I had to swim that frothing death trap back there. One might think you chose it to spite me."

Danae sucked her teeth. *The little . . .* she squelched the unladylike terminology that sprang to mind. "Fine. You're tired. What's next? When you're ready, of course."

Water at the front of the boat erupted in a geyser, and a glistening blur lunged at Praesidio. In a single motion, a blade of flame lanced from his hand, and he swept it in an arc before him. A needle-toothed, beady-eyed monster opened a blunt maw in a shriek. It dodged to the side and disappeared below the surface with a noisy splash.

"Stay down!" Praesidio said.

The ring of Culduin's sword grated against his scabbard somewhere behind Danae.

"Whatever you do, Danae," Culduin said. "Don't fall out of this boat."

Oh, sure. Simple enough. Danae's knuckles whitened from her grip.

The rear of the craft thrust skyward, and Culduin fell forward, onto Danae's back. He wrapped his free arm around her in a crushing embrace. His sword arm, he swept a level cut out to the side.

Danae flinched as something cold, but thicker than water, spattered on her face, hands, and with a woody patter against the hull. A long, flat beast dove back into the depths. Culduin righted himself, and part of Danae mourned his release of her shoulders. She wrenched one of her daggers from her bandolier.

"One of the giant eels you hunt?" Praesidio called.

Ikirra pressed a hand to her chest. "It must be. I have never seen one alive. Oh, no . . . I don't know—"

From the front left, the monster leapt at Praesidio's side. His Sword of the Sacred Fire answered in a cutting arc, and despite its ethereal nature, the blade struck with enough force to knock the attacker back.

The dazzling, erratic light of Praesidio's divine blade mingled with the *lumienne's* glow and blurred Danae's vision, but she thought she spied a deep rent in the eel's side where Praesidio's sword bit deep.

An instant after the eel sank below the water's churning surface, the creature leapt at Danae from the opposite side of the boat. She slashed with her dagger. The blade dragged across the underside of the eel's jaw.

Culduin lunged over Danae and ran his blade straight through their attacker. Praesidio narrowly ducked the point of the elf's sword. The boat tipped far enough to take on water.

The blade strikes cut the eel's leap short, and it fell, tail first. Its foul, toothy head and upper body crashed into the canoe, right in front of Danae. She kicked the beast in the head and sent it back into the water.

The canoe's rocking settled as all the warriors stilled.

In a trembling hand, Danae adjusted her grip on her dagger. She scanned the lake in a frantic circle. Her companions held blades at guard, but in time, even the water around them stilled.

Ten paces ahead, a flat, charcoal-gray shape breached the surface. It drifted onward and the right.

"Is that it? Do you think it's dead?" Danae whispered.

"I certainly hope so," Culduin said. "Did you see the teeth on that monstrosity?"

"Too well," Praesidio said.

With as sly a motion as she could muster, Danae sought Ikirra from the corner of her eye. Maybe suspicion colored Danae's perception, but it seemed to her that Ikirra wore the ghost of a frown. What did she have to frown about? Of all the reactions for the fish-girl to have . . .

The mermaid squinted at the floating eel, then dove into the water.

She surfaced beside the bow and clasped the canoe's edge with webbed fingers. "What a fight! We had best get you out of here. Eels tend to be solitary, but they're not the only flesh eaters in the river." She swam ahead. "This way."

Danae sheathed her dagger and clutched either side of the canoe, digging into the wood with her nails.

Praesidio glanced back. "Heavens, Danae, that expression could boil a river."

If only.

They paddled onward for a long stretch of hours, though Ikirra informed them they would not make it to the second whitewater before they would need to rest and make camp again.

"I cannot promise you another dry cavern at this point," Ikirra said. "Not for a while. But we should be able to at least make a small beach."

I wonder what charming denizen of this watery black maze will live there? Danae's face tightened. Culduin had certainly demonstrated his ability to survive multiple deadly scenarios, but Patrons ablaze, Danae was not going to walk into any traps where Ikirra's plans were for her to get eaten.

9

The Flute

*B*y the time they had reached the beach Ikirra had mentioned, Danae's rampant thoughts had filled her mind with predatory scrabblings and flutters. She crept from the canoe, her rump sore from long hours against the rough wooden floor and her leg muscles tight. The beach could not have exceeded twenty paces at its widest, and if Culduin slept in the space crosswise, his feet would likely have dipped in the water.

Praesidio offered another handful of broken bits of dried meat, two hazelnuts, and a shriveled fig to Danae and Culduin from his shrinking pouch of provisions. Danae took the food and savored the fig in tiny bites, which only intensified her stomach's constant growling.

The knight also offered a portion to Ikirra, who lay at the water's edge, nearest Culduin.

She regarded the food with a sidelong glance. "No, I don't

think so. But maybe I can find us all something more down-river. Or do overlanders always sup so lightly?"

Danae shifted on her bedroll, where she sat cross-legged. "No, this is conservation at its finest," she said. "No wonder my rear hurts. I think my tailbone has lost all its padding with the running and the fasting."

Culduin arched back to look behind Danae. "Maybe some, but not yet to any detriment." He shot her a roguish smile.

Danae gaped and backhanded Culduin's shoulder. He shrugged and popped a hazelnut into his mouth.

Ikirra puckered as though a sour taste filled her mouth before she submerged and shot downstream.

Contrary to Danae's assumptions, nothing crept from the dark recesses of the cavern to swallow them whole, and Ikirra did return with a gift of food. Sort of. It took Danae until both Praesidio and Culduin were nearly finished with their portion before she dared taste her first bite of the cured, minced fish the mermaid offered. Once she got past the mushy texture, the palatability surprised her. What Danae would not do for a good plate of her Mama's sausage and cabbage. But even the mushy fish beat hunger by a long stretch.

*C*ulduin wandered the water's edge, his companions deep in slumber, even Danae—at least for the moment. How long would it be before she woke in a sweat from night-mares or in frowning suspicion that some scheme was about to befall them?

Six days borne on the subterranean river and led by the mermaid, and no mishaps—Culduin regarded it as rare fortune. Why the constant exchange of tense glares between Danae and the mermaid, he could not fathom.

It mattered little.

Two or three more days traveling the underground route should put them over—or rather, under—the Kelmiri border, and then perhaps they could seek the closest surface outlet. As fascinating as he found the winding tunnels, the sparkling rock formations, and the power of water over stone, even Culduin began to miss the caress of open air upon his cheeks.

A low note caught his ear—or was it just the phantom of one? In this place where they heard little beyond their own voices and the rush of water, there were times Culduin fancied he heard bird calls or the sighing of wind through branches. But in the next moment, another note, soft but reedy, reached him. The tone soaked through him to settle in his very core and filled him with a thrill—an appetite. An impulse. He shifted the Sword on his shoulder, which had begun to thrum. Again, the pitches called, seemingly from a narrow passageway to the rear of their landing.

A quick glance around the sandy shore confirmed his companions slumbered placidly. A few steps toward the passage could not endanger that. In the tunnel, he could pass from the throw of the humans' lantern light, and his darkvision would serve him better in learning if anything but wild imaginings waited down the rocky corridor. He eased on silent strides after the woody notes, which crooned low but continual now.

The closer he stepped to the passage, the stronger the pull of the pitches became—though not music in the strict sense, their magnetism was undeniable. They filled Culduin with vitality and vigor he had not felt in a century, when the spryness of childhood's memory filled his limbs with spring and his actions with spontaneity unfettered by obligations. A corner of his mind chided him against leaving his companions, but the giddy majority of his heart quelled that stodgy warning. He marched into the passage.

The causeway opened into a round chamber with a still pool at its center, and upon a sloping stone that rose from the water,

Ikirra curled, a pale wooden flute to her lips. Her eyes were closed, and she played far more notes than Culduin had heard from the larger cavern. Many shorter, percussive notes flitted between her longer tones, and the music of her making reminded Culduin of water broken into hundreds of ripples, big and small, that expanded and intertwined. Her luminescent skin patterns brightened and dimmed in visual harmony with her playing.

His heart sped. His strides carried him to the water's edge.

Ikirra's eyes drifted open. "I did not expect you. Can you hear me in the other chamber? I did not wish to disturb you."

"Disturb me?" Culduin smiled in a hope of reassurance. "Not at all. Your music is very unusual."

"You don't like it." Ikirra put her flute in her lap.

Culduin shook his head. "Oh, that is not what I meant. It is very different than the melodies of my own people, but it is beautiful and full of power."

"You make music, then?"

"At times." A flush warmed his cheeks. "Chiefly, I like to sing."

The mermaid's face brightened. "I would love to learn some of your music. But I would have to keep your songs in my heart as mine alone, as my people don't approve of our kind embracing the art of others."

"That is a shame," Culduin said.

Ikirra nodded and put her flute back between her lips. She played another fascinating cascade of notes. "For now," she said, "why don't you sit and listen? My flute is gentler than voices and won't disturb the others." Her illumination shifted from its usual pale blue to a lavender hue.

When she began again, Culduin's legs folded beneath him, almost outside his will, and he sat on the beach, enveloped in Ikirra's song. In his mind's eye, he beheld waves upon a sandy shore, the crash of surf against rocks, the wind over the surface of turbulent waters. Drowsiness—no, more of a drunkenness filled his limbs. His eyelids grew heavy, and the tingle across his back where the Sword touched him increased to a vibration, as though the pitches of Ikirra's music resonated within it. He pressed the heel of his hand to his temple.

"No, no!" Ikirra pleaded in a voice both soft as a breeze and tempered as steel. "Don't spoil the song. Just listen. Listen . . ."

A shriek in Culduin's mind demanded he rise. Flee. But the notes of the reed flute swelled over him again, lavender light bathed him, and he swooned. He slumped to the side, despite his desire to fight the fall. It was as if a part of him stood outside the situation and bellowed warnings, but his body could not respond.

Ikirra's music swirled around him and pulled him down, down into darkness. Behind him, somewhere beyond Ikirra's cavern, shouting and clashing echoed in the faintest rumor.

And then there was naught but music.

10

A Muddled Mind

When Culduin opened his eyes, he lay on his side on a bed of something soft and cool, but his shoulders ached and a biting pressure plagued his hip. He shifted but found his hands bound fast behind him and his ankles tied as well, and his clothes—soaked again. Panic welled. He writhed on a bed of rust-colored moss in a cavern scarcely longer than his prone form. He was certain he would knock his head on the shaggy ceiling if he stood. On the left side of the niche, a narrow corridor turned right.

Clicking and vocalizations came from the corridor. As Culduin concentrated on the sounds, he found them mingled with the lap of water.

"You agreed to my price, and I don't care if the overlanders are put out. The other two should be appeasement enough."

The echoing nature of the voice made it hard to be certain, but Culduin assumed the speaker was Ikirra.

More chittering, clicks, and humming, seemingly from multiple sources, clattered from below.

Culduin blinked and fought to clear his mind. What was he hearing? Were those sounds the tongue of merfolk? Of course. Voiced syllables would be of little use underwater. Praesidio's Virtus must only offer understanding of Ikirra herself, not her language as spoken by others.

"Sword?" Ikirra said, her tone cross. "I gave you his sword."

Culduin's heart plummeted into his feet. He strained to check around his chamber and found no pack or weapons. No weapons . . . at all.

He squeezed his eyes shut. The time of his watch seemed so foggy. He had taken a watch, correct? Of course he had. And he had been wearing the Sword of the Patron during that time, as was agreed during watches. But now, not knowing where it or he lay, he swore under his breath. Danae's entire quest, crushed. There would be no denying his culpability if he ever saw her again. He was no better than his brother, after all—just as easily tempted to ruinous folly.

Ikirra huffed. "Well, I'm sorry. I don't know what they're looking for. Make the rest of the exchange and get them off our backs, then."

The speakers of the clicking language exploded in a fury of noise.

"Maybe the old man has it, or the girl. How should I know? I've done my part. I'm sure you don't really want to question Mother's terms. I *will* have my replacement for my last champion out of all this nonsense."

The chatter ended in a series of splashes, and all went quiet. Culduin struggled to sit, his legs curled under him and off to his right, his hands no looser than when he began twisting against his bonds. A glance to his ankles revealed some kind of dark, woven cord, perhaps a rope of grass or seaweed.

First things first, he needed to free either hands or feet. He wriggled his legs out before him and pressed his ankle against a shard of rock. It crumbled away at the pressure.

A gentle swish of something slipping through water caught his ear. He turned.

Ikirra peered around the corner of the cavern outlet with wide, silver eyes. A sultry smile spread across her lips. She snaked her way into Culduin's already-cramped space. Her shoulder butted up against Culduin's.

The elf wormed his way backward.

The mermaid smiled. "So shy." She reached for the side of his face.

"Do not touch me," Culduin said. "And I had better not catch sight of that fiendish flute of yours, or you shall find it smashed to slivers."

"Oh, my. You are in a bit of a bluster," Ikirra said. "Though it might be entertaining to see you accomplish such a thing, tied up as you are." She giggled low.

A dozen angry questions rushed to the forefront of Culduin's mind, but disarmed and immobile, what power did he have to demand answers? He would have to work another set of tactics to have a chance at freedom. He took a long breath, slowly blew it out, and relaxed each of his muscles from his scalp, through his neck, over his shoulders, down his back, through his hips and finally, his legs.

"My apologies. I let my vexation at waking up in a strange place get the better of me." He allowed his glance to linger unabashedly on Ikirra's feminine attributes. "Are your friends actually gone? Did you come to me alone?" he whispered in a husky voice. Culduin leaned toward Ikirra, his eyelids heavy.

Ikirra laughed lightly through her nose and closed the gap between them, speaking with her lips nearly brushing his. "Yes. Why?"

"Well, how cozy." Culduin wriggled his hands. He cast a disappointed glance down one of his immobile arms.

"Nice try," Ikirra said. "But you don't want me. I see it in your eyes."

Culduin fought to maintain a playful expression by fixing a pout over his frustration. "How could I not? Look at you. Was there ever a lovelier marriage of sleekness and beauty?"

The mermaid shook her head. "You've used up all your talents in swordsmanship and left nothing for lying—though that last one wasn't a complete falsehood." She reached up and fondled the edge of his ear, and her lip twisted in an unbecoming smirk.

Culduin's shoulders tensed.

She dropped her hand and sidled back. "It doesn't matter, though, because I'm not interested in you, either. Not like that. It makes it so much harder when you die."

Despair threatened to overthrow the elf's composure. "Please. I care not what becomes of me, but . . . have you no compassion? What of my friends?"

"Your friends." Ikirra raised a brow. "It's one of them who makes you more immune to me than most others. Thank goodness for that crystal sword that seemed to muddle your mind so much, or else I might never have gotten you out of the way."

Culduin gasped. "Out of the way of what? And the Sword! What have you done with it?" Fury boiled within him, and he thrashed against his bonds.

The mermaid's laugh echoed, dark and unfeeling. She opened her mouth to speak but only a series of pitches and clicks came out.

Culduin barked, "No games, or so help me I shall find a way to strangle you, bound though I am."

Only a quizzical glance provided Ikirra's reply. She clicked and whistled again.

"Can you understand me?" Culduin's voice tightened.

Ikirra huffed and glanced over her shoulder, a disgusted furrow creasing her brow.

And so the Virtus of the Sojourners had ended, abrupt and without warning. Culduin's stomach flipped. What did that mean for Praesidio, the vessel of that power?

11

Bars and Chains

*D*anae paced the circular chamber, lit from beyond its barred doorway by a single *lumienne*. Moisture snaked down shale walls and gave everything an itchy, moldy funk. But what did she care about dismal surroundings?

"Gone. After all that. Did we even have it a week?" She blinked back the sting of angry tears.

Praesidio stepped to her side and gripped her shoulder. "Peace, young learner. You lose count of the days, first off. And until we learn something of Culduin's whereabouts, hope remains." Swelling around his right eye had blackened it, and a crusty trail of blood ran from the nostril on the same side.

"I still don't understand how they got to us—he's never mismanaged a watch in the four months I've known him." She scoffed. "That's a lot of watches."

"Which is another reason I think we have cause to hope—" Praesidio bit off his thought at the sound of a splash and the grate of loose rock.

"Sounds like we have a visitor." Danae groaned. If the villains dared touch either of them again . . . Creo help her, she would unleash a Virtus that would make them regret their interference.

Out of the darkness beyond their cell, Ikirra emerged.

Danae crossed her arms. "Oh, look who it is. What do you want?" If she could have reached through the bars and throttled the fish-girl in that moment . . . well, it was definitely to Ikirra's benefit that a cell door between them.

Ikirra tilted her head, blinked slowly, and shrugged.

"I suppose you know nothing about the dozen mermen and their frog henchmen who attacked us in our sleep?" Danae seethed.

"I told you from the beginning it was a risk." Even from her low, serpentine posture on the ground, the mermaid gloated toward Praesidio. "The hauhetti would have been gentler had you come quietly."

Danae's molars ground. "I'm sure. Where's Culduin?"

Ikirra rolled her eyes. "You needn't worry about him. The eels are quick feeders, so he probably didn't suffer. Well, much."

Lies. They must be. "Not even your thugs could have thrown him to monsters. I won't believe it."

Ikirra laughed. "You northerners know nothing but root vegetables and frowns. Should I have one of the hauhetti snap your legs to convince you?"

The words punched harder than Danae suspected they might. So much of the world outside Dayleston had confronted her with wonders and horrors she had not so much as imagined a year ago. "Don't go anywhere." She turned to Praesidio and whispered, "Is there a way for us to talk that she won't understand?"

"Not without releasing the Virtus, and I do not believe this is yet the right time to do so." Praesidio winced as he spoke through battered lips.

She lowered her whisper further. "I don't know what to believe. Could Culduin have possibly lost a fight to these creatures?"

Praesidio shrugged his better shoulder. "Depends on how many, I suppose."

She clenched her fists. *He's still out there. Alive. Somewhere.*

"But what about the mission?" This time, Danae's eyes welled so suddenly she had no hope of restraining tears. They streamed down her cheeks and twisted her expression. "If Culduin had . . . *has* the, well, you know—then I can't deliver it to your people, and then I haven't lived up to my end of the—" Danae's sobs overcame her ability to speak. "And . . . Papa . . ."

"Hush." Praesidio pulled her shoulder toward his side in a paternal show of comfort, but the gesture only released the remainder of Danae's agony.

Her shoulders heaved. She buried her face in the rough weave of Praesidio's robe. Though she could feel the barbs of Ikirra's superior glare, she abandoned any effort at composure and groaned in grief what words could not encompass. Why did she ever leave home?

"Some burdens are too great for mere men, or even very headstrong girls, to bear," Praesidio said. "But Creo did not bring us here without reason. He did not separate us from Culduin without purpose."

Danae crumpled to the floor of the cell. Her new belief in the Creator's desire to guide her steps felt far too frail to take this setback in calm stride.

"You're more pathetic than I suspected," Ikirra said. "Sorry you won't make it to Bilearne, most likely. If it's any comfort to you, your transfer to the Tebalese search party will do nicely in ingratiating us to the temple of Queldurik. Thanks for that."

And with a slick splash, Ikirra vanished.

Praesidio wordlessly stood vigil over the long stretch of minutes while Danae opened the floodgates of her anguish—

raw emotion that had built up over so many weeks of continu-
ally dodging death or worse. Never in her life had she cried in
such a purge. After a last few shuddering sobs, Danae swiped
her sleeve across her wet cheeks. "So much for not knowing
anything about the 'overlanders' and their territories. Why did
she help us at all if only to give us up now? She could have been
rid of us in the first chamber."

"Because mermaids drive a hard bargain," a man, his voice
thickly accented but speaking the Western tongue, said.

A scalding sensation exploded across Danae's entire body
with such ferocity that she cried out. She curled in a ball. "Who's
there?"

Praesidio crouched beside her. "Danae, what's wrong?"

"Horrible . . . signature." She panted against her pain.

Someone laughed outside the cell. "So you're one of those,"
the Western speaker said.

Danae rolled to seek the perpetrator of her torment. Outside
the cell, she found a sable-robed figure with hunched posture
standing on the river landing. The *lumienne* provided too little
light to ascertain his features, though Danae caught sight of a
dark chin and gruesomely crooked teeth.

"Where is it?" the visitor asked in a hiss.

Danae hid beneath the shroud of her pain as an excuse to say
nothing.

The sable-robed assailant shot his hand through the bars and
grabbed the shoulder of Danae's tunic. He hauled her against
the grate so hard that the impact made her ears ring. "*Where is
it?* You do not yet know suffering."

"You will stop." Praesidio clutched his chest, at the spot
where Danae knew his silver phoenix emblem hung beneath his
robe.

"Don't trifle," Danae's attacker replied. He punched a
pointing gesture toward Praesidio, and the Knight of the
Elgadrim spun.

Praesidio staggered to regain his feet, but too quickly, his enemy swung his gloved hand downward in a raking gesture.

A scream burst from Danae's lungs. She felt as though an unseen force ripped all her skin from her flesh in a single, explosive motion. The last thing she saw before the agony overcame her was Praesidio's collapse to the cell's earthen floor.

$\mathcal{C}$ulduin's heart pounded, barely caged by his ribs. "Where's Danae?" he shouted.

Ikirra turned from him, called out in her percussive language, and then slipped back around the corridor's corner.

"Wait!" Culduin blurted but then followed it with a scoff. What use were words, even if she could still understand him?

He wormed his way to the end of his enclosure, the rock beneath the moss grating against his ribs, hips, and knees the whole way. How had a mermaid managed to get him to this spot? Had he come on his own power, totally entranced by her music?

Had he truly tried to feign attraction to this villainous schemer? How desperate had he become? The whole encounter turned his stomach. Wasted words, wasted time.

He reached the right turn in the corridor, and the outlet dropped off to a pebbled beach, where Ikirra gestured to a burly, sandy-skinned humanoid with a hunched back and the head of a monstrous frog. *Hauhettus.* Culduin groaned. If there were many of this kind about, that further complicated matters. Behind the hauhettus sat a pile of rusted chains.

The hauhettus brandished a harpoon, which he jabbed in Culduin's direction. "Stay place," the frog-man said in broken Elvish.

A conversation passed between Ikirra and the hauhettus in a strange combination of their own sounds. Clicks and whistles from the mermaid and croaks from the frog-man implied each speaker served as a one-way translator of the other's language. While their discussion stretched on, Culduin scanned his surroundings. The beach was narrow and promised terrible footing. The river offered the only escape from the chamber, and the chances of ending up lost remained an undeniable likelihood. Still, a solid kick to the hauhettus's knee or throat . . . Culduin scowled. Not with his feet still bound.

When the chatter wound down, the muscled hauhettus touched his bulbous fingertips together and bowed to Ikirra, who then leapt into the water and swam downstream and out of sight. The creature faced Culduin.

"Princess say take to pens." The hauhettus bent and lifted a clanking length of chain. He revealed several large blocks of iron welded to the links at intervals.

"Pens?" Culduin said. "Does that make me dinner or occupant?"

The hauhettus narrowed his bulging, red eyes. After a long pause, he said, "Not here for questions." He reached forward with one arm. Tight skin clung to stringy, exaggerated musculature. Every detail of the hauhettus's anatomy boasted raw power, with no fat to obscure the sinew.

Culduin twisted to evade the creature's reach, but the hauhettus dug fingers into Culduin's hair and clenched it tight. A quick wrench dragged the elf from the corridor and onto the beach. Culduin's scalp sent shocks of pain down his spine.

He landed on his knees. A sharp blow to the back of his head brought with it a shower of lights across his vision. Straining against the force of the hauhettus's arm proved fruitless, and so Culduin remained bent at the waist.

"You fight, I throw in river." The creature locked an iron collar around Culduin's neck. From it hung three of the block weights.

Scant comfort though it was, Culduin decided he must be

destined to occupy the pens, since he'd be easier to transport as hunks of meat than a fighting prisoner if he were meant as food. The weights around his neck made it abundantly clear that if the hauhettus delivered on his threat to throw him in the river, the iron would drag him to the bottom and facilitate a quick drowning. That is, if they did not break his neck before he hit the water.

Culduin's captor picked up his harpoon and used the smooth edge of the blade to cut Culduin's feet loose of their bindings, and then he employed the point as motivation. "Get up. We go."

Had Ikirra stripped Culduin of his chain mail, the jab would have likely ruptured his kidney. He counted the mere bruising a small mercy and staggered to his feet. For now, compliance would rule the day, which Culduin could only pray would buy him time for scheming.

The pens consisted of a series of a dozen chiseled chambers that ran on either side of a wide, still portion of the subterranean waterway, the first crafted culverts Culduin had seen since they had blundered into the network a week ago. Firelight flickered from sconces between each pen, and in the stagnant air hung the stink of chamber pots mingled with oily smoke.

Culduin's nerves thrummed to the point of giving him jitters. Would he find Danae and Praesidio in one of these cells? He squinted through the barred doors as they approached.

The first three chambers the hauhettus marched Culduin past imprisoned no occupants, just vacant bunks that stood three high on either wall. Although their emptiness pierced him, he drew in a breath to brace against the despair that hovered on the edge of his spirit.

In the distance, the rap of wood on wood echoed against the

hard walls. It seemed to drift from an archway blocked by a rusted portcullis. The orange firelight beyond the barricade glowed brighter than the low illumination in the pen section.

The hauhettus unlocked the fourth pen gate with a long-shafted key and pointed inside with his spear. Two ragged men in iron collars like Culduin's lounged on separate bunks, and only one of them turned a wary glance toward the gate when it opened. He wore a stained tunic and leather vest. In the rear corner bunk, another prisoner lay curled in a ball, almost entirely covered with a ratty blanket, save one dangling, dirty foot.

Culduin gingerly probed his neck where his collar of weights had begun to tear at his skin. His glance flicked to the river.

"In!" The hauhettus jabbed Culduin's ribs with the harpoon, and this time, the point found a path between his chainmail links and pricked his flesh.

It was not worth the risk. Not yet. Culduin shuffled through the gate, which the hauhettus slammed shut behind him.

The amphibious jailer turned the key in the lock. "You train with these. Very soon. Be ready." He tromped back the way they had come.

The man who had looked toward Culduin groaned. "Well, pox," he said in the Western tongue, though the nature of his pronunciation, especially the soft rendering of the letter "p," implied that the language was not his native tongue. "Looks like we might end up at the championships anyhow, team."

Culduin took stock of the speaker. His hooked nose and bronze skin, dark eyes and straight, thick hair, hinted at Da-Shirine roots, an estimation his accent supported.

"You speak western, elf?" the Da-Shirine continued.

"I do," Culduin said.

Another inmate rose from his sprawled pose on his bunk. His fairer complexion placed him anywhere from Radromir, through Velon, or potentially in Kelmirith. "Pox is an understatement. You better fight like a god, elf, if your getting captured drags us back into all this." He glared. "And if you don't, I sure as hell don't have your back."

"Come on, Davon," the third prisoner said from the corner. "You think he's any more thrilled about this than you are?"

Culduin started, then squinted toward the last speaker, who emerged from beneath the blanket and sat with knees drawn up and arms wrapped around them. Her ash-brown curls jutted in all directions around a pale, freckled face.

"They house you together?" Culduin said. "Odd."

"Thankfully." The Da-Shirine nodded toward the woman. "Bretta is my wife—I am shocked they allowed us this one mercy. I suppose so long as we win tournaments, this arrangement suits Her Ladyship."

"I fear you will need to catch me up," Culduin said. "Where should we start? With the tournaments, or with Her Ladyship?"

"The tournaments," the Da-Shirine said. "Best to get acquainted with the thing most likely to get any or all of us killed."

12

Seeking Signatures

*D*anae leaned against the stone wall of the circular prison cell, but her whole body, even her soul, however impossible, ached. At least Praesidio had regained consciousness. With the brutality of the signature she had suffered, she could hardly imagine what the Curse must have felt like.

"Please, Danae, try to concentrate," Praesidio whispered.

"Concentrate?" Danae moaned. "There's too much disaster muddling my mind right now. Too much—" Her grief threatened to pull her to pieces again. How could he be so task driven after the pain the black-robed villain had put them both through?

Praesidio clasped her face on both sides with his wrinkled hands. "You *can* do this. You must. Give no foothold to despair." The torchlight outside their cell cast the left side of his face in flickering orange light.

Danae pulled back from his grasp, rubbed her burning eyes,

and propped her pounding forehead on her knees. "I'm not sure how it was different. How do you describe how a signature feels?"

"Well, certainly you can admit a difference between that interrogator's signature and, say, mine."

"Sure." Danae chuckled darkly, even though it worsened her headache. "Yours, when you're being nice at least, is like a warm bath, whereas his, especially when he cast whatever Curse that was, felt more like being skinned alive."

"So perhaps you can find a defining trait of the Sword's signature by comparing it to another." Praesidio stroked her hair. "Focus. Breathe. Try."

Danae drew a slow breath and blew it out, then another. She concentrated on the ripple of water, somewhere outside their cell. Her mind stilled. She sought to recall the sensations she had experienced in relation to the Sword.

She grimaced. "Slithering."

Praesidio quirked an eyebrow. "Slithering?"

"Yes." Danae's mental search came into focus. "Being near it always made me feel like slimy tentacles were moving across my whole body."

"Perfect! You should be able to sort that from other signatures you encounter," Praesidio said, still in a low but earnest whisper. "Now, what you must do is reach out with your mind. Imagine yourself drifting from this cell, hunting like a predator for signatures, seeking the 'scent' of that slithering impression."

"You realize you sound like a lunatic," Danae said.

"Of course I do. You must try it anyway."

Danae's skepticism mounted. "Is there a Virtus I need?"

Praesidio shook his head. "Understand I've never done this myself, since I'm not a sensor. But as I understand it, those who seek signatures often pray for Creo's vision as they do so."

"At least neither the temple hunters nor the merfolk seem to know where it is either. That's some comfort." Danae closed her eyes and imagined the loathsome, crawling touch of the Sword's presence. *I can't believe I'm actually hoping to feel that again.* Though even if she found it, what they were supposed to do about it from their locked cell, she had no idea.

From behind lowered eyelids, Danae sensed movement, though it was even more abstract than her vaguest dreams. Distant, something akin to heading left, she brushed the violent, flaying presence she associated with the interrogator from the temple. She forced her search the opposite direction. After more probing in a pursuit that seemed to defy the passage of time, she drifted closer to an unfamiliar presence, this one like the swelling heat of flame mixed with an effervescent tingling—tingling always seemed to mix with the signatures one way or another.

Further into the darkness of the vision, a sliding, pulsing sensation, overlaid with an aura of sharp indignation, lingered just on the edge of her strange inner sense. She strove for it, but still, she could not seem to pull the signature into full focus. It could have been the Sword, but its faintness warred with Danae's confidence. Working toward it felt as though Danae leaned against a stretching, membranous wall that refused to yield.

Come back.

Danae leaned in harder. Her head swam and her stomach churned. But she had to know . . . it was not much further.

Come back! Danae!

The nebulous netherworld shattered, and in a crashing wave of dizziness and nausea, she collapsed against Praesidio.

"Your zeal is admirable, young learner," Praesidio said. "But don't push so hard so soon. You stopped breathing."

Danae pressed the heels of her hands into her eyes against the onslaught of pressure behind them. "I did?"

"You risk pulling your mind away from the material world entirely if you do too much with too little experience, Danae.

Your mind is not yet used to this connection to the supernatural world, and the realm between ours and the spirit world is treacherous. As always, very bold, very quickly."

"Half-hearted isn't in my working vocabulary." Danae tossed Praesidio a weary smirk. This small success in training warred with how little she still truly knew.

"No, I suppose it isn't," Praesidio replied. "I trust you saw some things?"

"Yes, though 'saw' doesn't represent it properly." Danae hugged her arms around her shoulders, against the chill settling into her flesh. "It's something like feeling your way in the dark. But I came up against something, and I couldn't push past it."

Her mentor laughed. "Your own limitations. I suspect your physical body was trying to warn you it couldn't probe to the depth you desired and still remember to do the little things— like breathe."

"Well, how do I widen that range?" Danae asked. "I think I was closing in on a recognizable signature, but it was too distant or intangible."

Footsteps outside Danae and Praesidio's cell crunched against gravel. Praesidio put his finger to his lips.

A hauhettus stepped up to the bars carrying a sack woven from dark grasses. "Lucky. Temple men want you fed." He threw the sack into the cell and marched into the unseen darkness.

Danae regarded the bag with a skeptical eye, though her stomach roared for the wax-wrapped cheese that poked from its mouth. "Do you think it's tainted?"

Praesidio lifted the bag, reached in, and produced a wine skin. "If you can stand to watch me eat, I'll sample each provision."

With the gauntness of Praesidio's cheeks, his hollow eyes, and the pastiness of his complexion, Danae doubted his fortitude to withstand a poisoning if the food was indeed meant to harm them. "With all due respect, Praesidio, I think I'd better play the part of cup bearer here. I acknowledge your knightly offer, but please . . ." She extended her hand.

Praesidio sighed. He handed her the wineskin.

Danae unstoppered the skin, and the tangy bouquet of tannins reached her nose, a welcome respite from algae and mold. "It might not even be awful," Danae said.

"The supporters of Queldurik's theocracy live well, by material standards," Praesidio replied.

Danae took one mouthful of the wine, a strong, dark vintage, and she waited. Other than warming her throat as it rolled down to her stomach, it threatened no remarkable effects. Neither did the cheese, or the hard tack, or the jerky, though she avoided thinking much about what sort of flesh the Tebalese had dried for it. After about a half hour of waiting that produced neither death, nor hallucinations, nor a sudden compulsion to tell Praesidio everything she ever knew, they deemed the food nothing besides nourishment.

"You realize," Praesidio said between ravenous bites, "if this proves habitual on the part of our captors, we're still going to have to go through this ritual every time."

Danae nodded. "In addition to making sure we keep our words few and low." She took another bite of meat and chewed it contemplatively. "I wish Culduin had a signature."

"Even if he did, you would no longer be able to sense it if—" Praesidio choked off his thought. His uninjured eye welled with a slick of tears. "I will refrain from making any predictions, at least yet."

"How can we even begin to guess what's true?" Danae blurted. "Nothing Ikirra has told us from the outset ought to be trusted."

"She is full of false turnings, that is certain."

"And if he's still alive, I believe if we find the Sword, we'll find him too."

"I will not rob you of this glimmer of confidence, young

learner, for hope is strength." Praesidio shuffled to his straw pallet against the wall and dropped onto it. "But remember, it can blind as well."

*B*retta climbed out of bed and padded to the Da-Shirine's side. She straightened the crooked neckline of a sleeveless shirt of indiscriminate color to position its fabric between her skin and her iron collar. Like the men in the cell, her pants ended at her knees in ragged tears. "I don't understand how anyone made a purchase or a trade this late. No one would be willing to break up a trained team now, with so little time before the championship."

Bretta's lilting brogue grabbed Culduin in the chest and squeezed. His breath grew short. "You're from Radromir?"

She tilted her head. "The highlands. How did you know?"

"Someone I care for is also from that land," he said. "Her manner of speech is much like yours."

"A highlander as well?" Bretta's face lit.

Culduin swallowed his candor. Grief and worry were making him sloppy. What proof did he have that these cellmates were to be trusted? "I do not think so, but I admit to knowing little of your geography."

Bretta frowned. "Oh."

"But what is this talk of sales and teams?" Culduin asked.

"Gods," the surly cellmate grumbled. "You're untrained. We're dead. Thanks so much for the death sentence, Points." He swung his bruised legs over the bed's edge and put his furrowed brow in his hands. Greasy strands of roughly shorn brown hair hung lank over his face.

Culduin clenched his teeth. The man must be Velonese, judging by his antagonism punctuated by a jab at Culduin's heritage. A Radromirian likely would not have known what to make of his ear shape, and one of Praesidio's people would have respected the allegiance between the Delsin and Elgadrim, despite how bleak current circumstances might have been.

The Da-Shirine sighed. "Don't mind Davon. He was beaten as a child by elves."

"What?" Culduin tilted his head.

"I'm in jest," the man added. "Anyway, it doesn't matter what he thinks—Her Ladyship historically has a good eye for gladiators, trained or not."

Culduin's back stiffened. "Gladiators? Is that what this is about? Do you all fight for her?"

Bretta nodded. "We hadn't lost a team member in two years, until two weeks ago—and that not even in a fight. I still say he was poisoned."

"That happens often?" Culduin asked.

"Too often to ever feel entirely sure every meal you eat isn't going to be your last," the Da-Shirine said. "What's your name, warrior?"

Culduin paused. Did it matter if he gave his actual name? The officials at the temple of Queldurik had never asked—but without knowing what had become of Danae and Praesidio, it struck him as best to remain stingy with information. "Theren."

"All right," the Da-Shirine said. "I'm Espowyes. Though folks mostly find it easier to call me Ennis."

"Ennis is a northern name," Culduin said.

Bretta slipped her fingers between her husband's. "When Ennis left Da-Shir to court me, he took a Northernized name to satisfy my clansmen. As if it somehow proved his loyalty."

Davon looked up. "You three can chat romance later. Theren, is it? You've got the gear of a warrior, judging by the mail. Can you stay alive in a fight without it? Pants and shoes are all you'll be allowed."

A spike of anxiety pierced Culduin's calm. "Truly? What's kind of madness—?"

"It's called blood sport, Points," Davon said. "The crowd wants a proper view of people's innards spilling when it happens. And it does. Often."

A grimace overtook Culduin's features. He studied Davon for a moment, noting scars across the man's chest and cheek, and crisscrossing, knotty marks covering his arms and legs. Davon met his gaze in a hard glare.

"You didn't answer my question. Am I going to die next week because of you?"

The elf crossed his arms. "If I have a blade or bow, I will do my part."

A clang interrupted the conversation. All three cell occupants turned toward the bars. The hauhettus, or another, for all Culduin could tell, held a wooden sword with a four-foot blade in a two-handed grip.

"Elf. You fight greatsword?"

Culduin eyed the weapon. "I have. It is not the weapon of my primary expertise but—"

The hauhettus opened the cell door. "Lady says is now. Time for training."

---

*T*wo hauhetti marched Culduin, Bretta, Ennis, and Davon down the corridor to the portcullis Culduin had spied earlier. They stopped in front of it, and Culduin peered between the grid of bars at the cavern within. On the cavern's left rose a terraced stretch of stone, occupied by a half-dozen hauhetti, two humans, and a man so huge he might have been a half-giant. The hauhetti stood guard, the half-giant sat, and the two men paced.

On the right side of the chamber, a straight, narrow channel of water ran, clearly cut with tools. Two mermen and Ikirra leaned on the channel's edge, talking in their clattering language.

The cavern itself stretched no fewer than three hundred paces from portcullis to hind wall, and deep golden sand covered the floor. Two groups of four warriors sparred in separate areas of the sand court, and occasionally, one of the individuals on the terraces would bark commands or rebukes. One of them also used the Western tongue, while another sounded like he spoke Thelenese, the language of Argent's easternmost kingdom. The echoes in the chamber muddled his words.

The hauhettus beside Culduin opened the portcullis by means of a winch that wound a chain around it. The second escort thrust the wooden greatsword into Culduin's hand.

"Better show all skills," he said. "Disappointing fighters make quick eel food."

Culduin weighed the weapon in his hands. It was poorly balanced and ungraceful, but not overly heavy, at least. Davon's remarks earlier implied contests would involve real weapons, not wooden wasters like the combatants before him now employed. The thought of dealing crippling wounds or death to other warriors, pressed into senseless entertainment against their wills, turned Culduin's stomach.

Ennis nudged him from behind. "They don't like delays."

With a nod, Culduin passed under the portcullis, and when his companions stepped inside, they took wasters from a barrel beside the entry. The mermen's eyes fixed on the entering team. Ikirra grinned and pointed at Culduin. One of her kinsmen frowned, while the other looked at her askance.

It does not matter what they think or want. Culduin clenched his fists around his weapon's wooden grip. *Bide the time.*

A wiry-framed man with a patch over his left eye called out, "Kiszchek's team, back to the bunks." He turned toward the arena gate. "Ah, and so it seems Princess Ikirra's vacancy has been filled. We'll see what sort of headache she's brought me."

Culduin's glance volleyed between the man with the patch

and the merfolk, but the swimmers exchanged fast words and pointed gestures, not even casting a single look toward Culduin and his new teammates. The man limped toward them in a gait that implied a significant difference in length between his right and left legs. He carried a thick bat in his gnarled hand.

When he drew within four paces of Culduin, he put the end of the bat under the elf's chin and pushed his head higher. "Hmph. Could be worse." He eyed the wooden weapon in Culduin's hands. "You're fighting with that? Bravado won't get you far here."

"It is what I have been given," Culduin said. "I have a perfectly good longsword amidst my own gear, as well as a bow and quiver I would be happy to substitute."

Patch laughed in a brash, humorless outburst. "Nice try. And besides, there are no missile weapons in the arena. You so much as throw a dirk and you won't like the penalty, I promise. Somebody get the weights off these slugs. Davon, you first. Let's get a look at what this elf is made of."

13

A Quarry of Four

"*T*ime for the games to end, little Creo-ling."

A wave of tearing pain across Danae's back wrenched her from the restless slumber she had finally apprehended after hours of tossing and turning on her thin pallet. She rolled to face her cell's gate, and at first, lantern light blinded her. After rubbing her eyes and tensing her muscles against the pain in her flesh, her sight cleared. The black-robed, hunched Curse Bearer and a robed-and-armored Inquisitor stood outside the bars.

"Please," Praesidio said. "I will stand in her stead."

The Inquisitor chuckled. "Oh, the noble knight comes to the damsel's rescue. We reject your Elgadrim chivalry."

Danae shuddered. "What do you want?"

"You know what we're looking for, besides you," the Curse Bearer with the brutal signature said. Beneath his hood's shadow, a pair of white lights flared. "Zechmaat already learned of your foolish errand, which you now know has utterly failed. So what is the use in resisting?"

Danae's back arched involuntarily against the twisting agony that ran from her skull to her tailbone and seemed intent on ripping the spine from her back. Visions of Papa's gaunt face, his hacking, gurgling cough, his black, web-like mark that encircled a triangular scar on his shoulder, all flashed through her mind. Her brother Weylan cast her an accusatory look, and her heart plummeted into her stomach.

"Such a shame, how your meddling has stripped them of everything. Driven them into exile," the sable-robed figure's voice droned in the recesses of her mind. "All the training your father poured into you, wasted here on an unmeditated flight of fancy. He will die, you will die, they will starve. Unless . . ."

"Don't, Danae!" Praesidio cried, but his voice sounded thin and distant. "Believe no bargain."

A pulse of chilling malice swelled from Danae's tormentor. *Creo, please. I don't think he'll hesitate to kill Praesidio if he interferes —help him see that.*

". . . unless you tell us where it is."

"I . . . honestly . . . don't know," Danae croaked. "Neither of us do. We think the merfolk stole it while we were sleeping."

The interrogator spat. "A fine tale to shield your elf friend with."

Pressure enveloped Danae's body, a loathsome, violating squeeze that seeped into her flesh, her mind, her soul, rooting through the inner fibers of her being in a ransacking assault. She wanted to claw, to kick, to squirm away, but her joints locked, and she could only endure. Only her eyes assented to opening, and she beheld the ebony-skinned face of the interrogator, his eyes white fire like Ba-al Zechmaat's had been, but with less restraint and greater ravening appetite. Their glow illuminated his narrow, bony features, his sharp nose and flaring nostrils, and the thicket of spiny teeth behind his thin lips. Another winged fiend. A Ba-al . . . what hope had she of resistance?

As suddenly as the restraining pressure began, it dropped away. The Ba-al gnashed his teeth. He turned to the Inquisitor. "She's useless. But the last place she saw *it* was with the elf, but the elf's gone missing—"

"Used as eel bait," Praesidio said.

The Curse Bearer scoffed. "So we're told. And now there's no one, not a mermaid war matron, nor this Elgadrim bag of dung, nor this little failure of an apprentice, who knows more."

"So we take these two back to Zechmaat for the pleasure of his sacrifice?" the Inquisitor asked.

Bile seared the back of Danae's throat.

"He sent me after a quarry of four," the fiend said. "I cannot return with half that."

The fiend sputtered a few more words in a guttural language Danae did not understand, then marched from sight. The Inquisitor chased after him.

Convulsive shivers overtook Danae, and she wished she had a blanket or some other heavy garment in which to hide, not so much for want of warmth, but for the wretched feeling of nakedness and filth that plagued her. The taste of salt on her lips alerted her that tears ran down her face. What safety was there in this ugly world into which she had blundered if her enemies could simply overpower her and scour her mind at will? Enduring the ritual plundering of her home city seemed utopian by comparison.

"We need to work on teaching you to shield your spirit in addition to honing your seeking abilities, do we not, young learner?" Praesidio whispered.

Danae rolled to a sitting posture, wrapped her arms around her bent knees, and buried her face in them.

"I'm so sorry there hasn't been time before this. Had I any

notion things would take this kind of turn, it would have been the first skill I taught you. Can you forgive me?"

"It's not your fault." Danae wiped her wet cheeks on her knees. "Every step of this journey, the warnings have been there that I'm dabbling in matters beyond me, but from stealing words from Papa's writings to insisting Archadion allow me to prove myself, I've bulled my way along. I'm getting a bit of what I deserve, I suppose."

Praesidio frowned, and his eyes welled. "No one deserves to have their mind rummaged like a slop trough. If any Curse is unforgivable, I say it is that."

"So it sounds like they're going to keep us here until they can find Culduin."

"Danae, please," Praesidio sighed. "I want him to be alive as much as you do. But I don't think he is the further acquisition that monster is worried about."

The weight of seemingly unalterable circumstances bore down upon Danae. Escape. It was the only option that remained. And the most impossible prospect of them all.

---

*D*avon's practice blade whistled in before Culduin had so much as taken a sparring posture, and only a clumsy swipe of the wooden greatsword prevented Culduin from suffering a sound blow to the head or neck. He backpedaled.

"We begin right away, I see," Culduin said.

Davon rolled his eyes. "This isn't fencing class in the royal court, Points."

After squelching the surge of irritation that swelled in his gut, Culduin swung the greatsword around in a two-handed grip, a high, level cut that Davon met in a left shoulder parry. Davon rocked back a step. His dark eyes flickered.

They exchanged a series of cuts and parries, which proved Davon a capable swordsman, but the way Culduin's attacks threw his opponent off balance spoke to the elf's superior strength.

I would be faster, too, Culduin mused, *had I not been saddled with this tree trunk of a weapon*. Had Ikirra assumed the Sword of the Patron was his primary weapon, since he had it with him when she led him to his capture? Surely she had been observant enough to notice how he, Danae, and Praesidio had rotated the weapon between them as they traveled with the mermaid as guide.

Danae. What might have befallen her in the past few hours?

A sharp impact exploded across the left side of Culduin's head. His ears rang. He staggered and fought to shake it off.

"Hold!" came the voice of the trainer. "That's a win for you, Davon."

Davon smirked and lowered his weapon. He swiped the back of his hand across a brow running with sweat.

Patch limped toward Culduin. "You'd best get your head in this, elf, or you won't last a round, and you risk getting three fine warriors killed to boot."

True enough—his concern for Danae had clouded his mind. Culduin stretched taller. "I will not allow it to happen again." He glanced to Ikirra, whose tight-lipped, disapproving stare skittered across Culduin's flesh in an arc of rankling energy. He fired as venomous a stare at her as he could muster.

"Bretta, you're up," Patch said.

Bretta pulled two lengths of chain from her belt. On one end of the links were handles, on the other, wood blades that curved in a semicircle about two handspans wide.

Culduin filled his lungs until his ribs could expand no further, then released the breath in a deliberate, focused stream. He imagined his frustration washing over his muscles and infusing them with strength and efficiency. As soon as Bretta had drawn within five paces, Culduin unleashed a diagonal swing, from high to low.

Bretta gasped and dove right, tucked in a roll. The wooden greatsword only missed her by a hair's breadth. She regained her feet and whirled her chain blades.

"Those are rather exotic for Radromir," Culduin said.

"We were teamsters." Bretta lunged at him with a spinning blade, but Culduin swept it aside in a parry. "We saw a lot more of the world than many."

"Ennis's horses?" Culduin swung; Bretta jumped back.

"Of course. He's the second son of clan Cho-Namis."

Culduin nodded appreciatively. A second son, just like him. But being a son of the most prominent horse lords in the nation of Da-Shir would give Ennis access to fine animals indeed. What had the position of second son in the family Caranaedhel earned Culduin, besides a long shadow to cover his modest deeds?

He mentally swept away the gossamer threads of connection he was already forming with these people. His only goal could be to leave them at the first opportunity. His next swing sailed in and caught Bretta's left arm.

"Left arm out!" the trainer called.

Bretta dropped the weapon from that hand and placed her arm behind her back.

She dodged Culduin's next six attacks in an elaborate series of twists and ducks. She came at Culduin with her remaining blade and her feet, but only one of the kicks made contact with his thigh. The attack lacked no strength; indeed, the muscle it met burned, but still he fought on.

The next blade that swung in inspired in Culduin a calculated risk, here in the practice arena where stakes remained low. He darted a hand in, gauging the rotation of Bretta's weapon, and grabbed it by the chain. A hard wrench spun Bretta halfway around.

A wordless roar of frustration burst from Bretta's lungs, and she countered Culduin's snare with wide roundhouse from her other leg, but Culduin's high block caught the attack. She staggered off balance.

Thrusting his arm back, Culduin tore Bretta's weapon from her grasp, and she pitched forward in the sandy footing. On her way down, Bretta elbowed the back of Culduin's knee with a sharp jab. His knee buckled. He spun on the opposite foot as Bretta sprawled, chest first, to the ground.

Culduin pressed the point of his sword between her shoulder blades and looked to the trainer. Without taking his eyes from the trainer's, he whispered to Bretta, "I apologize. It is not normal elven protocol to engage in combat with females of any race."

"You'd better get used to it." Bretta spat sand. "I won't be the only one out there, and I doubt I'm the best, either."

Patch stepped up beside Culduin, reached out, and helped Bretta to her feet. "That's more like it." The trainer guffawed. "For a moment I was beginning to worry Princess Ikirra had brought you on as bait."

_____

14

Submerged

"$\mathcal{P}$raesidio." Danae laid a gentle hand on the old teacher's shoulder. "It's time for your watch. I think."

In the subterranean cellblock, who could tell how many hours she had watched? Her level of fatigue simply warned her that she risked falling asleep and leaving them both unaware if she did not ask that Praesidio take over. She did not dare miss Culduin arriving as a prisoner.

The last three days had offered alternating periods of fitful rest and snippets of training. Praesidio only pursued the expansion of Danae's skills at times they could be reasonably certain their guard either did not understand or care what they talked about. Two of the hauhetti guards kept a suspicious eye trained their way throughout their shifts, but the third, a flaccid, flabby, pale creature with one eye missing and the other covered in a milky film, often dozed at his post. It was during his assigned times that Danae and Praesidio both remained awake. He instructed her in stretching her ability to hunt the Sword's signature and in shielding her mind.

Praesidio's eyes fluttered open. "That time again, is it?" His stormy gray glance had regained much of its keenness in the past day, and his sluggishness and pallor seemed to have improved as well, to Danae's relief. Another day and the swelling around his eye would likely be back to normal, though the bruising and bright-red broken eye vessel would remain a long reminder.

"I think I figured out why the signature of the Sword seems sort of odd. Warped, you might say."

Praesidio's brow lifted. "Is that so?"

"Yes!" Danae smiled. "It's because—"

Her mentor held up his palm, cutting her words short. "Might I suggest you lock this tidbit away in your mental vault, like we've been practicing? With your permission, I would like to probe after it to see how well you've learned your lessons. A morsel like this will be so vibrant that if you can conceal it from me, I will call you well trained."

She nodded. "Good idea." After sitting cross-legged in front of Praesidio, she envisioned walls of stone surrounding her, ring upon ring of an impenetrable keep with no gates. She imagined herself at its center, a staff drawn for defense, in case she might need to fend off a would-be gleaner of her thoughts. She imagined even her own skin made of supple steel.

"I'm ready."

She sensed Praesidio's effervescent signature, but it swirled around her at a distance. She could reach out to it if she so chose, but its energy did not encroach upon her mental walls. She and her mentor locked gazes, and while the intensity of his stare made her heart pound for fear of faltering under its strength, her fortress held.

Praesidio's signature metamorphosed and felt more like

warm, shifting water, and for an instant, Danae fought the temptation to allow its promise of comfort to sweep over her.

They will come in all guises, the marauders of thoughts. Those that seem to caress, to whisper, you must redouble your defenses against.

The recall of Praesidio's words, drawn straight from *The Tree*, drove Danae to shroud her fortress in darkness as well as stone.

Praesidio's signature dissipated altogether.

"Very, very good, Danae." Praesidio smiled. "Whatever blood in your veins granted you Thaumaturgy talent grows more potent every day. I had no access whatsoever."

"What do you mean by that?" Danae asked.

"You were fully insulated. I could pull no thought, however surface, from your mind."

"No, not that." Danae chuckled. "About my blood and my Thaumaturgy."

Praesidio's expression lit. "Oh, that. I just mean that somewhere in your ancestry, you have kin who have gifted you your divine talents. Only the Elgadrim and the elves have such gifts, so somewhere in your family tree, you will find one or the other. Or both."

"You mean I could be one of your kin?" Danae gaped. *Or one of Culduin's?* She restrained herself from voicing the second revelation with how melancholy Praesidio had become about Culduin's prospects.

"Possibly," Praesidio said. "But what of the warped signature? What's your guess?"

Danae scooted beside Praesidio and lowered her voice to the barest whisper. "I'm pretty sure it's underwater. It hasn't moved in days. Could it possibly have been dropped or lost?"

"Or is Ikirra telling the truth that Culduin has been given over to eels," Praesidio said, "and his remains are at the bottom of whatever dread place the creatures feed?"

Danae gasped. "D-dead people float. Don't they?"

"Not if they still have any armor or weapons on them."

A shudder overtook Danae. "Do you really have no hope?"

Praesidio examined the floor. "This place drains me of it, hour by hour."

Suddenly, her realization about the Sword's possible whereabouts took on such a bleak pall. Would the merfolk really throw Culduin, gear and all, to those spike-toothed monsters? One would think they would at least plunder his goods first. Could they possibly have seen no value in the Sword? And if it was at the bottom of some subterranean pool or river, trapped by water and darkness, how would they get to it?

"Do the merfolk live underwater most of the time?" Danae asked.

Praesidio shook his head. "No. They have lungs and need to come to the surface for air—like whales. They can stay under for much longer than we 'finless,' though." The disdain that crept into the old sage's voice was starker than Danae thought him capable. Yes, even the unflappable sage was prone to rankling. Their recent trials had proven that much.

"Praesidio." Danae cracked her knuckles. "We can't just wait for those Curse Bearers from the temple to decide it's time to wring our necks. I know it's crazy, but we need to escape. I think I can find *it* if we do."

After a long sigh, Praesidio rose and stretched. "Consider this carefully, young learner. First, know that I agree with you on both counts. But—what if we do find it? Are you prepared to face the darkest news about our elf friend? Or worse—learn nothing of his fate? Would you leave this place, uncertain, in the unlikely event we could even find a way to the surface?"

A sharp clang against the cell bars jarred Culduin from his repose. He sprang from his pallet, heart hammering.

Their trainer stood in flickering torchlight outside the cell, his bat in his hand. "Lucky day, fighters. You get to see the sun for a few."

Culduin straightened his tunic. "To the surface?"

"Tournament time, so yes," Ennis said.

"In five days," Patch said. "We've got to schlep you and your gear at an easy pace so you arrive with the strength to fight."

"About my gear," Culduin said. "You'll be returning my sword at least?"

Patch guffawed. "You'll fight with whatever her Ladyship fancies. You won't get anything with an edge until you're waiting to step into the ring. So doll yourselves up, my lazies. Ikirra will inspect you before we go, and then it's back to the surface."

A mix of relief and dismay swirled in Culduin's chest. The prospect of breathing open air held infinite appeal, but what if somewhere in the cave network Danae and Praesidio wandered, lost, potentially starving? Or had they, too, been captured? Submission to leaving for the gladiatorial championship threatened to abandon them to dire circumstances. Culduin's powerlessness over it all burned like a canker.

A sharp smack on Culduin's shoulder snapped his introspection in two.

Davon tugged his tunic over his head and threw it on his bunk. "Linens aside, Points."

Culduin furrowed his brow. "Pardon?"

"Inspection is in gladiatorial uniform," Davon said. "So lose the shirt and stop making us slow enough to invite Ikirra's ire."

Ennis also stripped off his tattered vest and shirt, and Bretta left her outer robe aside to wear only a short skirt of green leather and a sleeveless, laced vest of the same dyed hide.

Patch turned the key in the lock and stepped inside. He dragged a ball and chain for each of them from the corner, and while one of the hauhetti guarded the door, he clamped a shackle around each of their feet, then connected the group into a gang.

Following Ennis and Davon's lead, Culduin picked up the ball attached to his own ankle and carried it on his hip. Out of the cell they shuffled in lockstep to return to the practice arena.

Soon after their trainer had lined them up along the pool's edge inside the practice arena, a muscled, dark-haired merman with a goatee and unyielding gaze breached the surface of the water. He observed Culduin's team wordlessly. With a whispering sigh of water, Ikirra rose from the depths beside him. She pointed to Ennis.

The portcullis at the arena's end ground shut, and the hauhettus guard unlocked the team's shackles.

Freed of his bonds to the group, the Da-Shirine stepped forward and knelt at the edge of the pool. Ikirra studied him something like a wrangler at auction and then turned a short nod to the trainer. She waved Ennis away and then pointed to Bretta, who repeated the ritual.

Once Bretta had returned to her spot ten paces from the pool, Ikirra smirked, her eyes coy and mischievous, and she beckoned Davon. He advanced to the edge of the pool and dropped to his knees. Ikirra reached up, put her hands on his shoulders, and propelled herself toward him. They connected in a ravenous kiss for a long moment that drove Culduin's glance to the ground, the chiseled ceiling, the portcullis. An awkward eternity later, Ikirra drifted back. She hummed and clicked.

"She says win it all for her," Patch translated.

"I will use every trick, Your Highness," Davon said. "And you have prepared favors, should we earn them in battle?"

The merman lord screwed one eyebrow down and looked at Davon from beneath it.

"I've been overbold." Davon ducked his head. "Favors or no, it is a privilege to fight for your daughter."

"What's a favor?" Culduin whispered to Ennis.

Ennis spoke from the corner of his mouth without turning his head. "Items imbued with enchantments that can help a warrior in the final rounds—"

"Culduin!" Ikirra said.

The elf grimaced.

She beckoned with an impatient gesture.

Davon, on his way back to the line, leveled a dark glare at Culduin as they passed. "Pet name between you, *Theren?*"

Perfect. Just what he needed. This mistrust of the most volatile warrior in the bunch, right before they departed for the event. Culduin focused on the merfolk and took a few militaristic steps to the edge of the pool. By all that was honest in Creo's creation, he would not fulfill any role of plaything for this deceiver. He inclined his chin.

Ikirra leapt up and grabbed Culduin's hand, yanking on his arm and pulling him forward. He craned his head left as she aimed a kiss for his lips but instead caught his ear. She released his hand, laughed, then chattered in her chittering tongue.

Patch said, "She calls you stodgy. Funny."

"I fear she will continue to find me simply hysterical," Culduin replied. His glance flicked to Davon, whose jaw was set in a confrontational cast. "Besides, entanglements would cloud my mind and make me sloppy."

The merman stroked his whiskers. He clicked and uttered a series of baritone pitches.

Patch again translated. "He says, 'You sound at least like you have some sense to go with the muscle. I trust you will not disappoint my daughter or waste my investment.'"

"If the field is fair," Culduin said, "you should find me competent."

The merman king drew out two tones.

"And if it is not?" Patch said.

"Then we expect your favors will even the odds," Culduin said.

The merman burst into boisterous laughter. At the conclusion of his mirth and many rapid mer sounds, Ikirra's jaw dropped. She too laughed.

Culduin lifted his brows. *Do I want to know?*

Patch groaned. "He can see why she likes you. You've got some—"

"The point is made," Culduin grumbled.

The merman blew a gust of air and settled his lingering chuckle. He drew into a regal posture, his chest high and chin level.

Patch continued in his role of interpreter. "You will depart in two turns of the glass. I expect when I see you next, it will be to present me with the prize chest, or else, don't bother living through the last round."

15

So Close to Sunlight

"It's moving! Praesidio, what do we do?" Danae emerged from her deep concentration on the Sword's signature, though she hardly needed to descend to that state anymore, with as accustomed as she had become with connecting to the Sword's essence and watching over it. Its distasteful, groping slickness had become just another ill to bear in bad circumstances.

The Elgadrim knight looked up from studying the backs of his hands. "Do?" He gestured to the bars of their cell. "I don't know that there's anything we can do."

The cataract-plagued hauhettus guard reached through the prison door and grabbed the empty bag from their lunch. At least, despite the bleakness of incarceration, food arrived regularly. Never quite enough, but certainly more than they would have had on their own. The guard shuffled off, leaving their gate unmanned, as had become periodic habit in the last couple of days.

Danae darted over to Praesidio and crouched beside him. "Now or never, don't you think? If they move it too far, won't I lose it? We need to follow as best we can."

"Do you have some miraculous plan for dissolving iron?" Praesidio's tone bit.

Danae stepped back and propped her hands on her hips. "You don't need to be so snappish about it. You're the one who knows every Utterance in *The Tree*."

"And the other words of the text as well," Praesidio said. "Enough to know we don't simply throw Virtusen about at whim and will. Don't you think it matters to me, too, whether we recover this thing? You recall what it means for my people and the war."

"Of course," Danae said. "Which is why I don't understand why you won't try *something*. Anything!"

"Because Creo has told me one thing in all this time: wait."

"Easy for Creo to say, he who exists outside of time."

Praesidio interlaced his hands and lowered his head. "I do not care for Creo's directive in this moment either, but I've learned over these decades—"

Footsteps crunched outside the cell, and a torch-bearing Inquisitor came into sight. His pinching signature overtook Danae. "Time to go. His Eminence, Ba-al Zechmaat, requests the pleasure of your presence back in Garash."

Praesidio frowned. "Why now?"

"He doesn't answer to you, cur."

Danae's throat constricted. So they had waited too long. Was the Sword in motion because the Inquisitor's allies had found it? She retreated inward in search of it again—yes, it was definitely on the move, and no trace of the warbling that distorted its characteristics remained. Bare, clammy slime sent a shudder through Danae's torso.

The squeal of rusty hinges raked at Danae's mind, and she opened her eyes. The gate stood ajar, and the Inquisitor waited outside. He handed two packs to the hauhettus at the river's edge. Her pack. And Praesidio's.

The Inquisitor fingered his whip. "In the boat. Now."

Danae waited, assuming the Inquisitor would step in and bind them, but he did not advance. He carried nothing, in fact— no rope, no shackles.

A squinting glance into the dark beyond the servant of Queldurik revealed a slender gondola bobbing on black water. A lantern hung from decorative scrollwork on the boat's bow. Praesidio led the way to the water's edge, and the hauhettus kept his harpoon trained on the old sage's every step. Danae followed.

Her heart sped to a dizzying rate. It rocked her chest and pounded in her ears. Her skin flared with heat. With only two captors, still Praesidio did nothing. Their odds had not been better in weeks, and still, compliance seemed his sole intent. Danae breathed with deliberate slowness and depth.

All right. We wouldn't know where to go now even if we did get away. But may heaven and earth perish, I won't step behind another set of bars. Danae climbed into the rocking watercraft and perched on the rear plank too narrow to have been meant as a proper seat.

The hauhettus plunked their bags in the middle of the boat while the Inquisitor boarded. Lastly, the hauhettus joined them in the stern, unclipped a pole from the far side, and pushed off into the lazy current.

As they traveled, Danae divided her attention between the wet monotony of the cave tunnels, none of which had beaches or landings, and clinging to the Sword's signature. As best she could tell, the Sword had traveled farther ahead and up. Danae attempted to mark the time they spent on the river by counting the strokes of the hauhettus's pole, but after some seven hundred, she gave up.

By the time Danae's legs had begun to develop pins and

needles from the seat that cut into her rear, the boat pulled into a chamber with a little swatch of beach. The boat ground onto land, right in front of a rough doorway in the cavern wall. The Inquisitor's torchlight caught on flat planes of rock inside the doorway—the treads and risers of hewn stairs.

"Out," the Inquisitor said.

Danae all but leapt from the boat, but the hauhettus's spring exhibited the frog-like half of his nature in its speed and power. In a single bound, he placed his sinewy, sandy-hided figure between Danae and the doorway, harpoon at the ready.

The Inquisitor shouldered past Danae and led the way up the stairs, and the bestial guard compelled Danae and Praesidio to follow. The carven stairs wound in a serpentine fashion through jagged fissures in the rock. At times, they smoothed to a steadily inclined ramp. Always, they led the group upward.

Danae's thighs burned with the exertion after countless days of confinement. The only mercy captivity had extended her was time to heal her abrasions and bruised ribs from her plummet into the merfolk's domain. A deep breath no longer shot pain through her torso and shoulders. Up, up, up they climbed. The ascent threatened to stretch longer than the boat ride.

A filtered glow from Danae's left grabbed her notice. A passage branching from the sloped path they traveled definitely grew lighter farther in, rather than plunging into the usual blackness. She sniffed. Indeed, the air here seemed drier, less stagnant.

Praesidio marched on, dutifully following the Inquisitor. Tremors began in Danae's stomach and worked their way from her trunk and through her limbs. She had to improvise—there was no way to coordinate anything with Praesidio. Ahead, trickling water chattered, and by straining around Praesidio, she discovered a stream that ran across their path. In the water's voice whispered the hint of a plan.

Within a few paces of the stream, Danae spotted the stepping stones placed for crossing. The Inquisitor placed his foot on the first rock.

Danae snagged her toe on one of the many loose rocks in the passage and tumbled forward. She shoved the Inquisitor with all her might.

At the moment the servant of Queldurik lost his footing, Danae blurted, *"Incancunium laetir abedhaenno!"*

A sizzle of energy burst from her chest and ran down her arms to blaze from her fingertips. Lavender arcs of lighting entangled the Inquisitor like vines as he crashed into the water. He thrashed, kicking up an electrified froth, and screamed in a language Danae did not understand.

The hauhettus bellowed and rushed forward.

A flare of light and roar of flame filled the hallway. Praesidio spun, his Sword of the Sacred Fire borne aloft, and struck the hauhettus at the juncture of his shoulder and neck.

A musty, burning fetor filled the air. Danae gagged at the bubbling, charred skin around the hauhettus's wound but still scrambled to her feet and barreled past.

The frog-man's harpoon jab met Praesidio's blade of blue flame in a parry, which Praesidio followed with a thrust. The fiery beam emerged between the hauhettus's shoulder blades. The beast slumped to the left.

"Grab our packs if you can!" Danae yelled to Praesidio. "This way!"

The old sage fumbled with the satchels, yanking them free of the hauhettus's shoulder.

Back the way they had come, Danae grabbed the edge of the lit passage and hauled herself into it. She blundered up the shallow stairs. *Please don't let this be a* lumienne *in some chamber full of who knows what.* "Praesidio, you with me?"

"Yes," the old sage gasped, a few strides behind her. "What are you thinking?"

"Thinking? Not so much. Seizing opportunities."

"I fear it shows!"

Danae took the steps two to a stride until they ended at a landing. Sunlight shone through a doorway on the left, but it streamed in dusty beams, broken by a barred gate.

16

Ambushed

*C*ulduin sat cross-legged in the thick down of a velvet cushion, the covered cart rocking beneath him as it rumbled along the wide Garash-Cray Highway. He leaned his forehead into his hands.

Maker, I do not pray as often as I should—but I think now of only Danae and Praesidio's preservation in my absence. Forgive me for finding no way to fight my way back to them. I wish you could show me they are safe.

A clank of thin metal interrupted Culduin's halting prayer. Ennis straightened from having set a tray on the built-in shelf next to the elf's bunk in the cart.

"Try to at least push this food around a little," Ennis said. "The trainers won't make it pleasant for you if you keep fasting. Do you have some sort of religious restrictions on your food? Because they'll get you something you'll eat, if they've got it."

Culduin glanced over the meal—an ample portion of smoked fowl, some roasted barley, and a small skin of something to drink. "If you have to be a slave, being a gladiator appears less tortuous than some occupations one might land in."

"If you don't mind a stabbing or a mauling by wyverns always being a risk, then sure," Ennis said. He cracked a half-smirk. After casting his glance around the wide cart in which they rode—a massive, wooden vehicle with four plush bunks built into the walls, a sitting area, complete with upholstered chairs, oil lamps for light, blankets, and a floor carpeted in sheepskin—Ennis shook his head. "It's all part of the game. Each team is trying to outdo one another from the start. That's why we're part of this vanity parade. I swear it gets more opulent each year. Did you see the rolling water tanks the merfolk are traveling in?"

"Only a glance," Culduin said. He pinched a taste of the barley and placed it in his mouth. It showcased deft seasoning, but still, he could find no appetite, even after skipping most of the morning pastries and sausages. Perhaps it was his disgust with himself for leaving the tunnels without Danae and Prae-sidio—perhaps it was the threat of poisoning. Perhaps a bit of both. His shoulders slumped.

Bretta joined Ennis. "You fight like a soldier. Clean, precise —so I'm thinking it's not the contest that's bothering you. What is it?"

"Any sane person faces armed combat with some sense of trepidation." Culduin leaned back on his hands.

The cart rocked through a rut in the road, and both Bretta and Ennis stumbled, but they caught one another's arms and steadied themselves.

"You don't have to tell us anything," Bretta said. "But the battles are easier if you don't go into them burdened."

What reason did Culduin have to trust either of them? If the merfolk were in any way hunting for information on Danae and Praesidio, what would prevent them from using the bright-eyed Bretta as an accessory? But perhaps he was overthinking the situation. After all, Ikirra only wanted him so that she could take her gladiators to the final contest. Perhaps once she had him, she fell to ignoring his friends—though that would have left them lost, how far underground? The vague recollection of weapons clashing as he fell prey to Ikirra's lure rang in the back of his mind. No, she had not disregarded them.

"What do the merfolk do with outsiders they find in their cave network—those they do not intend to try as prize fighters?" Culduin asked.

Ennis said, "A select few they keep as personal slaves. The rest they trade with surface cultures for goods, especially sundries and food. There's only so much eel and algae you can eat, I hear."

A pulse of anger surged in Culdiun's chest. Lives as commodities. It was sickening.

"So Princess Ikirra lured you from a surface shore?" Bretta's tone was gentle.

"No," Culduin replied. "I blundered into a river cavern. Ikirra said she would lead me out. That turned out well."

"She used the flute, didn't she?" Ennis scratched his head and grimaced sympathetically.

Culduin flushed.

"If it's any comfort," Bretta said, "rumor has it she's never failed to lure any male she's set sights on."

Bretta's wording pricked Culduin's already-raw regrets. "Any chance I will ever see my belongings again? I had a bow I had made myself and a quiver gifted to me by my grandsire."

In a warm gesture, Ennis placed a hand on Culduin's shoulder. "Not unless you're blessed with a brand of fortune none of us has seen. Goods of that quality become valuable currency in surface bartering."

Culduin grimaced. The thought of his fine leather quiver exchanged for sacks of grain or bolts of fabric galled him. Worse, would Ikirra have named a price for the Sword? How quickly everything he had worked for on Danae's behalf unraveled. Irony mocked—the Sword could very well be in the hands of some banal oddities peddler who saw nothing beyond the weapon's exotic appearance. Or, more likely, the temple officials were taking it right back to Ba-al Zechmaat.

"Ennis is right, though," Bretta said. "You need to eat. If the trainers collect another full tray from—"

The cart lurched beneath them, and this time, both Bretta and Ennis fell to the woolen floor. Davon, who had been sleeping, pitched from his bunk. Shouting, in multiple languages— none of which Culduin could understand in the cacophony, warred outside.

A series of *thocks* punched at the left wall of the cart. Culduin bounded across the vehicle, which now barreled forward. Arrowheads protruded from side planks.

"We are—an attack? Highwaymen?" Culduin cried. He staggered for the door in the right wall of the cart, but as it had been from the start of the journey, he found it locked.

Davon rolled to his knees. "The opposition, most probably. They're starting early this year."

An object smashed against the cart roof, just over Culduin's head, followed by the tinkle of broken glass. The sharp bark of arrow strikes drummed again, also on the roof of the vehicle, followed by more bellowing. Fire rumbled to life. In the breaches where arrowheads had pierced the ceiling, Culduin spied the orange flicker of hungry flames.

Whether the choice would plunge him into a thicket of arrows, Culduin cared little—the wood and fabric of the bunk cart would kindle like tinder. He stepped back a few paces, then ran at the door, shoulder first.

The impact made his ears ring, but the planking did crack.

The ceiling smoked. Flames lapped through growing holes where arrows struck.

When Culduin backed up for another charge, Bretta and

Ennis joined him. He turned to the husband and wife, all the while bracing his legs shoulder width against the bucking of the cart rushing over uneven road.

"Ennis, you and I will shoulder the door—there is not room for three. Bretta, you follow behind. Davon, I suggest you join us! Ready . . . go!"

They rushed the door again, and the center plank gave way to Culduin and Ennis's combined weight. The frame cracked further.

Smoke thickened the air to a choking haze, and heat swelled from above. All four gladiators kicked furiously at the door between coughs, until the splintering wood burst asunder. With only a glance at the rolling steppes that sped by, Culduin jumped.

———

*D*anae gripped the iron bars of the gate and shook them like a crazed woman throttling an enemy. "No! Can't anything be simple? Ever?"

Praesidio picked up a stone from the floor, shouldered Danae aside, and smashed the stone against the flaking padlock on the gate latch. "Everything down here is so corroded, I doubt this lock will hold out long." He swung again, and the lock bent at the junction of the shank and the body. "Anything on your pack you might defend us with when someone follows us up these stairs?"

When Danae threw the flap to her pack open, the sweet, musty funk of thick mildew overwhelmed her senses, and she coughed. "Probably not." Her eyes watered. "Wait, what about the minor Virtusen for transformation?"

Another whack with the stone. Praesidio grunted and shook his hand. A flash of crimson betrayed where he had cut open his knuckles. "This is not really the time for flower petals to butterflies, you know. I'm surprised Creo even granted the lesser lightning."

"Well he did, so I can't be so off track." Danae stooped and picked up a handful of the gravely footing. "But what if I ask this be turned into caltrops? I have never seen a frog-man with shoes."

Between continued assaults on the lock, Praesidio chuckled. "Not the most direct interpretation of the Virtus, but why not?"

Danae closed her eyes and pressed her handful of untransformed gravel to her forehead. She clenched her teeth . . . could she remember the Utterance? She certainly had no time to look it up in *The Tree*, and judging by the smell of her bag, the book was probably molded beyond readability anyway. "Gardaphe . . . ennim . . . wait." Her brow prickled with sweat, and beyond Praesidio's ruckus, she strained her ears for hints of pursuit. So far, no one noisy pursued them, at least. *Creo, give me the words, I beg of you.*

The page in *The Tree* where she had read the minor Virtusen took shape in her mind. She could see the scrolled sidebar and the flowing text, divided by elegantly lettered headers. "*Gardaphe, seretennim! Gardaphe, seretennim et fil, perhominet,*" she whispered. Her fist clenched tighter around the gravel.

A burning, sparking pain exploded from Danae's elbow down, and she flung the stinging palm forward. Dozens of orange lights, bright as embers, launched from her hand and tumbled down the stairs. The pebbles, turned sharp and multipronged, bounced into the darkness below. Their light faded, but as Danae squinted after them, she could make out jagged shapes, just barely, scattered all over a dozen stairs.

"Well, here's hoping we don't need to go back that way. It should at least slow any pursuers down," Danae said.

With a swing and a grunt, Praesidio bashed the lock again, and the shaft finally gave way. "Or it might just make them angry."

"You mean angrier." She reached past Praesidio and threw the gate latch to the side, and it squealed in the most shudder-inducing way. "I'm used to that. Let's get out of here."

They hauled the stubborn gate aside, which groaned like it had not been opened in countless years. The exit led into a stone pit, deep as a well, but lined with abundant niches and outcroppings. Danae led the climb up, but when she reached the last of the natural handholds, she hesitated. Inch by inch, she poked her head above the lip of the chute.

Although a blanket of drab clouds hung over the skies, the light of day hurt Danae's eyes and stabbed her forehead with immediate pain. She shielded her eyes with one hand and surveyed the rolling landscape. The chute let out at the top of a stony embankment of a chattering stream, and on either stream bank, tall, young grasses rippled in a light wind. Clusters of magenta coneflower and wild indigo stretched to the horizon. Not an unwelcome soul spoiled her range of view.

Blinking, Danae clambered into the light of day, then reached back to grasp Praesidio's hand. Though his grip was tight, he did not refuse her help, and his weight pulled heavily on her arm as he hauled himself from the tunnel.

"Oh, Maker." Danae bit her lip. "Where do we go? Without Culduin, I haven't the slightest. You can't even tell where the sun is on a day like today. And what if he's still down there somewhere? Will the merfolk harm him because we've run?"

Praesidio sighed. "All questions I cannot answer, young one. Did you forget the risk when you decided to improvise this dash?"

Folding her arms, Danae scowled. "The risk of going back to Ba-al Zechmaat seemed worse—at least for us." She drew a long breath. "But there's one thing we've got to focus on, and I believe . . ." Her words hitched. "I believe Culduin would want us to get the Sword back if there's a chance of it."

"What of that?" Praesidio asked.

Danae reached with her mind, once again in search of the loathsome tendrils of the Sword's signature. Outward, farther, in a full circle all around her body, she imagined her mind spreading like a spill of molten metal. A thing of determination, unstoppable and pervasive.

Ahead and to her left, the faintest sense, like algae waving beneath a slow current, brushed Danae's consciousness. She grimaced, then pointed. "That way. I believe it's far."

"All right then, sensor," Praesidio said. "If you are certain we should press on, this is your quest."

Danae rubbed her temples. *May the Maker have liberated Culduin far ahead of us.* She tightened her pack and struck out after the uncanny aura she both needed and loathed. *We're getting back on track, Papa. Hold on.*

Their course paralleled a gravel highway that cut through the rolling meads of the southern Tebalese steppes—or at least Danae assumed. The weather had not yet grown warm, but compared to the chill of the tundra, or to a Radromirian spring, for that matter, it had a dry-but-balmy quality.

The bright flowers and the light breeze might have cheered Danae were it not for the constant connection she forced herself to maintain with the Sword, and for the unbidden memory of the wildflower wreath Culduin had once woven for her in a similar landscape. Her heart clenched. How much simpler the quest had seemed at that point. And how much greater devastation would she be facing now if she had listened to her heart and not her head when Culduin had offered that crown of blossoms. Her eyes misted, but she blinked it off.

"Are we, in fact, still in Tebal?" Danae asked.

"As best I can tell." Praesidio squinted skyward. "The northern wilds of Kelmirith and the southlands of Tebal are kindred in quality. But I have my doubts that anyone who might have taken the Sword would be bearing it into Kelmirith."

"Unless Culduin escaped with it."

Praesidio's expression grew pinched. "Danae . . ."

She lifted her palms. "All right. I'll stop. Really, I will."

"Can you tell if the Sword is still moving?"

Danae nodded. "I only have a vague sense that's the case—I can't tell how fast or any specifics. I wish I could separate my worry from Creo's prompting."

"Creo is not the author of worry," Praesidio said. "But he does sometimes call for haste."

17

The Team Intervenes

*L*ong grasses whipped Culduin's skin as he tumbled from the burning transport. Men's shouts, warring with the croaking language of the hauhetti, crackled in the dry air, mingled with the pop and snap of flame. Bowstrings twanged. Somewhere behind him, steel met steel.

He rolled over the crest of a knoll, and for a brief moment, relished the scent of crushed greenery beneath him. Keeping low, he pivoted his body to peer back over the knoll like a soldier in a trench. Davon, Bretta, and Ennis joined him.

A brief survey of the battleground revealed the rest of the merfolk's caravan had circled the gladiator transport, and their leap from the now-engulfed vehicle had not carried them beyond the perimeter of this hedge. A half-dozen men and hauhetti charged toward Culduin's position, round target shields raised high on one arm, and spears, cutlasses, and maces borne in the other.

Arrows whistled in from the south. A half-dozen bowmen,

wearing branches, face paint, and mottled clothing had remained well camouflaged in the tall bracken on the high ground to the highway's south, until now. One of the hauhetti guards charging for Culduin took an arrow between the shoulder blades. The creature hissed, convulsed, and sprawled. The remaining artillery pinged from armor and shields.

Culduin glanced behind him. The chain of carts and merfolk tanks surrounding them was not without gaps. Which seemed the least defended? The northwestern bend of the ring had the widest spaces between vehicles.

He leapt to his feet and barreled for the perimeter. The skirmish's cries, clangs, and twangs echoed on, and the hiss of an arrow past his ear made him flinch. Just a few more strides. No caravan members emerged to intercept. The driver of the middle vehicle tightened his contact with his pair of shaggy dappled horses and yelled something, however.

With a burst of redoubled speed, Culduin plunged for the scant gap between the rear of that cart and the muzzles of four black draft horses behind it. *Almost free.*

He pitched forward, a sudden snare grabbing his feet. Culduin twisted, but before he could break away, a second attacker clamped sinewy arms around his ribs. Two captors and he crumpled into a rolling heap.

A swift thrash liberated one of Culduin's legs from the man who had tripped him, but Culduin's other attacker grappled with his upper body, while the first threw his weight across his legs. They were surely both human.

The person on Culduin's legs panted. "I know you hate this. But don't. It'll just earn you a branding, and you don't have time to recover from that before the games."

The elf choked. *Ennis? Why . . .*

Davon knelt on Culduin's left bicep. "They have bloodhounds," he said. "They'll release them on you as soon as this little skirmish dies down." He thrust his arm into Culduin's line of sight, and the knotty tangle of scars across it filled the elf's vision. "Trust me. There's nowhere you can go, no matter how fast you are."

Self-serving bunch of . . . Culduin squelched the thought. Had he walked their path for as many years as they, would he not be interested in preservation first? He met both Ennis's and Davon's gazes. Behind flinty exteriors a real, tumultuous desperation roiled. How many times had Culduin seen it in the field, in the eyes of elves he tended with wounds whose severity they feared but fiercely wanted to survive? No, he could not abandon them. Not like this.

"Would she force you to fight without me? Would it even be allowed?" Culduin asked.

"Once the entry fee has been paid, it would be a dishonor to scratch," Ennis said. "But teams with less than four don't last."

Conflict raged in Culduin's spirit. *Maker, may Praesidio and Danae be together still.* "All right," Culduin said. "I will stay as long as I can be a help to you. But in exchange, if we live through the games, I must have your bond that you will allow my escape if the opportunity arises. I have friends to whom I must return."

The guards who had been closing on the gladiators charged up, their numbers lessened by two. "Get them to cover," one of the guards yelled. Two hauhetti grabbed Culduin and hauled him from beneath Ennis and Davon.

"Your bond!" Culduin cried.

Ennis, his face grim, nodded once.

The crowd of guards bustled Culduin and the other gladiators to the farthest caravan cart from the southern ridge. Not only the gladiator transport, but two other vehicles burned— one of which Culduin recognized as the wagon that carried their food.

He scowled. *I suppose I should have eaten more of that meal while I had it.*

*C*ulduin climbed from the back of the wardrobe wagon, where merfolk and hauhetti had hung various robes and ornamental costumes it was apparently expected the team owners and their entourage would wear to the gladiatorial championships. With their own wagon unsalvageable from the attack, quarters for the remaining five-day trip had been cramped, but at least dry and warm.

The wagons had once again circled, but at least not in a panic this time, and Culduin stepped into the slanting sun of what was a fine, spring morning. He lifted his chin to survey his surroundings, beyond the two lines of guards, as well as the coaches of the merfolk's various gladiatorial teams. The caravan parked in a semi-circle around the rear of the wardrobe cart. To the east, distant foothills rose against a sky dotted with pink and gold clouds, and through the haze that hung over them, Culduin could barely spy dark rock. With their easterly heading for the entire journey, he could only assume the range was the one known as the Ragged Pillars, which separated Thelenalon from the eastern borders of Tebal, Kelmirith, and Da-Shir.

Crowning the tallest foothill, perhaps two miles distant, a monstrous amphitheater rose above the flowered hill country. It cast a coffee-brown silhouette against a bright backdrop, and banners of every color and design adorned it. A road of slab pavers wound through the rolling terrain toward the arena. Clusters of carts, chariots, and tents dotted the roadside all the way to the amphitheater.

Behind Culduin, someone's stomach rumbled. He turned to see Davon joining him in the sunlight. Davon stretched and rolled his eyes. "They'd better find us a decent breakfast now that we're here. Cursed hired highwaymen—always hit the contenders and the food."

"So your team is viewed as important in this contest?"

"Important?" Davon scoffed. "We'll be the champions four years running if we can win this one without Nagat." He glanced around the group. "If they stop starving us. What is it, third hour from sunrise by now?"

Hardly half that. Culduin restrained comment. As miserable a life of servitude that revolved around blood sport must be, even on short supply, their captors kept them comparably well fed. Their days consisted mostly of lounging in the transport, eating, sleeping, and attending two sparring sessions that scarcely caused Culduin to break a sweat. But he had managed to learn the strengths of his companions in combat—Bretta relied on speed and martial arts, Ennis's competence lay in smooth proficiency with both saber and staff, and Davon hammered on his opponents like a man quarrying rock.

"I'm sure Ikirra will see to it you are fortified before she expects you to 'win it all,'" Culduin said.

The trainer with the eye patch emerged from behind a nearby cart and folded his arms. "All right, you ragged boars, time for the scrub up and final inspection. Your first fight is after the midday meal." He raised his voice. "Bretta! Ennis, get your lounging hides out here."

The couple bustled from the cart, and once they emerged, guards closed around the gladiators and escorted them toward the tank carts. Beside one of the lesser tanks, where members of Ikirra's court leaned on the top edge of the giant container, two basins with knee-high sides steamed.

"Bretta and Ennis first," Patch said.

Bretta fired a baleful glare over the assembled group of merfolk and humans who loitered around the tanks, chatting amongst themselves. Ennis took her face in his hands, pressed her forehead to his, and whispered words Culduin did not hear.

"Oh, come off it," Patch barked. "Same as every year." He grabbed Bretta's arm and pushed her toward one of the basins, where two female attendants stood.

When the attendants reached to disrobe Bretta, Culduin turned away. "Why the spectacle?" he asked Davon.

Davon sighed. "It's like the inspection of a steer before you buy it, I guess. Most of these folks will be wagering today, and they want to be sure they're not putting silver on stock with some kind of hidden flaw."

"We really have slipped to the level of livestock to them, haven't we?"

"The merfolk see everyone as their inferiors—you should be familiar with that attitude. Must gall you, as an elf, to be looked down upon."

"Listen," Culduin said through his teeth. "I don't claim to entirely understand the dynamics in Reidot, having never been there myself, but the Delsin have always been willing to live in harmony with any human culture that will agree to it. I fully intend to do everything I can to keep all of us alive. I cannot say I have the same confidence about your plans."

"I should have figured you were one of the southern types," Davon spat. "You have no idea. Elves where I come from have a word for people like me . . . *Daegth.*"

The elvish word for stain. Culduin blinked. "You have elven blood?"

"Generations back." Davon clenched and unclenched his scarred fists. "But since you people never die, I had enough elf neighbors still scowling about what my ancestors did and plenty of humans in my life suspicious enough to sell me off to this continual luxury I now live in."

"It is a misconception that we never die—"

"Gods, Points, I know that. But what difference does that make to us? A thousand years, forever? You still just laugh as we age and wither and burn."

"Culduin!" the trainer called.

A swell of nausea clawed at Culduin's throat. He abandoned his rebuttal to Davon's prejudice and approached the basin

Ennis had vacated. He reached down to remove a boot, but the attendant smacked his shoulder.

"You just stand." She worked at the tie on his tunic with sun-bronzed hands. A few dozen strands of gray shot through the black waves of her waist-length hair, though it was all bound into a tight plait that ran down the center of her back. The second attendant poured more steaming water into the basin.

Culduin closed his eyes and tried to think of home. Of fragrant fruit groves in midsummer. Of starlit nights browsing the forest with his brother and sister. Of anything besides the current circumstances.

Thank the Maker Danae is not with me. May she and Praesidio have found freedom.

The bathing proceeded with merciful speed, though the attendants were in no way tender in their application of soap and water. When they rinsed Culduin's hair, they simply doused his head with huge buckets full of water, heedless of whether he had caught a breath between deluges. The scrubbing and splashing made it *almost* possible for him to ignore the prattle that clucked amidst the onlookers while the attendants worked.

Once he was clean and dry, Culduin received a pair of clean trousers and his own boots, but the trainers inspected the men bare-chested, as Ikirra had the day of their departure.

"You're sure you've fought against blades?" Patch's skeptical eye roved over Culduin. "Nothing but a relatively new arrow hole in your arm—no scars?" He turned Culduin around. Again.

Culduin swallowed the story of his recent return from the threshold of Creo's halls, and how his restoration on the canyon's floor of Quel-Mahaar had likely cleansed him of the few scars he once had across his abdomen and chest. "I usually fight in armor."

"Even armor fails." Patch leaned into his face and spoke with low menace. "You'd better not embarrass me out there, Pretty One."

18

The Sword's Fate

*P*ost-inspection, the drapers in the entourage outfitted Culduin in a satin tunic, open to below the breastbone, and a long, plum cape. They fussed and giggled over his copper hair, brushing it into shining waves.

"Ah, you'll make a fine centerpiece," the male draper, a fair man of indiscernible heritage and mixed accents, said. He slipped several large rings onto Culduin's fingers.

"Centerpiece?" Culduin furrowed his brow.

"As we parade in." The draper fastened the gaudy brooch on the cape. "You'll ride on the tall platform cart, and Ikirra instructed us to make you worthy of the top tier."

The draper's female partner raked the top and front sections of Culduin's hair back and wove them into a slim braid. "Must make sure the competition sees the ears, mustn't we?" she said.

Culduin's scalp tingled under her neatly trimmed and painted nails. "Does it truly matter?" All he needed was a gladiator who shared Davon's prejudice to target him.

"Of course it does, you gorgeous thing," she crooned. "Fight well, and I bet Ikirra finds herself a new favorite."

Culduin grimaced. "I shall fight to stay alive, but if she asks, I maintain a distinct lack of interest in her favoritism."

"You'll change your mind," the draper said. He cast a sly look to his assistant. "They always do." The draper dusted a fine, metallic powder over Culduin's cheekbones, his nose, and his collarbones. He stepped back a pace. "Perfect. It's so nice when they give us one that makes it easy. Off we go, then!"

Last to arrive at the platform cart, the drapers and Culduin squinted up into the mid-morning sun. Atop the cart—a humongous, gilt, and painted vehicle with wheels taller than Culduin—stood Bretta, Ennis, and Davon. They too, had been outfitted: Bretta in a peacock-blue halter, short skirt, and thigh-high boots, as well as a feathered headdress twice the width of her shoulders; Davon in a severe, all-black array; and Ennis in an embarrassingly clichéd loincloth and beaded headband whose like the Da-Shirines had not worn in centuries. They sat upon a set of risers with railings at each level.

The draper pointed to the ladder at the back of the cart. "Up you go."

Culduin glanced about. The number of guards and trainers posted all around the area snuffed the fleeting notion of abandoning his word. He made the climb, and as he took his position on the topmost riser, Davon's black glare remained fixed into the distance.

---

*D*anae bolted from a hard slumber, her heart hammering. Again.

She blinked and tried to focus in the bright light of a high, full moon. Where was she? Mounded forms and stark shadows around her eluded her comprehension. Was she in her bed?

Fallen asleep in Papa's shop? No, she was outside—oh, right. Somewhere in the countryside of southern Tebal. Still.

A wash of needling diminished until nothing but the chill of the night breeze swept across her skin.

"Praesidio?" she whispered.

"Awake again?" he replied from behind her.

She turned and pulled her knees to her chest. "Another possible wave of a signature, but it's gone now. I wonder if I'm just having leftover phantom sensations from my dreams."

"This is the fourth time you've awakened to such a disturbance." Praesidio sat beside her. "I hesitate to dismiss it. Even more so as I think our situation over."

"What?"

"I find it hard to believe no one has come after us," Praesidio said. "The Ba-al that bargained for us in the tunnels did not seem halfhearted about his intentions. If we were meant to go to his master, would he not have known by which route the Inquisitor was bringing us to him?"

Danae rubbed her eyes. "Any chance the Ba-al went ahead of us and doesn't yet realize we've gotten away?"

"I suppose it's a possibility," Praesidio replied. "But it all feels as though it's missing pieces, if you ask me. Maybe you could hunt after the signature you felt as you woke?"

"I've tried." Danae shook her head. "I never get a strong enough sense of it to pursue it. That's what makes me question its authenticity. But we've really gained on the Sword, at least. Its signature is very strong. In fact, why don't we pack up now and try to make up more ground? Wherever it's going, it seems to have stopped tonight too."

"You've only slept an hour, at best."

"Now that I'm up, I won't really sleep the rest of this watch anyway." Danae stood and stretched. "Plus, that rabbit we snared last night isn't going to fill our bellies beyond breakfast. We need to find somebody to beg some real food from."

Praesidio tightened the braided belt around his robe. "All right. No peace for old men when they choose to entangle themselves in the affairs of the young and determined."

A muffled roar of exultant crowds echoed through the arched tunnels of the underground gladiator hold, where Culduin, Bretta, Ennis, and Davon sat in a dim, barred chamber. Once they had paraded past the throngs of cheering and jeering spectators who lined the pavement encircling the arena, all the gladiator teams had marched beneath the stadium to await their call to the surface.

"Careful. Keep pressure on that!" someone yelled from up the corridor, amidst the shuffling of many feet.

A cluster of men bearing a stretcher, probably the twentieth that had passed Culduin this morning, bustled through the causeway outside their holding area. An ashen warrior lay in the stretcher, and a thick trail of blood ran from his middle. Culduin shook his head as the men disappeared into the surgical area a few gates down.

"They're kidding themselves, aren't they?" Bretta stepped up beside Culduin, where he stood gripping a bar in one hand.

He offered her a sad smile. "He will have bled out before they can set him down. Why do they even bother pulling him from the field?"

"The rest of the team must be doing well enough that they think they'll make it to our round."

A curse echoed from the vicinity of the surgical area.

Can I survive this without adding to the bloodshed? Culduin swallowed against a tight throat. *Can I keep Bretta, Ennis, and Davon alive?*

More cheering, mixed with some booing and a rhythmic chant, swept over the audience above. Another set of footsteps

neared, though these had the steady rhythm of marching. Down
the stone ramp that led to the holding area, six hauhetti bore a
litter. Four men in the aqua livery of Ikirra's house brought a
chest on long poles.

Behind them, no fewer than a score of guards of mixed races
and species marched, all armed with polearms, nets, and short
bows.

Davon sighed. "Looks like it's that time." He hauled himself
to his feet.

Ennis took a place beside Bretta and clasped her hand.

"They leave little room for us to do something stupid,"
Culduin said.

"Who can blame them, when they're about to hand us actual
weapons?" Ennis whispered. "Not that I don't think about it.
Every single time."

The hauhetti stopped before the holding chamber, and one
of them parted the litter's side curtains. Ikirra reclined in a bed
of wet sea sponge. Bright white and aquamarine gems studded
her hair, hung around her neck, covered her hands. She smiled.

From the rear of the group carrying the chest, the team's
trainer spoke. "We will commence with the presentation of your
weapons. The time is upon us. Show them all; Ikirra's warriors
are champions."

The chest bearers brought their burden before Ikirra, who
lifted its mahogany and bronze lid on heavy hinges. The first
item she drew from it was a broadsword, its grip wrapped in
black leather, and a smooth, polished orb of onyx set in the
crosspiece. Ikirra chirped and clicked, then extended the grip of
the weapon toward Davon.

He reached through the bars and accepted the sword.

"Your stalwart companion," Patch said. "May it claim you yet
another championship."

Next, Ikirra drew a scimitar from the casket. Its blade
flashed pale blue in the low light of the holding area. The silver

handguard boasted two rows of sapphires. As the mermaid passed it to Ennis under words of ceremony from the trainer, Ennis nodded.

"Blue steel?" Culduin said.

Ennis grinned appreciatively. "Beautiful, isn't she?" The Da-Shirine tested the blade's edge, and his grin stretched wider.

Bretta received curved blades set on the ends of black chains, well oiled and smooth as she tested their spin.

Ikirra's gaze lingered for a long, silent moment upon Culduin. She blinked and chewed her lip, to Culduin's assessment, nervously. Indeed, her breath seemed a little short.

She reached into the chest with both hands, and with shoulder muscles straining, lifted a white satin-shrouded shape. It was huge—almost too unwieldy for her to rotate and offer an end through the bars. "Culduin," she said, in her strange coo-and-click rendering of his name.

He reached inside the satin sleeve and closed his fingers around the weapon's hilt. A clear orb, clutched in the cast talon of a raptor, fashioned the pommel. Culduin's heart thundered. The grip seemed to buzz, electrified, against his palm. Slowly, reverently, he slid the weapon from its shroud.

The entire population of the room drew a collective breath.

Culduin lifted the clear, five-foot blade, and colors like the rising sun danced across its surface. Saliva pooled in his mouth, forcing him to swallow and lick his lips. A feral giddiness filled his head and his limbs.

"Gods." Davon's whisper was the first to break the silence.

The clatter of applause broke out soon after. All eyes fixed on Culduin and the Sword of the Patron, and he stretched tall. He had never felt so tall in all his life. Nearly uncontainable vigor coursed through his limbs and core. The call of the battle-field carried the lilt of song.

"My inexpressible privilege, Your Ladyship," he said.

Ikirra answered with a smoldering twinkle.

From the arena, trumpets sounded, further speeding Culduin's heart. Part of him chafed like a racehorse awaiting the release of the gate, another warned: Control. Focus. Sobriety.

"Champions, it is time," their trainer said. "For your sponsor, to victory!"

19

Banners and Blood

*A*gainst the golden sunlight of midday, they stepped from the brick tunnel to the main arena, and the moment the aqua banners of Ikirra's house emerged, a roar overwhelmed the air. The din pulsed in Culduin's ears and surged through his veins. Tier upon tier of dark stone seats, none empty, offered thousands—no, tens of thousands—of reveling spectators. Many threw handfuls of flower petals, which drifted on the wind and to the sandy floor of the amphitheater. Overhead, an arching lattice gave the amphitheater a cage-like atmosphere.

The space, however massive, still constricted Culduin's spirit and awoke a flutter of trapped panic. His glance flitted across the sandy field of contest, already dotted with fresh pools of blood. Death waited to pounce out there.

The instinct to find the first escape rattled in Culduin's chest. He shook it off.

To Culduin's left, an enormous peninsula jutted into the

field, held aloft by ten-story arches. Upon it milled countless servants bearing clay jars, platters, feathered fans, and every other means of comfort and luxury. Culduin caught a glimpse of Ikirra's litter moving into place amidst the banners of a dozen other sponsors and dignitaries of territories little known to him.

Spaced at even intervals around the arena field of contest, wooden platforms flew each of eight teams' banners.

"This is the scenario where we are to capture banners without losing our own?" Culduin yelled over the arena racket.

Ennis nodded. "See the black banner with the kraken on it?" he bawled into Culduin's ear. "They're all offense. They'll come out fast and throw their whole team at one neighboring platform for the sake of a speedy banner capture. And the red group —just the opposite. They'll defend and try to let everyone else whittle each other down."

"How many do you need to win?" Culduin asked.

Davon chimed in. "Well, all of them."

"Will the teams continue to fight as they have in the past?" Culduin replied.

"Unless they have a new coach. Little need to change a strategy when it gets you this far," Bretta said. "Watch out for Greens. They usually distract with one team member and backstab with another."

"I'll take the first turn in capturing," Davon said. "You three defend."

Culduin balked. "No one should forge out alone—not if the Greens fight as you say. And how will we know who's who?"

"Get a good look now," Davon said. "And don't get delusional on me, Points. Do as I say."

As they took their places in front of the platform with the aqua banner, opposing teams emerged from other tunnels around the perimeter and assembled before their platforms as well. Portcullises ground down to lock with a loud *ka-chunk*. In the next instant, horns blared from somewhere high up in the tiers. Davon leapt forward and charged diagonally to the right.

Two gladiators from the platforms on either side of Culduin's came barreling in after Davon's departure, three of whom closed on the elf. In an overhand chop, a fur-clad, gray-complected warrior of Tebal brought his ax down.

Culduin met the weapon in a low parry, and when the ax's haft clashed with his blade, the wood sheared clean in two, sending the ax head tumbling into the sand. The Sword sang in harmonic overtones. The vibration buzzed through Culduin's hands, then up his arms, and filled him with elation that set his flesh afire. *An easy disarm. Good.*

The ax wielder gaped and backpedaled, bringing his sundered haft up in a level guard. Bewilderment washed over the Tebalese warrior's face. Culduin only glimpsed the reaction before the next two combatants surged in, fast enough that details of their race or origin came as a blur. Only the saber and the longsword in their hands demanded his focus.

He twisted away from the saber plunge while he swung upward to parry the longsword. Blade connected with blade, not with the arm-jarring collision of combat, but with another singing ring of Culduin's Sword. His opponent's blade split into two lengths of steel, leaving the swordsman with a hilt and about a handspan of blade. The rest of his weapon plunked down to kick up a cloud of dust.

In the background of it all, the crowd's roar swelled, but it hardly caught a thread of Culduin's attention.

His two disarmed opponents clambered to open the distance between them and the elf. He let them go. He spun the Sword overhead to haul it down for a low parry of the saber strike coming in from the left.

The saber wielder turned her own blow and avoided contact with the Sword. She glared from behind a leather mask with eyes of bright blue. With weapon held defensively, Culduin's last armed opponent backed. She glanced to the ground, then eased her way around the prone body of a bleeding warrior behind her.

Ennis's scimitar wore a matching crimson smear to the slash that ran across the felled warrior's chest.

"You two, get up here!" Bretta yelled.

Culduin spared a quick glance her direction to see she had ascended the platform. A demand rose in his gut that he should fell the retreating swordswoman—a voice of disdain clamored in his ears and sent surges through his limbs.

Madness and dishonor! Be silent, vile voice. He gritted his teeth and instead of striking, spun the Sword in a figure-eight series of flourishes, an overhead circle, and a few flashy one-handed exchanges. With the overwhelming waves that came from the weapon when Culduin parried, he feared the potential sensation of a flesh-rending strike.

Ennis and Culduin climbed the stairs on either side of the platform.

Already, in addition to Ennis's victim, five more warriors sprawled in the sand between Culduin's position and Davon's. Davon hammered on an opponent who held a fat-bladed khanda in a block, and around their melee, three felled warriors threatened to trip up the swordsmen's maneuvers. Davon had whittled the amethyst team to a single defender in a staggeringly short time.

A spry, wiry gladiator, no taller than about four and a half feet and carrying a rapier, sprang up the amethyst platform steps beside Davon. He snatched the banner from its pole. The crowd broke into tumultuous noise, whether whistles, accolades, or dismayed complaints.

Davon roared a string of epithets.

Davon's khanda-wielding opponent swung, but Davon caught the attack in a bind. They strove against one another, their arms shaking with exertion and sweat streaming, until

Davon pulled his free fist back and let it fly. Blood sprayed from his opponent's nose, and the victim stumbled over one of the corpses to his right.

Davon barreled past his felled adversary, vaulted up onto the platform, and plunged his sword into the back of the fleeing captor of the amethyst banner before the little thief could turn for a block. Wrenching the banner from the man's hands, Davon bellowed, then yanked his sword from his target's torso.

The audience catcalled.

"We can steal captured banners?" Culduin yelled.

"Yes," Ennis replied. "Whatever means necessary to get them all."

Another option aside from slaughter—did the arena terrain offer enough cover for stealth and theft?

Amidst the growing cacophony of the crowd, the crunch of feet reached Culduin's ears—unnaturally loud and superseding all other sounds for a moment. The Sword's grip warmed in his palm.

Culduin wheeled toward the footfalls.

Scarcely to be seen for the crouching stealth he employed in skirting the platform, a trident-bearing warrior crept within six paces of Ennis's back. He readied his weapon.

"Ennis!" Culduin charged. "Behind."

Ennis spun, and the attacker's thrusting trident scored his ribs and chest at an upward angle. Blood was slow to redden the superficial wounds.

Another downward swing of the Sword sundered the trident's haft like a wildflower stem. The momentum of Culduin's strike carried it to the edge of the platform, and his blade also cleft a chunk from their decking.

Ennis gaped. "What manner of blade—?"

The chattering, grinding, and cog-into-cog rattle of machinery echoed in Culduin's ears—again, strangely amplified. Wood groaned as the sound of a bow pulled near the bowman's ear, and then a cry: *Fire!* The voice reverberated more in Culduin's head than in his ears.

From the opposite side of the arena, a ball of shot that gleamed with curved blades protruding from its surface hurtled toward Culduin's platform.

Culduin rushed both Bretta and Ennis, and with a straining thrust of his legs, bowled them from the platform deck.

Half a blink before the blade-embedded ball of ammunition crashed into the platform and burst it to splinters, Culduin, Bretta, and Ennis bailed from the structure like rats from a flaming ship. They landed in a bruised pile in the sand. Shards of the ruined platform pelted them.

Ennis rose and grimaced, blood weeping down his chest from his trident scratches. "Perfect. As if fighting the goons inside this cage isn't bad enough."

"What do you mean?" Culduin said.

Bretta scoured her surroundings like a wary hare. "Looks like the game masters also have it in for us this year." She pointed across the battlefield to where a catapult stood on a rotating support.

With no platform to guard, surely there could not be any rule about keeping their flag in place. Culduin snapped up their aqua flag from the rubble of their platform, just as the catapult grounded and twanged again. Another blade-ball arced across the arena, devastating the black flag's platform, and so it seemed, two of its team members.

A cheer exploded across the arena, and Culduin's throat burned with reflux. Was it really possible so much of this audience reveled in the slaughter of those trapped in the ring? Skilled fighting they seemed to admire, but death was what they truly craved.

He squinted across the dusty expanse to where the catapult rotated on its wooden wheel. Flag jammed in his belt, he said,

"This way. Stay together!" Pelting strides carried him two platforms down the row.

The catapult released again, and Culduin skidded to a stop a dozen strides from the red-flag platform. Three blonde, towering gladiatrixes guarded it from the ground. They looked up as one, then scattered from the path of the incoming ammunition.

The moment before the ball struck, Culduin rushed forward, Sword high. With a crack and a boom, the shot hit, and the platform collapsed. Through the flying debris he barreled, striking at the biggest chunks with an arcing Sword and batting them away, and when the ruin came to rest, the red flag was in his grasp.

Bretta and Ennis held off the defenders in a flurry of parries, once the women regained their stances. The gladiatrixes swung maces, the weapons' heads fashioned with wicked barbed spikes. Culduin charged to Bretta's flank, sundering the first mace shaft his blade met.

The disarmed woman bellowed enraged words in a tongue Culduin did not know and threw her weapon shaft at him like a javelin. Culduin twisted, and although the sheared wood caught him along the forearm, it left only a superficial scratch.

A horn sounded.

Three arena guards stampeded on foot from the nearest portcullis, and they threw a net over Culduin's opponent. Heavy weights dragged her to the ground. "No missiles, maggot!" one of them bellowed in the common tongue.

Culduin backed away and held his blade level in front of his midsection. The guards dragged on the net, but the woman within thrashed and screamed inflamed words. A rap across the head from one of the guard's bats silenced her. A sweep of the area revealed Bretta and Ennis's opponents disabled.

Running strides hammered from behind, amplified in

Culduin's ears. He faced them, only to find Davon closing on his position. Davon clutched the purple banner in his left hand.

After a smirk at Culduin's banner, Davon said, "Good for you, Points. You got one. The trick is to keep them, and to do that, you're going to have to start spilling some blood."

20

Soul Reaper

The remaining five teams withdrew to the arena edges to regroup, since only one team, gold, still had a platform to defend after a rash of blade-shot attacks had lain the rest of the teams' structures to waste. Only Ikirra's team still had four members standing. While Culduin caught his breath, one of the game referees turned an oversized hourglass. Their time to strategize had limits, and they were tight.

"We need to bring all our strength against the other teams," Davon said. "Make a circuit of the arena and take them down, one by one."

"In the case of gold, it is foolhardy to rush their platform, since they still have three warriors on the field," Culduin said. "We enter that fight at an immediate disadvantage. Can we create for ourselves any position of strength?"

Davon growled. "Why?"

Culduin glared. "Calm your humors. I would much rather engage these combatants on our own terms, as much as that is even possible. Take their flags as the spoils of territory well defended."

After scanning their surroundings, Bretta chimed in. "What about the catapult dais?"

Ennis's eyes rounded. "Is that even permitted?"

"The game master declared no rule against it when the round began," Culduin said. "But you tell me. I am the green-horn here."

All but a fraction of the sand had passed to the bottom of the timekeeping glass.

Davon danced on the balls of his feet. "All right. All right. We take the catapult. Those artillerymen don't have an imposing look. But watch me for the sign to switch to an offensive."

Culduin contained further argument behind his teeth. A horn blew.

"Back at it, warriors!" the gamemaster bellowed, his voice echoing from somewhere on high in the arena.

Culduin's team clustered into a loose wedge, with the elf on the point that faced the center of the arena. They made a guarded move toward the catapult. The other four teams clashed with one another.

The groan and clatter of the catapult's release drew every eye, and the whirling ball of blades careened toward Culduin's team. They evaded, as one, to the left, and the ball of shot crashed into the sand many paces away.

Waste of ammunition. Culduin shook his head. *Who uses artillery against such a small, moving target? This is what happens when imbeciles use the tools of war for sport.*

Once their wedge drew too close for the catapult to target, Bretta and Ennis charged the dais, weapons high. Culduin and Davon maintained guard in case another team turned for them.

While teams across the arena jockeyed and fought, an uproar broke out among the spectators seated near the catapult. Bretta's chain blades whistled. Men shouted. The clash behind

Culduin lasted only moments before the crowd erupted into hoots and jeers.

He spared a glance back and found Bretta and Ennis with arms upraised. One artilleryman lay prone on the dais, one fled, holding his bloodied midsection, and the third had vanished.

Culduin joined his victorious teammates on the catapult platform, followed by Davon.

"Load it! Fire it!" the audience chanted in multiple languages that Culduin could comprehend, mingled with the babble of those he did not.

Davon surveyed the ammunition and smirked. "How are you at aiming one of these things, Points?"

"My training in artillery was limited," Culduin said. "And besides, do we not risk the guards disqualifying us if we use a missile?"

"They haven't made any move to kick us off here yet," Davon said.

"But we give the crowd minimal satisfaction if we do not engage the enemy," Culduin replied. "They will not stand for it."

From their new vantage point, Culduin could see that the gold team still held their platform, and they had felled two combatants from the green group that had engaged them. A remaining Green backed away. Purple and Red still battled; Red's single, hulking warrior staggered between the wicked halberd slashes of two opponents.

"Load it! Fire it!" The chant ensnared more voices with each repetition.

Ennis nodded. "Culduin is right. You watch; they'll find a way to force someone's hand."

An outcry from the stands arrested the group's contemplation. From across the field of contest, a winged, leonine beast barreled from behind a lifted portcullis, chased by an armored guard who slashed at it with a whip. The creature screamed through a hooked beak and spun to swipe at its tormentor with a huge front talon. Around its neck, it wore an iron collar, from which a length of chain hung. The links ran back into the darkness of the culvert from which the beast had been driven.

Another shrill raptor shriek ripped from somewhere beyond sight. The beast in the arena slammed to a halt, its caramel-brown wings extended in a mantling pose, and its plumage-tufted tail lashing back and forth like a striking serpent. It stared beyond the guard, back toward the gate, which ground closed. The whip wielder flicked his length of leather with a sharp crack.

Green eyes burning with hatred, the griffon reared and turned, then charged at Gold's platform. It bounded atop the wood structure. Two gladiators dodged away; one stood his ground and slashed with a short sword.

The griffon reversed with a thrust of his wings, and the sword stroke fell short. It landed on sinewy haunches, flexed its legs, then sprang at the gladiator.

Culduin averted his glance, but the platform guard's wail told enough.

"Points!"

Culduin spun toward Davon's voice. The halberd-wielding Purples pounded toward the catapult. The length of their hafts would grant them enough reach to engage anyone on the platform. He rocked on spring-loaded legs.

When the Purples drew within ten paces, a crazy surge pulsed from the Sword's grip and through Culduin's limbs. He took three running strides across the dais and leapt into the air, Sword high. On the way down, he hacked through the pair of halberd hafts and bowled their owners down with the force of the leap. They all sprawled in the sand.

Before Culduin could right himself, Davon piled on, throwing punches with the pommel of a dagger. In a sloppy brawl, Davon knocked what remained of a halberd from one Purple's hands, then spun and kneed the other opponent in the face. Culduin jumped to his feet and circled the Sword with a swish of ringing glory.

One of the Purples scrambled backward on hands and feet, but then he faltered and dropped onto his back. He lifted his palms. "Spare my soul!"

Culduin's mind raged hot.

Deprive him of it!

A wave of revulsion twisted Culduin's gut. He gripped the Sword with such force he thought his fingers would break. He stilled the slash pulling at his arms and instead leveled his blade point at the opponent.

"Your soul for the flags," he said through clenched teeth.

The Purple's face twisted in agony. He heaved for breath. And yet he reached to his belt and threw his handful of flags at Culduin's feet.

The crowd erupted in a discordant rumble of boos.

Davon snatched the flags up in a hand slick with blood. The Purple collapsed in a gale of sobs.

"Back to base." Davon turned for the catapult.

After scarcely avoiding tripping over the other purple team member, whose brutalized features told Culduin the tale of how Davon had defeated him, Culduin backpedaled toward the dais.

The elf fought the lurching impulse to vomit. *A reaper of souls. Such power will destroy me.*

21

Favor Bestowed

housands upon thousands of voices chanted, while thousands more roared as an underscore. Danae pulled her hood farther down over her brow. The long shadow of the dark stone amphitheater stretched over the road she and Praesidio traveled, a chilling blanket laid out by the sunset behind the structure. The pungent smoke of cook fires, wafting from dozens of encampments along the paved path to the amphitheater, reawakened the rumble in her fluttering belly. Boisterous singing from one of the tent clusters mingled with the more distant cheers, though Danae failed to sort any words from the tune, sung in a language very unlike her own Western Tongue.

"Why would they have taken it here?" Danae said to Praesidio, who shuffled beside her, his gray eyes wary and forever darting.

Praesidio rubbed his lined brow. "You're sure they have?"

"We're definitely closing in on it. It's been moving a bit, but never far enough to weaken its signature. Though there's been a shift—a thrill, like surges of excitement, almost. If a thing can be excited." Danae guffawed. "Heaven and earth, that sounds stupid, doesn't it?"

"Not at all," Praesidio said. "You forget, this is no ordinary thing. Closer to a mind than any other object you'll encounter, I daresay. And still very connected to Zechmaat's, I'd wager, so be careful."

Danae swallowed. "If I can feel it, can it . . . sense me? Or worse, could *he* know what we're up to?"

"That, I don't know. But even though I'm not a sensor, I can hear its inclinations when I touch it, so clearly, this Sword functions outside the expected nature of Curses and Virtusen." The old sage plodded toward an awning that extended off the side of a large red and orange cart on the right side of the road.

Under the awning sat a rotund, greasy man in a leather apron. He stirred a cookpot that hung on a hook over a fire. When Praesidio had drawn within six paces, the cook brightened.

"Cottage pie for your way to the arena?" he said.

Praesidio reached into his satchel and produced his leather coin pouch. "Two, if you please."

The man grabbed two rounds of bread from a woven sack leaning against the cart, dug at them with his fingers to hollow them out, and then ladled a scoop of root vegetables, gravy, and ground meat into the bowls.

"Who's your wager on tonight?" The cook took Praesidio's coin, gave it a brief bemused glance, then dropped it in his apron's bulging pocket.

Praesidio shook his head. "I'm not a man of the means to lose the little I've got. Just going to watch. My niece here, she's never been."

"If you were betting," Danae said, stepping up to take her bowl, "who would you put your money on?"

The cook swung a stubby arm toward the vehicles in his group. "Why, Prince Regnin's delegation, of course!" He then stage-whispered behind his hand, "That is, if they hadn't been taken out in the banner round and come limping back with only two. I hear the mer's group looks good, though they may be cheating. Hard to tell from the runners' reports."

Danae's chest constricted.

"The mer?" Praesidio said, his tone far more casual than Danae might have mustered. "Those odd, subterranean folk?"

"None other, as always." The cook grumbled. "But with a rookie in their fourth slot, it'll take the gods' humor for them win again." His attention shifted beyond Praesidio, and he smiled broadly. "Evening to you folks—cottage pie to warm your bellies on a brisk night?"

And so the cook's labor also shifted to another group of travelers that had come up behind Danae.

Praesidio kept moving, and Danae followed suit.

"Some kind of team sport, then," Danae said. "What could the merfolk have to do with that? There's no water in sight."

Praesidio scooped a bite of his meal with his fingertips and ate it. He nodded ahead and to the left while he chewed. "Take a look at the turquoise caravan across the way."

Danae squinted into the failing sun to find a line of opulently gilt and painted wagons and white tents flying blue-green banners. The huge cart to the rear carried two circular tanks of tight wood planks that reminded Danae of massive half barrels. Two silver-skinned individuals, one male and one female, leaned on the tank's edge and clattered to one another in the marine tongue.

Danae moved to the right side of the road and put as much pedestrian traffic between herself and the merfolk caravan as possible. Praesidio shadowed her.

"I don't like this," he said. "Something about the convergence of details feels suspect to me."

*C*ulduin's heart throbbed in his ears. Sweat streamed down his face, chest, and back. Or was that blood? No time to tell. Or care.

Somewhere in the muffled background, a dissatisfied audience catcalled about his team's lack of use of the catapult.

Purple: out by surrender. Green: dead. Red: dead. Gold— what had happened to Gold while he and Davon had seized their most recent flags?

Halfway across the arena, the two remaining gold team members barreled for the center of the field of contest, and the griffon pelted after. A few strides short of the field's middle, the creature's chain snapped taut.

Davon thrust the stash of flags into Bretta's arms. "Keep these here. Ennis, Points, with me. I'm not waiting for them to sic something worse on us." He lifted his black blade high and leapt from the catapult platform.

Culduin groaned. "Vainglory." Truthfully, the Sword thrilled in his hand, and it was all Culduin could do to stifle its pull into battle. After Ennis pursued Davon, he brought up the rear.

Ennis barreled straight for the left-most opponent, Davon for the right, and they met in a burst of steel clashes and grunts. Culduin scanned the conflicts for whether either of his teammates suffered a disadvantage.

The remaining members of the opposition wore closed-faced helms and ornate, burgundy- and gold-tooled pants, full through the thigh and gathered at mid-calf, and tall boots with soft soles laced up to the pant legs. Throughout the conflict, Culduin had assumed Gold to be a dark-skinned group of Tebalese warriors, given the gray cast to their skin, and dismissed the inconsistency in their wardrobe with that assessment. Now that he drew closer, however, he realized their torsos were not gray skinned at all, but rather covered with silky fur, subtly striped.

His'tabai? Culduin wondered. How any team had brought a species of warrior from a continent across a wide, tumultuous ocean, he could not fathom.

The his'tabai warriors had earned their place as the final combatants standing, for they spun, kicked, and pummeled Davon and Ennis with swift, lithe movements. They struck with pronged weapons in one hand and sabers in the other, and even Davon's fastest parries faltered at his opponent's sheer speed. Their footwork forced Davon to dance around them, which took him too close to the griffon. It screamed and lunged. Davon tumbled just out of reach.

Culduin's muscles twitched with the instinct to assist Davon, but reason restrained him. Davon was not a warrior one helped until even he could admit death was imminent.

Ennis's enemy held the Da-Shirine's blue-steel scimitar in a bind, then swept a leg at Ennis's knee. It connected with a crack, and Ennis toppled.

Culduin bounded in, the Sword high in a lateral guard. He landed, feet wide enough to stand over Ennis's prone form, as the his'tabai warrior completed the spin from his kick. Behind the visor of the closed helm, the gladiator's eyes gleamed wide and blue. He turned the downward sweep of his weapons and avoided contact with Culduin's glassy blade.

"Back!" Culduin yelled.

The his'tabai took one stride in reverse.

Culduin swung the Sword in a mid-cut. His opponent leapt backward, bending at the waist to barely pull his abdomen clear of Culduin's point.

The words of his early days of training echoed in mind. *Where blade challenges blade, someone will bleed. Do not let it be you.*

The his'tabai sprang, blades plunging in a downward thrust aimed at Culduin's neck and shoulder. Culduin twisted away.

He caught both saber and prongs against the jeweled crossguard of the sword.

The his'tabai pushed, and Culduin pushed back. Neither combatant wrestled the advantage from the other.

"Your sword to be mine!" the gladiator said. His accent and timbre grated like an untuned lyre. "Your heart as well."

They thrust apart and both took a few recovery steps back. Culduin's head pounded. Buzzing in his ears all but obliterated the noise of the crowd and the fight at hand. The very thought of his enemy pulling the weapon from his grasp surged through him like flaming pitch through a gutter and spout.

The fury broke loose, and Culduin stormed in. He feinted high, and as the opponent reached to block, he lowered the Sword and swept upward. The center of the blade cleft into his enemy's ribcage and kept going until it rang free of his shoulder. Blood flew. Culduin roared a nonsensical howl. The his'tabai collapsed in two pieces. A torrent that demanded further wrath, greater bloodshed, hammered upon Culduin's senses.

Ennis tried to rise, but his knee gave out, and he dropped to the sand on the opposite knee. Bretta rushed to his side and ducked under his arm.

Culduin wheeled toward the clash between Davon and the other his'tabai warrior. Davon, laying on his side in the sand, lifted his sword in a blind grimace as his enemy pounced. Culduin shrieked another battle cry and interposed. The Sword, blood-smeared and crackling with the glory of it, sliced through the attacker's wrist. Hand and weapon dropped to the ground. The helmeted warrior staggered aside.

Davon hauled himself to his feet, then wiped the blood from his eyes that had blinded his defense moments ago. A long cut that ran from his forehead to his ear still streamed crimson. Nonetheless, Davon drove his blade into the his'tabai's back. More gore sprayed through the opponent's visor. He lifted his weapon for another stab.

Culduin's racing heart whipped at him to escalate the carnage and hack again, but he shook his head against the urge. He thrust the point of the Sword into the ground.

Davon slashed his sword across the feline warrior's chest.

"Stop," Culduin said. A sardonic musing passed through his mind. *Am I telling him? Or me?*

Davon bared his teeth at Culduin.

"Davon, he's out! Stop."

The last member of the gold team wavered, took a few directionless steps, and dropped. Both his chest and handless arm pulsed blood, though the spray throbbed weaker with each subsequent beat.

Davon wiped his eyes again and spat. He ripped two flags from each of the felled gladiators, their colors splattered with the heralds of violence.

"Points, Ennis, take some flags."

Bretta handed three of the flags to Culduin, then grabbed his hand in a firm clasp as he took them. She thrust their arms into the air.

The audience burst with cheers, howls, and whistles. The Sword throbbed in Culduin's hand. There was no pain. No fatigue. No remorse.

Only victory.

*C*ulduin's team marched toward the open portcullis that would lead them back to the holding area under the arena, while festoons of flowers, loose petals, even gifts of strong liquors and choice fruits, rained onto the field. Most of the bottles proved a hazard to dodge, more than anything else, though Davon did scoop up two that managed to hit the sand and remain intact.

The fire of battle cooled in Culduin's veins, replaced by a

clinging sense of horror in its wake. Never, in all his years of fighting for his people, had he gloried in the death of any opponent. It had always been a necessary and lamentable evil. So when the dozen guards surrounded him warily at the gate and their leader requested the group's weapons, Culduin surrendered the Sword with a hint of revulsion and relief. How could the blade be so seductive and so vile all at once?

The guards escorted them past their holding cell and to a room of iron tables, its floor glistening with fresh blood over the crust of old. The stench wedged in Culduin's throat and made him cough. Tables of rude implements of treatment that might have been mistaken for tools of torture lined the wall. A pair of apron-clad Thelenese men stepped forward.

"Each of you, sit, and we'll see what we can patch up before the next round," one man said.

Maker have mercy. Culduin's head spun. *More rounds. There are more rounds.*

Culduin staggered to one of the tables, and the worker squeezed out a rag in a bucket of rusty liquid. He stepped toward the elf.

The sight of the wet rag snapped Culduin back to his current circumstances and calmed the tempest in his mind. He lifted his hands. "Not to worry. My hurts are clotted," he said. "You'll do them no good swabbing them." *Especially not with that infection waiting to happen.*

The worked shrugged. "Suit yourself. It's your hide if Ikirra doesn't like that you're still bloody when you go out again."

After surveying his teammates, Culduin said, "Davon, any chance you would donate one of those bottles you picked up to your associates' treatment?"

Davon snorted. "Nobody's hurt so bad as to need to get liquored up."

"That is not what I mean. If you put that brew on fresh rags, your wounds have a better chance of actually getting clean."

The second worker glared. "Look, you stick to swords and we'll do the stitching, all right? Shut it before we burn it shut."

The tramp of unison footfalls rang in the hall. Culduin leaned to peer through the doorway. A quartet of turquoise-clad servants approached with Ikirra's draped palanquin propped on their shoulders. Culduin sat back and groaned.

The servants crouched to fit the litter through the doorway. When they brought their burden to a halt near the tables, Ikirra parted her curtains.

She clicked and cooed, and the hauhettus at the lead of the litter bearers translated. "Her majesty says, 'A fantastic display, my daring warriors. I have come to bestow upon you my favor for the final round.'"

Ikirra opened an ebony box, bound with silver, and pulled from it a silver chain with a hazelnut-sized orb hanging from it. The surface of the orb swirled with orange and yellow. She clicked some more.

"For you, Culduin, the most potent of my favors, for the most potent of my warriors," the hauhettus translated. He rolled his eyes.

Davon coughed. "Are you kidding? He didn't show up to fight until the last—"

A hauhetti guard cuffed Davon's ear. "No one asked your opinion of the princess's judgment, cur."

"If you find yourself beset, just throw the orb," the translator continued. "Where it lands, I promise you, no opponent will remain standing. Just be sure to get it at least a dozen paces from yourself."

"Oh, great," Davon said. "So if we just happen to be too far from him, then what, we get to see how well it works from a personal standpoint?"

"It's not going to matter to you," someone in the doorway said.

Culduin craned to see past the litter, where there stood a

lean, hungry-eyed man with long, white hair that ringed his head while leaving his crown gleaming bald. He polished his fingernails on the chest of his floor-length velvet robe.

The hauhetti all bowed. Their leader said, "Lord Game Master, we did not expect you so soon."

"I like surprises," the elderly game master said. "Ikirra, you have quite a warrior on your hands, with a most remarkable weapon."

Ikirra ducked her head demurely, and her translator conveyed her humble thanks.

"However, after seeing what he can do at the end of the flag round, I think the crowd would love to see what he can do on his own, and under pressure." The game master pointed to the other members of Culduin's team. "Take these three away and rack them on the south side of the arena."

He stepped up before Culduin, and an acrid cloud of hard liquor and pipe smoke wafted from his breath and clothes, nearly as overpowering as the rotting blood on the floor. "Compassion seems to drive your swordsmanship, which we don't see much here. For the final round, the longer you take to rescue your friends, the . . . well . . . taller they become."

Culduin clamped his teeth shut. From the cold glitter in the game master's eyes, he imagined any plea for decency would provide only humor.

Ikirra squawked, but before her servant could provide translation, the game master cut him off. "I make the rules here," he snapped. "You bring the teams. For their sakes, you'd better hope you gave your favor to the right fighter."

22

Cornered

*B*oiling anger heated Danae's chest and quickened her breaths. She glared at the turquoise banners along the roadside and imagined engulfing them in flame with her mere disgust.

"Well, if that little liar is here and so is the . . . you-know-what . . ." Danae clenched her fist. "Fair warning. If I run into Ikirra, I might get distracted by violent compulsions."

Praesidio sighed. "Try to focus, Danae. I don't know what we'll find inside that arena exactly, but vengeance is unbecoming a Thaumaturgist, and—"

"—and not her province," Danae tacked on. "The Lay of Lament, right?"

Praesidio's smile confirmed her recollection.

"All right." She scooped a bite of the hearty dish in her opposite hand. She hesitated upon seeing the amount of grime under her nails, but appetite won over squeamishness, and she put it in her mouth. "At least we won't be hungry for once."

The closer they got to the arena, the thicker the crowds on the road became, and the harder it became for Danae to sort the Sword's signature for an increasing density of supernatural noise. Amulets around the necks of passersby flared with little sparks of energy, and the rare man or woman emanated a creeping aura Danae began to recognize as the stench of a life committed to Curses. A faint thrumming from somewhere behind them snagged her attention, and after the third instance of noting it, she bent her concentration upon it. It faded immediately. Thankfully, no guards or hangers-on near the merfolk caravan appeared to cast any notice toward her or Praesidio.

The road led them around the north side of the arena, where Praesidio paid three silver for each of them to pass the gate.

"It's a good thing we got our packs back, or else we'd be starved and climbing some side fence to get in," Danae mused.

Praesidio's mouth pinched tight. "Fortunate indeed." The skeptical edge of his tone took Danae by surprise.

"What?" she asked.

"You mean this doesn't feel too easy to you?" Praesidio asked.

"What are you say—"

An uproar in the arena drowned any hope Danae had of finishing her sentence. Bells clanged and horns blew, and somewhere amidst it all, a thunderous screech tore through the air. It scattered gooseflesh all over Danae's arms.

"What was that?" she yelled to Praesidio.

The tension around his eyes mounted. He did not like what he was hearing, from what Danae could tell. He shouldered his way up the ramp, choked with spectators, that led into the lowest level of seating. Danae scrambled after, scarcely able to keep pace with her mentor in his surge of urgency.

They reached a guarded gate at the end of the tunnel, where well-dressed men and women held out sealed scrolls to the guards. One of the men, armored in scale mail and a tall, crested helm, nodded and ushered a couple clad in velvet and jewels through the entry.

When Praesidio approached the guards, the gatekeeper with his hand on the iron latch of the gate curled his lip at Praesidio. "Credential?" His tone conveyed his thick skepticism that Praesidio would produce one.

"How much must I pay?" Praesidio asked.

"Without a family seal on the list, you couldn't carry enough gold, old man," the gatekeeper said.

More cheering erupted and muddied the next exchange of words between Praesidio and the guard. Pulses of the same elation Danae had felt earlier while focusing on the Sword ran through her limbs, strong and dizzying.

"We need to see what's happening!" Danae blurted.

The gatekeeper rolled his eyes.

"Then go to the commoner level where you belong!" a woman called from somewhere behind Danae.

Though the sneer in the woman's voice raised Danae's hackles, she swallowed a retort. "What levels?" she asked the guards.

"Five, six, and seven. Take the ramps at the outer promenade," the second guard answered.

Danae hooked an arm through Praesidio's elbow. "We need to get a view as soon as we can."

He sighed heavily. "Very well. The outer promenade just inside the first gate?"

While the guard nodded, Danae towed Praesidio back the way they came, through a throng of men and women of high or haughty bearing and their heavy-laden servants. So much jostling. The overpowering clouds of fragrances, the scratch of furs and fabrics. Danae led with a shoulder and gave up any concern for manners. Still, progress through the crowd came only a few steps at a time.

It was all she could do to keep from breaking into a run when they reached the ramp up the outer perimeter of the arena. Overhead, carved arches and fluted columns provided magnificent scenery in the light of hundreds of lanterns suspended along the way, but Danae cast them only a cursory glance. More cheers. Collective gasps. And the bone-jangling screech—something like a raptor's cry, but far too loud, and intermingled with a throatier undertone. They all whipped at her sense of urgency like a slaver.

The long ascending ramps set her heart galloping and made her breath short, but she pushed on through the fire in her legs. Praesidio kept up, but his burst of vigor had begun to wane. Perspiration ran down her back in a stinging trickle.

Or was it truly just a bead of sweat?

The heat of exertion spread an itchy mantle across Danae's back, but something more than that troubled her. Somewhere to their rear, someone or something clawed at her with a thorny insistence. She pushed it from her mind. More speed—that was what she needed now.

When they reached the fourth switchback in the ascent up the ramps, Praesidio grabbed the shoulder of Danae's cloak. "I . . . cannot." He panted for breath.

Danae spun. Praesidio's pallor and sunken eyes made her gasp. His hand on her shoulder trembled. "What's happening to you?" *Is this the same man who ran for two days straight after we left Garash?*

"The climb," Praesidio rasped. "Suddenly got so hard."

Danae swiped the back of her hand across her brow and forced the loose tendrils away from her eyes. Ever since he had spent that watch contending with the Sword, he had seemed more frail, but this was even above and beyond that.

"I'm sorry, Praesidio," Danae said. "I'll slow down. Let's try to take a look at what's on this level."

At the next hallway leading toward the arena from the outer promenade, Danae forged her way. Dozens of plain-clad men and women held baskets, trays, and fans along the hall. None seemed to wear any uniform or defining garb. They chatted idly with one another. Some stood queued to receive loads of pastries or goblets of bubbling wine, and thus laden, marched for a doorway.

Danae spied a pair of servants, a man and a woman, where the man leaned far into the woman's personal space. She giggled and blushed. He twirled a lock of her hair. An empty basket and tray leaned against the wall behind him. Danae swept up to him and grabbed his serving vessels.

"Take a break for a bit, you two," Danae said.

The manservant cast Danae hardly a glance. She handed the basket to Praesidio and led him to the queue. "You going to be able to carry that load?" she whispered.

"I hope so," Praesidio said. "I suppose you can tell I feel awful."

She handed him her waterskin. "Well, get a drink. Maybe it will help." While he sipped at the water, Danae searched their surroundings for any suspicious figures, or even those who perhaps seemed too familiar. Whatever stymied Praesidio, it was smart enough to blend in.

Frenzied suppliers loaded the trays brought before them in a constant stream, and in moments, Danae bore an unwieldy load of flagons of nearly black ale. She gritted her teeth in a smile and worked her way toward the elaborate gate that separated the servants' hall from the inner arena, or so she hoped.

Another outburst crashed over the crowd like an avalanche. The Sword's signature washed across Danae in a twisting, spasmodic surge that seemed on the brink of flying out of control. It twisted her gut like she was back in the hold of *The Sea Bear*.

She and Praesidio passed the gate with their burdens, and they found themselves in a caged chamber amidst jostling servants. An attendant closed the gate to the cage. Just as Danae's panic set in, the floor lurched, and the cage rose. The grinding of chain and pulleys sounded somewhere overhead. They shimmied their way up a stone chute.

When the cage bounced to a stop, the bars on one side looked out to a colorful crowd. Another attendant opened the gate, and the servants all shuffled out like nothing remarkable had just happened. They emerged into the dying light of dusk, bolstered by rows of lanterns, and the far side of the mahogany stone structure cast an arched silhouette against the deep crimson of the western sky. Crisscrossing bars domed the amphitheater. Before them, a peninsula of rock, thirty paces wide and at least two-hundred long jutted into the arena.

The gate attendant directed Danae to Lord Somebody on the front left who wanted *selamboche*. So now she at least knew what she carried. A momentary flash of home, of Garrett's explanation of the Tebalese fine ale, and loneliness flitted through Danae's mind.

Concentrate! Danae chided herself. She wormed her way through the crowd, all bedecked in jeweled finery, richer than any she had ever imagined in existence. Following the lead of other servants milling the peninsula, she announced in feigned rasp, "*Selamboche?*"

Spectators, mostly men, lifted a hand to hail her and take a heavy flagon from her tray. She juggled it to keep it from tipping, and when she reached the railing at the platform's end, she peered down into the arena. Her glance swept the scene, where a cluster of heavily plate-mailed warriors charged from one side, and on the opposite, a massive, winged beast with the body of a great cat strained against chains. Behind the beast, three people, two men and a woman, hung on a wooden device, their hands and feet lashed with taught ropes.

And between the beast and the warriors . . .

With brilliance beyond that of any earthly blade, the Sword flashed, scattering torch flame and sunset in arcs of ethereal wonder. Copper hair loose, chest bare, and muscles banded, the warrior swinging the Sword cleaved through the charging pikes of a half-dozen swine-headed assailants.

Wonder and dread crashed over Danae in an avalanche. Her tray tumbled from her hands. A woman shrieked something about her gown, but Danae could only gape.

Someone grabbed her arm. She snapped a startled glance to behold Praesidio.

"You clumsy buffoon!" Praesidio barked at her. "That mess'll come out of your wages, you know!" He dragged her back from the extent of the peninsula.

"What'll we do?" Danae stammered. "We have to . . ."

Praesidio leaned in. "We have to keep one noble from killing you for destroying her dress and another from noticing who's made the mess." He jerked his head right.

Danae glimpsed a palanquin held aloft on short pillars, and amidst its turquoise and silver cascades of fabric, a lavender-haired maiden—no, monster—chewed her nails.

She's anxious? Danae's face flamed in fury.

Danae gathered her tumultuous emotions. "But the . . . you know!" she whispered to Praesidio.

"Of course I know. I see. But—"

A cacophony of shouts clattered at the gate end of the peninsula, at the same moment an explosion of needle stabs raked across Danae's flesh. The door to the platform lift burst open. Servants and nobles alike dodged to the edges of the platform, and through the space they cleared, two pony-sized, wiry-haired, foamy-mouthed hounds charged.

"Blast their tracking!" Danae cried.

Behind them, a black-robed, stooped figure wove his hands in an intricate pattern, and a nimbus of green light swirled around his ebony knuckles, palms, and claws. Praesidio writhed.

In a stumbling scramble, Danae fled the charging hounds, back to the extent of the platform.

"Danae! We'll be trapped . . ." Praesidio shambled after her in a halting gait.

She skidded to a stop at the brass railing that encircled the peninsula. On the hounds came, just behind Praesidio. Danae glanced over the dizzying, ten-story drop to the sandy, bloody field of battle below, where Culduin continued to fend off attacker after attacker.

Danae charged back to Praesidio, rounded him, and shoved him toward the railing. He fought her direction, but she prevailed in bringing him to the brink of the peninsula.

Praesidio, his face awash in bewilderment, caught her glance.

"Sorry about the rough handling," Danae said. She dove at his ribcage. They slammed into the railing with breath-buffeting force. The lead hound lunged. Their master bellowed. Danae threw her weight—and Praesidio's—over the rail.

They tipped, headfirst. The plummet, however planned, still wrenched Danae's insides.

A moment into their fall, Danae loosened her grip on Praesidio.

"*Arineth—*" she began.

Praesidio caught her intent. In unison, they Uttered, "*Arineth da'et plumie.*"

Their descent slowed to a gentle drift, and both Danae and Praesidio righted themselves to land, feet first, on the sand.

Praesidio shook his head at Danae. "Insufferable creature of habit."

"Well, no hounds at our throats, right?" Danae panted. She glanced up, toward where the beasts leaned over the edge of the peninsula, barking and snarling.

Forty paces ahead, a line of boar-headed warriors jabbed spears toward an opponent.

"No," Praesidio replied. "But this does still plunk us in the center of a gladiator battle."

23

Rack and Reunion

he Sword sang in Culduin's grasp, exultant and repellent all at once. Its song, though unheard, resonated in the elf's chest, made his heart pound, and lent him speed beyond any he had felt in his limbs before. Nothing could withstand the blade's keen edge, not iron, not bone. It sighed through everything it touched and cleaved its target asunder.

After the first four boar-men had fallen to Culduin's strikes, the remaining warriors of the final round resorted to dodging instead of parries. He spun and ducked their spear thrusts. The rear-most warrior pulled a throwing ax.

A moment of outrage surged through Culduin. Once again, missiles from one side but forbidden the other—

The ax came hurtling toward Culduin, and his indignation nearly cost him an abdominal wound. He hopped back, only in time that the ax should scratch and glance away.

A mix of cheers and boos washed through the crowd.

Ka-chunk.

Bretta shrieked. Ennis groaned. Davon spat a curse.

Too much time fending off distractions. Somewhere behind him, beyond the tormented griffon, his teammates' racks pulled tighter, the threat of ripping them limb from limb becoming more imminent with every moment he played at sparing the boar-men. But if he let go to the compulsion to slay them, wanton and crazed, would his spirit ever cool again?

From the direction of the dignitaries' section of the audience, an uproar spread. From the corner of his eye, Culduin caught a swift motion—something falling from the peninsula. Maybe one of the debauched bloodthirsters above had blundered too close to the edge.

The boar-men charged in a wedge formation, sword wielders coming in low, and the rear two holding long pikes high for downward thrusts. Even the broadest arc could not catch them all. Culduin drew the Sword of the Patron back, his palms buzzing. *Do not be the one to bleed.*

Further commotion echoed from the dignitaries. Shrieks. Fainthearted dismay.

The Sword rose with all the splendor of a swift sun and mowed through the front-most of Culduin's attackers, either blade, limb, or ribcage. His heart swelled with the thrill of dominance. Through a haze of collapsing opponents and no small quantity of blood, Culduin tucked and rolled. Two pikes that came down found no mark in the elf's flesh. The third shot fire across his right thigh.

He snarled and wheeled toward the cur that dared mark him.

Ka-chunk.

More cries erupted from Culduin's comrades.

Another collective exclamation from the crowd wrenched Culduin back from his boiling rage, while the heat of his own blood poured down his leg. His gut lurched. Had one of his fellows lost the fight to the rack?

More motion near the dignitary platform warred for his attention as Culduin righted himself from his tumble. The remaining boar-men stared, wide-eyed and incredulous, but not at him. Past him. They stood, rather than charging in for the kill.

Cut them down! the Sword demanded.

What could warrant such a sudden halt? Why the gasps and tumult that spread through the spectators?

Culduin dared look.

Descending from the platform's lip, a black-robed figure drifted, black, bat-like wings extended to slow his fall into an ominous landing. Culduin caught only a glimpse of the creature's cloven-hoofed legs before two running individuals captured his notice. In the lead—Culduin choked on a gasp— came Danae, strides pushed to their utmost extent, her cloak and strawberry braid flying behind her. Nearly at her hem ran Praesidio. How in the Maker's dominion . . . ?

The boar-men gathered their wits and made another charge at Culduin. He dodged. His one-handed swipe with the Sword deprived one of the boar-men of his leg, from mid-thigh down.

Patron's ablaze! Survival. The team. Now Danae. Culduin held the Sword in a low block, panic plucking at the edges of his composure.

And of course, the voice of the Sword shouted over all. *Conquest!*

The arena air vibrated with the discordant strains of outrage and disbelief. Praesidio called forth his Sword of the Sacred Fire, and with its blade of blue flame, cut a smoking gash across the boar-man farthest from Culduin. This left only one increasingly faint-hearted opponent, of those the game-masters had thrown into the ring. At Praesidio's approach—or maybe at the threat of the winged fiend closing with alarming speed—the last tatters of the boar-man's resolve disintegrated. He fled.

Culduin's gashed leg pounded with the pace of his heart, and his knee weakened. The fiend's dash outpaced Danae and Praesidio's speed, and its strides swallowed the distance between them at an alarming rate. The griffons' screeches behind him haunted his ears. The chaos, amplified and layered in his mind by the Sword, threatened Culduin's grip on reason.

Block it all out. Think. Your own thoughts—not the Sword's. Who can I save? How?

The favor.

He reached to his chest with his off hand, grasped the orange orb suspended there on the silver chain, and yanked it free. A sparking flame sizzled at the place where the bauble had separated from the necklace.

A deep draught of air aligned his scattered thoughts. He stared down the fiend, some forty paces away, but perhaps fewer than a dozen behind Praesidio. It would have to do. Cranking his arm back, he let the favor from Ikirra fly.

The light of thousands of torches glinted off the favor in countless motes of light, and the sparking fuse left behind it a trail of white light. Or perhaps Culduin's heavy bleeding was stretching and magnifying light in fascinating ways. He could not be sure.

Ikirra's favor arced over Culduin's friends and hit the sandy arena just a pace in front of their pursuer. In a concussive burst that blasted everything into momentary silence, the bauble exploded. The fiend flew backward and crashed, headfirst, into the bloodied sand. Praesidio and Danae flew forward, but with less force. Danae rolled and regained her feet. Her mentor dove and slid, but after a firm shake of his head, clambered to his feet again.

Though the compulsion to open his arms to Danae tugged, the mechanical twang of the racks drove Culduin to more sober choices.

"Follow me!" he yelled to Danae, and he made a wide arc around the chained griffon.

An avian screech from the recess reminded Culduin of the second creature he suspected lay in wait. The griffon he could see lunged after him.

He lifted the Sword of the Patron.

"Peace, griffon," Culduin yelled in Elvish. "I will free you and the other, if you will but carry us three free of this place."

The griffon skidded to a halt. "How?" the beast said in the hollow, creaky speech of their kind. His flanks heaved and his probing jade eyes conveyed only mistrust.

"My blade can sunder your chain."

"I will not go alone."

Culduin huffed. "I can make short work of the other griffon's restraints as well. Are you both fit to fly?"

Danae caught up to Culduin where he had slowed. "By the Maker, Culduin, what are you doing? We need to get out of here!" She glanced back across the arena, where the fiend still lay prone.

"Nice to see you too." Culduin smirked. "I am attempting to enact such an escape."

"Yes." The griffon's elvish was heavily accented with an edged, avian timbre, but understandable. "Save my mate first," the griffon said. "They torture her to make me fight."

A weight of sorrow, even amidst dire circumstances, dragged on Culduin's heart. "All right. Then you help me free my companions as well."

The griffon looked up at the lattice of bars across the sky. "You had better be right about that blade of yours."

Culduin dashed past the griffon, and when the beast did not lunge and rip him or Danae to shreds with beak and talons, the crowd bellowed its disappointment. Limping strides, lessened by the Sword's fire in his veins, carried him to the recess, where behind the portcullis, a man in full plate held a glowing brand at the ready. The griffoness already bore three blackened insignias on her shoulder and rump.

Culduin hacked through the portcullis in three strokes, then through the tormentor's feeble parry with the branding iron in one flick of his wrists. The man groveled.

"Stay down and you need not perish this day," Culduin said. He faced the griffoness, whose hackles stood on end, and whose posture rumored an imminent pounce. He spoke to her in measured Elvish. "Your mate has agreed to help us free of this place if I release you."

The griffoness hesitated. "No force can break these chains."

Danae guffawed. "Did you not just watch what happened to the gate?"

"Your point is taken," the griffoness replied.

Culduin severed the chain that ran from the griffoness's iron collar to the ring in the stone floor.

She bolted in a streak of molten gold, and Culduin's stomach lurched. Would she just abandon them, with no regard to the ancient bond of unity between his kind and hers?

Once she cleared the recess, she snared Danae and Praesidio, one companion in each of her talons, as her twenty-five-foot wings thrust her skyward. Danae shrieked, and Culduin did not blame her. He dashed back for the arena.

All around the perimeter, guards and warriors issued from every gate. With a surge of panic-driven speed, Culduin pounded back toward the griffon and cut his chain. Javelins stormed in. The ratcheting of the catapult echoed on the far side of the arena.

The moment the chain fell slack, the griffon wheeled on Culduin, and for a horrifying moment, he despaired of the beast ripping out his throat. It surged forward. Strong talons caught Culduin around the chest and legs.

In a dizzying lurch that stole all sense of orientation, Culduin left the ground. Sanity beckoned him skyward. Compassion insisted one last, desperate rescue.

24

The Gratitude of Griffons

he tight bind of Danae's clothing, gripped along her back by the griffoness, cut into her underarms and ribs, but of her woes, this was least. Her legs dangled and swayed with nothing but a hundred feet of empty air beneath them. The griffoness pumped her wings with sinewy power, and up, up they spiraled, beyond the range of javelins, too fast for the catapult to take aim. But where was Culduin?

The griffoness flew the perimeter of the gridlock dome of the arena. The stands sped by in blur. The spectators blurted unintelligible exclamations, and Danae sought the source of their astonishment. Or was it directed at her unexpected contribution to the insanity?

A clatter of wood echoed from her left, and Danae strained against her tight clothes to see. Two men and a woman hung from some sort of tables, set up at a raked angle. Culduin hacked at levers and mechanisms around them. He freed the first man from his restraints.

The griffoness banked, and Danae lost sight of Culduin's efforts.

"Your friend had best get up here soon," the griffoness squawked.

They climbed and dove and banked and evaded, and none of the few arrows that reached their height found a mark in man or beast. A gold blur streaked across Danae's vision.

"This way!" Culduin cried.

Danae craned to find Culduin not gripped in talons, but astride the griffon. He swung the Sword of the Patron, and it passed through the bars of the dome. Another stroke cut a second, long slice. A third completed a triangle, and his griffon flapped his wings forward, launching the beast and rider backward and out of the path of a ten-foot section of dome that broke free of the rest. It plummeted to the arena floor, where guards scrambled to dodge it. A band of clear twilight sky beckoned them.

Culduin's griffon grabbed the edge of the sundered lattice with his front talons, hauled himself through the gap, then thrust into flight once again. Danae's griffon had a more awkward time, her talons full, but soon she joined Culduin beyond the arena's dome.

They shot into the heights with a speed that whistled in Danae's ears, and she teetered between elation and utter terror. The Sword's signature trumpeted in a brazen swell of triumph. The arrogance that underscored it marred what should have been unspeakable beauty, and Danae marveled at conflict that raged within the weapon's complex voice.

"Which way?" the griffon said.

"West," Culduin yelled over the wind.

"Shouldn't we go a way that leads anyone watching astray?" Danae called to him. Or did traveling west do that? Blazes, she wished she knew where in the world they were.

"Culduin's choice is best," Praesidio said.

Danae sought his voice and found her old friend clutching the griffoness's neck, dangling at the beast's shoulder. He struggled but managed to haul himself astride the creature.

Culduin nodded. "Better to forge for friendly territory with as much speed as we can. Stealth is a laughable hope."

They soared through the darkening sky, over the rolling steppes, and in just minutes, the last rumors of the arena crowd faded, and not long after, they lost sight of the arena over the horizon.

Danae dared heave a breath of relief. She cleared her mind and opened her awareness to any signatures that might be within reach of her notice. Only the smooth, wall-like presence of Praesidio's shielded signature and the quieted pulse of the Sword spoke to her inner senses.

"Praesidio, can the Ba-als fly?" she asked.

"No," Praesidio said. "Not by physical might alone. They use their wings to glide or to slow a fall, as we saw, but they're not made for pure flight."

"They don't deserve it," the griffon said. "There are some I would never share a sky with."

Danae chewed her cheek. Even if the fiend could not fly, it was only a matter of time before his Hounds of Queldurik tracked her again. Twice they had proven great speed in closing the gap between predator and prey. In fact, Praesidio's suspicion about their trip to the arena had proven to her that she was particularly bad at determining whether she was being followed.

She needed to improve her skills at shielding her signature—and remembering to do so.

"Is keeping sensors from finding my signature like keeping a Curse Bearer out of my mind?"

"Much the same."

To Danae's relief, much of Praesidio's usual color had

returned to his cheeks. "That fiend was doing something to attack you while we were in the arena, wasn't he?"

"Indeed. I suspect, even as early as when we were climbing the ramps, his assault began. It was as if he was constantly stuffing me into a stifling bag, if you can understand what I mean," Praesidio said. "My assumption is that he was working hard to prevent me from calling on any Virtusen."

Danae furrowed her brow. "But *The Tree* says that Creo is greater than any agent of the Darkness—even mightier than the Darkness himself."

"But sometimes, the agents of darkness are still mightier than the mortal vessels of Creo's power. Every Thaumaturgist has his weaknesses and limitations, and it takes a life of meditated surrender for us to release those to Creo and prevent them from being exploited by those who hate the Maker and his servants." Praesidio cast her a sober glance. "Do you have an idea where your weaknesses lie, young student?"

Danae pondered the question, and it rumbled in her middle. Her cheeks flushed. "Probably in my impatience."

Praesidio smiled, his eyes lit with a twinkle of sympathy.

The griffons banked right and descended toward a towering bluff.

"Landing now?" Danae asked. "We haven't fled very far."

"We have a decision to make," the griffoness said.

The griffons spread their wings wide, lowered their haunches, and fanned the plumage on their tails until they slowed to nearly a stop. The griffon landed. The griffoness set Danae on her feet before she too, touched down.

Danae's legs buckled like her bones had turned to gelatin. Her head whirled.

In a single bound, Culduin was at her side. He caught Danae with one arm, and in the other, he still gripped the Sword, though he pressed the blade point first into the ground and appeared to be leaning on it. "What's wrong?" His clear blue eyes searched her.

Danae, albeit shakily, regained her feet. "I guess flying just doesn't agree with my constitution—at least not the first time. Not that it wasn't lovely, after the terror settled." In a sudden wash of emotion, her breath caught and her lip trembled. She grappled Culduin in a hug. "I'm so glad we found you."

He lowered his cheek to the top of her head and sighed. "Me too."

In chirps and whistles, the griffons conversed. Danae examined their fascinating interaction, despite her lack of understanding their native language.

The male of the pair circled the griffoness, eyeing each of the raw brands on her body. The set of his jade hawk eyes maintained a stern countenance at all times, but clearly, he regarded her wounds with further consternation. The griffoness's replies came in a mellower tone.

"Any idea where we are, Culduin?" Praesidio asked.

Danae cleared her throat and stepped back from the embrace. She wrapped her arms around her middle and surveyed the horizon.

"Some," the elf replied. "My companions in the gladiator championship informed me that the arena was built near major trade routes that run into both North and South Deklia, so the subterranean journey took us beyond the Ghilter Fens. The closest city to the arena, about a day's travel east, would have been Scraga." He wrinkled his nose.

"Not someplace we want to go for provisions, then?" Danae ventured.

Praesidio laughed derisively. "Not unless we fancy landing ourselves right back in the arena—or in worse straits. I'd venture Scraga is the most wretched place on the continent."

"A due west course should take us into Kelmirith and hence,

Bilearne." Culduin put his fingers on Danae's lips just as she drew a breath to speak. "About five weeks on foot."

She exhaled and her shoulders sagged. "That's a lot of time for the Tebalese—or the merfolk's warriors—to catch up with us."

"The world becomes much smaller when you fly," the griffoness said.

Danae clenched her teeth. *Thanks. Must be nice.*

Culduin tilted his head. "What is your meaning?"

"We intend to fly into the setting sun to return to the nesting peaks of our kind—this is what you call 'west,' is it not?" the griffoness said.

Praesidio nodded.

"We will bear you on your way."

The griffon squawked, but his mate just ruffled the thick fur around her neck and shoulders at him and blinked.

"In gratitude for our freedom to return there."

Danae clapped her hands over her mouth. "Really? By Creo's mercy . . . you mean it?"

The griffoness regarded her mate. "I'm not sure Kli-Chak entirely shares my sentiment, but he holds on to many reasons to hate humans."

Culduin bowed, his fist clenched over his bare but blood-smeared chest. "It would be an infinite honor if you would grace us with any amount of travel as your riders."

"Only after Crienna has had some time to heal those new wounds, though," Kli-Chak said. "I may owe you my gratitude, but not at her expense."

"Time is what they lack." Crienna blew a puff of air at her mate and fluffed her neck ruff. "You saw what chased the girl and her father into the arena."

Danae choked on a breath, then cleared her throat. "Oh, no, Praesidio isn't my father. My teacher." A swell of melancholy pulled her glance to the scrubby ground. "No, my own papa is far off. And dying."

After shifting his weight to his unscathed leg, Culduin wrapped a muscled arm around her shoulders. "Fret not, Danae. With the griffons' help, our chances of reaching him in plenty of time increase more than I think you imagine." He looked to Kli-Chak. "I should be able to dress Crienna's wounds, and I will keep a close watch on them as we travel. You have my word."

Kli-Chak harrumphed. "Might want to dress your own first."

A quick survey confirmed a small gash on Culduin's abdomen, a large slice across the leg he favored, and a half dozen other nicks, scratches, and bruises—though the bruises were harder to assess through the clotted grime of the battlefield.

Danae grimaced, though more in sympathy than distaste. "Kli-chak is right that you both need a bit of tending."

Culduin cracked a sheepish smile. "Fair enough. What do we still have to work with?"

---

*O*nce Culduin had done what little he could for Crienna and himself with water and a few bandages gleaned from Praesidio's gear, Danae unfurled her bedroll and spread it on the least-rocky section of the bluff she should find.

"No, no," Crienna said. "We are not weary, and we see well at night. We will go now and give your hunters less chance of closing in on you."

"But I will take two," Kli-Chak said. "No taxing Crienna in her state."

"Oh, stop," the griffoness said. "You heard the elf. Of the atrocities they could have done to me, branding was among the least. But if you wish to take two riders, so be it." She nodded to

Praesidio. "Elder man, it would be my pleasure to bear you on your way."

Praesidio touched his fingertips to his forehead and closed his eyes. "I am in your debt, noble griffoness."

Danae licked her lips and swallowed a lump in her throat. Having been scooped up and swept away by a flying lion-bird was one thing, but voluntarily climbing aboard carried with it a new dose of hesitancy.

Culduin, now dressed in one of Praesidio's spare long tunics over his pants and boots, held a palm out to Danae. "After you, fairest of us all."

"Oh, the pleasantries are getting awfully thick around here." Danae blushed but concealed it by bending and lifting the wrapped bundle that once again shrouded the Sword. Clumsily, she hauled it over her head and settled the blade on her back.

"I can still carry it, if you like," Culduin said. His glance lingered on the blade with a smolder that gave Danae the impression of appetite.

"No, it's all right," she said. "I should do my share."

Culduin's lips tightened.

Kli-Chak crouched and blinked at Danae. "If we're going, we should. The moon has flown enough of its course tonight already."

After a long moment of consideration, Danae dried her sweating hands on her tunic and forced a step from legs that wanted to lock. Kli-Chak looked on with his piercing, inscrutable glare.

"I'll be right here with you," Culduin said. "It might even be fun."

She eased up beside Kli-Chak and grasped a handful of the griffon's thick ruff. His warmth spread through her hand and up her arms. Before she knew it, Culduin had grasped Danae around the waist and settled her astride the griffon. He sprang up behind her. Reaching his arms around her waist, Culduin clasped two large handfuls of the griffon's neck fur as well.

Danae's heart and stomach swirled with a mix of fluttering anticipation, queasy exhaustion, and nameless unease, so she took a deep breath to steady her nerves. As if it were not staggering enough that she sat only moments away from hurtling through the sky on the back of a creature many would contest even existed, she also confronted the press of Culduin's broad chest to her back and his steady arms barring her in on either side.

She wondered if Culduin could feel the hammering of her heart as he pressed so close. Or did he only feel the bulk of the Sword between them?

Long before she was ready, the griffons lurched into flight, their powerful wings thrusting them over the bluff's edge with dizzying suddenness. They plummeted toward the lowlands of the steppes, where a meandering river flowed.

Danae's voice froze in her throat, and though the desire to cover her eyes raged through her limbs, the instinct to cling tight to the griffon's ruff made louder demands. Just when it seemed the flying mounts would crash into the water, its chattering current dappled with the light of the full moon, Kli-Chak opened his wings wide and arced upward once again. Danae's stomach seemed to have plunged into the river. In a matter of moments, the pair soared high above the depths of the rolling wilderness. In every direction, Danae beheld starlit sky.

"Are you all right?" Culduin asked, the brightness of a smile in his voice.

Danae swallowed the bile in her throat and sucked a deep breath. "Yes." Her voice quavered. "Just fine."

"Do not worry," Culduin said, his head over her shoulder to overcome the rushing wind. "I have you."

A wan smile worked at Danae's cheeks. She had to admit, the assurance of Culduin's battle-strengthened arms on either side of her brought her a warm security. Once she was able to recover from the takeoff and settle into the splendor of the flight, Danae mustered the courage to shift her gaze downward.

She gaped at the dark landscape flowing past. The full moon continued its own flight over the open lands of who-knew-where and cast the world below in a luminous palette of azure, amethyst, and cobalt. The stark, barren hills, sporting a mantle of little more than sloe and sagebrush, grew more treed with junipers and mesquite as they progressed west.

The griffon thrust along with sinewy power in every beat of his wings. The warmth of the fur on his broad back made for a comforting ride—far more pleasant than bumping along in a leather saddle. While she did not yet dare unclench her white knuckles from the beast's thick ruff in order to point, Danae did comment often, her words spilling from her lips.

"Look at how far we can see! If it weren't so dark, I'd bet we could see straight to Kelmirith from this height," Danae said.

"Perhaps." Culduin chuckled. "Perhaps."

"And how fast we're going! It's hard to tell, but I'm guessing we're putting leagues upon leagues behind us by flying. Nobody is going to believe this story when I tell it."

Culduin leaned even closer to her, the warmth of his breath tickling Danae's ear as he spoke. "There is nothing like another's awe to rekindle amazement even in the unamazed hearts of the elves."

Goosebumps swarmed down Danae's neck and shoulders. "Unamazed? How is that possible?"

Culduin leaned around Danae to catch her glance. His eyes sparkled like embodied starlight. "Perhaps the edges of my joy have been rasped away by two centuries of experience." In a hushed tone, he then added, "Or perhaps I am simply distracted by gentle beauty far closer at hand than the landscape that flows by down below."

Danae overheated. Perhaps the moonlight masked the hot

blush that flared in her cheeks. Had anyone ever called her beautiful before? Did she believe it? A long moment of silence hung between the two riders. She groped for an answer.

He will master you.

Danae started.

"What is it?" A flicker of concern crossed Culduin's features.

"I . . . I don't know." Danae faltered. Had he not heard the words? She wrenched her eyes away from Culduin's—too much wandering in desolate places and fleeing from one doom to the next was scrambling her good sense.

But did she also imagine that the Sword of the Patron, once again her burden to bear, seemed to shudder on her back, if only for a moment?

25

Blackened Land, Blackened Thoughts

*D*anae groaned and shifted on Kil-Chak's back, her shoulders burning and the constant sense of the Sword's sneering, groping presence barely held at bay by the shield she constructed around her mind.

"How many more days to Bilearne, Culduin?" she asked. "I don't mean to whine, but this has been a really long week."

Culduin rubbed her shoulder with strong fingers. "I am not as well acquainted with the geography of Kelmirith as I might be, but I would guess another three or four days." He raised his voice. "Am I right, Praesidio? Was that not the southern fork of the Ingre Sira we passed this morning? If so, we have made impressive progress."

"It was," Praesidio replied. He shifted his gaze to Danae. "Even in this balmy breeze, you look ready for a sick ward. The Sword grieves you, does it not? Your shielding is not helping?"

Danae shook her head. "Not enough. It's like pushing on a

falling pile of rubbish all day. The minute I stop, it tumbles down over me and buries me in filth."

"Pass it to me, then," Praesidio said.

She lifted the rope strap.

"No need to weary yourselves," Culduin said. "I'm happy to relieve you both of the burden."

Praesidio muttered something, perhaps in his own tongue, that Danae could neither hear nor translate. A hard expression punctuated a long pause. "No, best I should bear it and fly at a distance from her, or else she gains little benefit from passing it."

"It doesn't bother you, Culduin?" Danae asked.

He shrugged. "Not particularly. I don't have a palpable sense of any malice from it, as you and Praesidio seem to."

"Aren't I lucky to be so gifted?" Danae sighed.

Crienna maneuvered below and to the right of Kli-Chak, and Danae reached the Sword down to Praesidio.

"All talents come with certain burdens," Culduin said. "If it serves you best for Praesidio to take it, far be it from me to assert otherwise."

Once free of the blade's weight and its infectious presence, Danae shifted her attention to the copses of budding trees below. Branches wore a dusting of pale green as their buds swelled into tender new leaves. The air hummed with a promise the Sword's ugly voice had masked as the life breath of spring coaxed the slumbering landscape from beneath the gray shroud of winter. Birds flitted through air, chirping and disappearing through the tangled branches of Kelmirith's forests. The fresh smells of herbs and spring rain drifted on a lazy breeze, and Danae drank it all in with relish.

As the day wore on, however, the humid, fragrant air grew increasingly stale, and the landscape went from fresh and dew-laden to dull and clouded in haze. The farther west they flew, the more the murkiness thickened, until finally the reek of smoldering fires choked the air, and the forestlands wore a veil of smoke. Soon, however, the dense tree cover faltered, for through it was hewn a broad lane, where wagons and the tramp of many feet had churned the earth into a rutted scar. The ravaged track led to a dark smudge upon the horizon, from which the smoldering murk seemed to issue.

They flew onward, and soon, the smoke thickened enough to obscure their view of the ground.

"We ought to fly lower and learn what we can about what has transpired here," Culduin said.

"But we could be seen, flying much lower. Do you think it's safe?" Danae asked. She felt suddenly small and cold.

"That, we cannot know." Praesidio drew closer on Crienna, and with him came the added unpleasantness of his burden, like stench upon stench in a slum. "A part of me hopes that perhaps we will find only a forest fire kindled by spring lightning, or perchance, only a large roasting pit, remaining after a large meal for many. But the highway cut through these lands gives me cause to worry otherwise."

Culduin set his jaw as he surveyed the landscape. "Safe or not, there could be either information here we need, or unfortunates who require help."

"True enough. Griffons, if you would kindly descend so that we can see the ground better," Praesidio said.

"We do not wish to be seen by many men," Kli-Chak said.

Praesidio nodded. "This is understandable. You are entirely welcome to keep whatever distance necessary, should we need to land."

The griffons spread their wings and drifted lower. Danae pushed down the sick feeling that crept into her throat over the possibilities of what they might find in the distance. Culduin had neither his bow nor longsword to draw in case of conflict. The smoke thickened further the lower they flew, until Danae's eyes watered and the foul air made her cough.

Finally, they drew near enough to see the blackened patch of land, and it was nothing so innocuous as Praesidio had hoped, but the ravaged remains of a village. The jumble of charred timber and toppled stonework bore the fresh wounds of warfare, the ground littered with riven swords and broken shields. A tattered black standard, emblazoned with a red triangle and gargoyle's head, fluttered on the gray breeze. The attackers had spared no effort in kindling every house, barn, wagon or haystack. Danae looked to Praesidio and found his eyes aflame. The knight bade their mounts land in the desolation.

Danae slid from Kli-Chak's back. Her boots crunched and squeaked against blackened wood.

Culduin also dismounted, and on wary strides, forged into the bleakness.

Praesidio rubbed his temples and propped the Sword against a nearby ruin of a tree trunk. "I can't think with this blasted thing throbbing in the back of my mind." He proceeded to root around in the rubble a dozen paces from Culduin.

Danae grimaced. A foreboding that hung in the tainted air of the village nagged her. She picked up the blade and slid it across her back. *Somebody better be paying attention to this thing.* Faint, hissing laughter wove with the breeze. Danae spun but found no one in sight, other than her companions.

Her strides came slowly as she waded through the black wounds of war. A sudden numbness of spirit overcame her. Danae stared at the chaos that had toppled so many lives. A discomfiting sensation of weightlessness and detachment from the charred village around her swirled through Danae's chest and shortened her breath. She turned a befuddled gaze from Praesidio to Culduin as they picked through separate sections of the ruin with scrutiny. What could there be to find, other than a repetitive refrain of death and destruction?

Smoke billowed on the soft breeze of spring that should

have been speaking words of new life to the people who once inhabited the barren scene. Danae drifted from one crumbling home to the next decimated shop, and impressions of childhood laughter, of parents toiling, busy but content, all these echoed in her mind with a tinny timbre. Scorched furniture lay overturned within the rubble, the tools of many trades scattered in the streets, the earthenware dinner dishes of families not unlike her own strewn in shards underfoot. As her eyes lingered upon an iron cauldron, which hung crookedly in the remains of a fireplace, her feeling of detachment cracked. She bit her lip as tears seared her eyes. Not tears from ashes and murk, but tears of grieving. She swept them away with her sleeve.

Your father is taken.

Danae swiped at the air as though a droning insect whined in her ear.

You are too late . . . too slow . . . you were foolish to believe . . .

The wind picked up and swirled a cloud of ash into the air. In its shadows, Danae saw faces. She rubbed her eyes. *Too much constant danger must be making me see things.*

The cloud shifted. No, there *were* figures, shaped by the dust. A broad figure grabbed a leaner one by the throat and dragged it away before the ash lost form and settled to the ground. Another gust brought smaller human forms, children by their proportions, who slashed swords. But larger assailants grabbed and subdued them. The ash cloud rode away on the wind.

Danae's heart pounded. Her stomach churned. Turning abruptly, she returned to Culduin and Praesidio. She studied them through a blurred stare.

"I have seen no dead in this place, Praesidio." Culduin turned over a charred beam with his foot. "Neither do I see graves or a sign of a pyre."

"I have noticed this same lack of evidence," Praesidio responded, the fury in his eyes having cooled. "I am hopeful that my people saw this assault coming and were able to move the residents of this village to safety. Better the loss of homes and livelihoods than the loss of irreplaceable lives."

Danae blew a bitter laugh through her nose. "You don't really believe that? Nobody's here because they've all been hauled off to the slave ships, more likely."

Praesidio blinked. His brow furrowed. "Danae, I think you had best—"

"Admit it!" she thundered. She aimed a swift kick at a chunk of charred debris in her path. "Your women and children probably shovel coal into their altar fires as we speak!"

Culduin approached Danae with slow steps, like someone who nears a cornered animal. He placed his hand gently under her chin.

"Why indulge such thoughts?" Culduin asked. "It is simply the bleakness of this scene that unsettles your spirit."

Danae batted his hand away. "What would you have me do, then, Culduin? Just close my eyes? Make up some fanciful story to crowd out the ugly truth?" She shot a bitter sneer to the elf. "Is this how the elves endure the woes of their long years? By simply wrapping themselves in a cozy history—as they choose to remember it? By composing long ballads that only see the heroism and forget the suffering of the small and the weak?"

Culduin recoiled, brows knit and jaw slack.

Mirthless laughter tugged at the recesses of Danae's attention once again. She pressed the heels of her hands to her ears. *It's just the wind. Don't be ridiculous.*

"Miss Baledric," Praesidio said. "It is unbecoming a servant of the Maker to rail. The task before us will take more fortitude than this to complete."

She flung her arms wide. "Complete? What's the point? It has already been so long . . ." Danae shouted, her voice choked with tears. She fled from her companions, her sobs dying in the emptiness.

Danae stumbled through charred sundries and chunks of

collapsed buildings, block after block, until her knees buckled beneath her, and she sank to the ground. All her fears burst through the breach in her composure, and her anguish poured from her soul as wordless groans. Her body shook with sobs. Tears streamed down her cheeks, unchecked.

What if all her efforts over the past months truly had been for naught? What if her father had already succumbed to the Curse driven into his body by the marking knife? Had the ash cloud shown her Drex coming back for Papa? Her brothers failing in defense? Perhaps the Tebalese zealots of Queldurik had already taken Papa away, to some unknown place, to channel the dark energies wielded by their malevolent priests.

She had no guarantee Praesidio really even knew the antidote to all of these horrors. Why had she ever agreed to undertake this impossible task, only to miss the last few months with her father before the unthinkable befell him?

One dreadful scenario after another ran rampant through her mind, and with every thought, the Sword grew heavier. It pressed into her back. Mocked. Scorned. It was too heavy to carry all the way to Bilearne. It was too far. Too hard. A fool's hope.

She clawed at the strap and hauled it over her head with weakened fingers. Let the Tebalese have it. What did it matter? The world would war on. None so small as Danae could sway events so monumental. She thrust the Sword of the Patron from her back, flinging the shrouded weapon into a mound of ash, as far away as she could manage. Not nearly far enough. Miserably, she dropped her tear-dampened face to the ground, heedless of the soot that would cling to her skin all the more for her weeping.

She sobbed in silence for a short while before Culduin approached, though he slowed to a stop when he reached the spot where she had flung the Sword. He lifted the weapon, his gaze locked upon it for a long moment before he slipped it over his shoulder.

Danae did not speak. She turned her head away from Culduin.

The elf waited in silence. He shifted his weight from one foot to the other . . . then back again. His restlessness grew from shifting to pacing a short track in the dusty earth.

"Go away," Danae croaked.

"Pardon me?" Culduin replied. To Danae's surprise, his voice was as hard as steel and sent a chill down her spine. She heard the creak of Culduin's teeth as he ground them together.

"I . . . I need some time alone."

"I must speak with you, Danae. You have wronged me."

Danae slowly pushed herself to sit upright but still did not face Culduin. "I'm overwhelmed. Please don't expect me to talk."

Culduin marched to her side. "No, you will not wield words as a scourge and then dismiss me because of troubles you concoct in your own head." Even without facing him, Danae could tell the elf's posture was rigid, like a snake coiled to strike.

"In my own head?" she countered. "Look around! I see plenty of things to feel more than troubled about."

"But this place is not the heart of the matter."

Danae bristled. "Near enough! It's a pretty clear picture how the war's been going while we ran all over creation—and for what?"

"You exaggerate—"

"Don't dismiss me, Culduin," she broke in.

"How can I *not* dismiss your melodrama, when now you buckle under the fear of things that have not even come to pass!" Culduin said. "The miles that stretch between us and Bilearne are few as compared to how far we have come, and this is no time to crumple beneath a load you unnecessarily pile upon yourself. Can you not look to hope, rather than fear?"

Danae huffed. "Hope? Here? Sorry, but I just don't see it."

Culduin lowered his voice but spoke slowly, as if Danae might misunderstand. "Did you not hear Praesidio and me? There is yet the chance the people of this place never faced attack, that the Elgadrim foresaw their danger and intervened."

"Don't treat me like I don't know anything and like I don't listen, Culduin. I know I'm not the student of war you are, but even I can see it's bad tactics to divide an already-small and struggling army to save people who aren't strategically important." Danae focused on the distant tree line.

"Just because *your* countrymen rolled over to the inevitability of occupation does not mean that all men are so weak willed and ready to abandon their kin to save their own skins!"

Danae's blood boiled in a sudden surge. As if the elves had taken any notice of her people in countless generations.

"What do you know about it? Yes, the mountain tribes betrayed us, but we in Dayleston fought and bled like the best of any country's soldiers! Queldurik's zealots march even across the lands of the great Elgadrim . . . why should I hope that my . . ." Her words stuck in her throat like dry bread, but pride insisted she set her jaw and blink back the tears.

A crow flew over. Its caw echoed in the silence.

Culduin stood, his arms folded, as if waiting for Danae to finish her sentence. She dared not speak another word, lest she come unraveled and begin to cry again. The longer she stayed silent, the more she could sense Culduin's pulse quickening.

The wind hissed over the blackened ground.

"There is more to your black mood than you will say!" Culduin thundered. "Speak! Or else, do not hobble our journey with your foolishness."

"Foolishness?" Danae shrilled. "Don't trouble yourself with my worries, Master Caranedhel! It's not your father whose life is at stake here!"

For a moment, Culduin's steely mask of fury cracked, and

tears welled in his eyes. "Do not trouble myself?" His words came in a husky whisper. "Have I done anything *but* trouble myself on your behalf, from the moment I laid eyes on you? You ingrate! How dare you?"

For a fleeting moment, Culduin's barb of truth stung Danae, but she doused the spark of remorse in a torrent of temper. "So now it's my fault that you have left home and kin on this endless, maybe even *pointless* mission?"

Culduin gaped for a moment, but then his posture stiffened. His eyes flamed. "Are you so shortsighted that you only understand the scope of your own little life, Danae? There is so much more that the recovery of this Sword represents."

The Sword. The cursed hunk of metal. Why had Culduin insisted upon picking it up before he spoke with her? She was sick of the burden of it and tired of the elf's obsession with it.

"Oh, and *you* are the endlessly noble, all-seeing scholar of world events, so above all the rest of us that you don't look at this quest through the lens of what you might gain." Danae hauled herself to her feet. "Go, forge your link in the chain of elven history, Culduin. Finally, cast a black shadow over your older brother. Do what he couldn't! Bask in the fame of being the one to recover the great Sword of the Patron." She challenged him, nose to nose. "No, no, of *course* there's nothing in this for you!"

Staring full into his face, she hardly knew her gentle friend, her healer, her guide and companion. His countenance melted her anger and struck fear into her: real, raw, fight-or-flight fear. Why had she let so many careless words fly at an elf warrior? His pulse throbbed visibly in his temple. His crystalline eyes were at once hard and wild. Perspiration dewed his lip.

She dropped back a step. "We . . . we shouldn't be trying to talk about any of this right now. I'm a mess and can't even understand what this argument is about, and you . . . I don't even recognize you right now." Danae spoke more carefully with each word. His fey mood chilled her.

"Not again!" Culduin bellowed, his voice seeming to shake the very ground Danae stood upon, ringing in her ears. "You will not dodge your way out of this! On all matters between you and me, you duck and dodge, and I will brook it no longer!" He clutched her sleeves at the shoulder. He lowered his voice and leaned down, eye to eye. Strands of his wind-blown, copper hair brushed her cheek.

Danae dared not breathe.

"You will face the truth of what we can attain through might," Culduin whispered. "Choose now, Danae, will you cower in weakness, or will you play your part as I grow into the craftsman of my destiny?"

Her face blanched. What dark secrets had the Sword spoken into Culduin's soul? While it spoke to her only of repugnant filth, what had it been washing over him? She trembled in his grasp, so terrible were his blazing eyes and inescapable the iron clutch of his hands on her shoulders.

"Let me go!" The words came out more breath than sound. Danae's heart galloped wildly in her chest.

The vice of Culduin's hand only clenched more tightly around her upper arm.

"You must let me go!"

"Must I?" He took a step that forced her back in a stumble. He stepped again, and she faltered back until she bumped into the scorched remains of a building. The molten anger in the elf's eyes transformed into something even more unnerving as a crooked, sinister smirk twisted one corner of his mouth. His eyes, crazed and aflame, roved over her, from head to toe. "Under whose command? You *choose* to have no power here, Danae, and that is a very foolish choice indeed. Power belongs to those who have the courage to take it."

He will master you.

The foreboding echo lanced through Danae's memory. Her eyes bulged, and she could do nothing but shake her head. Culduin's expression departed entirely from the encounter. It was as if the life, always so vibrant in his eyes, vanished under a thick layer of flash-frozen ice. His pupils dilated. His cheeks flushed. His jaw tightened and the muscles bulged.

"You should take the Sword off, Culduin." Danae forced the words. "I think it's . . ."

His fingers tightened on her shoulders. "Why do you and Praesidio keep insisting? I am fine. It is the two of you who are so undone by the thing."

"I think, maybe, we're just better equipped to notice." She reached up and slid her fingers under the strap over Culduin's shoulder.

The elf's eyes widened to white-rimmed. He wrenched Danae aside so that she stumbled. Her wrist twisted and fired pain up her arm, but she kept a grip on the Sword even so.

Culduin spun and grabbed the weapon bundle she had dragged from his back. He strove against Danae for it. Despite the shooting pain of her twisted wrist, she fought for it with every ounce of desperate might she could muster. The elf shoved. Danae toppled onto her back but hooked her leg around Culduin's knee as she fell. Her grip on the Sword and her footwork pulled Culduin off balance with her.

His weight landed square upon Danae's torso, buffeting the breath from her lungs. The Sword barred her chest and shoulders. While Culduin pressed the weapon toward Danae's throat, she shoved back with all her might, barely keeping the assault at a stalemate. If he got that blade any higher . . . his weight and the sword's unyielding steel would crush her windpipe for sure. The horror of it all summoned screams Danae could not utter.

Indignation and exertion left the elf's face, suddenly replaced by a stony mask—all except his eyes. Danae could put no name to the look in his eyes, but it stabbed cold terror into her heart.

26

The Dismissal

*I*n a brawl against a crazed elf warrior, Danae may have had no power. But Creo did.

With a clarion voice she never could have mustered on her own, Danae blurted the string of ancient words that had long come to her aid. *"Lumitannat is distanir, kelenith ve sinithwe!"*

The syllables burst from her lips with palpable force, much more potent than any other time she had uttered them. Her hand flared and crackled with pale lavender-white energy. She reached under the Sword to fumble an open palm onto Culduin's chest. As a sound like a thunderclap tore through the air, the elf's lean figure launched from her as though pummeled with a battering ram, crashing to the ground and rolling over backward, not once, but twice.

The Sword of the Patron came to rest some five feet from his body. He tried to push up on trembling arms but collapsed back to the ground. Residual arcs of electricity snaked across his body until they dissipated.

At once, Praesidio came dashing around the corner of a crumbling house and skidded to a halt. He gaped.

Danae sat up. The charge of energy faded from her hand, but she still turned her palm over in mute examination.

"What is going on here?" Praesidio glared at the Sword and each of his traveling companions in turn.

Danae gazed at the old sage, unblinking and dazed. After an agonizing pause, she dropped her arm to her side.

"I don't . . ." Danae's body broke into trembling, and she hugged her knees to her chest. She could not look at Culduin.

Praesidio stalked over to the Sword of the Patron and snatched it from the ground with a snort of disgust. Once Culduin clumsily rolled to his back, he coughed and turned his head to the knight.

"What do you have to say about all of this, Master Caranedhel?"

The elf merely dropped his wrist to his forehead as he gasped to catch his breath. Praesidio huffed.

"Clearly, I will get no useful answers from the two of you," he said, more muttering to himself than conversing. "But I can piece things together well enough. There has been a wealth of foolishness indulged here, and I advise the two of you to search your souls for the balm for it. For now, this Sword shall not touch your person, Culduin. And Danae, I think you had better use the rest of this day in meditation to clear your head."

The Elder Knight then turned on his heel and stalked off, taking the Sword with him.

---

*D*anae sat with her back propped against a tree, wrapped tight in her cloak, but still her body trembled as she relived the day's events in her mind, in unstoppable repetition. The crazed look in Culduin's eyes, the harsh words they had stabbed into one another. It all seemed to nestle into the pit of her stomach and twist her insides until they ached. What had gone so amiss in this dreary place? They should have just kept flying.

"Danae?" Praesidio called.

So he was back. She peered over her shoulder. The old knight stood a dozen paces away.

"We make camp here," he said.

The last thing Danae wished to have all around her was the stark reminder of the wages of war. "Here? Isn't there—"

"Most of us are in no shape for further travel today. And there is work to do." Praesidio turned toward the ruined cottage where Culduin sat against a broken wall. "Master Caranedhel, follow me."

Praesidio stormed back toward the village center, and Culduin limped after with nary a word of protest.

Alone and in doubt, Danae curled her body tighter, thankful for the vigilant watch of Crienna and Kli-Chak. Her occasional glimpse of the griffons' paced track around the camp spoke to the sharp eye they kept for intruders.

Well, if they were traveling no farther today, no use sitting in the wind. Spring had not warmed enough yet to make idleness outside pleasant. With shaking hands, Danae fumbled with her oilskin tent to pitch it.

The faint ring of metal upon metal, distant but unmistakable, pierced the stillness. Danae clutched a dagger's hilt on her belt. Another battle? Dread threatened to drown her. She would fall easy prey. She had no heart to stand her ground—perhaps she could find a hiding place before the conflict barreled closer. Where were the griffons?

She peered between nearby tree trunks and found Crienna and Kli-Chak sitting in the thin shade of a tree that had sprouted small, bright leaves. Crienna preened her wing. Kli-Chak dozed. Did they not hear?

Danae focused on the sound again. Still, metal clashed. But the longer she listened, the more she realized: This was no chaotic clash of swords but a rhythmic clang of the smith's hammer. But who could be crafting in this desolate place, she could not imagine. Praesidio must be up to something.

She blew out a sigh of relief and finished tightening down her tent. Slowed by a weariness of body and soul, she crawled inside.

With the occasional ring of the hammer calling like a church bell through the stillness, she drifted into the slumber that overtakes the utterly spent.

The next morning, Danae awoke, stiff and cold, the smell of smoke mingling with the damp aromas of dawn, though the odors of burning summoned a rumble in her belly. Food cooked somewhere nearby, and her appetite demanded that she emerge from her nighttime cocoon. She poked her head from behind the tent flap. A little fire crackled about fifty paces away, over which roasted three hunks of meat, and yet another cook fire warmed an iron kettle hung on a long hook, staked at a diagonal into the ground.

Praesidio sat near this outdoor kitchen, his copy of *The Tree* resting open on his lap, his face haggard. What was he sitting on? It appeared to be some sort of long, narrow, crudely fashioned box of scarred wood, banded with black iron. Something he must have dug up in the rubble of their forsaken campsite.

After a final stretch, Danae approached Praesidio with slow steps. She eyed his expression, wary of potential rebuke. Despite his worn appearance, a smile brightened Praesidio's face as he looked up from his reading.

"A fine morning to you, Danae. The griffons have brought us fresh game to help soothe our empty bellies. And I found a teapot and some tea, if you can believe that! I'm thankful for this unlikely chance to prepare it." He rose and lifted the kettle from its hook. "Care for some?"

Danae nodded. She perched gingerly on the far end of the box from where Praesidio had been sitting and shuffled her feet in the dust. A budding headache pressed at her temples.

As the old sage poured her a bit of the well-steeped tea into a pewter cup, he tilted his head, sighing and blinking slowly.

"Do not fret, young learner. We can talk in due time. For now, warm yourself, and perhaps just listen." Praesidio flipped back a page in his volume as he sat and began to read aloud.

"*Behold, the soil of the soul is made fertile in forgiveness. But the wise man does not sow before the bitter frosts have well passed, for he knows the blossoms of emollient words are tender. You, Creo, know the time of planting and of harvest. Open our eyes that your wisdom might take root in our hearts. Let us not spend our seeds in haste and find our fields become fallow places for thistles and thorns to grow.*" He closed the book, set it aside, and took a lingering sip of his tea.

Forgiveness. Danae mulled Praesidio's meaning, shrouded in the words of *The Tree*, rather than calling the words his own. Reconciliation? Ludicrous. Some breakdowns of character . . . displays of inner intent . . . he had not even seen what happened.

But the wise man does not sow before the bitter frosts have well passed . . .

Whose bitterness? Danae wondered. The knotted feeling overtook her stomach again, but she gritted her teeth against it. She sipped her tea, staring darkly over the lip of her cup, when Culduin slipped past Praesidio's shoulder and up to the fire.

Danae's muscles tightened, and her heart accelerated. An anxious flutter arose in her chest.

The elf looked at neither of his companions but silently busied himself prodding the game for doneness. He cut a long strip of it with his knife and turned to depart. His foot snagged on a charred beam that lay near the fire. A few fumbling steps saved him from sprawling in the dirt, but the edges of his ears flamed crimson as he hurried out of sight.

Praesidio and Danae finished their tea and ate their own share of breakfast, exchanging only sporadic small talk about the spring weather. Just as the awkwardness of another stilted silence settled over them, Kli-Chak approached. Finally, a respite from the Elder Knight's quiet scrutiny.

"Man of the south?" the griffon creaked in his unsettling, hawkish voice. "It appears a great flock of men, clad in skins, assemble to the . . . north?" He glanced off to his right.

"That is north, yes," Praesidio said. "Could you tell what they are doing?"

"Much cutting of wood. Building of towers that they can pull along on . . ." Kli-Chak lashed his tail. "I don't know men's ways well. Not enough to say for sure what they fell the trees to make."

"Probably machines of war," Praesidio said more to himself than in conversation. "Siege towers." The lines in the old man's weary features deepened. "You have gone to great risk to learn this, my winged friend."

"Do we need to go north?" Danae's earlier flutter threatened to escalate into trembling.

"More west than north," Praesidio said. "When we set out, we'd best give that encampment a wide berth, and then hasten for Bilearne." He patted a palm upon the casket where he sat. "Good griffons, do you think Crienna will be able to manage the hauling of this cargo, as well as bear a passenger?"

Kli-Chak eyed the box with his keen glance. Ruffling the thick hair about his shoulders, he nodded abruptly. "If it's needed, we shall manage it. We are ready to depart as soon as you are."

With a flutter of his wings, the griffon turned from Praesidio to settle back down next to Crienna. They exchanged a series of quiet clicks and whistles, but Danae withdrew her attention from the creatures and steered it to the casket beneath her.

"So keeping the Sword in a box will be better than carrying it wrapped?"

The old sage regarded the crude vessel, and he hunched as though multiplied weight settled over his already-stooped shoulders. "It will prevent anyone from having to touch the weapon, which is important. I should have been more wary, for all our sakes," Praesidio said. He rubbed his fingers over his brow. "Can you forgive me, Danae?"

"Forgive you? For what?"

"I alone knew the depth of the danger the Sword posed to each of us. I should have found a way to limit how much we handled it much sooner." Praesidio clenched his hands in his lap.

"Of all people, Praesidio, you're the last one who deserves any blame," Danae said. "There wasn't time to do anything other than run."

"Let it be a lesson to all of us, then. I never anticipated how great a risk the Sword's voice posed to someone who cannot hear it as clearly as you or I do. A gain of speed does not always out-value the usefulness of due diligence." He heaved to his feet. "Anyway, enough proverbs for now. I scavenged about the ruins here, and with Culduin's help, managed to piece together this box. Tell me, is the Sword's signature dulled for you?"

Sure, none of them might need to handle the Sword directly now, but had the damage not already been done? And what if the Sword was not a true root, but merely an excuse for what poison lurked in the soul?

"And here I thought I was getting better at shielding," Danae said. "It's muffled, if that's the right word."

"That's a start, then," Praesidio replied.

*P*raesidio used what rope they had available to create handles on the sword casket, and although he worked steadily, the process took a long, uneasy chunk of the morning. He refused to share the task with either of his younger companions.

Culduin had not attempted to address Danae in any way, but his presence alone sent shudders through her flesh. She did not want to contemplate what might have been had she not called the Virtus to her aid.

Under his crestfallen look, did the demons of power mongering and mastery still linger? Was he sorry, or just feeling the sting of reprimand? Just how far would he have gone to keep her from taking the Sword?

But then again, what of Culduin's accusation that Danae had become a slave to her doubts? She steeled her mind against the notion and focused instead on tightening buckles.

---

*T*he morning wore on, and Culduin had run out of tasks to perform at his absolute slowest pace. Whose command did they wait upon to move? Was Praesidio lingering in this forsaken place just to torment him with the constant whisper of his weakness? He could hardly stand living within his own skin. Flesh that had betrayed him and nearly driven him to disaster.

Culduin clapped his hand to his forehead at the nausea that welled up and threatened to expel what little breakfast he had managed to choke down. They needed to move on. For many reasons. He swished saliva in his mouth and swallowed to quell the burn in his throat, with small success. He would have to speak to her at some point. The elf pressed his hands to his thighs, stood, and crossed camp with trembling steps to where she sat, beating soot out of yesterday's tunic. Her back was to him, but not once he drew within a dozen paces.

Danae turned only partly and eyed him over her shoulder. "Please. Don't come nearer."

Culduin closed his eyes. A gust of breath deflated him until his shoulders sagged and his spine curled. "I just wondered if we ought not move on."

"I'm not ready yet," Danae replied. "I still have soiled items. I'm not packing filth." She folded the tunic and picked up a pair of breeches smudged and blackened on the knees and up one side, likely where she had collapsed on the ground in her woe.

He noted her hands' trembling.

"It's not like you to linger over the nonessential," Culduin said.

She whirled and lanced him with a tortured look. "What do you really know of what I'm like or what I should be like? Leave me alone!"

Culduin stepped back a pace. "I meant no harm." He glanced to the southeasterly sun. "The day wears—"

"So what? Move on today, tomorrow, does it really matter?"

"I cannot understand what has gotten into you."

"Me? Have you looked in the glass?"

Culduin clenched his fists. Indeed, he had reflected on his own warped image of late, and he neither understood nor liked what he had seen yesterday. He had become alien to himself, so starkly different than the elf he had known himself to be. Before the gladiator ring. Could he ever find his way back? Had his missteps closed those paths to him?

"I do not believe I am what you accuse me of being." The words came out in a whisper. "Something inexplicable—"

"Don't!" Danae screamed with such shrill ferocity that Culduin startled. "Until you can take some responsibility—"

Praesidio marched between them. "Enough of this foolishness. Culduin is right—we have frittered enough time away here. As soon as the griffons have returned from their scouting, Culduin will ride with me on Kli-Chak, and Danae, you will ride Crienna as she bears the casket."

The casket. Danae sat upon it, clutching her sooty clothing to her breast, her eyes hard and frantic like a cornered beast.

Could it be that a mere containment of iron and wood might not prove enough? Culduin squinted at the box.

Danae gestured to the lid of the box. "Praesidio, don't you see?" A sudden welling of tears spilled over the rim of her chestnut-colored lashes and ran down her cheeks. "He can't break its hold on him." She shook her head, then sniffled. "I can't be in constant danger." She rose and pulled the cloak around her. "We're close enough to Bilearne that you can find the way now, right, Praesidio?"

"Not without either utilizing the course of the river or the road," the sage replied. "I rarely have need for cross-country travel, at least not in my homeland."

"So that means we'll get there." She closed her eyes and took a shuddering breath. Her lips quivered in a tense frown. "Your help doesn't outweigh the risk, Culduin."

Culduin's stomach imploded. His knees melted. He grabbed a low limb of the tree beside him to prevent an embarrassing collapse. "Just so—you dismiss me? It is not advisable—"

"I've thought about little else all day." Danae opened her eyes, slick with tears. "Are you really *sure* you wouldn't lose control again?"

In desperation, Culduin sought Praesidio. "Please, stand on my side! The roads and rivers are far too dangerous. If to keep the Sword from enemy hands is your wish, then you cannot make choices according to fear."

Praesidio did not speak, but the ache of fathomless suffering creased his forehead and drove away his previous livid fury.

"I'll go myself, without either of you, if I must!" Danae took a step back. She stared, wide-eyed, at Praesidio. "If you're going to insist we still follow this . . . unstable . . ."

Alone? So close to the enemy's encampment? Culduin gulped down his panic. He spread his hands and took a single step toward Danae. She recoiled as from flame. A sob wedged in Culduin's throat, but he fought it back before it betrayed him audibly. There were no words that could fully convey *I did not mean any of it.* Certainly none Danae was of a temper to believe. He grasped his temples as though to hold his unraveling fibers together.

A warm hand clasped his shoulder. "I won't let her run off unaided." Praesidio's voice came in a husky gravel. "But for now . . . you know where we're headed."

Culduin heaved a beleaguered breath. He straightened and looked south through a haze of welling tears. Without another word, he marched into the late morning sun.

*D*anae turned her back on Culduin's departure. Her shivers and quick breaths only subsided once she could no longer hear the slightest rumor of his footfalls. She wet her dry throat before she sought Praesidio. "Will the casket slow Crienna down much?"

"You should have seen Crienna returning from their hunt. This, at least, has handles." Praesidio's eyes crinkled with a smile, though Danae saw it for the façade it was.

She busied herself for the next half hour with reordering her equipment in her pack. When that got tiresome, she practiced the minor Virtus Praesidio had shown her that would mend a tear in cloth.

After her third successful attempt, the griffons landed about fifty paces from their campsite.

"So it was him," Kli-Chak said, padding toward them.

Praesidio tilted his head. "I beg your pardon?"

"The elf," Kli-Chak snapped. "Why does he march southward without you?"

Praesidio closed his eyes and breathed out in a long stream, then deferred to Danae.

Her pulse quickened. Kli-Chak raised his hackles, and Crienna's posture was wary.

"We, uh, didn't really need him for the rest of this trip," Danae fumbled.

"Then our obligation to you is also concluded," Kli-Chak said.

Crienna chirped low, but he screeched back a reply that silenced her.

"Our debt was to the elf, and our allegiance ties us to his kind, not yours." Kli-Chak opened his wings. "There is far too much human trouble between here and your intended landing for my comfort, and therefore, we sunder ourselves from you."

Danae choked. Her glance volleyed between Praesidio and Kli-Chak, but the sage did not lift his downcast eyes. "But, please. This is when we need you the most, if we're in danger of enemy army seeing us."

"If Culduin has no need to journey west, then our agreement is spent." His ruff fluffed bigger, and he thrashed his tail. He exchanged rapid clicks with Crienna.

The griffoness blinked and cast a last glance to Danae. "Farewell. Take care—in addition to the northward enemies, more humans boil like ants, a day's walk to the south."

Both griffons spread their wings and launched skyward. In mere moments, their flight carried high above the trees.

Praesidio squinted skyward after them, then turned for his gear. "We had better get moving. Three days flying will become more like a fortnight on foot."

"Did you have any idea they'd abandon us?" Danae asked.

"Abandon us? Do you think I did?"

Danae groaned. Why could he never answer the simplest questions? "Well, maybe you wouldn't have called it that, but you knew they'd leave! Why didn't you stop me from messing that up?"

Praesidio lowered his chin and gazed at her from beneath his brows. "So you would have kept Culduin here in order to retain faster transportation?"

"No. I mean, that's not . . ." Danae tramped in a circle. "Whose side are you on?"

"The side of truth." Praesidio grasped one rope handle on the Sword casket and lifted one end. "And of temperance. Grab your side. It's not getting any earlier while you sort through the scope of your decisions."

---

*T*he next morning, Praesidio sat beside Danae as she scanned what pages of her copy of *The Tree* she could still read after its dousing in the merfolks' domain.

"Care to help me draw some water at the river?" the sage asked.

Danae jumped at the chance of respite from her reading. Some days, the words within the tome of wisdom spoke with clarion authority when she read, but this morning, as with every other time she paused to read since the day at the burned village, very little made sense to her. She closed her book and stashed it in her pack, rising, stretching, and following Praesidio. He ambled along, less dependent on his staff today, much to her relief. They moved side by side beneath the swaying branches of silver-barked birch trees, whose tiny, bright leaves opened to drink in the spring sun. The peaceful song of the wind through the branches tugged at Danae's soul, but her heart was like hard clay to little rain.

"Danae," Praesidio began, his voice guarded. "It's important we delve into the incident from the other afternoon."

Danae raised an eyebrow. "The incident?"

Praesidio's face grew stern. "Do not presume to play games, young one. If you are not ready, say so."

"No, no . . . it's not that." Danae took a deep breath and blew it out again. The knotty swirl of panic, anger, and shame, now growing all too familiar, rumbled around in her core.

After a pause, Praesidio continued. "I received Culduin's side of the tale as we worked on the casket, and I wish your opinion of what happened after you fled from us."

Danae's throat constricted. She squeezed her eyes shut against the memory of the elf's cold, uncharacteristic stare. Still, her gut shuddered. "He should have left me alone. Given me some time to unload so many pressures that have built up on this journey."

Praesidio raised his eyebrow.

"I was in no condition to discuss anything!" Danae added. "Yet he kept pressing, and then *blamed* me! Said I invited worries onto my own back, and that I was too small-minded to appreciate the scope of this whole mission."

"And everything you said? Each thought you expressed was sober and inoffensive?" Praesidio asked.

Danae's next words crumbled from her lips. "He . . . it still wasn't—"

"*He* had the Sword on his back. If we are only going to focus on Culduin in this discussion, perhaps that detail bears examination."

Danae clenched her teeth. Looking at the ground, she resumed her heading for the river's edge. She pulled out her waterskins and thrust them roughly below the surface of the rushing current. Praesidio knelt beside her and dipped his vessels.

"Danae, no one deserves a scare like you've had. But it is

crucial that you find your way through the fright and your feelings of betrayal if you are ever to discover a path to healing."

Danae pulled her skins from the river with a loud splash, threw them over her shoulder, and stalked back toward camp.

He doesn't understand. How could he? It's not about words . . . Of all the insane events since she had left home, never had her fear of death been as intense as when Culduin forced the Sword toward her throat.

Trapped. Helpless.

She pressed the heel of her hand against her eye. With a grunt, she forced the spike of horror back down.

Once Danae had collected her emotions again, she looked back over her shoulder. Praesidio remained on his knees at the water's edge, his head in his hands. His drooping frame spoke of weariness and defeat.

Grief clawed at her. *I'm sorry, Protector,* she thought. *I just can't. If forgiveness is necessary for us to carry on, we might have a problem.*

27

Not Just Reinforcements

ow could he have been both blind and weak? All the potential grabs at might and splendor that had arisen in his imagination, how childish, foolish, and impossible they all seemed. Now. Now that the blade was out of reach and its hypnotic hues could not lure him. Even as his thoughts lingered on the sing of the blade as it cut the air, the tiniest thrill fluttered in his stomach, the swirling intoxication so akin to the spark of romance.

No, not romance. Lust. He forced the thrill away with a grunt of disgust. It was aberrant, the sensation. Deviant. Meant only to lead him into destruction, and yet, how did it still arise in his flesh, even when he knew the poison for what it was? And still, the memories of wielding the Sword in the gladiator ring swelled within him with gripping potency. Perhaps he did not hear the Sword in the way Danae and Praesidio did, but he felt it. Deeply.

Culduin tramped through the budding underbrush of

Kelmirith's countryside, gladdened at least a little to see some of her tender blooms unmolested by the enemy's progression through the country. Would even a blade remain standing after Queldurik's hordes waged their assault? How much of the ancient soil would they stain with Elgadrim blood?

Though his destination, if it was indeed Delsinon, lay more due south, Culduin had taken a more south-southwest heading in his indecision. His previous companions would shortly be long out of reach, but somehow, keeping the angle between their courses relatively acute seemed the better choice, at least for today. It was better that he forded the Arin farther west at this time of year anyway, or so he told himself.

At nightfall, Culduin made forlorn camp under sod-sweeping boughs of a weeping cherry. He lay on his side, his vision fixed one moment on the tiny pink buds not yet ready to burst into full splendor, the next, blurring the limbs to gaze beyond. A breeze stirred his verdant bed curtains. The taint of sulfur, smoke, and iron prickled in his nose. He blinked. Sniffed again. No, it had not been a figment.

The smells intensified until a low murmur of voices that ebbed and flowed like a tide mingled with the sighing breeze. At times, the sound of a distant multitude rose, then died away again. Culduin rose to his feet and fingertips to creep forth from his bower. He skulked low, hunting the voices, following his nose and ears.

He wended his way through thickets and over a chattering stream, and all the while, the voices swelled. Their rumble became chanting—its sound dark and impure. It chilled Culduin's bones. Something very wrong lurked beyond sight.

He sought cover as he worked his way up a hillside, from one tangle of blackberry canes to the next swatch of dense laurel. Ahead, the woodlands thinned, and the orange glow of firelight danced between the black boles of the trees. Silhouetted against the firelight, two men stood.

Great. Culduin grumbled inwardly. *Perimeter scouts, I wager. But it is nonsensical—the front lines are farther east of this place. Reinforcements, perhaps?*

He crept left, giving the scouts a wide berth. The chanting, somewhere ahead, continued and amplified. Thankfully, it masked any misstep he might make in last autumn's dew-dampened litter underfoot. His strides carried him silently toward where the foliage failed, distant enough from the scouts to maintain the hope of secrecy. He hunkered even lower and progressed at a near crawl.

The woodlands gave way to a clearing, around which the remnants of a tumbled granite wall circled. Creeping forest trailers reached from the edge of the clearing to grope their way up the walls. At the major breaches in the ruins, two banded-mailed guards stood watch, weapons bare in the moonlight. But the throng within the ring of stone gripped Culduin's heart with crushing dismay.

Countless misshapen apparitions teemed in the ruinous courtyard. All bore some semblance of mannish features, though some stood hunched with the ridges of their backbones stretching their skin in tight prominences. Some had hide and pinion wings like Ba-al Zechmaat's. Others stood tall and brazen, the figures of women unclad and gleaming, but with cold, glittering eyes, sneering expressions, and tentacles for hair. In the midst of all these creatures, at intervals, stood robed reptilian creatures, their crocodilian heads bared in the torchlight. They all roared and chanted in mingled languages.

In the center of the crowd, the shell of a watchtower rose, its nearest side crumbled away, and all of it heavy laden with a brown tangle of choking vines. The crumbled wall revealed an interior level of the tower, and from the dark recess of this structure, another figure emerged.

A hush fell over the multitude. Culduin's heart pounded in his ears.

The individual in the tower stood no taller than a formidable man, but an aura of malevolent authority pulsed from him in waves. Chills ran down Culduin's arms and back. The figure wore a long, trailing robe of deep green, hemmed in mahogany, a helm with two ridged ram's horns, and smoke-colored plate and chain armor. His eyes burned a brighter green than his raiment, and he swept the crowd with his gaze. His face, chiseled and ancient, offered them all a toothy grin.

He lifted a staff, topped with a bronze gargoyle head, and spoke. The language was fluid, like waves of black velvet, but at the same time, oily. Beside the tower, a dragon-kin spoke moments after, in the croaking, guttural language of their kind. From the dragon-kin's address, Culduin pieced together a greeting and the name Queldurik. After speaking the name, the dragon-kin turned to the man elevated in the tower, who touched his fingertips to his forehead and bowed. The crowd mirrored this gesture.

Maker have mercy. The remnants of Culduin's dinner burned the back of his throat. He gulped the acidic herald of his horror with a grimace. *It could not be . . .*

The man in the tower raised his hand in a casual gesture that suggested humility, though it seemed at odds with the stark fear his simple presence inspired. He spoke again, and as the dragon-kin interpreter followed with his language, Culduin fought to glean pieces of the speech. The thrum of the crowd's responses to the oratory frustrated his efforts, since the fiends in the courtyard inevitably roared their approval before the dragon-kin was done translating. Words like "campaign," "end," "Elgadrim," "map," and "victory," came through clear. As did "destroy," and "triumph." As the speech giver concluded a particularly spirited segment, the crowd erupted into a chant.

"*Achru, Queldruik: jukta, poulch-ven, Supreghat!*" the dragon-kin repeated.

This much, Culduin understood. *"Hail, Queldurik: comman-der, course-charter, Almighty!"*

Culduin's legs weakened. Reinforcements? If only this was so mundane. No, this was a legion of fiends—likely bound by the dragon-kin in their midst—ready to swarm into the war. He scanned the clearing—how many creatures comprised the throng? Four thousand? A single fiend posed a match for a dozen ordinary troops. How many of the Allied forces would carry blessed weapons, capable of hurting the beasts at all?

Danae. How far had the griffons borne her and Praesidio in the past day? Did Culduin dare hope for their safety? Should he try to warn them of the maelstrom poised to strike? What good was a message of doom against the type of host Queldurik himself would command?

Poor Danae. Toil upon toil, and now a worse war than anyone dared imagine raged ever closer to her destination. As much as he ached to find her again and see her safely behind the entire allied army, deep down, he knew she would reject his help.

But there were other places he could take his terrible knowledge, perhaps to more significant benefit. In his own people, there was greater hope than mere messages. If only Culduin could make them hear him.

A twig behind Culduin snapped.

"You," a man barked in the common tongue. "Don't move."

28

Crows Mustering

C ulduin's head drooped. The grate of cogs whispered in his ear, behind him in the dark. Maybe ten paces? *Stupid. Stupid! How long did I crouch here like an old stump, waiting to be tripped over?*

He bent his elbows and raised his palms, while easing slowly around.

A mechanical *ka-chunk* rang out, and Culduin dropped flat. A crossbow bolt whizzed over Culduin's prone form. He got to his hands and balls of his feet, dug his feet into the soft earth, and sprang the direction the bolt had come. Culduin rushed the crossbowman's midsection.

They collided before the man could draw the sword on his hip, and Culduin drove the soldier backward until they slammed into a tree trunk. In the next instant, he grabbed the archer's arm, yanked it straight, and jammed an upward thrust of his palm against the man's elbow. The crack, while sickening, was effective.

The archer's cry might as well have been a signal horn.

Voices rang out, from both Culduin's right and left. He wasted no effort in puzzling out their words. He punched the bowman in the gut, dodged a wide swing, and then elbowed his opponent in the face. The man dropped.

Culduin relieved him of his sword, then bounded away from the edge of the clearing and deeper into the woods.

"Spy! Elf spy!" Shouts in common and dragon-kin pierced the woods.

He pushed for more speed. Arrows hissed past. The tumult behind him grew.

A quick glance revealed at least four men pursued him on foot. He barreled onward, when ahead, he beheld several bestial shapes. Horses! Picketed for the night, so it would seem. Culduin cut right to strike a path for the mounts. Beside the nearest beast, he found a bow and quiver, which he yanked from the horse's pack. He nocked a poorly crafted, ugly, graceless arrow on a bow whose pull was weaker than he had used as a child. He rolled his eyes, then let the arrow fly, followed by a second. The first felled his lead pursuer with a hit to the right eye. The second hit another in the shoulder.

"*Cha-thrathrita* fletching," he grumbled.

The horses threw their heads up and pivoted nervously. They were all the stout, shaggy beasts with erect manes native to Tebal, all bridled, but none saddled. Culduin yanked on the knot of the closest mount's reins, tied in a highwayman's hitch, so it blessedly released. He sprang to the animal's back and drove his heels into the horse's barrel.

They thundered through the moonlit forest, kicking up clods of earth as they went, but the sound of further hoofbeats rumbled behind them. They burst into another clearing, when Culduin's mount screamed and stumbled. His leg grip prevented a fall from the horse's back, but the horse hobbled, lamed by the shaft of an arrow protruding from his hindquarters. Cheers and the pound of hooves neared.

A whooshing somewhere above sent Culduin's hope into his stomach like a ball of shot. If they had sent dragon-kin—or worse—fiends after him, this was over. He placed another arrow upon the nock, still urging his poor horse forward with legs and seat, and aimed toward the starry heavens. A winged blur descended and extended golden talons. Culduin scarcely succeeded in redirecting the shot before the beast grabbed his arms and lifted him from the horse's back.

Culduin laughed aloud. "Crienna! How . . . ?"

"When Kli-Chak and I saw this awful rabble gathering, I felt terrible about you being alone. It looks like I was right that you'd need us."

"We're not safe yet." Kli-Chak swooped in from the right. "Speed, Crienna."

Crienna's wings beat with sinewy might, and the wind whistled in Culduin's ears. Westward they flew, between marches of pines and through tight valleys. With his limited ability to turn, Culduin could not hunt the skies for pursuit, but with the griffons' great speed, he doubted even Queldurik's summoned abominations could have kept pace.

---

*D*anae paced the edge of the campsite, the chirp of spring peepers singing in chorus, punctuated by an occasional bullfrog interposing his comical baritone. Pale light filtered through the new leaves above as dawn neared. Five days of southwestward march had offered them encounters only with the wildlife of Kelmirith—rabbits, squirrels, red-tailed hawks, and even an elk or two. Spring had taken hold of the lands around her with both hands, and everything was green and supple.

She could almost forget that somewhere in the eastern distance, a war raged between armies. Over their time of traveling together, Praesidio's history and current events lessons had flowed in a near-constant stream, and while Danae was grateful for the education, the weightiness of the times she was living in did have a way of hanging on her like a wet mantle. The Sword's indignant, muffled presence further weighed upon her mood.

"Glad to see you ready to move on."

Danae jumped at the sound of Praesidio's voice when it broke the stillness from behind her. She spun his direction, heart hammering.

He held his jaw tight and lips in a line. His glance flicked over his shoulder.

"What is it?" she said.

"What is what?" Praesidio sniffed.

"The look on your face. You didn't like something you heard or saw while you were away from camp."

He pulled up his hood. "The weight of so much, that's all."

Danae's cheek pulled her mouth into a doubtful twist. *Guess I'll keep my eyes open. He's dodging.*

She shouldered her pack and grabbed the sword casket's rope handle. Praesidio took on the burden of the opposite side and nodded. They plodded onward, over a smooth but weedy road. With Praesidio's greater height and length of stride, the long box bobbled between them, since Danae marched double time to keep up with her mentor's long, brisk steps.

No history lessons this morning. No chatter at all. Something was wrong.

Danae kept a sidelong watch on Praesidio as they walked. A flutter of wings from a tree ahead caught her ear, and apparently Praesidio's as well, as he snapped his gaze to it. A black bird swooped across their path, beat its wings, and disappeared through the canopy.

A quarter-hour later, two more birds, blue-black of feather, took to the sky ahead of them. Praesidio's weathered fist clenched tighter around the rope handle.

"Ravens?" Danae said.

"Crows." Praesidio's tone carried a foreboding edge.

"And that troubles you because . . ."

"Who said it troubles me?"

Danae lifted a brow. "Your face."

Praesidio softened. "I've seen too many this morning. A fair flock of them passed overhead while I was away for my daybreak meditation."

"I take it that's a bad sign?" Danae's stomach clenched.

"When men poise on the brink of battle, the crows muster for gleaning," Praesidio said.

"But aren't the armies fighting to the east?"

The clop of hoofbeats on packed dirt interrupted their conversation. Somewhere ahead, a few horses approached. Not many, and not fast, at least. Still, Praesidio took Danae's arm and led her off the road and into the brush, at least a dozen paces back into the snagging blackberry canes and myrtle.

A light, airy buzzing rose on Danae's skin. It recalled a tickling breeze, but the leaves around her were still. Praesidio nodded to a thicket of dense branches. He moved behind it, half-covered from view, so Danae followed suit.

A handful of tense moments later, soft voices joined the hoofbeats and the prickle in Danae's skin. Women's hushed tones and the occasional high chirp of a child wove in and out of the murmur. Three horses, ridden by armored warriors appeared at a bend in the road, and a train of women, children, and elderly followed on foot. Perhaps a score of them, all told.

Danae looked to Praesidio, but his gaze fixed on the group, not her. His hand, which had gripped his staff until now, relaxed.

"These are my kin," Praesidio whispered.

"One of them has a signature," Danae whispered in return.

The old sage held a palm out to her, then emerged from behind the thicket. He returned to the road, a dozen paces ahead of the riders and their following.

"Hail, Elgadrim." He touched fingertips to his chin and then his chest.

The riders drew their reins in. Over long linen tunics, they each wore a matching tabard of purple and white, emblazoned with a crown that surrounded a blazing sun. Leather breast-plates covered the riders' chests, with wide bands of matching brown leather hanging from a belt. Hardened straps overlapped their shoulders. Above their brassy greaves, the men's legs were bare.

The central rider removed his bronze helm and propped it on his knee.

"Step forth, stranger," the soldier said, using the Western speech as Praesidio had.

The group following the soldiers huddled tight, casting one another wary glances. Danae took stock of them from her place in the thicket.

The women wore mostly long gowns that gathered at the throat and left their shoulders bare, though most also hung mantles or scarves across their bodies against the briskness of the spring morning. All of their clothes had a fine, tailored appearance, but dark smudges and ragged tears marred every gown or tunic.

A curly-tressed child piped up, her tone questioning. The old man beside the child hushed her, although Danae could not understand the language they spoke, even if the girl had continued. The elder took the edge of the bright sash that crossed his tunic and wiped tear-streaked grime from the girl's cheek.

Praesidio took another step into the road. "What brings such a pilgrimage into these unpeopled lands?"

The soldiers' mouths tightened. A stony look volleyed between them.

The middle rider inclined his jaw, and he gazed down at Praesidio with light eyes. "It is not the way of the Risen King's soldiers to speak of our plans to vagabonds on the road. But I will tell you this, no passage lies ahead. Turn to some other way."

"It is my full intent to come before Aeleronde the Fair," Praesidio said.

The soldiers exchanged amused smiles.

The man on the left chimed in. "The road ahead is closed to all, stranger. As we spoke, you must turn to some other way."

"*Chen conquinarest ne prova sinsa Bilearne,*" the curly child said, her eyes round.

Praesidio's chin jerked higher. "I assure you, I am no stranger, and I must know details of the shift in the fighting."

The middle soldier frowned. "But you speak the tongue of the West, not that of those who inhabit fair Kelmirith."

"*Beste, che falle aderren mis gathe oineccet, purretin, e fiernen,*" the second soldier said to his comrade.

Danae balled her fists. She really needed to make time to study the Virtus of the Sojourners.

"Now, if you would make way," the center soldier said, "we have a long day of travel ahead of us that we would not make longer for these poor citizens in our company." He nudged his horse with his heel.

Praesidio blew out a growling breath. "*Bastec e thesta honi nahitza.*" He lowered his hood, reached into his collar, and produced his phoenix talisman. "Again, I must know the details of the enemy's movements. I speak in the Western Tongue out of courtesy for my companion." He waved Danae toward the group.

All three soldiers' eyes rounded. In unison, they dismounted and fell each to one knee, their gazes downcast.

Without looking up, the middle soldier said, "Sincerest apologies, Lord Protector. We had no intention of dancing about the truth. I did not suspect—"

Danae stopped at Praesidio's side.

"You had no way to guess, as my garb is uncharacteristic and my speech foreign." Praesidio nodded. "You may rise."

Danae narrowed her eyes and summoned concentration to drown her unease. She focused on the bubbly signature that whispered to her senses. She could only place it as centered in the vicinity of the soldiers, since the Elgadrim citizens followed at enough of a distance to make that clear. Her sensing skills still lacked the polish to single out the owner.

The soldiers regained their feet, but only the middle man met Praesidio's gaze. "I am Sir Lucius Vermillion, a knight in my errancy, ordered to escort these kinsmen to safety. I have been forbidden to speak in more detail than this."

Danae scanned the townspeople, who fidgeted and whispered to one another. The black grime on their faces and clothes, the occasional bandages . . .

"Their homes were burned, weren't they?"

Sir Lucius's comrades gripped the hilts of their swords.

Praesidio raised his palms. "Soldiers, no need for concern. This girl is my protégé."

Sir Lucius's eyebrows arched. His glance flitted between his two men and Praesidio before it settled on Danae. "Yes, my lady."

The two other soldiers relaxed their stances, but their eyes still flashed with wary attentiveness. Praesidio caught Danae's eye and heaved a reproachful sigh.

She shrugged an apology but then turned to Lucius. "We've seen at least one example of what Queldurik's hordes are doing."

"Then you have seen only a fraction of what they have done. I must assert, we are not safe here in the wild lands. The enemy has roving squads harrying any and all they encounter on the roads." Sir Lucius drew a deep breath. "You are welcome to come with us, where you will find food and beds."

"Will there be any other Protectors where you are going?" Praesidio asked.

"Sir, aye, there will," Lucius said.

Danae's heart fluttered in her chest. "Praesidio, the . . . well, what about the errand you've charged me with?"

Resting a light hand on Danae's shoulder, Praesidio nodded. "If the child among the citizens here speaks the truth, as blurting children are wont to do, we may find more than we bargained for between us and Bilearne. I believe our best course would be to follow Sir Lucius and his men."

Danae drew a breath to protest, but Praesidio held up his hand.

"I do not question your valor or urgency," he said. "But neither is enough to protect you from enemy armies."

Danae swallowed her complaint. What options remained if the front lines of the war had shifted nearer?

Sir Lucius's men nudged their horses onward while Lucius called something back to the crowd following behind. His tone sounded reassuring, and Danae noted many glances from the group had shifted from fearful to merely curious.

After returning to the thicket for the sword casket, she and Praesidio fell in behind the soldiers. They left the road and pressed into the tangle of the forest, where brambles and under-growth clawed at their every step. Worse, though, were Danae's raking fears that not just knowledge, but an entire war now stood between her and Papa's cure.

29

In Elgadrim Hands

*A*s the group picked their way through the budding forest, Sir Lucius eyed the narrow box Danae and Praesidio carried. The casket complicated their passage through the untamed lands of Kelmirith. While she and Praesidio fought their way through a partial gap in a cluster of laurel, Lucius shook his head. Nervous heat crept up Danae's neck while the knight stared.

"We could lash this . . . burden . . . of yours to a horse, if you would prefer?" Sir Lucius said.

Praesidio grunted as he hefted his end of the box higher. "That won't be necessary. Our pace is no slower than what the children of the group can manage."

"What's in the case?" a dark-haired, green-eyed soldier asked.

Danae's middle clenched. They barely knew these men, and they knew nothing at all of the refugees following. What if the Sword's voice was finding chinks in each of their armor even while they walked? They could not risk any—she shook her head. This fear, it was the Sword talking, even from within its case. She fortified the shielding around her signature and her mind. This journey was difficult enough without the Sword's uncanny influence.

"That information is classified," Praesidio said, to Danae's relief. "In fact, should we encounter trouble, I entreat you to protect this case, even before you defend our lives."

The second soldier blinked. "If it's so valuable, should we not know its contents?"

"You aren't listening very well for a knight." Praesidio glared. "Citing article twenty-three, section six of the knight errancy code, none of your company will ask questions of our doings, and we will not be searched. That is, unless you have someone of higher authority than myself in your number to dictate differently."

Silence fell over the three knights. Green Eyes swallowed.

Sir Lucius nodded, but concern lined his features. "As you command, Lord Protector. Sir Servius, Sir Arrius, is this order understood?"

"Sir, we serve our king and obey," they both replied.

They pressed on, and Danae lagged enough to let the soldiers move a dozen paces ahead. She whispered to Praesidio, "They don't have the slightest idea what's in article twenty-three, section six, do they?"

Praesidio chuckled. "At their age and level of experience? Likely not. But it will serve to keep them and any superior in their midst, short of Lord Sorex himself, from probing about the contents of our gear."

The fine morning clouded over by midday, and a drizzle turned their journey drear and wet, with the sun's position impossible to discern through the dark of trees and clouds. The path the knights struck carried the group on winding side trails, across streams, and through the shelter of green valleys. Trees here in the central Kelmiri countryside bore full leaves, and it was not long before Danae stowed her heavy cloak. The perfume of lilac and azalea hung thick in the air. So despite the wet squish of Danae's boots, the travel was not altogether unpleasant.

Had Culduin journeyed somewhere safe? Well, he could take care of himself, so there was no use in pondering things beyond her control. Danae focused on keeping her strides in rhythm with Praesidio's, as much as their winding course allowed.

As the gray day turned pink with a shrouded sunset, the troupe of travelers crested a hill to look down upon a clearing, where a half-dozen canvas pavilions and scores of smaller pup tents dotted the landscape. A swift river ran by in foamy waves on the far side of the camp. Curls of smoke rose from three fires at the center of the encampment, and the smell of roasting grain wafted on the damp breeze. Danae's stomach rumbled.

Women, children, and elderly Elgadrim milled between tents, some toting water, others wood. At the four corners of the encampment, squads of four soldiers, clad in similar tabards as Sir Lucius's company, stood at attention, spears in hand. A member of the nearest squadron turned his focus to the rise and raised one hand.

Lucius and his men halted their horses and mirrored the gesture. Only when all the knights had dropped their arms to their sides did Sir Lucius lead the group down the slope. They approached as a soggy, solemn bunch, with little chatter between them. If the rest of the group felt anything like Danae did, fatigue had long ago stolen any motivation to converse. Her neck and shoulders ached, and every blink increased her craving for solid sleep.

Praesidio sighed as they ambled down from the hilltop. "Ah, Bilearne, the Jewel of the Valley, that I should have seen her before the crows of war gather."

"Creo's mercy and might surround thee," the knights replied as one.

Danae recognized the prayer, drawn from the pages of *The Tree*, from a time when Praesidio's people were still young and called themselves the Vareinor, Creo's chosen among men, and not Elgadrim—the forsaken ones. History's repetition resurrected the ancient writing.

Lucius circled his horse to ride up beside Praesidio. "My men and I have a duty to see to the housing of the refugees. Shall we make arrangements for you and your student as well?"

"Shelter me only if supplies are abundant," Praesidio said. "My primary need is to speak to whomever is in command here. Perhaps you could offer Danae shelter and water for washing in the meantime?"

Danae glanced around the encampment, which was tidy but somehow bleak. "What about the, uh . . . cargo?"

"I will take it with me," Praesidio said.

Danae's insides jumped and her muscles tensed.

Her mentor's eyes softened. "My student, don't be afraid. We're in the safest place we've been in a long time."

"Servius, Arrius, please lead the refugees to the intake pavilion for their supply bundles," Lucius said. "I will see to the Lord Protector's requests."

The two knights rode back to the refugee group, dismounted, and began addressing the people in their own tongue.

"Commander Sorex's pavilion is on this side of camp," Lucius said, "so it's logical for me to present you there first, Lord Protector. From there, I can see to Danae's needs." He offered Danae a smile, warm despite their spare acquaintance.

She smiled back. A day's travel did not offer her much evidence to say she yet knew Lucius, but he seemed conscientious as a soldier, polite, and competent. A revelation broke into her consideration of the man—the other soldiers were now far enough away to narrow down who the signature-bearer was. Danae stretched her senses, seeking the fizzy sensation she had managed to ignore for the latter half of the day. Its source was ahead of her. Not behind. And so it was Lucius who had the affinity for Creo's gifting. Someone who might understand the challenges of learning the nuances of Virtusen and Creo's will.

Danae stuffed down the notion. What time did she have for friends on this journey? After today, she would likely never see Sir Lucius again. And for all she knew, Lucius may have already been fully trained in Thaumaturgy, only able to offer his sympathy for her struggles.

"This way," Lucius said, reining his horse toward a three-peaked pavilion to the right side of the camp.

She gripped the handle of the sword casket, and flutters of anticipation rose in her chest. Would this be the moment where Praesidio's brethren would recognize her participation in the quest and agree to teach her fully? Or was there some chance the plan would fail at this critical juncture?

Praesidio clucked his tongue, snapping Danae back to the present. "Sorex? I shouldn't have intoned his name before—you know how it is, speak of the devil . . ."

The two men laughed, and Danae chafed at the sense they shared a joke of which she was ignorant. It fanned the sparks of her unrest. Praesidio's insinuations did not inspire confidence about this Sorex, whoever he was. Danae doubted she had the fortitude to endure another brute like Archadion, back in the annex at Myslapten. Perhaps it was a good thing she would have time to bathe and settle her nerves before she might need to participate in discussions.

At the entrance to the pavilion, where the flaps hung closed, a soldier stood guard. Though his helm and armor made him mistakable for any other member of the force, his young face caught Danae off guard. The boy was likely younger than she, by several years.

A rush of anxiety rolled through her middle. *That guard is probably Tristan's age. Is my brother standing guard at some Tebalese tent somewhere?* Or more likely, hauling wood and supplies, work that often fell to slaves. So many reasons she needed to get home.

After a brief exchange between Sir Lucius and the guard, a voice inside the tent barked a single word.

Praesidio bowed to Lucius. "Take my companion to Helvia, please." He then turned to Danae. "I will come to you as soon as I am able." He took the handle of the sword casket from her hand, turned, and ducked through the pavilion entry.

Danae stared after him, flexing and extending her sore fingers. Just like that, the Sword passed from her reach.

"My lady?" Lucius said. "If you will come this way, I can find you a place to clean up and rest."

"What?" Danae pulled her attention from the pavilion.

"Your teacher, he said—"

"Yes, yes, I'm so sorry." Danae's cheeks flushed. "I'm out of sorts, so I hope I haven't been too rude."

Sir Lucius offered a soft smile. "I sense that you've seen a bit of an ordeal. Come. Our hospitality will not be lush, but there will be soap and likely a few portions of dinner remaining."

After picketing Sir Lucius's horse, they made their way across the camp to the pavilion where the refugees had preceded them. Inside, many of the Elgadrim who had followed Lucius and his men to the encampment stood near a set of tables where they received one burlap parcel each.

Danae hugged her arms around her middle and listened to the conversation that flowed between the refugees and those helping them. No familiar word met her ears. Sir Lucius led her straight across the pavilion to the end of one of the supply tables.

"Begging your pardon for the interruption, Mistress Helvia," Lucius said.

A tall woman, her mahogany hair tied back in a knot at the nape of her neck and a canvas apron tied over a pale-blue gown, turned from stacking burlap bundles behind the table and met the knight's glance. Her eyes then flicked to Danae, and a quizzical sparkle lit within them.

Lucius placed a palm over his heart and half-bowed. "Protector Praesidio of the Knights of the Phoenix asked that I place this young woman under your care."

Helvia smiled. "What adventures has he sent my way today?" Her words carried a heavy accent, but the Western tongue was clear. "Your trip here appears to have been long. Do you wish to bathe?"

Somewhere outside, someone shouted. Every soldier in the pavilion looked as one to the exit.

"My apologies, my ladies." Sir Lucius bowed. "It appears I am summoned. Mistress Danae, the good people here will make sure you are shown a place to rest for the night, if I am unable to return and see to it myself." He spun on a heel and joined the handful of soldiers cutting a brisk course to depart.

"Of course. Thank you. Um . . . Creo go before you, Sir Lucius," Danae said. The tension in her shoulders mounted, and her mind buzzed with questions. The calls to arms that emptied the room of soldiers piled more weight onto her overloaded spirit. While she stared toward the tent exit, wondering how long Praesidio would be gone, a tap on her shoulder sent a jolt of panic through her. She wheeled around. Her heart thudded.

Helvia held out a burlap bundle. "This will have a blanket, some bread, bandages, and a few other comforts inside. I can also see to procuring clean garb. The bath?"

Danae blinked until her hammering heart slowed. "I . . . uh . . . yes? Thank you. Where should I go?"

A smile brightened the lady's face. "This way." She waved Danae toward the corner of the tent where folding screens cordoned off a segment of space. Helvia folded one section of the screen back and gestured to the gap.

Danae poked her head around the screen to find a metal tub behind it—barely large enough for an adult to scrunch inside, but at least the water within was clean and steaming. A handful of rough towels sat folded on a crate beside the tub.

"You should find soap in the bundle of provisions," Helvia said.

Many of the refugees that had arrived with Sir Lucius's company had filtered from the tent, presumably to whatever accommodations the camp had to offer, and with the departure of the soldiers that had been present, only the supply workers remained. A bath behind a screen—still awkward amidst strangers, but Danae accepted her proverbial beggar status in the situation and stepped into the bathing area.

After a hasty scrub that washed an alarming amount of travel scum from her skin and hair, Danae stood shivering beside the tub while she dried off. When she lifted the first of her stained garments from the edge of the tub, she grimaced at the stale funk that emanated from them. She held up her under-garments and frowned. Should she use the bath water to return them to wearable condition? As it was, she could scarcely bear the thought of lacing back into their grime.

"Miss?" Helvia's voice, near the screen. "New garments, if you desire them."

Danae heaved a sigh of relief. "Yes, please!"

Several cream-colored swaths of fabric flopped over the top edge of the screen.

Just as Danae finished dressing and emerged from behind the bathing area, Praesidio stepped through the pavilion entrance.

He headed straight for Danae. "I see my timing is good. I hope the bath has refreshed you enough, because you are to accompany me to a meeting right away."

Worries awoke from their short slumber and skittered through her limbs.

"Don't worry." Praesidio tossed her a wink. "I'll do most of the talking. Come. We're expected on the opposite side of camp."

Danae trotted after Praesidio, who set a swift pace between the rows of tents. "What kind of meeting is this? To learn of the enemy army's movements?"

"That, I've already discussed with Lord Sorex," Praesidio said. "It seems Tebal has covertly moved a mercenary force of North Deklians and a mixed bag of other ruffians in from the southwest, which is the force now coalescing south of us, just outside Bilearne. Most of our army is engaged closer to the Kelmiri-Tebalese border, cut off from any kind of tactical retreat to the city."

Danae squinted while Praesidio talked, doing her best to formulate a mental picture of battle lines and borders, with only minimal success.

"We thought for certain any bolstering force the enemy brought to bear would be comprised of dragon-kin and summoned creatures, but no intelligence we've received points to such things. At least we have that going for us, for the time being."

"Summoned creatures?" Danae swallowed.

"Lesser fiends, something like Ba-al Zechmaat, but not as powerful."

They arrived at another canvas pavilion, smaller than the intake pavilion where Danae had bathed, but appointed with banners and tassels. A guard in a bronze, brush-plumed helmet and armor of overlapping plates stood at the entry. He gripped a spear that exceeded his height.

The guard touched his fingers to his chin and chest and bowed lightly. He grasped the edge of the tent flap and pulled it aside. "Welcome back, Lord Protector." His glance flicked to Danae, but just as quickly focused elsewhere.

Praesidio gestured with an open palm to the entry. "After you, my lady."

Her mouth terminally dry, Danae pursed her lips and stepped through.

Inside the pavilion, multiple oil lamps burned and lit the space with a warm glow. A huge table at the center held a vellum map, and colored stone markers of several sizes clustered in four locations on the map's surface.

A towering, armored man leaned on the table, but he raised his glance at Danae and Praesidio's arrival. A frown deepened the creases around his mouth. His sharp, blue-eyed gaze settled upon Danae.

"A little premature, don't you think, Praesidio?" He scanned Danae from hood to heels.

Danae's stomach overturned, lurched, and twisted. Thank goodness she had not yet eaten.

"Better the robes of an acolyte than some frippery that would only make productivity more difficult," Praesidio said. "Lord Sorex, may I introduce you to Danae Baledric of Dayelston, follower of Creo and pursuer of Thaumaturgy?"

"This is the Curse Bearer Archadion's letter spoke of?" Sorex narrowed his eyes.

"Not anymore," Danae blurted. "I understand now the cost of such power."

Sorex tilted his chin higher. "Do you now?" His gaze was chilly but not outright disdainful as Archadion's was. That had to be an improvement.

Praesidio chuckled but also tossed Danae a cautioning look. "She has made much progress, even while in constant peril." He crossed the tent to a side wall where a tapestry lay over some crates. "If you wouldn't mind assisting me, young learner."

"Of course." *With what? I wish he would prepare me for these sorts of encounters. How am I supposed to say the right things?* Perspiration dampened her back.

Danae scuttled to Praesidio's side as he flipped the tapestry back. The wooden casket they had carried across the wilderness sat alongside the taller crates.

"Did Archadion's letter also detail the arrangement I proposed for Danae's further education?" Praesidio bent and grabbed a handle of the casket, and Danae followed suit.

They walked the sword case back to Sorex's table.

"He made veiled references to some quest you laid upon her," Sorex said, "but withheld details for fear of the communication being intercepted, as are too many of our scrolls of late."

They hefted the casket onto the table's surface.

"Danae played a pivotal role in the task we asked of her, in exchange for full instruction in Thaumaturgy, that she might use this knowledge to heal her father," Praesidio said. He faced Danae and whispered, "Steel yourself. Ready to open this?"

Danae shivered. If it would help her take the next step to getting home, she could endure the Sword's full signature again, couldn't she? After a fortifying breath, she nodded.

Praesidio unhooked the latches on the sword casket and removed the lid.

30

The Fruit of the Quest

a wave of fury pummeled into Danae like a storm of nails. She recoiled a step and gasped aloud. The Sword's hot indignation pounded on her skull. Even so, she clenched her fists and returned to the table's edge.

Sorex reached a gauntleted hand inside the case, lined with scavenged, rusty metal, and pushed aside the burlap wrappings at one end of the bundle within. The clear jewel, clutched in a golden raptor's claw that composed the pommel of the Sword of the Patron poked from the coverings. Lord Sorex's eyes rounded. He pushed more of the wrappings away, grasped the hilt of the Sword, and lifted it from its housing. The burlap fell to the table to reveal the glittering, glass-like blade.

The signature pulsing from the Sword shifted from thrashing anger to oily scorn.

"How is this possible?" Sorex asked, his tone hushed and reverent. His initial awe gave way to a furrowed scowl at the weapon.

Praesidio smiled. "So few thought it could be accomplished, but my companions and I have indeed retrieved the Sword of the Patron, wrested so long ago from its rightful master."

"Companions?" Sorex said. "You've brought only one."

Praesidio turned to Danae.

She squelched the sick tightness rising into her throat. "We had help from a gnomish guide, who was slain by the enemy, and . . . an elf as well. One of the scouts of the Delsin, named Culduin Caranedhel."

Sorex nodded. "Your Elvish rendering of his name is well turned for a northerner."

"He was in our company long enough to straighten my accent out," Danae said.

"Quite some time, indeed," Praesidio said, "and an invaluable help along the way. But now that you see the success of this quest, I bring Danae before you to ask your witness to her fulfillment of her part of the agreement."

Sorex rotated the Sword, his gazed fixed upon it. Motes of light reflected from the blade and danced across his tense features and onyx-black hair. "You traveled with a Carandhel?" he said. "What, to make amends for losing this Sword in the first place?"

With every mention of the elf's name, Danae's stomach grew a shade queasier.

Praesidio stepped in. "Please, Sorex, this is no time to stir the embers of an unrelated grievance. While the time this sword spent in the hands of the enemy is regrettable, in Creo's great design, there was purpose in even this." He turned his gaze upon Danae and let it linger.

Both Praesidio and Sorex focused piercing attention on her. Danae cringed beneath the weight of their undivided scrutiny.

"But Archadion's letter dictated that the quest needed to bear fruit if the terms were to be met." Sorex tested the edge of the blade, and his brows lifted.

Danae's breath hitched in short gasps. She pointed to the weapon. "Is there really a question? You hold Mystrin's sword in your own hand."

Praesidio placed a hand on Danae's shoulder. "The quest, while performing a needed service, served as a framework. A test, if you will. The fruit we seek is not this thing, but borne by you."

Oh, riddles now? Danae suppressed a groan. The possibility of the last six months of striving unraveling right this moment gripped her throat. *What does he mean?*

Both Elgadrim men watched her and waited, seeming content to allow her to flounder.

The fruit of the quest, if not the Sword . . . a test. A framework. Danae squeezed her eyes shut, and the memory of her mental battle with Ba-al Zechmaat splashed across her mind's eye. It was in that moment that she truly grasped the scope of what serving Creo meant, and only her willingness to surrender to that life had saved them from a fiery death that day.

Until that moment, she had believed she served no one other than herself and her family. As she contended with Ba-al Zechmaat, the truth of her condition grew clear. And now, before Lord Sorex, the delivery of the Sword complete, hope brightened like once-stormy sky now pierced with streaming glories. The trembling in her limbs slowly drained away.

"Yes!" she cried. "It's my surrender—my willingness to do Creo's work with my gifts. And coming to really understand that Creo is the source of power that's pure. Opening my eyes to that. That's the fruit of the quest, isn't it?"

A broad smile broke across Sorex's face. "*Misin Solemeturum! Misin Fellbraetius! Alerr Misin Pretoratenius!*"

Danae squinted. The words had the ring of Utterances, but contained too many unfamiliar Elvish words for her comprehension.

Praesidio faced Danae and clasped both her shoulders in his hands. *"Misin Solemeturum. Misin Fellbraetius. Alerr Misin Pretoratenius.* We welcome you into the fold of Creo's devoted."

31

Allies at Home

A light pulse from the talisman of passage vibrated against Culduin's chest, and as he glanced down, the silver sword and quill emblem emerged from the invisibility that shrouded it in times he journeyed outside Delsinon's city limits. The air around him warped and wavered.

"Fly straight, good Crienna," he said. "You will be tempted to do otherwise, but it is a product of my people's enchantments that protect the city. I will help you know where to land."

Curving bridges of wood and stone, homes with tall windows and private gardens, and the expansive royal and military compound at the city's north-most corner faded into view, emerging from the leafy canopy below. The sugary aroma of honeysuckle in the spring air tickled Culduin's nose. He breathed deep.

From the north, a lithe, pearlescent creature broke a circling flight course and shot for Culduin and the griffons with a burst of speed. Crienna's muscles tensed under Culduin's seat.

"No need to worry; just a patrol. She will escort us within the city."

Kli-Chak squawked. "We have no need to enter your nesting place."

"But my people would feed you in gratitude for your help and give you a warm place to sleep among your own kind," Culduin said.

"Our exchange of debts is now even," Kli-Chak said. "We require nothing more than to be left alone to hunt and return home."

Culduin swallowed any further argument. Whatever Crienna's opinion, Kli-Chak was resolute, and only a fool would argue with a resolute griffon.

The pearly flier neared—a slender young dragon of similar years to Culduin, if he recalled correctly.

"Hail, friend elf! Who are these?" the dragon called in a low, feminine voice.

"Hail, patrolmistress," Culduin replied. "Iriscendra, correct? My mount is Crienna, and this is her mate, Kli-Chak. They have spared me much danger and toil but wish no entrance to the city. Shall we land outside the north gate for my entrance and their departure?"

The dragon nodded. "Well, your face is new to me, but you're a good guesser. I'm Iriscendra. The north gate's a fine place to land and get the guards to scribble in their books."

They banked and made their descent, through the slender reaching branches of beeches, birches, and dogwoods, into the sun-warmed woodlands outside Delsinon, and to the broad thoroughfare that led to the gate. The griffons touched down, and Culduin slid from Crienna's back. His knees wobbled.

"Not usually a flier?" Iriscendra arched a scaled brow.

Culduin steadied himself. "Many days of riding have robbed me of ground legs, it would seem. I'm glad it is you who has found us, though, for you are in a position to know. Is High Lord Ecleriast in the city?"

Iriscendra tilted her head. "Who does the asking?"

With a bow, Culduin introduced himself. "I have flown in haste from northern Kelmirith on a matter of negotiation between the Elgadrim and our people."

Iriscendra nodded. "Aha. Well, I'm pretty sure Vin—I mean, Lord Ecleriast knows some other Caranedhel than you."

"Likely my father, who serves as one of the king's ambassadors," Culduin said.

"The Elgadrim's plight isn't news to him, either, but it's not my place to speak on where *all that* stands." She rolled her sapphire-blue eyes. "Bring your patience, that's all I'll say."

"It is good news to hear that Lord Ecleriast is at least at hand," Culduin said. "In such dire times, the odds were not with me in that being the case."

"He's gotten better at following the king's orders in his old age; otherwise, I daresay you wouldn't have found him home." Iriscendra turned for the gate.

Culduin faced the griffons. "You have my utmost gratitude for the speed you have lent me. If you indeed won't stay, I wish you good fortune in your journey to whatever eyrie you call home."

Crienna ducked her head. "It has been an honor, Culduin, our liberator and friend."

Kli-Chak nodded, and Culduin accepted that as the best he would get from the bristly creature.

"Farewell, then. Feast on whatever game you prefer, short of the silver hart. You'll find yourselves at elven bow point far too quickly if you make a meal of him."

"We appreciate the warning," Kli-Chak said. He ducked low, spread his wings, and with a thrust that blew Culduin's hair into his face, launched skyward. Crienna followed. The two griffons wove through the canopy and into the blushing western sky.

Culduin marched for the gate, where two mail-clad elves stood guard, slender halberds in hand.

"Welcome home, Master Culduin," the first guard said. "Of the house Caranedhel, we understand? It has been many seasons since you passed Delsinon's gate."

"Too many," Culduin said. "But if I have my way, I will not tarry." He held his talisman forward on its silver chain. "May I pass?"

"You may," the guard said. "The blessings of the Maker be upon you."

"And you as well." Culduin passed through the gap between the white gates, his eyes lingering on the flawless spirals of their designs, as fluid as wind and water, but harder than adamant.

"Good luck, young Culduin," Iriscendra called. "If you can't get audience with Lord Ecleriast tonight, do yourself a favor and wait till nearly luncheon tomorrow." She, too, took to the sky and sped beyond sight.

Culduin tread the block-paved streets of Delsinon, drinking in the sounds of flute and water, of laughter and song, of quiet industry and greeting. Wholesome scents of fresh cucumber and the first berries of spring greeted him, and he plucked a plump blueberry from a roadside shrub as he passed. If only the ripeness of spring came so soon and lingered as long in the rest of Argent. He savored the sweet crispness of the berry as he walked.

He sighed. If only Danae could have seen more of Argent's beauty while they traveled together. A pang of worry tightened his chest. Ultimately, he was helping her the best way he knew how. He had to remember that.

Over the footbridge that spanned Caelnethe's Rill, around the corner of the Duillion silver smithy, and up the winding hill path to the low cane gate at his father's homestead he passed. Each step came as familiar as his own skin, but older, richer, and more poignant since he had left them for his years in the army. Hanging bell flowers dangled from the arching trellis as he mounted the two smooth stairs to the veranda. They dusted him with pollen as he passed.

Culduin stashed the Tebalese bow and quiver in a dense pocket of foxglove beside the steps. Countless years he had spent swinging with his mother in this very place, but now, it was more memory than home. He reached up and rapped lightly on the carven ash-wood door.

"Well, I cannot imagine. I am not expecting anyone," came the male voice from inside, and a wave of comfort filled Culduin's heart.

The door swung open.

"Culduin!" His father beamed on the doorstep and reached his arms wide. "Not even a message before you show up on the doorstep? Your mother may switch you, in her dressing gown and hair down as she has it." He pulled Culduin into a tight embrace.

Culduin laughed. "Dire times leave little time for couriers, Father."

Father eased Culduin back and looked him over. "Well, it seems you have returned to us not a moment too soon, you lean vagabond. What is this array? And you without even a pack. Have they ceased outfitting patrolmen in the north?"

"The loss of my belongings is too long a tale to tell in the doorway," Culduin said.

Behind his copper-haired father, Culduin's mother appeared, in the satin robe and flowing pants she always wore around home. She pulled her golden waves together at the nape of her neck and fastened a clasp around them. "I thought I heard your voice, but then again, I am always wishing such things. Come in, come in, my dear one. You have not brought your brother?"

Culduin's stomach tightened.

Father shot Mother a glance.

"Of course not, which means we can focus on pampering you," she said. "Come in, come in. Some food, some rest, and songs await."

---

*C*ulduin drained the last of his mead from his cup and savored the warmth of a full belly, but he soon pushed plates and cup aside and leaned toward his father across the table. "Father, what of the negotiations to procure Lord Ecleriast's help in the war on the humans?"

Mother cleared Culduin's dishes. "Oh come, business so soon? Maybe another mead will mellow your nerves?"

Culduin smiled. "I will take another mead, for there is nothing like it outside the city, but I fear I cannot talk parlor fancies for even moments."

Father tapped his lip with his fingertips. "Not much has changed since our last letter to Luidriana and Thalius. His Majesty hesitates to commit forces to an unrelated threat, even to those who were once allies."

"Once?" Culduin blurted. "They are still allies, and we would have others among men if we would look for them."

Father scowled. "Why this insistence?"

"The Elgadrim are beset. They need us."

"What can we do?" Father asked. "Goblins breed faster than we can cut them back, and the Tebalese seem to take particular pleasure in elven blood running down their altars. How is our involvement anything better than suicide?"

Culduin sat back. "Our abstention is a sure invitation that the enemy hosts should turn their ire upon us next, once they have laid waste to the most noble of men. They need Vinyanel Ecleriast."

"Oh, they do?" Mother said. "For what? To berate the Tebalese and their monsters into submission?"

"Prickly reputation notwithstanding, he's the best choice," Culduin said. "To wield the Sword of the Patron."

"Are the Elgadrim still spinning that piece of lore in vain hope?" Father sighed. "The last we heard, they had sent a single member of their elder knights on errancy to fetch it. No word has come to us since."

Culduin locked gazes with Father. "But we did fetch it."

Mother stopped, plates in hand. "We? What are you talking about, Culduin?"

"Oh, heavens." Culduin pressed a palm to his forehead. "How to condense it. Well, that knight they sent on errancy? I was with him. As well as his student." His throat constricted. Was Danae all right? She must be. He must maintain his trust in Praesidio's wisdom or else lose his direction completely.

Father cast Culduin a quizzical look. "There is more to your tale."

After a deep breath, Culduin continued. "The three of us confounded Ba-al Zechmaat long enough in the Great Temple of Garash to run with the Sword." His heart thundered. "A remarkable weapon, beyond anything any literature can describe."

Mother placed a cool palm to Culduin's forehead. "Are you well? You mean to tell me you've been to Garash and back? And you saw this supposed Sword?"

"Not only saw, Mother, but held in my hand. Wielded even, by strange happenstance. But last I knew, it was on its way to Bilearne with Danae and Praesidio. I fear they will meet with great obstacles in their hope to pass within the city walls."

"Then let the Elgadrim wield it themselves," Mother said. She lifted her dishes again and swept toward the kitchen. "History has not been gentle with allegiances between the Forsaken Ones and elfkind."

"Father, it is impossible to put it into the hand of even their most seasoned," Culduin rose and paced the room, thinking aloud more than pleading. "Those with the maturity are too old in body. The thing is corrupt. A temptation and abomination all at once. And yet someone must take it in hand. Someone strong enough not to let it steer him." A swell of regret washed through Culduin as his insane treatment of Danae in the razed village flashed across his mind. He clenched his teeth.

Father stepped to Culduin's side and put his hand on his son's shoulder. "Why now?" he asked in a low voice.

"Because Queldurik himself is leading a battalion to Bilearne."

"What?" Father's posture stiffened. "You are certain of this?"

"As certain as I am that I behold you now," Culduin said. "My own two eyes I trust."

For a silent moment, Father rubbed his temple with his fingertips. "Desna, help me find Culduin something suitable to wear." He clasped Culduin's shoulder. "We must request audience with his Majesty himself."

32

Alchemist's Apprentice Again

"So you'll be able to instruct me fully now? I'll be able to return home soon?" Danae focused an earnest gaze upon Praesidio's face.

Sorex set the Sword back in the case. His smile faded to his previous severe expression. "This is all well and good, but we need you on the front lines right now, Praesidio, not holed up in a library. In fact, by the time we can pass Bilearne's walls, there may not *be* a library."

She clasped Praesidio's hands. "I can learn anywhere, in whatever time you can spare."

"Young learner, I fear you don't understand the gravity of the current situation or what you will require in instruction." Praesidio sighed. "An army stands between us and Bilearne's Academy Arcana."

Frustration kindled a burn in Danae's chest. "I don't feel like you're listening to me."

"I fear you will find complexities at home that will require as much training as we can cram into your head. But even if I had every Virtus, every bit of theology, and all the rites that you need to commit to memory, would you have me sit with you for weeks on end to recite all of it to you?" Praesidio tilted his head.

Danae stammered. "That's . . . I mean—"

"I would, were it possible. But I have just learned my kinsman have both an army before them and one behind. I am foremost in the House of the Phoenix, who are charged, at all costs, to preserve the life of the Risen King, Aeleronde the Fair."

"So the timing of my needing your help is utterly disastrous." Danae's heart picked up speed, and her thoughts volleyed from one half-formed worry to another.

"The world presents us with many needs," Sorex said. "The zealots of Queldurik build their designs to hasten our downfall."

"But . . . but . . . we've brought the Sword. Doesn't that mean we—I mean, you have the means to end the war?" Danae panted for breath. Dark spots flashed in her vision.

"As it stands, the Sword has no wielder, and until the council agrees to a course of action regarding it, we remain quite far from any end to the war." Praesidio circled his fingers on his temple and shuffled across the pavilion.

Sorex scowled after Praesidio. "If the holdouts might agree to bestow the Sword upon one of our own . . ."

Praesidio leveled a stern gaze upon him. "You cannot begin to imagine the depth of the thing's corruption. That one of our knights might wield it was a foolish proposal before we knew what we were dealing with. I am convinced that not even the mightiest among us has the strength of body and mind to use it without becoming corrupt himself."

"Well, now that the Sword is here, is this council going to meet again to decide what to do?" Danae twisted the tie of her robe in tight fists.

Sorex paced. "In addition to the rest of the council currently being inside the city walls, there is no point in discussion when we don't know if the Delsin are even amenable to sending Lord Ecleriast."

"Because while I have traveled, the council has entreated the Elves?" Praesidio's tone was heavy with reproach. "Rarely can one answer a question that has not been asked."

The two men stood in a silent standoff.

Danae pressed her lips together. So the Elgadrim had put little stock in the Sword's retrieval, but beyond that, a deeper hesitancy seemed to underpin Sorex's mood.

"Come, Danae," Praesidio said. "Many questions remain that have no answers tonight. I will take you to whatever quarters they have found for you."

No hope of real knowledge that she could bear home and halt her family's disaster, and a Sword brought to a place to be of no use—a Sword that had cost her the greatest friend she'd ever had—pain pierced Danae's heart. She squelched the thought.

She followed Praesidio into the dark of night, where no one could see the tears that rolled down her cheeks.

---

*D*anae bolted awake to dull, flickering orange and a complete lack of recognition of her surroundings. Voices whispered in a jumble nearby, in a language she did not understand. She blinked and cleared her vision. A tent. She shared a common tent with a handful of other women, who all sat up on their pallets. They shared her confusion, judging by their expressions.

"What's happening?" she asked.

Her tent mates turned uncomprehending stares to her.

"Ugh." Danae threw aside her coverlet and grabbed her boots. After wrenching the first one on, she hopped toward the tent flap while pulling on the other.

The shadows of passing figures and the shifting dapple of firelight shone through the tent's thin canvas. She poked her head out.

Elgadrim workers and refugees alike marched on purposeful strides between tents. No one uttered a word, and their silent urgency sent a shudder down Danae's back. A hiss broke out to the left, and she spun toward it. Steam and smoke billowed up from where an Elgadrim woman stood with tipped, dripping bucket. Further down the row, another fire drowned in a cascade of water.

Praesidio approached from behind her tent. "Ah, you're still here." He grabbed her arm. In a low voice, he added, "You must go to the intake tent with the rest of the camp. It's the safest place." He turned to march on.

Danae grappled his arm. "Safe? What's going on?" she shrilled.

He pressed a forefinger to his lips.

Suddenly, the prospect of being separated from Praesidio in the growing bustle closed around her like a fist. She swallowed further words.

"I know it's difficult, Danae, but there's no time to explain," Praesidio said. "Please, do as I say. I will send word if I can."

"Don't send me away—let me go with you," Danae pleaded. "I don't know anyone here."

Praesidio fired a ferociously stern glare at her. "No, Danae. You have no idea what you even ask."

"Why must you treat me like a—"

"Enough!" Praesidio hissed. "Because you're acting like one. Go to the pavilion. I promise to return at the first opportunity." He took a few brisk steps but wheeled back and raised a cautioning finger to her. "And if I find out you tried to follow me, the Patrons as my witnesses, I will teach you *nothing* after this is all over."

Danae clapped her mouth shut and watched Praesidio disappear against the current of an oncoming crowd of tousled refugees. Numb, she joined its flow. Their relative silence was eerie.

When Danae at last arrived at the great pavilion, she fell into line with all the frightened inhabitants of the camp, young and old. Grandmothers and mothers spoke gently to soothe crying children. Danae could not help but wonder if these women, their brows creased with worry, really believed their own words. A soldier ushered people through the open entry.

When Danae reached the pavilion, Sorex's iron gaze caught her own from inside. He dismissed the woman he spoke with and marched toward Danae on long strides. She froze where she stood.

What could he possibly want with me?

"Mistress Baledric!" he called in his rumbling voice. Many of the worried Elgadrim around her paused and stared. Before Danae could respond, he continued. "You are skilled in the craft of alchemy, are you not?"

Danae swallowed hard but could summon no saliva to wet her parched mouth. "I've been an assistant to my father since I was twelve, but I'm no master."

"I don't have time to debate you on your self-appraisal!" Sorex said. "Are you familiar with explosive compounds?"

Danae winced at his brusqueness. "Yes. I've experimented in the area. But not since—"

"Since the Tebalese invasion made such production ill advised?" Sorex said.

Danae nodded.

"Excellent." Sorex grabbed Danae's arm and dragged her from the queue of refugees. "The last thing your country needs is a bunch of crazed Tebalese getting their hands on a formula for explosives, had you gotten far enough to devise one."

Sorex plowed away from the crowd and to a smaller pavilion, deep in the center of camp. A thin plume of smoke drifted upward from an opening at the pavilion's apex, seemingly the only fire still burning in the camp. "We have need of you to assist our chemist. Praesidio thought you would be of use in this matter."

Throwing the tent flap aside, he gestured for Danae to enter. "Helvia! I've brought you an assistant. I will be back at the dawn bell for the first load." With that, he turned and disappeared into the crowd, leaving Danae on the threshold, a lump growing in her throat.

33

Blast-Shot

A woman with deep-brown hair, tied in a simple knot, and a familiar face emerged from behind stacked crates and sacks piled high throughout the tent. She wore a gown, simple of cut for Elgadrim fashion, covered by an apron made of chain mesh, and long gloves that covered most of her arms. Her patient, dark eyes roved over Danae.

"So Praesidio's intended acolyte is also a chemist?" Helvia asked.

Aha. The woman at the intake tent who had seen to Danae's needs the evening before.

"A better chemist than acolyte, for the foreseeable future," replied Danae. She sniffed at the faint scent of sulfur hanging in the air. "Will *you* tell me what's happening?"

Helvia shot a quick glance to the corners of the tent and then out the door. "The enemy's raiders hit a caravan far too close to this camp." Helvia towed Danae by the arm. "We don't think they've located us here, but the lords thought it best if all the refugees were gathered and guarded, just in case."

"But they've plucked me from being guarded to mix compounds?" Danae inquired.

"And tinctures, for those may also be needed in due time. But for now, Lord Sorex has instructed me to produce as much of a certain compound as I can with supplies that didn't make it to the city." She pulled out a tattered parchment, its lettering faded and edges charred.

"Explosives," Danae said. "What for?"

Helvia lined up bags and jars of ingredients in an orderly row on the large metal table in the center of the room. Danae read over the parchment, cross-referencing the words on the sheet with the packages of ingredients before her. She smiled at Helvia's precision and orderliness, so much like her own.

"This compound has many applications. I shall never complete the work in time without experienced help," Helvia said. "In one form, we call it blast-shot."

Danae lifted her eyebrows. How could such a thing work? What was in it? "That sounds . . . devastating."

Helvia nodded. "If we were in the city, we'd be making it to load into catapults and ballistae on the walls to lob at siege engines. Here, we'll rig the charges a little differently to create a protective perimeter around the refugee camp."

Danae rubbed the back of her neck with a trembling hand. "It'll be something like making really, really large match heads."

Helvia smiled. "I suppose so. That at least makes the whole process seem less frightening. The real challenge will be getting the components both stable enough to transport yet volatile enough to explode when they should."

Danae gave Helvia a leery grin. "Well, where do we start? I wish we had been able to do something like this when the Tebalese came for my home city. The siege towers were our undoing."

Helvia nodded as she handed Danae a similar apron and set of gloves to the garb she wore. "Put these over your robes."

Once Danae had arrayed herself in the work garb, and all the necessary items sat in exactly the places Helvia preferred, she joined Helvia at the tableside. The Elgadrim chemist stood over Danae as she pointed to the different components on or near the table. She set a large wooden frame on short legs upon the tabletop. A wire mesh screen provided a bottom to the frame.

"Use this scoop to get a level measurement of that." Helvia pointed to a barrel full of slate-gray powder that stood between them.

Danae scooped and leveled the ingredient. The fine powder stuck to everything.

"Now, pour it into the screen."

"Are you sure you wouldn't rather show me the procedure first?" Danae asked.

Helvia shook her head. "I don't have time to show you and then have you try. If you do it, you will understand and remember sooner. Every motion counts in this business. Pour it."

Danae dumped the powder into the screen, but a fine layer remained in her scoop. She knocked the measuring device against the wooden plank on the side of the screen. Helvia clapped her hand down on top of Danae's.

"Never bang. What are we making?"

Danae ducked her head. "Right. Explosives."

Helvia continued to instruct Danae in how to smooth a variety of powdered components through the mesh screen to sift and combine them. Some of them made her eyes burn, and the silt in the air made her cough. Over time, the skin on her arms and face stung more and more as though someone had scrubbed her with a wire brush.

"Oh, this is nothing," Helvia quipped as they continued to work. "Should you choose to bathe after we are done with all this mixing, certainly, you will get clean, but it will burn like no hot water ever could." She grabbed Danae's wrist. "Do *not* bang."

The wee hours of the night crept toward dawn, but industry and nerves kept Danae's sleepiness at bay. Amidst it all Danae learned new tricks for the proportions of ingredients to maximize the blast, while she contributed some of her own expertise in the wrapping of the sulfurous paste that would help them get to their destination with the least chance of catastrophic mishap. Most uncanny, however, was the thin, paper-like layer Helvia produced from a flat case with a lock. They placed a sheet of the film between the shot's outer wrap and the pasty fill.

"What does this do?" Danae asked.

"It provides the spark to ignite the blast." Helvia tucked the bundle she worked on shut.

Danae lifted and turned one of the supple sheets over in her hands. "What's in it?"

Helvia shook her head. "It's only dire circumstances that make it so you're seeing this at all."

No later than the third toll of the dawn bell, Sorex strode into the work area. He evaluated the large trays of a dozen nondescript packages, his face grim.

"This is a start," he said. "Keep building until you can't. I have a feeling we cannot make too much." He waved toward the trays, and three knights in emerald tabards came forward to lift the first batch of shot.

Danae tensed as the men turned with their loads, despite her knowledge it would take far more than brisk walking to upset the compounds. The knights departed without a word.

Chewing on her curiosity, Danae struggled to keep her questions locked behind clenched teeth.

As Sorex exited the building, he called back over his shoulder, "I shall return for the next load at the third hour after midday."

Helvia sighed and leaned against the makeshift lab table behind her. "No time for thank yous when raiders are spotted."

Danae shook her head and rolled her eyes. "Pleasantries don't seem to be his main area of expertise. He could have at least given us some news."

"What you don't understand about war, you make up for in your competence in chemistry." Standing, Helvia took a bite of jam-marbled bread, rather than breaking for breakfast. She handed Danae a palm-sized meat pie from a tray a young girl had set at the lab entry.

Danae felt her face reddening. "Thanks. I owe it all to my father. He's a great teacher." Her eyes misted, and she took a large bite of her pie. She closed her eyes. "It's good."

Helvia smiled. "A wise father is a treasure beyond worth." She handed Danae a parchment and a quill and ink. "Make a copy of the blast-shot formula, and then when we are both working in a good rhythm, maybe you could tell me about this great teacher of yours."

---

*D*anae jolted awake, and shadows shrouded the room around her, with only the light of a small lamp in the corner flickering beside where Helvia sat. She pressed the heel of her hand to her temple in the hope of stilling her dizziness. She swung her feet to the dirt floor.

A boom, followed by a rumble, ran a tremor up Danae's legs.

"That's two." Helvia rose and picked up a pack from behind her bed. "Grab your things from under your bed and follow me."

"Two what?" Danae asked.

"Blasts. Didn't you feel them?"

Maybe the first is what woke me up. Danae nodded.

"One blast can be a fluke, but two likely means someone is encountering our perimeter mines," Helvia said. "Time for us to bring up the rear." She grabbed the locked box that contained the strange paper components of the explosives, as well as the parchments with the copies of the shot recipe, and tucked them under her arm.

Danae surveyed the pavilion, noting that only a few crates remained, compared to the jumble of supplies it housed when she had fallen asleep. She fumbled under the cot and found her pack there, stuffed full.

"We're leaving?"

Helvia handed Danae a leather breastplate.

Danae tilted her head. "This isn't mine."

"The chances aren't small that you'll need it," Helvia said. "Follow me, quickly."

The two women darted through the pavilion exit.

Outside, dusk had fallen once again, and the camp was still. Danae spotted no other refugees, soldiers, or Elgadrim of any sort. To the west, distant voices rode on the wind.

"Where is everyone?" Danae whispered as she jogged after Helvia.

"Most everyone else has been evacuated ahead of us, but now that we know this position has been compromised, it's time for the rest of us to go. My lab had better make it to the next encampment!"

"I slept through an evacuation? I must have been more exhausted than I thought."

Helvia quirked a sad smile. "My people have learned the art of silent flight over many generations of dodging genocide."

Another blast and cries pierced the evening stillness. A weird stillness, indeed, where no bird sang or cricket chirped. Danae breathed slow draughts of air while they pressed toward the eastern edge of camp. Her heart jolted.

"All the tents are still here. And your lab wasn't empty," Danae said. "Are we sure everything of value was packed up?"

Helvia narrowed her eyes, but then the spark of understanding brought a soft smile to her lips. "Don't worry, nothing interesting remains here, but the raiders don't know that. The smattering we're leaving will give the raiders who don't get blown up something to pick through. It slows them down."

Helvia glanced over her shoulder, then rounded an outer tent.

A chill swept over Danae—no, a bubbly signature. As she stepped behind the tent, she almost collided with Sir Lucius.

He stepped back and bowed, though a smile tugged at his lip. "Welcome, Lady Alchemists."

Two Elgadrim men in civilian tunics and wraps stood behind Lucius, as did Lucius's horse.

Helvia nodded. "This is all of us. Off we go. Stay single file, friends, unless you fancy being the next thing that goes *boom* in the night."

The group melted into the dark of the trees outside the encampment with Helvia in front and Sir Lucius leading his horse at the rear.

What a tramping noise we're making. Surely the raiders will find us. Danae's heart thundered. *No, don't be hysterical. Our group is small, it's dark, and they are not that close. But where did they take the Sword? Praesidio had better have it.*

As they pressed onward, unspeaking, Danae pushed her mind to the familiar comfort of the bedtime stories of her childhood, stories her travels had revealed as not only fancies to enthrall a child's heart, but history, however ancient. Would the people of Bilearne survive to make such tales for generations to come? Her daydreams slowly shifted from the rustic lyrics of simple Radromirian legends to the sophisticated rhymes and meter of the Elvish ballads she had learned under Culduin's instruction. The clarion sound of his singing voice flooded her mind.

Enough of that. She shook the melody from her head.

Sir Lucius spoke low from behind her. "That song you were humming. Elvish, was it not?"

Danae's eyes widened. "I was humming?" She averted her glance to the new grass underfoot. "I suppose it was, then."

"Many hopes rest on the charity of the elves," Lucius said. "Don't you think?" His glance held a knowing gleam, and he seemed to eye Danae with a certain reverential appreciation.

Another distant boom echoed.

Danae hesitated. "If you trust them."

34

Heated Negotiations

anae marched in the midst of a small company of soldiers and other support workers over hilly terrain all day and well into the night. The farther they traveled, the sparser the forests grew. The steeper, rockier hills more than replaced the diminishing undergrowth in making the travel arduous, nonetheless. Well after midnight, Danae caught the scent of smoke on the air. After another half hour of walking, the thrum of crowds drifted on the ashen breeze. An occasional crack of stone on stone punctuated the distant rumbles.

Danae searched her companions' faces, but they all apparently had a lot of practice maintaining a complete lack of expression. What went on behind those emotionless Elgadrim eyes?

They crested a rise, and about two leagues in the distance, a city filled a rolling valley. At first, the city itself captivated Danae's attention. Its walls, loftier than she could guess, reflected the blue light of a full moon. Turrets rose above the walls, and from their pinnacles fluttered a multitude of banners, all emblazoned with symbols, whether the Tree of Creo, or the Phoenix of Praesidio's order, or a wyvern, or a quill, plus many others Danae could not discern in the distance. Upon closer inspection, it became clear than many of the banners had ragged edges, torn or burnt.

A multitudinous cry echoed in the valley below.

Spread before the city walls, a dark swath of boiling battle darkened the land. Fires burned at the feet of the city walls. Metallic clashes, distant but unmistakable, rang from the combatants. A mechanical *ka-chunk*, somewhere to Danae's right, caught her ear. Though not close enough to be startling, the fact that Danae could hear it at all wedged a knot in her throat.

A flaming comet streaked toward the city and smashed to smoldering bits against one of the turrets. The burning remains rained down into the city. The reek of charred cloth and rotting blood wafted over her.

She stared down into the valley. "Is that . . . ?"

Helvia stepped up beside Danae. "Bilearne, yes."

"I think I'm glad I can't see more, here in the dark."

After resting a hand on Danae's shoulder, Helvia sighed. "Take heart. I don't see any siege towers in the fray, which must mean our last batch of shot served well. Come."

"Haste," Lucius said. "We are far out from the fighting, but I dare not risk blundering into a perimeter squad. Queldurik's minions don't differentiate between soldier and civilian."

Danae found a last burst of energy under her growing fatigue as Lucius led them farther east. The sounds of battle faded from hearing. To her dismay, the funk of old blood returned, after they had marched at least a couple of miles. They worked their way up a rise where a bank of scrub oak and sycamores blocked Bilearne and its woes from sight.

A ring of stout stockades crowned the hill ahead, and inside,

Danae spied the peaks of five pavilions. Torches burned bright at intervals along the barricade. They traveled a worn track up the hill. The air was hazy with smoke.

Once they had drawn within twenty paces of the stockade, a guard in a dirty wyvern tabard and his arm in a sling opened a gate. From inside, two more soldiers brought a stretcher and followed along the outside of the wall with it. Before they vanished around the corner of the stockade, Danae noted a sheet draped over the entire contents of the stretcher.

"You there," the wounded guard called. "What's your business at the field hospital?"

Looks more like a morgue than a hospital. Danae stared after the departed stretcher.

Helvia responded. "Lord Protector Praesidio sent instructions that I was to bring his acolyte here in the event we had to break the refugee camp."

The guard appraised them as they all approached the gate. He nodded and gestured to the opening. "I hope you expect to be put to work. We're losing more wounded than necessary, owing to a shortage of surgeons and attendants."

They passed the gate into a churned corral of tents and makeshift surgeon's tables.

Smudged and bloodied men bore stretchers from one location to the next in the crowded hospital, hustling with wounded sometimes so gruesomely maimed that Danae had to look away to contain the scant contents of her lurching stomach.

A runner burst from one of the tents, nearly smacking Danae with the flap. He bellowed a long string of words.

Helvia grabbed his sleeve. "We'll help you find it."

Sir Lucius halted his horse. "My good companions, now that you are safely within these walls, I must seek the commander here to find how I might rejoin my company." He surveyed his surroundings. "Clearly they could use every soldier available, and more."

"Of course," Helvia said.

Lucius met Danae's gaze. "Keep safe, my lady." He clasped her hand, bent low in his saddle, and pressed her fingertips to his lips.

Her cheeks warmed. "Um. I'll . . . do my best."

"Until we meet again." He wheeled his horse and headed at a trot across the encampment.

Danae followed Helvia to another tent. "Can we get news of the assault here?"

Helvia led the way inside the tent and lifted a lid off a crate within. "From the looks of things, I'd say any news isn't good."

Danae wrung her hands. "But the Allies are keeping the enemy in check?"

"For now." Helvia moved to the next crate. "The runner needs poultices, clotting agent, and bindings. Help me look."

*K*ing Saransaeloth paced the polished floor in front of the faceted crystal throne of his audience chamber, a long, calligraphed sheet of vellum in his jeweled hand. "Well, one thing is for certain: the Elgadrim Knight who penned this is the preeminent flatterer of our time. The Maker forbid Ecleriast actually reads this. His head's big enough as it is." He pushed a loose strand of hair, pale as corn silk from his eyes, then rolled up the vellum.

"So if I may be so bold," Culduin said, his glance downcast. "If Lord Protector Praesidio has sent this missive, it must mean that the Sword is now in Bilearne. High Lord Ecleriast could retrieve it there."

"But he did not say as much, not in definitive terms." The king squinted into the distance. "You swear upon your honor that this knight did not send you to argue his position?"

Culduin lifted his chin. "On my honor. My time with Praesidio proved him faithfully bent on the greatest good, and my decision to come before you was my own."

A smoldering, peacock-sized bird bobbed its way along the central aisle of the hall, between two rows of white-barked apple trees, bright with pink blossoms. It pecked at the soil beneath the trees, and tiny embers drifted to the ground from the crest of plumage on its crimson head.

"Someone see to it that creature does not burn down my apples of elvenkind," Saransaeloth grumbled as he returned the parchment to an ivory scroll tube, capped with bronze phoenix medallions. "But what you must also understand, Caranedhel the younger, is one does not just send a single warrior to a conflict of this magnitude, lest we appear stingy and placating."

"Or worse," Culduin's father added. "We send Lord Elceriast into a fight so far gone that we simply endanger him."

"The destruction of the sham-god Durik will be a service to the world at large, but even so, if I commit soldiers, there is an outspoken population of the Delsin who will criticize me for it." Saransaeloth pinched the bridge of his nose. "And if the Celevonese denounce our actions—well, you had better hope this War of the Risen Age ends at Bilearne, for we will find no help from our eastern brethren if Durik marches upon us."

"Quel . . . ahem . . . Durik marching his army upon us is sure if we do not send forces," Culduin said. "I saw the fiend host."

Hands clenched behind his back, the king pivoted and paced. "This host is the development that makes the strongest argument for action."

"Yes." Culduin clasped pleading hands. "The allies need a stroke that will cut the heart from the dark army's offensive. Even at dragon speed, I fear we risk being too late."

The king sighed. "Then let us hope those who love me for it outnumber those who will throw stones. Scribe!" He held out the scroll tube. "Pen our response to Protector Praesidio and the High Council of the Elgadrim, that our Windrider Battalion and my Formenar Legion will come to their aid. Affix it to Praesidio's blasted bird and let us have it done. Now, if you will excuse me, Masters Caranedhel, I have rebuttals to formulate."

Culduin's father bowed.

Culduin's pulse quickened. If the Formenar Legion was to provide soldiering support, there was call for those so inclined to join the cause. A chance for amends, if he could live to see it, loomed.

Culduin extended a palm. "One more thing, if I might, Your Majesty?" He drew a long breath against dizziness.

Father grasped Culduin's shoulder. "This is important, correct?" he whispered.

Saransaeloth turned back to him. He lifted a brow.

"As a former scout for the Formenar Legion, may I request assignment to this company, to depart with the Windriders as soon as they are mustered?" Culduin cleared his throat. "The survival of those caught up in Bilearne's trial is of personal concern to me."

"Personal concern makes for bad soldiering," the king said.

"I understand, Your Majesty," Culduin replied. "But years of regret and forgiveness unsought make for bad living."

A smile quirked the corner of Saransaeloth's mouth. "Request granted, Sergeant Caranedhel. Creo shield you."

---

*P*raesidio slammed his palms on the map table, making all the markers jump.

"Does this really come down to a paranoid power grab, then?" He pushed wild strands of hair away from where they stuck to stubble on his cheek. "That the Radromirian girl endured months of hardship just for this council to decide Mystrin's Sword should stay locked away and forgotten?"

One of three large crystals, hanging from stands like

lanterns on the opposite side of the table from Praesidio, flickered yellow. "Paranoid? More than half of us consider it perfectly reasonable that to pass such power into the Delsin's hands could have long-term implications even the wisest of us cannot foresee."

Praesidio gritted his teeth at Councilman Gannaro's words. The disadvantage of not being able to gather the council in body grated on his nerves, but the logistics of gathering them all in the command camp outside Bilearne were unworkable, even with Thaumaturgy. Persuasion was always more difficult without the benefit of a face-to-face meeting. But circumstances being what they were, Praesidio would take even a discussion by the Crystals of Discourse.

"So it is our fear of the unknown that hobbles us?" Lord Sorex said.

At least Praesidio had him in person.

"The current encroachment of the conflict prevents a proper agreement to be drafted, debated, and delivered," Councilman Albin said, via the pulse of his green crystal.

Praesidio paced. "Because none of you had time to sit down with a quill in the six months since this notion arose."

"The recruitment of Velonese soldiers to our cause occupied my every waking moment, Councilman Praesidio." Archadion's tone took a condescending pitch as it reverberated from the orange crystal to Praesidio's right. "*Some* of us have been about the war at hand while others chased after some miracle panacea."

"With your approval," Praesidio said. *The gall*—

"We've all learned over the years how useful it is to gainsay you when you've gotten your mind set on something," Albin said.

"The best place for the Sword is in the vaults," Archadion said. "Or do you deny that it is a holy relic worthy of such a place of honor?"

Easy for those a half continent away to say. "I'm sure the Bilearnian vault is currently *quite* accessible." Praesidio focused a blistering stare on the crystals, as if his fellow council members might feel his frustration. "Before this conflict ends, we may find the vaults plundered and Bilearne again in ashes. We need a dramatic turn here."

"Once the War Sages on the wall clear the way for the final companies to pass the gates, you will have your turn of the tide," Gannaro said. The light from his crystal waxed and waned in a slow cycle. "The walls are strong, and with our troops out of harm's way, we can bring the full force of our defensive mechanisms against the enemy."

"They've ransacked every village, farm, ranch, and caravan between here and our borders. Do you truly believe we will outlast them? If you do, I say your overconfidence will be the Elgadrim's downfall."

"Praesidio, you act as though you have been the only mind bent on this war, when in fact, you have been latest to the preparations," Albin said. "The High Philosopher had the presence of mind to stockpile supplies for many months."

Praesidio sat on a stool and folded his arms. "So that's the strategy. Outlast the siege. When disease and hunger begin to steal children from their mothers, is that when you will think again?"

Praesidio met Sorex's gaze. Outside the makeshift war room where they debated, the tramp of a company of soldiers, awoken from too short a respite, rumbled by. Sorex shook his head and dropped his chin.

"Get your head out of poetry and speak sensibly, Praesidio," Archadion said. "One weapon, even a supernatural one, cannot best an army."

"And you accuse me of not looking to the future and the potential of arming the right warrior with this weapon," Praesidio said.

"And you ignore the danger of the thing's corruption, corruption you yourself reported to us." Archadion's orange crystal flared bright, then deepened to nearly red.

Praesidio dug his fingers into his scalp. "Now I know this conversation is over, since we've resurrected the hysterical conspiracy theory of elven darkening and domination."

"This council has already come to the majority conclusion that it is our duty as knights to lend our aid to the current course," Albin said. "I conclude this debate and admonish you to seek the commanders in your quadrant for orders." The green crystal went dark.

Yellow and orange did likewise, before Praesidio could interject another thought. *The fools.* He eyed the Sword, hanging in its new, galactite ore scabbard from the rack at the rear of the tent. *Better than any vault is the hand of a warrior from whom a weapon would not likely be taken.*

Thankfully, a council majority did not yet equate to law. That much would keep Danae out of trouble when Praesidio sent her on one more crazed intervention.

35

A Trace of Her Signature

*D*anae crouched in a patch of wild cranesbill. She harvested a handful of plants and added them to her basket, atop the purple dead nettle she had the luck of finding on a streambank earlier that morning.

Boom.

In the distance, the rumors of battle rode on the wind when it came from the southwest. Despite the seeming calm of the woods around her, the ash in the air and the periodic call of a horn offered stark reminders of the danger that loomed so near.

Back at the field hospital, they needed no runners to tell them when the fighting rose to fever pitch, because the flow of wounded would surge. At the first waning of wounded arrivals, Danae had sighed in relief, only to learn that such a drop in deliveries merely meant the field of battle was likely too choked with carnage for fight-worthy soldiers to turn their attention to the wounded.

So much blood. The hospital was bathed in it. In the hope of preventing further deaths, Danae hunted herbs she knew would aid in clotting. If there was even time to process the plants when she returned.

At least she could only hear the impacts of the biggest catapult loads from this distance. The hospital offered enough pained screams to pierce her soul for a lifetime. To add the tenor of combat to that might have undone Danae entirely. She shuddered at the thought of soldiers hewn and gasping their last, just a league or less from their homes and families. Did the Tebalese bring slaves, like her brother, to the front lines?

She sawed at a second patch of cranesbill, when the snap of brittle footing jarred her. She spun, knife in hand.

"Ho there, friend, don't fear!" A hooded man stepped back, hands raised.

Danae's hammering heart leapt. "Praesidio! Where have you been?" She sprang to her feet and dashed to him.

He tipped his chin high enough that she could see his shadowed face. "Oh, I cannot say. My time away from you has involved quite a bit of diplomatic wrestling." Though a twinkle lit his eyes, deep circles darkened them, so much that Danae almost mistook his fatigue for bruising. Every crease in his face had deepened over the days since Danae had seen him last.

"It seems Helvia has made good use of your skills." He stepped forward and picked up her basket of herbs and blooms.

"I'm so glad you seem all right. Any news?" Danae said.

The gray-haired man sat heavily on a nearby boulder. He cast his glance around the landscape. With a beckoning gesture, he leaned forward to speak in hushed tones.

"The commanders will have my head if they discover I've spoken of things, but battle has come to a standstill, for the emissaries of Queldurik have delivered terms to High Philosopher Aeleronde."

Danae's eyes narrowed. "Terms? But I still heard booms of impact, even just now."

Praesidio smiled wearily. "That would have been the Elgadrim's answer to the terms."

"So the king rejected them. But how?" Danae searched Praesidio's expression. "The hospital has looked like a slaughterhouse for days. Not just Elgadrim, but Velonese soldiers, and even some Da-Shirines."

Praesidio heaved a long breath. "Yes, the losses have been staggering as the enemy's mercenaries slipped behind our forces. But the Allied reinforcements—the Velonese and Da-Shirines you have seen—flanked the enemies and took some of the pressure off. Since then, we've focused on opening ways for companies to withdraw and pass the gates. Our warriors have done an exemplary job of keeping the enemy line back from the walls. For now."

Sighing, the sage shifted uncomfortably on his perch and continued. "The enemy holds the northern roads, and he knows Kelmirith's farmers and herdsmen are scattered to refugee camps. Even if our remaining troops make it within the safety of the city, Queldurik knows he need only dig in. Either starvation or their superior numbers will eventually undo us."

"Is there no hope?" Danae shivered.

"As Creo is sovereign," Praesidio said, "there is always hope. But sometimes it is hope from without, not within."

"Help from without?" Danae asked. "Who could possibly come to your aid now, with the roads held?"

Praesidio sighed heavily. "There are some for whom roads are of no consequence, but so far, we have no definite answers. So in the meantime, it is to hope alone we must cling. But frankly, it is your help I have come to seek, in giving my hope its best chance."

"Me?" A rustle of leaves caught Danae's ear, and in the next instant, something heavy and sharp hit her knife hand. She yelped. A brown blur tore past her face.

In a flurry of feathers and beating wings, a bird launched for the treetops. Hot pain arced through Danae's hand and up her arm.

Before Praesidio had jumped to his feet and ignited his Sword of the Sacred Fire, the bird was gone.

Danae cradled a bleeding hand. She squinted skyward. "What in the . . . that bird just stole my knife!"

Praesidio gawked. "My apologies. I was so slow—I must be more in need of rest than I thought. Here, let me see your hand."

With a wince, she extended the wound to him.

Praesidio took her hand gently. "Stole your knife? This gash looks like a raptor's work."

"But why would a hawk take . . ." Danae's stomach twisted. "The hawks in Tebal."

Pressing his cloak to Danae's gash, Praesidio muttered. "This bodes evil. I fear you are no longer safe in the field hospital."

A clammy sweat arose on Danae's brow. "But where can I go? And where's the Sword?"

Praesidio stared into the sky. "We cannot stay here. Come." Whether he was exhausted or not, he spun on a heel and headed back the way Danae had come.

She trotted after him. "But I thought you just said I'm not safe at the hospital."

Without turning back to her, he said, "I did. But before I send you off, I'll need to enlighten you to my plans. Hurry."

---

*B*a-al Hilekar drew his fingers from the basin of hazy water and opened his eyes. At first, he winced at the daylight that flooded his vision. He wavered on unsteady legs. The return to corporeal sight after employing the Basin of Seeing always required some recovery, but what he had witnessed more than compensated him for the momentary discomfort.

Finally, a heading. The Elgadrim swine had once again failed in hiding his underling. Zechmaat's demands would soon be met.

After drawing his deep hood up over his head, Hilekar stepped outside his tent. Here in the daylight hours, a lull hung over the encampment. He huffed. Clearly the priests had not yet succeeded in their attempts at improvement upon the dragonkin's sun tonic. Nocturnal mercenaries were mostly more trouble than they were worth.

Bah, let the lizard-men rest while we're held in reserve. Soon, we'll unleash our might and crush what remains of the humans' sad effort at defense. Hilekar smirked at the prospect of Bilearne returned to ashes.

He paced the camp, his ear attuned for noise in the canopy. How far away could the blasted falcon be?

Finally, after Hilekar had made a leisurely circuit of the camp, three hundred tents strong, the falcon's cry shrilled close by. He reached his black gauntlet high, and the bird alighted. It hopped on one foot while juggling a plain knife in its other talon. Hilekar took it by the blade and allowed the falcon to settle into a more stable perch. A grin pulled at his cheeks.

He crossed back to the eastern side of camp, where three huge crates with iron grates for one side sat. He hooded and tethered the falcon on a post beside the boxes. Hilekar's sharp whistle woke the inhabitants.

The three wire-haired hounds snarled and slavered at the bars. Hilekar reached into the bucket near the left crate and drew out a handful of morsels—an ear, a finger, a shriveled nose. It seemed the interrogators had been at work. He tossed each hound one of the nibbles, which they each gulped in one sloppy bite.

"Very well, my pets." He extended the leather-wrapped knife grip toward the first hound's bars. "Get a good draught of this."

Once each hound had gotten a nose full of the knife grip's

scent, they burst into raucous barking. Indeed, these beasts hungered to follow the girl's magical trail now that he had presented its essence. They slammed their shoulders against the bars and dug at the floor with long claws.

Hilekar laughed and pulled the pins from each of the crates' latches. The hounds burst out and charged across camp, the lead beast baying with an invigorating howl.

"Trail's hot again, boys." Hilekar belted the knife and broke into a run in the hounds' wake.

---

*P*raesidio led Danae to the laboratory tent, where Helvia cinched a knapsack shut.

Helvia looked to the tent entry. "Oh, you're back."

"Yes," Danae said between heavy breaths. "I've brought as much cranesbill and—"

"No time for chatter," Praesidio said. "I must get Danae and . . . it . . . out of here." He glanced over his shoulder.

It? Danae's pulse quickened further. "It's here? Not back with your people, safe?"

Praesidio rolled his eyes skyward. "Why does everyone seem to think this thing will be safe in Elgadrim hands? Are we not besieged in part because the enemy hunts the Sword?"

Danae bit her lip. "That's why the offensive made a sudden charge for Bilearne, isn't it? When Ikirra learned of our heading, that scheming—"

"Stewing over the past won't help in the present," Praeisdio said. "Accept the lesson and take the next step. Now, where is your pack?"

"Here." Helvia pulled the pack from under Danae's cot. After that, she drew out an enormous scabbard made of smooth, black wood or stone, with flecks of sparkling silver riddled through it.

Danae beheld the pommel atop the housing, the clear orb and talon holding it, and her stomach flipped. "I don't sense its voice at all."

Praesidio nodded. "Our smiths and Thaumaturgists toiled to create a new scabbard for the thing, one that binds the Sword's voice." He took the weapon from Helvia. "Take your gear, Danae. We must go."

"Already?" Helvia asked. "I thought you planned to enact your plans in the morning."

Danae reached for her breastplate but cringed at the sharp pain that lanced across her gashed hand. She ducked her head through the collar and fumbled with the side buckles.

"Oh, what's happened?" Helvia squinted at Danae's bloodied hand. "You'll at least need to wrap that before you rush off."

"No time," Praesidio said.

Helvia scoffed. "Nonsense, old Protector. It's still oozing."

After a sigh, Praesidio conceded. "Be quick." He took a position by the tent exit while Helvia scrounged for salve and bindings.

"Where will we go, Praesidio?" Danae gritted her teeth against the sting of the salve Helvia smeared on the wound. The pain rippled over her entire body.

"Best not to speak of it," he said.

Danae sighed and conceded the point.

While Helvia wound a bandage around Danae's hand, her skin continued to thrum with discomfort. The sensation worsened moment by moment.

It wasn't that big a cut—

The scream of tearing fabric drowned Praesidio's next words. Danae yelped and wheeled toward the sound. A knife yanked back through the canvas tent wall behind Helvia.

"This way!" Praesidio yelled.

Empty crates flew. Crockery clattered. One, two slate-gray beasts barreled into the tent through the knife slash. Helvia grabbed Danae by the shoulders and hauled her out of their path.

A rush of pelting pain battered Danae. No, not arrows or shot, not even phantom sensations from her hand wound—a signature. She knew it from her captivity in the merfolk's kingdom.

"Get up! Run!" Helvia cried.

Danae scrambled on hands and knees away from the snarling hounds. She caught a glimpse through the slash in the tent. A third hound clambered over scattered supply crates, and behind it, a hooded figure brandished a wicked, curved knife. A camp guard lay at his feet.

Blue-white light flooded the tent. "Run! I will hold them," Praesidio boomed. "Take this." He shoved his phoenix talisman into Helvia's hand.

Helvia hauled Danae the rest of the way to her feet. Praesidio lunged into the center of the tent and swung his sword of the Sacred Fire. Hounds barked in a mix of pain and fury. He swung his off hand in a slash from right to left, and the beasts flew back as though pummeled by a battering ram.

Danae dug her feet in against Helvia's dragging. "We have to help him!"

Praesidio and the hooded knifeman charged one another. Praesidio swung a downward chop, but the knifeman caught it against his blade.

Caught it? Danae choked. What weapon could catch the flaming blade of an Elgadrim knight? The sword's blue light glinted from a dark chin and snarl of pointed teeth inside the hood of Praesidio's opponent.

With another thrust of the knight's empty hand, the hounds convulsed and fell to the tent floor, thrashing and yowling.

"*Go!*" he roared.

Helvia hauled on Danae's hood. The rough wool of her collar burned across her throat.

Cringing from the wretched signature's assault, Danae accepted Helvia's direction. But just as she turned, the enemy's knife flashed in an upward cut across Praesidio's torso. An arc of blood sprayed.

Before Danae could scream, Helvia shoved her from behind. "Go. It's the only way."

She staggered the direction she had been shoved. Helvia came alongside her and thrust her pack into her arms.

Half blinded with tears, Danae ran with a drunken gait between tents. Helvia dragged her in a zigzag pattern until they burst through the stockade at a point Danae had not even realized was an exit.

"Don't look back, Danae," Helvia cried between gasps. "Just keep running."

36

No More Running

*S*tupid! Danae berated herself. *Why didn't I realize what I was feeling? You'd think I'd know a hound's signature by now.*

Danae barreled down a rocky hillside, sure she would break an ankle over the terrain, but Helvia's pace was unrelenting. How could she just leave Praesidio? Only when she took her eyes off her feet for a scant moment did a flash of comprehension flicker under her bewilderment. Helvia ran with the Sword on her back.

They fled to the bottom of one valley, through a rill, and up another hill. Only when they had cleared that next rise did Helvia slow to a stop.

"What's going on?" Danae threw her hands out to her sides.

Helvia heaved for breath. "This wasn't the plan."

"I certainly hope not."

Helvia lowered stern brows. "In case you're wondering, it also matters to me that we had to run."

Danae swallowed her anger.

"And if you ask me, we need to quit running. If those brutes survive this fight, they'll keep coming after us, won't they?" Helvia's hazel eyes held Danae's, intense and full of concern.

Please don't let them survive. Danae blew a long exhale. "Yes. This has been my life for far too many months."

"Then stop running," Helvia said.

Danae gaped. "Are you kidding? I'm no warrior."

"Neither am I," Helvia said. "We need to outsmart them."

"Well." Danae stared out over the empty hills ahead. "They're after me and the Sword. Maybe we should get their two targets as far from each other as possible."

"If we had soldiers to protect both, that might make a slim portion of sense, but as it is, it won't help." The Elgadrim chemist shifted a bag at her side that Danae only then recognized as a quiver and short bow.

Danae dropped her chin into her hand. She scoured her mind for ideas. But only the sight of Praesidio reeling from the huntsman's slash would arise in her mind's eye.

"We set a trap," Helvia said.

Danae blinked. "I don't have anything that would slow down one of those hounds, let alone their master."

A sly grin curled one side of Helvia's lips. "You sure?" Her glance flicked to Danae's bag.

After lowering the pack to the ground, Danae hesitated. "What if the hounds are already chasing us? We don't have time to stand here."

"Check the pack."

Danae flipped the top flap open and uncinched the bag. Inside, she found a sack full of what might have been three small loaves of bread. She peeked inside the sack. Tied, oilskin wrappers created familiar bundles.

"You put blast-shot in my pack? I could have blown myself up with the running!"

Helvia shook her head. "This is the more stable kind that needs to be ignited."

A twig snapped. Danae jumped.

Just a squirrel bounding across branches.

"All right, this is a start, but can we walk and plan?" Danae closed her pack and shouldered it again. "I'm getting jumpy."

Helvia pointed to the southeast. "Do you see that bridge over the river valley?"

Danae squinted in the direction Helvia indicated. "Um . . . yes. The haze makes it a little hard to see."

"We should make for the bridge." Helvia started toward it. "If we attach the shot to the bridge right, we have a chance to blast everything from beneath them. Perhaps send the hounds—even the huntsman—to their end."

Danae chewed her cheek. "If the huntsman is the same as I left behind in Scraga, he has wings."

Helvia stopped to stare at Danae, her head tilted and eyes narrowed. "What in creation pursues you?"

Danae shrugged. "I guess you don't steal a sword from a greater fiend without making some otherworldly enemies. But I like the plan. I just hope we can pull it off."

"Speaking of which . . ." Helvia pulled the scabbard and its belt from her back. "I return to you the object of your quest."

Danae pulled the strap over her head and across her body. The Sword on her back, while oversized, felt . . . unremarkable. No slimy tentacles or roars of disdain. Relief spread through her as they accelerated to a run.

The bridge was farther than it had looked when Helvia pointed it out. At the top of every hill, Danae's lungs burned for air and her legs shook. Sweat soaked her back. On the way down each slope, she staggered, only half in control of her strides. In the valleys along the way, they splashed upstream in whatever creeks they could in an effort to confuse the trail.

Finally, they reached a neglected road, paved with flat stones but riddled with weeds between them. They ascended the slope that rounded one of Kelmirith's rolling hills. They turned one of the road's sharper corners, one that arced around an outcropping of layered shale.

"Halt!"

Danae's throat clamped closed and squelched a yelp.

Four men pointed weapons toward her and Helvia, about forty paces ahead of them on the road. Two held swords, two held crossbows. But they all wore tabards of purple and white, their heraldry depicted the crown and sun of Bilearne's knights. A faint bubbling sensation . . .

"Sir Lucius," Danae said to Helvia. "What are he and these other knights doing out here?" Would they complicate matters if they realized she and Helvia had the Sword with them?

Helvia shrugged. She raised her voice. "Good knights, we are no threat."

The group lowered their weapons halfway and approached. The swordsman on the right cracked a small smile.

"My lady, we meet again," Sir Lucius said.

A taller, older knight with grey-shot, short brown hair led the group closer. "You know these women?" He adjusted the gold-emblazoned sash across his armor.

"Sir, we met on the road to the north of here," Lucius replied. "But why they have departed the field hospital, I do not know."

"Please," Helvia said. "Our errand is urgent. May we pass?"

The senior knight pursed his lips. "These lands are perilous. What could be so urgent to risk traveling unescorted?"

"Our escort was . . . otherwise detained." Helvia narrowed her eyes and studied the knights one at a time.

"I fear I must ask you to be plain," the knight said.

Helvia grasped the chain around her neck and produced Praesidio's talisman from her collar. "I fear I must decline, as our errand is also of utmost secrecy." She held the talisman forward.

The squad of knights cast one another a variety of looks, most with eyebrows raised.

"The surveillance of this quadrant is my sworn duty, my lady," the knight said. "I can only let you pass if one under my command accompanies you."

Danae's breath hitched. She glanced to Helvia. The chemist offered a gentle nod of reassurance.

"Then any such knight shall also be bound to secrecy until released from that bond by Lord Protector Praesidio," Helvia said.

"And we need to go," Danae said. "Now."

The commander sighed. "You bear the token of authority of one I cannot gainsay, although it is my desire for the warning in my depths." He turned to the right. "Sir Lucius, because you are known to these women, I assign you to act as their sheildmaster, wherever their errand leads, unless it is somehow to betray the Elgadrim."

A spike of offense jolted Danae. She scrunched her brows.

Lucius grinned. "I cannot imagine such a mission being in the hearts of these fair travelers. And so I swear my silence and my protection."

Somehow, Lucius's bright smile softened Danae's worries. And the sword he carried would not hurt to have along either.

The commander bowed. "So be it. Sir Lucius, find us at our usual camp when you have seen their errand completed. Creo shield you and guide you to success."

Lucius bowed to the remainder of the squad, and the soldiers continued past Helvia and Danae down the hill. He turned to the women. "Lead on, then. I shall keep a sharp eye for dangers."

Helvia pressed onward, up the hillside road. "Very good, knight errant. Sharp eyes and fleet feet are our chief needs now." She broke into a brisk jog again. "You should be able to return to your squadron tomorrow."

Danae followed Helvia's lead, and Lucius fell in beside her on the outer edge of the road. His glance roved the length of the huge scabbard on her back. "Once again, my lady, you are strangely burdened. May I relieve you of some of the weight you carry?"

So you can learn what it's like to have a target on your forehead? Danae's cheeks flushed as a bolt of nervousness lanced through her. "Uh, I'm not sure what you mean. I mean—thank you. But I'm fine."

Lucius shrugged. "As you wish."

After a few more snaking turns of the road, they closed in upon the stone bridge. Colossal archways supported the causeway that crossed churning rapids. At each end of the bridge, rectangular turrets stood sentry over the expanse, but only the rusted remains of band hinges hung from the stone. The gates they once supported had long rotted. Vines as thick as Danae's arm climbed up the stones from the riverbank, and their branches hung in a tangled curtain on the bridge's southward side. About a third of the way across the bridge, a full-grown aspen had taken root in the center of the way. Generations of slow determination had thickened its gnarled trunk. Its grasping roots had cracked the rocks around it.

Helvia gasped with each step she took along the final rise that led to the bridge. "The vines . . . will help. Hide the shot bundles." She mopped her brow with her sleeve.

"Bundles?" Lucius said.

"Part of a trap we are setting," Helvia replied.

They stopped at the end of the bridge, and Danae considered the crossing. "We'll need to spring the trap well into the middle of the stretch. This thing must be at least three hundred paces long!"

Helvia nodded. "No time to waste." She tramped through the vines that crisscrossed the roadway with Danae close behind.

When she reached the rogue aspen tree, she halted. "The stone may be weakened here because of the roots."

"I could help better if you would offer me details on what you are planning." Lucius frowned.

"You can help," Danae said. "We definitely need a watchman posted somewhere you can see as much of the road leading up here as possible."

Lucius brightened. "Ah. Very good. I will take position on the far half of the bridge. I believe that commands the best view of the valley."

Once Lucius had taken up his post, Danae rolled her head and stretched her shoulders, but the tension from care and carrying still remained. At least they could work with less scrutiny. She handed her bag to Helvia.

While Helvia placed the first packet of explosives near the deepest crack in the stone, Danae scanned the distance, hazier with smoke to the northwest. Just how much of Kelmirith burned? Or was that smoke the product of a greater concentration of flame at Bilearne itself?

"Any sign of them?" Helvia placed a twisted vine over the shot packet she had placed.

"No." Danae shivered. "But don't worry. I'll know when they're close." *This time.*

37

Springing the Trap

*B*etween the two of them, the women found strategic niches for each of the shot bundles, although every twig that cracked underfoot while they searched sent a new surge of worry up Danae's spine. But each sound came from only Lucius's or Helvia's movements.

After placing and covering the last bundle, Helvia dusted off her hands. "Creo permit that we have chosen well." She scurried to the far end of the bridge and ducked into one of the turrets. Danae followed, with Lucius a few paces behind.

"Who or what are you so nervous about?" he asked.

"Enemies," Danae said. "We'll let you know if it turns out they're still following us. With any luck, our trap will prevent any of us from getting tangled up with them." She slipped through the turret door.

The only light inside gleamed through narrow arrow slits in the walls. Helvia took a position near the slit that faced back the way they had come, and she drew the bow from her quiver. Bracing it against her foot, she strung it.

Lucius took a guard position outside the door.

Grabbing his arm, Danae shook her head. "No, that won't work. You have to come inside." She towed him through the door before releasing him and taking up a position at the arrow slit beside Helvia's.

She watched there for a few moments, then switched to one that looked out over the valley. How long would they have to wait for their pursuers? Would the huntsman delay, building his own scheme? Danae found her bag on the floor, flipped it open, and pulled out her bandolier of daggers.

For all the good it had done her in previous altercations with hounds.

Eyes fixed on the trap, Helvia said, "Calm your heart. Pacing and fidgeting won't help you respond to peril."

Danae blew out a breath. "I'm sorry. I'm just not used to letting people who want to kill me catch up."

Sir Lucius's eyes widened. "Who wants to kill you, now?"

Helvia cracked a sympathetic smile, which she offered to Danae. "There's always the chance that they fell in the fight."

Although Danae wanted to believe that had been the case, the wound Praesidio had taken mocked her hope.

"I beg your pardon, my ladies, but—"

"Too much knowledge in these circumstances is worse than too little," Helvia said.

Lucius stood straighter, with a soldier's practiced posture. "Will you at least tell me where you intend to go? How else can I convey you there safely?"

Danae studied the volley between Lucius and Helvia. Though Lucius seemed earnest and polite, he also seemed green. He lacked the calm assurance Culduin had with a drawn sword. Danae bit her lip. She forced her attention back to the bridge and rebuked any further thought of the elf.

Helvia sighed. "Very well. We are making for the ancient tollbooth at marker sixty-seven on the Southwest Road."

"And then what?" Lucius asked.

"And then you will be relieved of your duty and can return to your squadron."

Danae looked sidelong at Helvia and her businesslike tone that bordered on curtness. It clearly convinced Lucius that further questions would hit the verbal equivalent of a stone wall.

Midday passed, afternoon wore on, and dusk cast lavender light over the river. The women had fallen to taking turns watching, although the time Danae spent sitting in the turret with naught to do but think tormented her worse than staring into the wild distance in search of anything that moved. Why had Praesidio failed to catch up? Were it not for the trap, she would have insisted upon leaving hours ago.

When Helvia did not watch, she wrapped her arrow points in strips of cloth and soaked them in lamp oil.

Lucius spent the time both watching and reading a copy of *The Tree* at intervals, until at dusk, he put his volume away and met Danae's glance with an awkward smile.

"Well, it seems we're wanting for a privy here." He flushed. "I'm going to . . . well. Step out a moment?"

Danae chuckled. "Such things happen."

"Maintain cover," Helvia said.

Lucius swallowed and slunk out, making for the tree line on furtive strides.

Danae leaned to Helvia and whispered, "Where are we *really* going from here? And how do we know when we should leave?"

Helvia matched Danae's low voice. "I told Lucius the truth about the toll booth. There is a hidden way, built to evacuate the king in a time of disaster. We can follow it into Bilearne."

"Is it far? Would it be possible we could outrun them, especially if the way is hidden?"

"Don't get skittish. If we keep running, we risk leading an agent of evil to our most secret evacuation route," Helvia said.

Danae pushed a scraggly tendril away from her face. "I can see how that—"

"Shh!" Helvia locked an intent stare out the northward-facing arrow slit. She continued in a whisper. "I think we've got one hound and his master on their way."

Danae joined Helvia at the opening. In the deepening dusk, a dark figure and a pony-sized animal, nose to the ground, ascended the abandoned road to the bridge.

Of all the timing, for them to show up while Lucius is . . . indisposed.

Helvia crouched to the floor and picked up one of her wrapped arrows. "Warn me if they get close to the trap zone."

Danae's breath tightened. A prickle of the two approaching signatures rose on the back of her neck.

The hound reached the end of the bridge first, and it snuffled around, doubtless following a trail that doubled back and twisted, with how Danae had roved most of that end of the causeway in search of advantageous locations for the shot. Could it smell the powder too? Would it sense any danger in the metallic scent of the compounds?

A flare of light jolted Danae away from her intent watch. She steadied her breath—it was just Helvia's arrow, now aflame. But with the falling dusk, the light would illuminate the arrow slits in their turret. Danae's mouth went dry. Where was that knight?

Helvia took up a place at the slit that faced the bridge.

Creo, please don't let them charge us when they notice the light! Danae left her scouting position, threw her pack over her shoulder, and strapped on the Sword. She hovered near the turret door.

Helvia glared through her opening, bow in hand and arrow at the ready. "Come on, come on," she muttered. "Closer, you villains."

The standstill filled Danae's limbs with trembling.

In a swift motion, Helvia nocked the arrow, drew back, and released. Darkness flooded over the turret interior, and Danae blinked hard, as though it would make her eyes adjust faster. Sweat rolled down her temple.

Outside the turret, the hound burst into raucous barking.

Helvia hissed something in the Elgadrim tongue and fumbled with another arrow, flint, and striking steel.

Danae flew to the watch position while Helvia reloaded. The arrow she had fired lay on the ground, about four paces from the tree—the shot must have fallen short. The cloaked huntsman peered from behind the aspen tree trunk, his fist tight around the hound's collar.

Snick, snick, snick . . . Helvia fought with the flint. Still no arrow alight to follow up the first. It was taking too long!

The huntsman took a step from behind the tree. A wave of needling blanketed Danae, weak, but loathsome nonetheless. It carried with it a pulse of bemused mockery.

Anger burned in Danae's chest. And then an idea. Finally, a Virtus she could both remember *and* use.

She focused her attention on the spot she knew a bag of shot lay hidden, just three paces from the huntsman's feet.

The huntsman released the hound's collar. "Flush them out! Tear them to pieces."

The beast bounded across the bridge. In a blur of motion, a figure charged past Danae and Helvia's turret and pounded toward the hound. He brandished a sword.

Maker's mercy, Lucius, not now! Danae clapped a hand to her forehead.

"What's happening?" Helvia glanced up from her flint.

Danae's heart pounded. "Lucius ran out to meet the hound. He's going to get mauled."

Helvia muttered and struck her flint faster.

Lucius and the hound clashed in a blur of shield, blade, and teeth, about halfway between the tree and the turret. With furious strokes of his blade, Lucius slashed. The beast snapped and growled, but also backed up a handful of steps.

"How big is the blast radius?" Danae said.

Helvia grunted. "Wedged in stone like this? Hard to say. Won't matter if I can't get a shot right."

One step at a time toward the center of the bridge, the hound and Lucius battled on, deflecting one another's attacks. Lucius slashed with the edge of his shield, and the hound yelped.

The coming night and the flicker of the arrow flame confounded Danae's ability to discern details.

"Where's the rest of your pack of maggots, little knightling?" the huntsman yelled. He stood back from the fray, his arms folded across his chest, and the sight of his smug posture seared Danae's throat like bile.

We need to spring the trap.

Danae scanned the trap region as it related to Lucius's position. The hound had pushed Lucius a few retreating strides. Dark patches stained Lucius's tabard on his chest and leg. Was he far enough from the huntsman to be safe? Would detonating the trap now miss the hound completely?

Creo, please shield your knight. Danae fixed her stare on the packet of shot closest to the huntsman.

"*Calletminera mextonen,*" she whispered.

The light vibration of power ran through Danae from her scalp to her toes, and in the next moment, a flicker of flame sprang up from the crack in the stone that ran behind the huntsman.

A blinding flash.

Ka-BOOM!

The explosion hit Danae like a punch to the chest an instant before she heard it. She spun away from the arrow slit and covered her head with her arms. Blazing sulfur stung her nose.

Stone fragments pelted the outside of the turret with a gritty chatter.

In the next moment, Helvia's arrow finally sprang to flame, and she leapt to the opening. Her bowstring twanged. This time, another *ka-boom* shivered the ground beneath their feet.

The shiver in the stone grew to a rumble. Splitting, cracking, rattling. Danae caught Helvia's glance with her own wide-eyed stare.

She flew back to the arrow slit.

Through the clouds of dust and smoke, Danae found two shapes slumped on the bridge, closer to the turret than a gaping rent in the bridge. The silhouette of the aspen tree leaned at an unnatural angle. One of the slumped figures was inhuman—probably quadrupedal. But who was the other?

"Now what?" she asked. Her voice sounded stuffy, muffled by ringing in her ears.

"We run."

Danae gawked. "What? That's like sacrificing Lucius, if I didn't already murder him!"

Helvia grimaced. She peered at the bridge.

At least the barking and snarling had stopped.

"That's him, on our side," Helvia said.

Plus the hound that Danae could sense from its cutting signature. But it didn't matter. Danae bolted from the turret, rounded it, and charged onto the bridge. By the time she neared Lucius, he had hauled himself to his hands and knees. Danae skidded to a stop beside him.

"Can you get up?" She grabbed his arm.

He coughed. Open claw rents on his arms and chest wept dark blood. "I . . . think so."

The hound stirred. It whined. Then snarled.

Danae hauled on Lucius. "Come on!"

Between Danae's dragging and Lucius's unsteady effort, they brought him to his feet and staggered down the bridge.

Helvia emerged from behind the turret. "This way!"

They all fled the bridge with Helvia in the lead. Danae glanced over her shoulder as they barreled down the road. Flickers of flame licked over the brittle vines that clung to the remains of the bridge's middle. The hound regained its feet but immediately collapsed again. The smoke and darkness cloaked any sight of the huntsman, alive or dead.

Helvia guided the group to a steep downhill slope, paved with weathered stones and bordered by a low wall on the right side. She pulled Danae and Lucius down to duck beside the wall.

While Helvia panted with her back to the wall, she and Danae exchanged uncertain glances.

Shhhhhk BLAM!

Danae dropped to the ground. Gravel rained upon them. When the downpour of debris stilled, Danae dared peek over the wall.

Flames devoured the vines on what remained of the bridge. Stone cracked and rumbled in what reminded Danae of a high-lands avalanche. The aspen tree tipped farther, then plummeted into darkness.

Fire must have spread to the third packet of shot and set it off. The three blasts had reduced the middle section of the bridge to a gaping ruin and scattered rubble in a wide radius.

Helvia plucked at Danae's sleeve. "Stay down, but let's go."

They shuffled along, bent at the waist, to maintain cover, but Danae could not help but look back. On the far side of the breach in the bridge, a dark lump sprawled on the ground. There was too much dust and smoke to be sure, but Danae suspected that lump was not stone. Was it just a phantom of her dread, or had that lump just moved?

38

Secret Stairs

utside the ruins of a square, two-story building, Danae handed Lucius another bundle of bandages.

"Make sure you change the dressings at least once a day. Tell the medics you could use yarrow balm when you get back to the army." Danae surveyed the patched-up knight. Although his tabard was much tattered and stained with dried blood, Lucius's armor had prevented worse mauling. Only two of the wounds had required stitching. In the dead of night, with only one lantern to work by, the task had proven tricky enough for Danae's rudimentary surgical skills.

"I am in your debt, Lady Danae," Lucius said. "I hope, some-day, we shall meet again, and I can learn the details of this night's strange circumstances."

"We shall see if Creo interweaves your paths again," Helvia said from her seat on the ground, her back to the outer wall of the toll building. "Until you hear otherwise from Protector Praesidio—"

Lucius raised his palm. "Yes, I know, Mistress. I'll speak to no one of what I saw."

Danae offered Lucius his pack of supplies. "I'd like it if we did see each other, in better times."

He grasped the shoulder strap of the pack and slid it on, the motion of his wounded arms stiff. "My thanks, my lady. Until that day, may the Maker lead you safely, wherever urgency sends you."

Helvia nodded a weary goodbye, and Lucius set off, down the disheveled road. Once he was out of sight, she stood. She waved Danae after her as she passed the empty doorway.

Within the remnants of the toll building, Danae took up a watch post by the marble-framed doorway. She had jumped at every shadow the whole way from the bridge to their odd destination, although no huntsman or hound had materialized.

Helvia set the lantern on an iron hook in the left-hand wall, then began clearing rubble and roof tiles from the center of the floor.

"Before our diaspora," she said, "our people collected tolls to maintain the roads." She pushed aside a beam that crumbled from dry rot when she moved it. "Someday, we'll breathe life back into all this. Be good stewards of Kelmirith again."

Danae stifled a yawn. The deep of night did not betray whether the hour was very late or very early. All she knew was that her legs ached. She worried that Lucius, even with light wounds, might meet too great a trial between the toll building and safety.

And her heart quavered at the possibility Praesidio had not survived the huntsman's attack at the hospital camp. If not Praesidio, who would teach her the depth of Thaumaturgy she needed? But while she ruminated on these concerns, a pang of guilt prodded her. What were her worries as compared to those of an entire people who faced slaughter? Perhaps she should just be grateful the Tebalese had only occupied her homeland, not emptied it.

"Now, to see if this mechanism still works," Helvia said. She had cleared debris away from a large circular groove in the floor. In the center was a smaller circle, and between the two shapes, straight cuts rayed out like spokes, as if a giant wagon wheel had been carven into the floor.

As Danae inched closer, Helvia crouched and blew on the center circle. Grit tumbled away to reveal another carving. Lantern light flickered over the details, but Danae could not make sense of them as she blinked burning eyes.

Helvia pulled the chain from inside her collar once again and lifted Praesidio's talisman over her head. She set the medallion on the carvings in the center circle, then rotated the phoenix until it settled into depressions.

The floor shuddered beneath Danae's feet.

Helvia scuttled back. The stones between the two circles sank downward, each section farther down than the one before it. Before Danae's eyes, the circle carvings and rayed grooves became a set of spiral stairs that descended into blackness.

"What is this?" Danae cast a skeptical glance down the stairs.

"A passageway," Helvia said. "For the purpose of evacuating our king, should the need arise." She stepped down the first two stairs and retrieved the phoenix talisman from the center circle.

"So this is how we're getting into Bilearne." Danae unhooked the lantern. "I'll be relieved when I can deliver this wretched weapon and get to the next phase of my learning."

Helvia continued down. "Your fate, that of the Sword, and this whole war are a machine with many moving parts. I don't understand most of them or how they work together, but Creo's plan for all of it will grow clear over time."

Danae followed Helvia, a frown tugging at her lips. "Time is not my friend right now."

A sympathetic smile creased Helvia's cheeks. "Nor is it any mortal's, in truth."

The stairs ended at a three-way tunnel, all of them dark and riddled with cobwebs that shimmered in the lantern light. Barely two people could walk abreast in the passageways. Danae swallowed. The cool, dry air hung still.

"I've had just about my fill of tunnels on this adventure," she whispered. Dusty air tickled her nose, and she sneezed.

In the intersection between passages, Helvia pushed on an iron lever poking from the floor. Grinding stone shivered more silt from the walls. Between the bridge explosions and the shedding walls here, grit had settled into every crevice of Danae's clothing.

The stairs rose back to the surface and formed a grooved pillar behind them. The sense of confinement gripped Danae's gut.

"You know the way?" she asked.

"No." Helvia held up Praesidio's talisman. "But the talisman will show us." She scanned the narrow strips of wall between passageway entrances, stepped forward, and pressed the medallion to one of the walls. As it did in the center of the hidden staircase, the phoenix emblem clicked into depressions Danae had not spotted.

In the left-hand tunnel, a torch sprang to life with purple flame. Then another, farther down the passageway. Additional lights bloomed into view, and soon, the tunnel glowed with a soothing light.

"Our Thaumaturgy was greater in days of old," Helvia said. Eyes alight, she led the way into the tunnel.

And so it progressed with every intersection they encountered in a vast network of tunnels. As soon as Helvia illuminated the next path, the one behind them would wink out. Aside from the cobwebs and dust they stirred with their steps, the journey turned nearly pleasant. Along the arched passages,

Danae caught sight of swirling mosaics that depicted noble kings and queens, boats on a river, rolling countryside, birds, and beasts. They passed many doorways, always with lintel and posts that bore elaborate scrollwork and runes, but Helvia never stopped at any of them. Abundant beauty graced even something as mundane as an evacuation tunnel.

Although beautiful, the route stretched on and on. Danae's legs weighed heavier with each step, and she battled her eyes against closing. Just as she thought to suggest they take a respite, however, a murmur reached her ears. She stopped.

"Wait, do you hear that?" Danae strained her ears over the rustle and clink of Helvia's clothing and equipment.

Helvia turned back. "What?"

"Voices? Do I hear voices?"

Helvia chuckled. "Of course you do. We're headed into the city, after all."

The prospect of finally emerging from the tunnels breathed new determination into Danae's aching feet. Passageway by passageway, murmur grew to bustle, and then bustle to chatter. Open portcullises and iron gates stood at the entrance to every new hallway. Danae glimpsed barrels, sacks, and crates in many of the side passages, and sometimes open baskets of bread and produce.

They turned the corner to a much wider corridor, one that emptied into a room buzzing with activity. The mingled odors of blood, an acidic compound Danae could not place, honey, and mold caught her notice.

"The chambers ahead are what we call the Underkeep." Helvia yawned. "It sounds to me like my brethren have put them to use."

They reached the threshold of the chamber and found it lined with cots and pallets, every one of them filled with a battered soldier. Elgadrim women and men in yellow robes wove between the beds, sometimes examining wounds or administering water. Tables of bandages, metal knives, saws, scissors, and a hundred other supplies occupied every corner.

Helvia grabbed an empty sack from the floor nearby. "Let's just make your equipment a little less remarkable before we wade in here, what do you say?" She stepped behind Danae and tugged the sack over the jeweled pommel and ornate cross guard of the Sword.

Danae's nerves tightened and filled her limbs with jitters. "You mean there's some chance we're not even safe here?"

"Without Praesidio beside us, I think it's just best to take a wary approach," Helvia whispered, close to Danae's ear.

A short man with a bald head, his yellow robe splattered with blood both old and new, halted near the women.

"Mistress Alterreon!" he said, eyes wide. "I would have called for you ages ago had I known you were here. Creo's blessing be upon you this morning."

Helvia bowed her head and touched her fingertips to her chin. "May the healing of Laraniss be with you, Master Enyis. I have only just arrived."

"To our good fortune, then," the man said. "I greatly covet your counsel on a remedy, if you are not otherwise engaged."

"Not at all," Helvia said. She turned to Danae. "Just find a spot to settle down and rest. We'll address our next steps with regards to your . . . mission . . . as soon as possible."

Danae blinked dry eyes while the balding man bustled Helvia into the hubbub. She shuffled to a dim corner, mostly full of crates, sank down to the floor, and sighed. So she had made it to Bilearne, and yet her delivery of the Sword and saving knowledge for Papa seemed as far away as ever.

A distant boom rumbled through the floor. Maybe Danae was just as trapped as Papa was.

39

Danae Before the Council

*C*ulduin took a position along the woven wall of the personnel carrier and sat between two soldiers he had never met. Although the carrier held fifty of his warrior brethren, conversation was scant. Many of the soldiers busied themselves with mundane tasks, such as adjusting fletching, rewrapping sword grips, or tightening buckles and laces.

He drew a series of long breaths. The carrier looked much like a giant basket with a wood floor. *They have used these before. Of course the carrier is sturdy enough.* Still, tension knotted his shoulders.

About thirty paces to the right, an archery commander latched the gate to a second carrier, similarly full of soldiers. The elven Chancellor of War had determined that in addition to sending the Windrider Battalion and Formenar Legion to the Elgadrim's aid, that the Windriders would bear one hundred archers to bolster Bilearne's wall defense. And thus, Culduin received his wish to travel to the front lines, faster than he guessed possible.

A shadow passed over the open green where the carriers sat, and Culduin glanced up. Silhouetted against the morning sun, a winged shape banked and approached in a slow descent. In a gust of leathery wings, a sapphire-scaled dragon settled beside the assembled force. The beast's rider, a tall elf maid wearing a long blonde braid down her back, dismounted from the beast's dragon saddle. Her navy-blue plate armor gleamed, despite a few dents. She offered the soldiers a smile, then picked up the heavy rope attached to the side of the carrier. After dragging it to her mount, the sapphire dragon took the rope in its foretalons and clamped it to an iron ring on the underside of its barding.

The flitting glances many of the soldiers cast one another while this all progressed told Culduin that he was not the only warrior new to being airdropped into battle. He wet his parched throat with a stingy mouthful of water from his waterskin.

Over the next quarter hour, three more dragons and their riders arrived—a green dragon, an amethyst, and a black. The green dragon took up a position on the opposite side of the carrier Culduin rode in. The amethyst and black managed the second detachment of troops. Once the Windriders had affixed, checked, and rechecked all the lifting lines, they remounted.

"Grab your grips. Here we go!" the blonde rider yelled.

Culduin clamped his fists around rope handles that poked up from the floor on either side of him, as did all the other soldiers. The dragons jumped into the air and thrust their wings in synchronization. The carrier lurched upward. Culduin was not sure his insides came along with it.

In a series of nauseating surges and dips, the dragons bore the personnel carriers high over Delsinon, then continued to climb as the group headed north.

The soldier next to Culduin sat with his head between his knees and hands trembling.

"First time in the air?" Culduin asked, as much to distract himself from his own flipping stomach as to ease the elf beside him.

The soldier took off his steel helmet with one hand to reveal sweat-soaked brown hair. "Is it so apparent?"

"No shame," Culduin said. "I have flown before, but this is unexplainably more terrifying."

Once the dragons had gained an altitude where the spring air was downright cold, they leveled off and settled into a rhythm that diminished the carriers' bobbing. Only a day of this to endure before they plunged into the uncertain perils of war. If the Sword was indeed in Bilearne, Danae could not be far from it. Culduin uttered a silent prayer that despite the odds, he would find his way to her side once again.

A boom and rattle jarred Danae from a dead sleep. She sat up. Blinked. All around, cots bearing young men lined the fieldstone walls. Where had she ended up? Right, the underground keep, somewhere in Bilearne.

Men and women in yellow robes bustled between cots, just as they had been before she had settled her heavy head on her pack and sleep had taken her. For how long? Who could tell in this underground chamber, lit with lanterns and glowing orbs set into the walls?

Danae stretched her cramped neck and rubbed at a sore left shoulder. No matter how far she had traveled or in what dreadful places she had slept, it seemed her body would never learn to do without a mattress.

Helvia entered the chamber from around a corner, and she worked a pestle into a bronze mortar.

Danae staggered to her feet and found plenty more sore joints to add to her neck and shoulder. "Helvia, a question if you please?"

"Oh, you're awake." Helvia smiled. "I'm glad you got a chance to catch a bit of rest."

Danae picked up the Sword scabbard and lifted the strap over her head. "Who do you think is supposed to receive this? If Praesidio isn't here now, I think I had better proceed without him."

Helvia's smile dissolved. "Perhaps you should give him until morning to find his way to us."

Another boom vibrated the floor under Danae's feet. Dust and grit trickled down from cracks in the ceiling. A nervous flutter filled Danae's middle. "How long is that?"

"It is now about one hour until sunset."

Danae pursed her lips. Delay another half day? "No, I don't think I should. Who knows what turn things might take before then."

"Danae—"

"Really, Helvia," Danae said, her tone curter than she intended. "Where should I start?"

Helvia dropped her gaze to the mortar and pestle. "I am not well acquainted enough with your quest to counsel you, but for the tug in my heart. But if you insist upon seeking recipients for the Sword, I would start with the High Council's chamber. If you exit this complex, you will find it three blocks down the street, on the right. It has a long colonnade across the front."

Simple enough. "Perfect." Danae grabbed her pack from the floor. "I'll check back as soon as I've finished there to see if there's any news of Praesidio." She started for the stairs at the far end of the chamber.

"Be careful, Danae," Helvia said. "There's a war going on out there."

Danae nodded, then jogged up the wide flight of stairs she

assumed would bring her to the surface. She reached the top and found another wide, low chamber that ended in a set of gates comprised of vertical bars connected with scrollwork, iron leaves, and flowers. Two soldiers stood at their center. From beneath their brush-plumed helms, the soldiers cast Danae a quizzical look but then pulled open the gates enough for her to pass. The floor beyond the gates sloped upward. After a few dozen strides, Danae found daylight and open air, though the breeze smelled of smoke. Her eyes watered.

When Danae emerged from the Underkeep, she found a surface courtyard ringed by two-story walls, and upon the walls perched a panoply of gargoyles. Some had mannish features, while others more bestial, but all faced outward like an army of still sentries keeping watch over the courtyard. A set of gates that matched those she had passed underground offered the exit to the city of Bilearne.

Somewhere beyond the walls, gargoyles, and gates, the din of battle—the faint ringing of weapons, the boom of impacts against ground, wall, or architecture, and sometimes, a roaring chorus of voices—throbbed in the distance. Danae gripped the scabbard strap across her chest and forged toward the gate.

Once outside the courtyard, Danae marched along what appeared to be a residential district, full of two-storied struc-tures with pitched, tiled roofs, and arched glimpses into gardens full of greenery and fountains. The warm smells of roasted grain and grilling meat wafted on the spring breeze, at times overtaking the more sobering odors of conflict outside the city walls. After a couple of blocks, the structures shifted from homes and gardens to stately marble buildings with tall columns, friezes, and meticulously carved adornments. Bilearne was a place of symmetry and order, softened at times by water and bough.

The fourth block she reached offered just one, massive building, surrounded by the arched colonnade Helvia had told her to expect. Behind the arches, she found three separate sets of bronze doors, cast with square panels and heavy pull rings. Draperies shrouded tall windows between each set of doors. Danae sucked her teeth at the lack of opportunity to at least peek in a window in preparation.

Both the first and second set of doors Danae tried did not budge, even with a hard tug on their rings. When she reached the third set, she blew out a long breath.

Maybe they'll all be locked. If so, I guess I won't have to do this alone after all.

She pulled. The door swung open.

Pox.

Danae lifted her chin and stepped through the doorway.

Inside, she found a foyer that ran the length of the building, lit with hanging lamps that reflected from the polished marble floor. The ceiling loomed high above. Architectural details divided the ceiling into embellished squares. Along the right side of the foyer, many doors, much like the entry in design, stood shut. A pair of men in black tabards stood on either side of a wood lectern, about halfway down the foyer from where Danae entered. The soldiers stood at tall attention.

The door latched behind Danae with an echoing clack. She winced.

The soldiers turned their heads her way. They glanced at one another before one of the men approached her, halberd in hand. He spoke, but as usual, Danae could not understand.

"I'm sorry," she offered in the Western tongue. "I don't know your language."

The soldier placed a palm over his heart and made a small bow. "I beg your pardon, Mistress. I inquired what your business is here in the High Council Complex."

Danae's pulse picked up speed. "It's . . . complicated. I'm Protector Praesidio's student, and we were on a journey together. We've lost contact with one another, so I came here to seek guidance on how to complete our task." Has she said enough? Too much?

The soldier nodded. "I can present you to the members of the Council who are here, but I offer no guarantee of whether they will give you audience. Their minds are much burdened with the siege."

It was almost possible to forget that a siege plagued the city wall, here, deep in the untouched recesses of Bilearne.

Danae swallowed. "A presentation is all I can ask. I understand."

While the soldier led Danae though a set of doors and up a set of lushly carpeted stairs, she could only scoff at herself. *I understand. If that isn't the greatest overstatement of my entire life.*

At the top of the stairs, they reached a small, circular landing and another door, which the soldier opened for Danae. She stepped through, though her knees quaked with each step. Inside, she found a long chamber, once again with a slick marble floor. At the far end of the room, a dais rose to support an ornate throne, carven from white wood with the likeness of coiling vines and flowers spreading across the arms and back. Two smaller seats stood on either side of the throne, and behind these, the late afternoon sun gleamed through a dazzling stained glass window that depicted the familiar image of the spreading tree of Creo. The ceiling above the dais rose in a high dome.

Between the entry and the dais, two columns of upholstered benches flanked a central aisle. The soldier led Danae forward. From the frontmost bench on the left, a white-haired woman rose from where she sat with two men. She swept toward Danae and the soldier. Everyone's attention fixed on Danae. Her neck warmed.

The soldier and elder woman exchanged words while Danae tried not to fidget. The woman nodded, the soldier bowed, and he turned for the exit.

"Greetings." The woman focused her attention on Danae. "I

am Lady Hadriana. You are a companion of Protector Praesidio?"

Danae nodded. "Is he here?" She wriggled her tongue in a sand-dry mouth.

The other Elgadrim men broke off a quiet conversation and joined Hadriana. All three Elgadrim wore long robes—Hadriana's cascaded in shining plum folds. The men sported deep green and saffron.

Lady Hadriana gestured to the man in saffron. "This is Councilor Albin. In green, Councilor Gannaro."

Councilor Gannaro lifted his chin. "We have not had contact with Protector Praesidio in three days. I see our hope of news may be in vain." The wrinkles around his lips deepened.

"Have you spoken with him more recently than we?" Albin asked. His dark eyes glinted with a hard mixture of emotions Danae could not quite identify.

How long had it been since she had fled the field hospital? Two days, unless she had lost track of one in the blur of fear, flight, and exhaustion. Danae scanned the faces of the three Elgadrim dignitaries before her. Any confidence that had brought her before them evaporated.

"It's likely we both lost touch with him at a similar time," Danae said.

Gannaro eyed something over Danae's shoulder. She glanced back but caught sight of nothing notable in the room, still the empty rows of benches, columns, and tall doors.

Ah, the Sword. Her gut tightened at the thought of being the first to broach the subject.

"It is our understanding that Praesidio accomplished a task our people have been working toward for some time," Gannaro said. His steel-gray brows puckered, perhaps with worry. "Are you the acolyte he spoke of? The one who accompanied him on his most recent expedition?"

A spike of anxiety drove into Danae's heart. Why all the dancing around?

"Uh, I believe so? If the expedition you're speaking of led him to Garash."

The three Elgadrim exchanged glances.

Lady Hadriana blew out a stream of air. "For the Sword. Tell us, is that what you carry?"

Danae hesitated. Why had she come here alone? She should have waited longer for Praesidio.

"Mistress, you have nothing to fear from us." Albin placed a wrinkled hand on Danae's shoulder. "If you are indeed the bearer of this blade, you have come through great toil to bring it here, and we understand your reluctance to be plain. I will offer the first specifics, if that will help. Have you come to deliver Mystrin's Sword, for whatever reason Praesidio could not accompany you?"

A weight lifted from Danae's shoulders as the reality of her burden's identity emerged.

"Yes." She pulled the scabbard's shoulder strap over her head. After tugging the sack free of the pommel, she held the scabbard forward. "This is the Sword of the Patron."

The three elders fixed wide-eyed gazes on the Sword's beautiful hilt, from the clear gem set in the pommel to the jeweled and engraved cross guard.

"May I?" Lady Hadriana reached out her hands.

Reluctance tightened Danae's hands around the scabbard. She chastised herself. *What do I have to fear from Praesidio's people?* Archadion's harsh words echoed after the thought. *You believe you have something to offer the Creator of the Universe that he does not already possess?* Again, she rebuked the thoughts. *If I don't give it up, no Thaumaturgic teaching. That was the deal.*

She placed the scabbard in Lady Hadriana's hands. *I'm coming Papa. Soon.*

With reverent care, Lady Hadriana took the weapon, grasped the grip, and slid the blade halfway from the scabbard.

Wrath!

Danae quailed at the electrified pain that arced through her head.

Unworthy!

The raw fury of the Sword's voice pounded upon Danae's spirit. She covered her ears, but still, the fury raged on. But just as suddenly as it had begun, it ceased.

When she opened her eyes, all three Elgadrim elders surrounded her, close and with faces taut with dismay. Lady Hadriana had sheathed the blade again.

"Mistress, are you unwell?" Gannaro met her gaze.

Danae shivered. "The Sword. It has such a dark, hateful voice."

Albin took the scabbard from Lady Hadriana. "That settles it beyond doubt, does it not?"

"I'm sorry, settles what?" Danae asked.

"We thank you, Danae Baledric of Radromir," Albin said. "You have toiled and suffered to prevent great evil from exploiting a power no being but Mystrin himself was meant to wield." He beamed. "You have put an end to a great and grievous sacrilege."

Hadriana took Danae's hands. "You never need suffer the corruption of this weapon again. You have done well, and our words of thanks are but frail emissaries of our gratitude."

"We shall see this artifact secured." Gannaro came alongside Albin.

A ball of dread pummeled Danae's chest. Head spinning, Danae drew a long breath to prevent a thousand words from spilling from her lips in the wrong order. "So you're just going to . . . keep it here?"

Gannaro and Albin nodded. "Well, in the Temple of Creo,

but yes. The council reached this conclusion in our last communication with Praesidio."

Danae blinked. That did not sound like Praesidio's designs, as far as she could tell, but then again, how much of his mind was a mystery to her, even after months of travel and survival together?

"Again, our deepest thanks, and congratulations on this worthy accomplishment," Hadriana said.

The door at the rear of the chamber banged open.

Danae spun.

A trio of disheveled officers, led by Lord Sorex, marched down the center aisle. Splattered mud, soot, and grime marred their attire. Shadowed circles darkened Sorex's eyes.

"Members of the council," he said on his way to the front of the chamber, "I have come to order the evacuation of Bilearne."

The council members dropped their glances to the floor. Albin raised his eyes again first. "For what cause?"

Sorex stopped at his side. "The outer wall is breached."

40

Praesidio's Bond

*E*vacuate? Now? In that kind of chaos, I'll never find *Praesidio.* Danae could not draw a decent breath.

"Our troops are falling back to the second wall, even as we speak." Sorex's gaze swept the council members. "With your approval, I will dispatch heralds to inform the women, children, and infirm to proceed to the Underkeep and evacuate using the westward tunnel into the foothills. The Underkeep staff is prepared to outfit them with the preordained supplies."

Albin pursed his lips. "The perimeter of the secret stairs is secure?"

"As much as it may be," Sorex said. "Scouts and runners will prevent their discovery."

Danae's heart pounded. Sorex had been at one of the perimeter camps before. Or at least on that side of the conflict. "My lord, a question?"

The shouts of a multitude boomed somewhere beyond the Council Chamber walls, too close. Horn blasts followed.

Sorex squinted at Danae. "We've met, I believe?"

She met his gaze. "Yes! I helped Praesidio retrieve the Sword of the Patron. Have you seen him?"

Sorex's expression clouded. He waited several moments before speaking. "Last I knew, he was at the field hospital."

"Is he all right?" Danae grabbed Sorex's hands.

One of the officers who had entered with Sorex cleared his throat. Another nodded his head toward the door.

"Many pardons, Mistress, but I am needed elsewhere. I have no recent news of your mentor's . . . condition." Sorex withdrew on long strides. "All of you, hasten with evacuation preparations!"

Danae stared after Sorex and his companions.

More horn blasts rode above the roar of men.

Gannaro bowed to Danae. "As you have heard, Mistress, we must take your leave. May Creo shield you as you depart."

The elders turned, Sword in hand, for the front corner of the chamber, toward a door beside the dais.

"But—" Danae choked on her words.

Albin glanced back.

"Praesidio said I'd be able to learn Thaumaturgy in exchange for helping with the Sword," she finally managed to blurt. "I need to save my family! What about that?"

He lifted a shoulder. "What Praesidio has promised is his own bond."

Danae's heart galloped in her chest. "What if . . . maybe something has happened to him?"

Hadriana tilted her head. "I'm certain you must understand how we cannot have our attentions divided at such a time as this."

Jaw slack, Danae could find no counter.

"Creo keep you, young mistress," Gannaro said.

Albin opened the side door, and just like that, the elders and the Sword were gone.

41

In Search of a Surgeon

*C*ulduin ducked behind the pedestal of a fifteen-foot marble statue depicting High Philosopher Aeleronde the Fair. The ground rumbled beneath his feet, as though from the footfalls of gargantuan beasts. Had the enemy's fire giants proceeded so far into Bilearne already? The main gate had fallen less than a quarter hour past.

Corporal Malkendrik ducked alongside him, followed by Privates Aeralyn and Ralam.

"I hope their retreat to the inner wall remains tactical," Malkendrik said. "I should have stayed behind to help rally them."

Culduin sighed. "I expect your bardic inspiration will be applied soon enough. But for now, please lead the others to deliver our scouting report to the detachment."

"Without you?" Aeralyn lifted one blonde eyebrow. "With all due respect, Sergeant, what is your aim?"

"I have one more source I am hoping to find here within the

city walls, who should be able to give me some insight to fulfilling the Windrider phase of our operations." Culduin peeked around the pedestal's corner. "I cannot delay the scouting report by having all of us hunt for one or two individuals in all this mayhem."

Thunder rumbled in the leaden sky above. A few raindrops spattered the street.

Aeralyn drew the hood of her olive-green cloak. "Understood."

Malkendrik frowned. "I hope you will not leave the cover of the inner wall, sir. The outer city looked like a bloodbath."

Culduin's stomach twisted. Danae would not have found any reason to be on the battlefront, would she?

From down the street, the murmur of conversation and the shuffle of feet grew. Culduin and the three elves in his scouting company pressed their backs to the pedestal. He peered around the corner. A crowd of twenty or so women and children approached, many of their faces careworn. Some of the adults carried lit lanterns, which cast pools of warm light against the dusk.

"Malkendrik, what are they saying?" Culduin whispered.

After a period of narrow-eyed listening, Malkendric whispered back, "Their talk is mostly about the evacuation and someplace they are supposed to go called the Underkeep."

Culduin clenched his teeth. If the Elgadrim had called for an evacuation of the city, to whom would such an order apply? He had to start somewhere.

"Very well," he said. "Scouts, keep sharp. Maker willing, I will see you after this siege is repelled."

Once the three scouts had made a furtive departure, Culduin followed the cluster of Elgadrim at a distance. Wind gusted. Lightning flashed, and soon after, the rumble of thunder rolled in answer. All of Bilearne huddled in wait, with no hope of avoiding the wrath of the storm.

*D*anae gasped for breath. How could this be happening? All of this toil, risk, and time lost to the Elgadrim's indifference? She never should have left Praesidio when the huntsman appeared at the field hospital. But what good would she have done there—to be slain alongside him and the Sword truly lost? Perhaps if Culduin had still been with them. She chided the notion as foolishness.

With heat rising into her face, Danae spun on her heel and marched from the main council chamber. She forbade the tears that threatened to brim in her stinging eyes. By the time she reached the bottom of the stairs, her stomping strides had turned into a run, and she fled past the foyer guards and into the street. Cloud cover and twilight cloaked everything in a smoky pall.

Only after a block of blindly barreling down the street did Danae realize the sky poured sheets of rain upon her. Lightning flashed in a dark sky, and the thunder's peal came in an instant. As if mocking in response, a boom resounded somewhere in the distance, adding war's thunder to the atmosphere.

Danae skidded to a stop in the drenched street and threw her head back. "What now, Maker? I tried learning magic on my own, and look where that got me! Are my failures going to hunt me forever? Will I ever make a choice that doesn't end in disaster?" She swept rivulets of rain from her eyes, only to have them blur again.

Danae resumed her route toward the Underkeep, her steps weighed with grief and fear. Maybe she should backtrack through the tunnel and return to the field hospital. Someone there must know what had become of Praesidio. Without him, she was adrift.

The clank of metal caught her ear. Shouts. Not just the distant thrum of a multitude, but nearer. She pressed on but found more rumor of skirmishes on the wind, between thunder clashes.

The closer she got to the Underkeep, the more crowded the streets became, full of Bilearne's people. Women in graceful gowns that fastened at their throats, children in simple tunics or wraps, and the elderly hurried through the rain. When she had drawn within a block of the Underkeep gate, she found a great crowd converging outside the complex. Hundreds of people huddled under and around a canvas pavilion erected on the north side of the gate. Torches sputtered in sconces on the Underkeep's outer wall. The civilians must have been perched in wait for the order to leave the city.

Danae swiped at the streams of rainwater running down her cheeks. She shivered in the spring chill. Shouldering her way through the throng, she made her way to the gate, which was shut.

The guard spoke the expected gibberish. How weary she was growing of strange places and incomplete plans.

"I'm a guest of Helvia the chemist," she said, her tone weary.

The guard looked her up and down.

"Evacuees are to report to the pavilion for supplies," he said in the Western tongue.

"I'm not an evacuee," Danae said. "At least not yet. I'm not sure what I'm supposed to do. Please let me go to Helvia."

The guard pursed his lips. He glanced over his shoulder.

A rush of footfalls approached from Danae's left. She blinked rainwater from her eyes and turned.

Two soldiers, their tabards emblazoned with the Elgadrim heraldry, parted the crowd. They bore a stretcher, and the soldier they carried stained the canvas beneath him deep red. Trickles of bloodied storm water left a crimson trail behind them on the pavers. Sparing Danae no notice, they hastened for the gate. Another soldier with a wounded man slung over his shoulder followed shortly thereafter.

The gatekeeper opened the Underkeep entrance for those bearing the wounded, and Danae followed at a wary distance. The gatekeeper drew a breath as to speak, but then released it and waved her through with a look of resignation. When she passed the gates of the complex, she discovered a grisly transformation had overtaken the courtyard.

For as many wounded had occupied the Underkeep when she had left, four times as many dead and dying filled the courtyard. The soldiers she had tailed to this point fairly dumped their cargo and sprinted back out the gate. She wove between bodies, struggling to find a path to the stairs, so choked was the place with mangled soldiers. The stench of death hung over the dark courtyard like a low fog, and Danae's shoes stuck in thick puddles of coagulating blood. Even in the rain, crows perched on the outer wall, upon the gargoyles that studded it and leered at the world beyond. She tripped over a stiff arm in her path. She regained her feet but barely avoided sprawling into the carnage.

Danae clapped a hand over her mouth and squeezed her eyes shut against the scream rising in her soul. Just then, a firm clasp took her other hand.

"'I am greater than the world's horrors. I do not drowse, nor am I deaf to the cries of my children,'" a woman whispered.

Danae did not open her eyes, but she took a deep breath. Helvia. Thank the Maker for Helvia.

Unconsciously, she mouthed these words of encouragement, over and over, and soon, between the firm clasp of Helvia's hand and the timeless truth of Creo's proclamations, her panic drained away. Finally, she opened her eyes.

"I am relieved you've made it back here before the battle has found us," Helvia said.

Danae struggled to swallow. "How are there so many wounded?"

Helvia took Danae's arm and led her toward the Underkeep entrance. "Let's get you out of this rain."

Danae assented to Helvia's leading, which spared her the need to study the litter of wounded to find her way. Once under the cover of the entry, Danae swiped her cold sleeve across her face. "Things look so much worse than they did just an hour ago."

"They are." Helvia proceeded down the ramp and then through the inner gate. "Our army took heavy casualties when the outer gate fell. Between making space to move the evacuees through, covering the dead, and ordering those still awaiting treatment, our surgeons are buckling under the load."

Danae's stomach churned. How far away was the conflict? It had been no trick of Danae's ear that it seemed closer, more distinct. "Can your forces expect to hold this second wall?"

"The enemy is far more zealous than we expected." Helvia sighed. "Tomorrow brings a new dawn, though. I don't know what it will bring, but always, the rise of the sun is the herald of hope."

Inside the Underkeep, healers and their assistants dashed in all directions, piling blankets on the wounded and moving them from cots to stretchers. Numb, Danae drifted to a spot along the wall, beside the stairs. The ground shook. Silt rained down and stuck to her wet skin, clothes, and hair. Perhaps the council had ordered the evacuation too late, and the convoluted westward tunnel would simply collapse on all the powerless people just trying to flee. Or else, the Tebalese might pour in and cut them all down like rows of wheat.

Helvia stopped at a stack of crates and picked up an armload of bandages. "You should go, Danae. Nothing holds you here."

Danae turned hard eyes to her only companion through all the chaos. "Nothing waits for me beyond Bilearne's ruined walls. Everything I left home for dies if I go now. Praesidio promised me . . ." She swallowed the rest. It felt so childish, yet at the same time, it meant everything. "Are you leaving?"

Helvia shook her head. "More wounded will come. And someone I care about more than all of them is somewhere out there. I can't leave him, until I know for sure otherwise."

The crushing weight of loneliness bore down on Danae's shoulders like a rock slide. She squeezed her eyes shut, wishing all the uncertainty and fear of her circumstances away. If her fortune would not change, perhaps she could just shrink out of existence. The more she tried to act, the less she seemed to control. What hope was there?

Totally devoid of ideas or the energy to hunt for more, Danae placed her back to the wall. She slid to the floor and wrapped her arms around her knees. Under the guise of drooping her head, Danae quietly wept her eyes dry.

---

*T*he groan of the iron gate pulled Danae from a long stretch of numb silence. The drone of many voices filled the air. She rubbed blurry eyes and surveyed the Underkeep chamber, which she found no longer full of cots and pallets, but Elgadrim civilians shouldering burlap satchels. Many of the women, children, and aged members of the crowd had a haggard look, their faces smudged with soot. And some of them, blood.

Once the gate swung open, the crowd parted for four splendid knights arrayed in crimson tabards, gleaming helms with red horsetail plumes, and ankle-length capes. They tramped through, the light of broad day streaming in behind them and silhouetting the figures against the outside. Their tabards bore the same device as Praesidio's silver amulet: the rising phoenix wreathed in flame. No other wounded had entered the Underkeep with such ceremony. She craned to glimpse what they carried between them as they trundled down the stairs.

When the knights reached the bottom of the stairs, a rasping voice from upon the stretcher they bore grated out a few words.

"Stop. Take me . . . beside the gate."

The knights hesitated.

"Fools! Do I not seem urgent? Back up!"

The knights obeyed, and the few remaining medics clambered after them.

Danae peered into the stretcher and gasped.

"Praesidio!" she blurted. His face, ashen in color, gleamed with cold sweat, and his eyes were glassy. Angry, garnet slashes glistened through rents in his black-and-silver robe. The linen of the stretcher around him was saturated with red. "Somebody! Do you have any more clotting agent?"

An aged medic to the rear of the knights shook his head. "Not for days, miss."

Praesidio shifted onto one shoulder and grimaced. He caught Danae's gaze with eyes that struggled to maintain focus.

She wanted to pour out her woe about the council's claim on the Sword, to plead with Praesidio to still teach her, to share her fear and burdens, but as his life blood leeched away, she held her tongue.

"Danae . . . where is it?" His speech broke off as he reeled and coughed.

Danae froze. Shame at her hasty actions heated her cheeks.

"The Sword." Praesidio's bleeding chest heaved. Dark blood spilled from his mouth and stained his chin crimson.

Her eyes burned. "The council decided to—"

Praesidio groaned. "I know their position."

Danae surveyed his wounds. "Were you here fighting all this time?"

Praesidio shook his head, though weakly. "They brought me

here for better surgeons. The fiend . . ." His words petered to a gurgle.

"Praesidio?" Danae grabbed his shoulders.

The old man's eyelids fluttered. His breath came in rasps.

One of his stretcher bearers spoke up. "Mistress, we must deliver the Lord Protector to a surgeon with haste, lest we lose him."

Danae clapped her hands over her mouth. Her glance volleyed around the chamber, where she found none of the surgeons who had worked around the Underkeep before. "But who? Does any surgeon remain?"

The nearby medic sighed. "We have established a surgery ward, out of public sight, but they have their hands full. It may be some time."

"Time?" Danae's voice pitched higher. "I don't think he has much. He's a Knight of the Phoenix—doesn't that—"

The medic's and stretcher bearers' askance expressions silenced her.

"I can see to his wounds." The voice came from behind her.

Danae's heart wedged in her throat. This was no stranger who spoke—this was the voice that had coaxed her back from the grave, from drowning and crushed ribs and a concussion. His words came in lilting Elvish. She spun. Just a few paces behind her, she found Culduin, his features flawless, patient, and expectant.

"I have been a field surgeon for many decades," he continued.

Culduin wore a pristine suit of chain mail, a royal-blue tabard, and a set of silver shoulder cords. On his back, he carried a shield and bow. On his hip, a lithe scabbard and sword.

Her initial relief to have his help washed away ahead of a flood of worry. Culduin wore a soldier's uniform.

"What?" she stammered. "How are you here?"

Culduin dipped his head. "The story must wait. I am deeply

relieved to find you well." He redirected his attention to the medics. "Show me where I can work. Quickly."

"This way," the medic said. He led the stretcher bearers, followed by Culduin.

While Danae trailed after them, she berated herself for her failure of a greeting at Culduin's arrival. Would she ever learn to still her emotions before she opened her mouth?

The medic parted a way through the crowd and deeper into the Underkeep. He reached a doorway, where he placed his hand on a palm-sized rune graven into the right-hand post. The rune glowed yellow, and the oak door swung open.

Inside the chamber, row upon row of tables bore soldiers with the most grievous of wounds. White shrouds covered almost half the patients. In the corner, the chatter of metal teeth grated on bone. Although Danae could not see past the surgeon there, the mere sound of his work brought bile to her mouth. Three more yellow-robed surgeons stood over other tables, their arms and fronts splattered in layers of brown, red, and green.

The stretcher bearers found an empty table on the left of the room and worked to transfer Praesidio's limp form to it.

Culduin turned to Danae. "Ecleriast will be here, possibly within the hour. Where's the Sword?"

I wish people would stop asking me that. Clammy sweat broke out on Danae's lip and brow. "In the Temple of Creo, so I'm told," she said, her eyes downcast, as much to avoid Culduin's glance as to seal out the horrors of the surgery ward.

Culduin stepped up to the edge of Praesidio's table. "I had intended to help ensure the blade got into Ecleriast's hands, but if I go, Praesidio will die." He flashed Danae a sorrowful look. "He still may."

The noises of the surgery ward faded to murmurs, and the rumble of battle above came to Danae's ears as though through deep water. *He's dying. And for what? He saw something in me, but now he's torn to shreds from my defense. I owe it to him to make this right.*

Danae clenched her fists. "If anyone can save him, it's you, Culduin. I'll figure this out. I'll get the Sword to Ecleriast."

Grabbing a pair of shears from a side table of surgical tools, Culduin slid them under the soaked bandages across Praesidio's chest and snipped. "Hurry, Danae."

Danae turned for the door. She swallowed a hundred questions with each step. On her way out, she passed Helvia, who entered the surgery ward with a knit brow and tight lips.

Even if Praesidio did not survive, Danae could at least give his people the hope of Queldurik's destruction, whether it was a hope they wanted or not.

42

A New Bargain

Smoke poured from a district of Bilearne only a half-dozen blocks, at best, from where Danae emerged from the Underkeep. Armed only with daggers and directions to the temple, she steeled her resolve with deep breaths and a drive for haste over hiding. Glass smashed. Weapons clanged. Men and worse screamed in agony. Chills ran through her, her heart pounded, and sweat ran down her temples.

A huge shadow blotted the sun on the cobbles around her, and she quailed against a building, for worse than the shadow was the sizzling signature that accompanied its coming. With wide eyes, she watched a gargantuan creature fly overhead, and although she had never seen a dragon anywhere but her mind's eye, she harbored no doubt that the orange- and yellow-scaled, broad-winged monster above was indeed one of these legendary creatures. The dragon's rider leveled a lance as he flew into the distance, and the dragon folded its wings to dive steeply beyond sight.

Danae stole on. As she closed the distance between herself and the government district, she witnessed three smaller dragons wheel overhead, as well as a dozen other creatures she could not name. A wicked, man-faced, bat-winged beast with the body of a lion engaged one of these smaller dragons, lashing its barbed tail and swinging dagger-sized claws, and Danae only paused long enough to see the dragon rider run the abomination through with her lance. The creature's body crashed to the ground several blocks away.

She ran through the streets, closing her ears to the swordplay that encroached, ducking and dodging from one hiding place to the next.

Just as Danae stepped into the street to make the next dash, a group of a half-dozen Elgadrim civilians scuttled from a side street, their eyes fixed skyward and their faces drawn and pale. Three knights urged them along. Danae skidded to a stop. One of the knights met her gaze.

"Mistress!" Sir Lucius said. "Why are you in the streets? Peril closes in!"

Danae shook her head and strode forward. "No time to explain."

He caught her arm as she attempted to pass him by. Danae's chest tightened. *Didn't you hear me . . . ?*

"Knights, carry on," Lucius said to the Elgadrim group. "I must resume my shieldmaster duties."

The smash of stone upon stone split the air and sent a tremor through the street. One of the Elgadrim young ladies whimpered. Lucius's pair of companions nodded and jogged onward with the frightened group between them.

"Lucius, really." Danae tugged her arm free. "I have to go."

He matched her pace. "I can see that. I shall guard you along the way."

"You're not bound to me."

"Not formally. But the Code compels me to be sure you do

not face danger in these streets alone. Will you accept my protection?" He searched her face with an earnest glance.

She sighed. "I'll ask one better. Guide me to the Temple of Creo?"

Lucius smiled and drew his shield from his back. "I can do that."

After a handful more twists and turns through Bilearne's alleys and streets, they stopped beneath the portico of the city guard headquarters that overlooked the central plaza. Directly across the expanse, the Temple of Creo rose, a triumph of architectural wonder. Twin spires jutted toward the heavens on either side of concentric lancet arches, each arch graced with friezes of mythical beauty. Windows of stained glass marched down each side of the building, and flying buttresses arced outward between them. The buttresses connected to the greensward around the temple through massive sculptures of Creo's Patrons.

In the street beside the building, a man in deep-purple robes stood in the bed of a cart, rearranging the vehicle's contents. The gray draft horse hitched to the cart stood with its head high and nostrils flared.

Another purple-robed man emerged from the temple. He carried a silver case in his arms, which he handed to the man in the cart.

"We've a large job still ahead of us," the case deliverer said.

The other man nodded. His companion turned back to the temple.

Danae frowned. "What's happening?"

Lucius watched with pursed lips before replying. "The knighthood is probably evacuating relics in case the city falls."

Oh, great. Danae ground her teeth. How would she get the Sword out from under a couple of emergency curators?

"Will you talk to them and find out for sure? Maybe ask them if they've seen a big, black scabbard?"

Danae scanned her surroundings for alternate routes to the temple. No need to tell Lucius that she would make a search inside while he engaged the guards. The route across the plaza left Danae bereft of nooks to hide in.

"We can speak with them," Lucius said.

"Honestly, I'd rather let you do the talking," Danae said. "It's . . . awkward, being an outsider in times like this."

Lucius smiled, his eyes warm with sympathy. "I'm sure I'll just be a moment." He set out across the street toward the cart.

Though her racing pulse made her dizzy, she waited and watched. One of the men emerged from the temple, delivered an armload of . . . something . . . and retreated inside. Lucius reached the cart and exchanged words with the Elgadrim man there.

The next time the man doing all the heavy lifting emerged, Danae drew calming breaths. The temple door boomed shut, the goods bearer back within. The man in the cart rearranged the crates, boxes, and satchels, all the while conversing with Lucius.

After a quick fumble through her own bag, Danae produced her dilapidated copy of *the Tree*. She leafed through it quickly until she landed on the Lay of the Sojourners.

Enough bumbling around deaf, right? Under her breath, Danae pronounced the Utterance for the Virtus of the Sojourners, her focus flicking between the foreign words on the page and the men near the cart.

As she closed off the last syllable, a buzzing pressure swelled behind her eyes. It radiated out to her scalp until she was sure her hair must have been standing on end as though she had just rubbed a wool cloak over it.

". . . wouldn't mind your help, Sir Lucius." The soldier added another crate to the cart.

"It's about time we got a hand," the cart man said. "If they want the vault emptied, that's no small task."

The porter glared. His glance then flicked around the perimeter of the plaza, hot with suspicion. He shielded his mouth with his hand and spoke in a voice too low for Danae to hear.

Danae hugged her arms around her shoulders. Bounced on the balls of her feet. The foreboding sense of time running out bore down upon her like deep winter snows on the rooftops of the highlands. The men continued exchanging whispers peppered with knit eyebrows and shifting glances.

Enough fooling around. She dropped back to the rear of the guard headquarters and skirted the plaza under the cover of the nearest buildings until she reached the structure beside the temple and farthest from the cart. At last, Danae bolted toward the temple and bounded up the smooth stairs. She pulled on one of the high, gilded doors, and it swung easily for its grandiose size. Danae dove through the doors.

She paused only briefly in the narthex to catch her breath. No immediate sounds of intervention came from outside. She spared only slight notice to her surroundings. Pastoral frescoes graced the segmented ceiling, and while Danae longed for the artwork's tranquility, she uttered a prayer of thanks for her preservation as she sped beneath them.

Danae pressed onward to the main sanctuary, eerily quiet compared to the thrum of battle outside. The colored light that streamed through the stained glass on the south wall splashed across the altar platform and glinted from the golden candelabras flanking it. At the back of the platform, a set of spiral stairs wound to a landing and a door.

Where now? Am I on a fairy chase? Danae stilled, closed her eyes, and reached out with her mind in search of the Sword's slimy signature. A tingle of nervous perspiration wet her lip.

Indeed, ahead and above, she encountered a smoldering anger, couched in blackness and insult. She shuddered. Somebody left the Sword outside its scabbard, and for once, that was a good thing.

Danae brisked down the center aisle, between the empty rows of pews. She stepped quietly across the altar platform, then ascended the carpeted stairs. She placed her hand on the door handle and her ear to the dark wood panels.

Silence beyond.

A cry erupted in the street. Weapons clanged—close. Danae threw open the door.

Inside, a long, narrow room of shelves, cases, and pedestals sat in disarray, like some eccentric collector was halfway finished moving out without having bothered to pack up his belongings. At the farthest extent of the room, Praesidio's rude casket for the Sword occupied a pedestal far handsomer than its contents.

Danae ran for the casket and threw it open with an irreverent squeal of hinges.

Conquest! Wrath!

The Sword's fury, frantic and writhing, struck her with such force that she sprawled backward. The indignant fury boomed in her head.

Danae fought back waves of nausea as the voice of anarchy hammered upon her. It cried out for a worthy wielder, and its bloodlust was stark and horrifying. Shaking and sweating, Danae recovered her feet.

Outside, men's voices lifted in the tenor of panic. Someone screamed with the intonation Danae had grown to know as the cry of severe wounding.

"Creo, shield my heart and mind as I bear this blade one last time," she whispered, fixing her gaze on the rear wall of the vault, where a wooden frieze of the tree of Creo, full of leaves, stout of trunk, and deep of root, hung. "Silence this sinister voice."

You were not so unlike it, once.

Danae started.

Meant for my glory but steeped in Darkness.

She gasped. But her path now, though imperfect, sought light, rather than indulging ignorance.

"Thank you," she said. "Thank you for showing me. Thank you for using me, frail and petty as I am. Help me serve you and get this Sword to a worthy wielder of your choosing."

Danae lifted the Sword and slid it into the new, glittering, black scabbard that lay in the case with it. And in that moment, the blade went mute.

She bolted awkwardly through the door with the five-foot claymore in her arms, charged up the center aisle of the sanctuary, and dashed to temple doors. At the doorway, she skidded to a halt.

Behind the cart, one of the purple-robed Elgadrim, the one who had been carrying items from the vault, lay facedown in a pool of blood. The driver took a wide swing with a short sword but utterly missed his target.

A leering fiend, its eyes aglow with yellow-green light, stood beside the cart. Its signature stabbed into Danae, a horrifyingly familiar hailstorm of malice.

The driver staggered as though his limbs were too heavy for his strength. Blood painted half his face crimson, and he dragged his left leg at an awkward angle.

To the fiend's left, Lucius brought his shield around in a sweeping arc, and its edge slashed across the monster's ribs.

Danae froze. She hugged the Sword to her chest. Could not breathe.

The fiend roared at Lucius, yet without looking, clubbed the short swordsman with a fist. The man crumpled. He twitched on the pavement.

"Don't come out!" Lucius screamed.

The fiend raked both sets of hand claws downward. Lucius threw his shield in the path of the strike, but the claws cut deep rents in the metal. The knight's legs quaked beneath him. Closing his fists, the fiend wrenched Lucius's shield from his arm with an ugly snap.

Half kneeling, Lucius lunged with his sword, but what looked like a sure strike glanced off the fiend's abdomen.

Danae shook. She stared at the sword in her arms. She grasped its grip in her right palm.

"No, Mistress! Go back in—"

The fiend drew a curved stone dagger from his belt and arced it across Lucius's face in a single motion. The knight slumped.

Pounding heat rocked Danae's skull. She pulled the Sword from the scabbard.

Maggot! Worthless. Thief and deceiver.

No, it was wrong. She had grown so much over the seasons with Praesidio. Danae pushed its vile words from her mind. She squared her shoulders, lowered her chin, and glowered at the fiend.

"I'm done running from you," she said.

The fiend turned to face her. It licked a splatter of bright blood from a knuckle on its knife hand. A cold smile revealed his spiny teeth.

"Oh, my girl, don't be silly now," the fiend said. "I've seen you with knives. And you're not much better with spells. The explosives, now that was a nice trick, but not yours, of course. And now you're all alone."

Danae was sure her heart would explode. The world around her seemed hazy, but the fiend, too crisp, with edges of razor and flint.

"You've made your last mistake, coming here." Danae weighed the Sword in her hand and found it to be surprisingly light for a blade as tall as she was. She glanced at her boots and found her toes on the marble of the temple's doorstep, but her heels rooted on the tiles of the narthex.

Was she really going to charge out there and attack this fiend who had been following her since she had fled Garash? After he had just laid three Elgadrim knights to waste in the amount of time it took her to walk through the temple?

"You've proven your tenacity, Danae Baledric, and you know you're running out of time." The fiend blinked slowly, with feline assurance. "A shame you've allowed all these messy affairs that aren't your problem to interfere with what you're after."

Danae steeled herself against the thread of questions that unwound in the back of her mind. "I'm not interested in anything you have to say, murderer."

"It's really very simple. Give me the Sword, I call off the hunt, and your life goes on however you wish to order it. Aren't you tired of being hunted?"

Steel rang against steel, borne on the smoky wind.

"It seemed a lot more complicated the last time I was offered a deal by one of you deathmongers."

The fiend chuckled. "You've been dealing with scum, servants, and underlings until now. I have authority: the Sword in exchange for our sudden ignorance of you."

She took a step backward into the narthex. "Oh, that's all there is to it? All right, come get it." Danae lowered the blade into her left hand and held the sword level, in a posture of offering.

The fiend snarled. "Don't toy with me. You can't stay in that church forever."

And so that *was* what Lucius meant by telling her to stay inside. Poor Lucius, for his bravery and willingness, was he now just another victim in Darkness's path? She glanced to where he had fallen.

With slow, soundless fingers, he pressed a fold of his sash to the wound across his face. He wasn't dead. Yet.

Danae swallowed. *Focus.* "Your offer might be tempting if all I wanted in life was for you to leave me alone."

The shouts of men echoed against stone architecture. Battle's rumor crept closer to the plaza. The sunlight dimmed, a breeze wafted by, and the street brightened again. Danae dared not spare a glance anywhere but the fiend's contemptuous face.

While they stared one another down in a seeming stalemate, his knifing signature strengthened across her arms and back, but also, other sensations crept in. Buzzing, sizzling—not painful, but distracting.

Shouts erupted from her left, seemingly behind the guard headquarters. A woman and a tiny girl, tattered but in Elgadrim fashion, staggered into the plaza. The woman protected her head with one arm while clutching the little girl's hand with the other.

Behind them, two footmen followed, both clad in the paneled armor and skullcap helms common to the Tebalese. The leading soldier, shorter than his companion, carried a bullwhip.

"Lash 'em again," the second soldier bellowed.

The bullwhip wielder glanced over his shoulder.

"Do it!" came the command.

The girl shrieked and cowered against the woman. They stumbled and clutched one another.

The bullwhip soldier stopped, took a wide stance, and unfurled the whip. When he reached back, he lifted his chin, and sunlight fell upon his face. His teenaged, freckled face.

Shock punched all the air from Danae's lungs.

Tristan! Don't! her heart screamed, although her voice would not.

43

High Commander Vinyanel Ecleriast, Lord of the Windriders

$\mathcal{T}$ristan brought the whip down with whistling speed. Much of its length slapped across the woman's back, but the very tail curled around and caught the little girl across the cheek. She wailed.

Finally, Danae found her voice. "Stop it! Tristan, don't listen to him!"

His glance snapped to her. His eyes rounded. He shook his head. Then drew the whip high again. Blood ran in a stream down the little girl's face.

Danae charged into the street, past the fiend. "Don't be one of them!"

The whip whistled again. *Crack!* Screams.

"He'll do as we say," the second soldier snarled.

Stomach acid bubbled into Danae's throat. A full vomit threatened to follow. She reached for Tristan's whip arm.

"No, that's not true." Her voice came out as a rasp. She closed her fingers but grasped nothing. Tristan's arm misted from her touch.

His face twisted into sneer before he began to laugh. The soldier laughed. The fiend behind her joined them. Then the soldiers and the women turned to vapor and disappeared, leaving only the fiend's scornful guffaws.

Danae spun, horror and fury blurring her vision.

"You want so many things," the fiend said. "Which gives me so many ways to break your heart."

Danae clenched both fists around the Sword of the Patron. Her breath came in hissing gasps through her teeth.

The manic chills of warring signatures bathed Danae's body in a flood.

Explosions rocked the air in the distance, mingled with roars and many shrieks, much closer. Beneath the din of battle, the gusting of her breath, and the low chuckle of the fiend, the angry, disgusted voice of the Sword demanded bloodshed.

For the first time, Danae agreed with the voice, if the blood to be shed belonged to the monster before her.

The fiend wove his claws in an intricate pattern, and a cylinder of green light formed between his palms. "You choose the path of pain."

Danae screamed, wordless, and charged.

The fiend unleashed a bolt of green light from between his hands, and it struck Danae in the chest. Crushing agony threw her backward. She landed flat on her back with a gust of breath and a crack of ribs.

Before she could sit up, the tromp of footfalls closed in. The fiend loomed. Punched another green bolt toward her.

Danae rolled aside, vaguely aware of the pavers' explosion where the magic bolt hit. Fragments of pulverized pavement pelted the back of her head and neck.

She scrabbled on one hand and her feet to try to stand. She swept the Sword in a weak arc.

The fiend gathered more pulsing green light.

Danae got to one knee, and the sunlight dimmed. A shiver swept over her. The shadow did not simply pass but hovered over her and surrounded her in a chill pool of gray.

The fiend's gaze shot skyward, his eyes bulging. His magic winked out.

The hair on the back of Danae's neck stood on end, and she froze, daring not to look up.

Whoosh—a gust of wind knocked her prone. Immense pressure enveloped her, buffeting the breath from her lungs.

The fiend snarled as he tumbled back. He grabbed with claws and scratched with wings to regain some footing. Amidst the fallen Elgadrim knights, he finally recovered his stance.

Lightning for you, you monstrosity! Danae lifted a hand and pointed tense fingers at the fiend. She croaked the first words of the Utterance.

The fiend snarled in an expression of utter hatred. He leapt to the side and wrenched Lucius from the pavement, throwing the soldier over his shoulder.

Danae's words petered to a stammer.

With Lucius covering most of his back, the fiend retreated in a half-dozen bounds. His strafing signature dissipated with his departure. Two other pulsing, bright sensations remained.

Black haze at the edges of Danae's vision threatened to plunger her into unconsciousness.

"You there!"

This was not the voice of a simple man in the streets. The command in it grabbed her heart in a fist. She froze, clutching the sword beneath her.

The air around her undulated with the deep breaths of a massive creature. The clatter of metal impacted with pavement, and then footsteps advanced toward Danae, their rhythm slightly uneven.

Her stomach clenched, and had she eaten anything that day,

her gut would have ejected it all over the pavers. She cringed on the ground, opening only one of her eyes that she had squeezed shut.

What was I thinking? She shifted her body over the Sword.

"Girl, face me," the commanding voice barked. "Are not all civilians to be evacuated from this city? Or are you some rogue who would prey upon the misfortune of those who must leave all behind?"

Deep in Danae's core, beneath the rest of her ready to die of terror, something bristled. Prey on misfortune? No, that predator had turned tail and run, bearing Lucius as a shield for his cowardly retreat.

That tiny shard of bristling temper gave her the strength to rise and turn around. Before her, a dragon crouched low, its silver scales reflecting the sun like a million tiny mirrors. Its brilliant green eyes looked on as her temper melted and her knees knocked.

It cocked its head and adjusted the fold of its shimmering, white wings against its sides.

"Proceed gently, Vinyanel," the creature rumbled in a surprisingly serene voice, different from the first who had addressed her. "Can you not see the girl is nearly overcome with terror?"

As if the proximity of a seventy-five-foot dragon was not enough, its speech made her woozy, and lights began to dance in her vision. Its signature still pressed upon her like the inescapable weight of deep water.

In her panicked observation of the dragon, Danae completely missed the advance of the rider, who strode slowly toward her, removing his golden helm. A second signature, somehow sharp and bright, if something could feel bright, preceded him. She now saw the elf's face, obviously older than Culduin, but only more robust as the wages of additional years.

Platinum-blond, straight hair fell about his shoulders, and

his violet eyes pierced her to the core. His gaze seemed to perceive every thought she had ever entertained and every inkling she ever would. A slight bend at the bridge of his nose provided the only flaw in his long, noble features. Ebony plate mail covered him from head to toe, emblazoned with lacquered tooling on his gauntlets and the edges of his breastplate. On one leg, the armor bore a complicated network of rods and hinges.

Reaching his hand toward her, he too spoke, his baritone flowing like the waters of a deep yet swift river. "What do you carry, Mistress?" He nodded toward the glassy blade in Danae's arms. "I do not believe it is a burden meant for you."

Danae's tongue clung to the roof of her mouth. She swallowed but still could not speak. After another gulp, she finally croaked, "I don't believe I'm at liberty to say."

The elf huffed. "Do not toy with me. It is something I have come to acquire."

You and a whole evil army, then. Danae winced at her pert thought. She glanced at the weapon. "I'm about to give up the object of my last hope. The last thing I want to do is give it to the wrong person." *Again.*

The elf pressed his fingers to his temple. "Do you doubt that time is of the essence? I am High Commander Vinyanel Ecleriast, Lord of the Windriders. And that is the Sword of Creo's Patron, or I am a purple gnome."

Danae's mind reeled. How much she wanted to fling the Sword to this elf and be done with it. But she found mistrust protested in a louder voice than even weariness. "I probably seem silly to you," Danae replied. "If you'd come with me, I can be sure of what I'm to do."

The elf warrior narrowed his eyes. "Come with you where? The thread that binds the fate of the Elgadrim stretches thin indeed."

Anxiety clutched at Danae's already-frayed nerves. "I know. This would be an especially costly mistake, though." She knew whose opinion she could trust, but would she find him able to offer it by the time they arrived at the keep? "Please follow me."

After retrieving the Sword's scabbard from the temple entry, Danae resumed her course for the Underkeep on weak legs. By some miracle, the heavily armored elf and his mount came in tow. She led them through the streets, and though he walked with a limp, his strides pressed her to a near jog to stay ahead of him. When they arrived at the Underkeep, the people within parted like oil before a spray of water. Danae hustled ahead of the imposing elf warrior, down the stairs, to the surgical ward.

Culduin labored with a needle in his teeth and his hands working with metronomic precision at closing a wound on Praesidio's side. Praesidio was still breathing, though each gasp was shallow and labored. His face had gone from ashen to green.

"Praesidio?" she called gently.

Nothing.

Culduin shook his head but did not look up from his careful attention to the knight's plight.

Vinyanel threw his gauntleted hands into the air. "Woman, do I appear to have an overabundance of time? Surrender the Sword, or thousands more than this Elder Knight shall die because of your dalliance."

Danae closed her eyes and took a moment to listen to what Creo might say to her heart. *Please, Lord and Master Creo, don't let me be at the center of a misstep now. Show me what to do.* Nothing. Danae sensed nothing. She squeezed her eyes tighter. *Please! Help me.*

Culduin finally raised his gaze. His eyes bulged. "And here I thought you would only come back with the Sword."

"How bad are Praesidio's wounds? Do you know yet if he'll live?" Danae asked.

"Mistress, how distractible can you be?" Vinyanel thundered.

"I offer you one more instant to offer the Sword to me before I yank it from your hands."

Danae's whole body shook, and she clutched Praesidio's table to steady herself. "In the absence of Praesidio's opinion . . . Culduin, do you know this elf?"

Culduin laughed, and its sound was like bells at a summer's dawn. "This is none other than High Commander of the Windrider Battalion, Vinyanel Ecleriast, here to deprive Queldurik himself of his long-misused head."

Danae stood tall, defying the jelly that filled her legs, and extended the Sword to the black-armored elf. "Well, then. Sir, I pass this to you, although I'll warn you, not everyone agrees this is the right course."

"Where great power is concerned, myriad opinions tend to arise." Lord Ecleriast grasped the scabbard.

"You'll forgive my wariness, I hope." Danae released the Sword. "But you understand, the thing was too hard won to simply drop into the hands of the first elf who showed up on a dragon!"

A smirk creased Vinyanel's cheek. He clenched the Sword's hilt and drew it.

Instead of emitting the violent signature Danae braced herself for, the Sword shuddered. No sense of groping, slithering tentacles filled her awareness, but rather, a craven sense of dread.

Vinyanel resheathed the weapon. "Thank you. I did not come all this way to dull my blade on Queldurik's minions." The High Lord of the Windriders frowned at the scabbard. "Your days of abasement end today. You will serve Creo again, mark my words." He draped the strap across his body. After a slow and regal bow, he turned with a flourish of his sable cape and marched from the room.

Danae shot Culduin a glance, then followed Lord Ecleriast to the surface at a distance.

The High Lord of the Windriders placed his hand upon the waiting dragon's sleek silver hide. "Now the real test begins. Majestrin, we hunt Queldurik, Lord of Lies!" He bounded into his dragon's saddle, then settled his helm on his head. With a great thrust, the wyrm launched into the air, bending the trees of the courtyard and sending those soldiers who stood there to their knees. The Sword of the Patron, which Ecleriast held aloft, glinted multi-hued in the sunlight. The dragon pumped his wings and shot to the north.

Culduin stepped up behind Danae and rested his hands on her shoulders. "Much better in his hands than mine," he said.

An awkward moment stretched on. Danae's relief at Culduin's arrival in Bilearne warred with her lingering wariness over whether he really meant what he said about the Sword. She glanced back toward him. "I didn't know if we'd ever see each other again."

"I am grateful our paths have converged." Culduin's face was grave.

"How's Praesidio?" Danae searched Culduin's eyes.

"Still with us, for now." He stretched his shoulders. "I had to remove the lower lobe of one of his lungs, as mangled as it was. It's no wonder the Elgadrim surgeons could not stabilize him."

Danae's eyes widened. "That sounds really risky."

Culduin nodded. "The next couple of days will be crucial."

A trumpet, bright and clear, called in a fanfare, not far outside the Underkeep wall.

"I pray it is Creo's will we should see one another after today," Culduin said. "Will you please minister to Praesidio in my absence?"

"Absence?" Panic welled from Danae's core. "You're not going anywhere . . ."

The trumpet sounded again, and Culduin stripped off his bloodied top-layer tunic to reveal his blue tabard, emblazoned with the crossed sword and quill. The livery of the Delsin army.

"My division assembles." Culduin's eyes misted. "Thank the Maker you got back before the call." He picked up his sword and quiver from the ground beside his boot.

"You're going to fight? What?" Danae cried. "But—what if Praesidio . . . I . . ."

Culduin took a step back toward the courtyard exit. "I must. My brethren, none of whom have hunted the Sword, nor traveled as a companion to any Elgadrim, have agreed to lend their blades—maybe their lives—to the cause. Can I do less?" He clenched his teeth, and his cheeks flushed.

"You can't, not now." Danae's hand flew to her mouth, trembling. "Don't listen to me. Of course you have to. Go." She covered her face. "Go!"

"Promise me you'll remember me for who you knew me to be, when I was myself." Culduin did not wait for her reply, but his running footfalls receded as the trumpet broke out a third time.

44

Allies or Enemies?

Thunder rumbled, adding its voice of threat to the shouts of battle that drowned Bilearne's first bailey. Raindrops spattered Culduin's cheeks. Nonetheless, he stared down the shaft of his arrow, choosing a Tebalese target amidst the throngs of armored men hauling a wooden siege tower across the bailey, toward the city's inner wall.

"Loose!" he cried in the loudest voice he could muster.

Arrows flew from a hundred bows on either side of him to join his own in a storm of defense, down into the enemy lines below. Shields spared some of the assault, but dozens of soldiers dropped or reeled when arrowheads pierced them.

What a grim reality, the mounting death toll of war.

A swell of heat flared over Culduin from the left. He ducked behind the protection of the parapet while the armies of Quel-durik returned a volley of bolts and arrows. Culduin glanced aside and glimpsed a pillar of flame erupting from the siege tower that had ground closest to the inner wall. An orange-scaled, fire-breathing dragon sped away from the inferno, his elven rider hunkering low against him for cover.

Culduin sprang back to his gap, and the elves around him mirrored his motion, all fitting arrows to their strings and pulling back to their cheekbones.

"Loose!" The command rang again.

The cloud of arrows felled yet another wave of enemy soldiers, and immediately after, an emerald dragon made a low sweep, parallel to the wall. The gush of steaming acid that poured from his maw flooded a cohort of Queldurik's warriors. Those enemies on the fringes of the target area screamed in agony, splashed with the corrosive liquid but still living to suffer its devastation. In some cases, it was better to bear the brunt of an assault.

Yes, Queldurik's minions were quickly losing heart, though Culduin had to admit there was no pleasure in witnessing it. The sharp stench of melted armor, weapons, and flesh turned his stomach.

From the distance, a division of mercenaries from North Deklia churned through the breach in the outer wall like sand through the narrows of a glass. The enemies ushered in ladder after tall ladder, borne on the men's shoulders. Lightning flashed. For an instant, all stood in stark brilliance or shadow.

Culduin yelled, "Archers! Take down those ladders as soon as they are in range. Before, if possible." Already enough villains had slipped over the inner wall prior to the elves' arrival, and too many more risked danger to Bilearne's rich stores of knowledge, as well as to those citizens who had remained to assist the wounded in the Underkeep.

Citizens and travelers alike.

The thought squeezed Culduin's heart, but he shook it off and loaded two arrows to the string.

The groan and hiss of bellows, clouds of smoke, and shouts in the Elgadrim tongue rose from somewhere beneath Culduin, within the infrastructure of the wall. After a mighty cry, spouts midway up the wall erupted with smoking pitch. As far as Culduin could see, the mouths of gargoyles vomited boiling liquid down upon those nearest the wall. A great concentration of the assault fell upon a cluster of Tebalese men running a battering ram at the gate below and to Culduin's right; men, he noted, that only ran the ram at the suggestion of a fiend wielding a scourge.

Odd. He is one of the few fiends I have seen on the field, Culduin thought. *Are they holding them in reserve somewhere?*

Allied soldiers followed the dousing from the murder spouts with a volley of flaming arrows, and a channel of fire raced all along the wall. The smells of charring mixed with the already-nauseating stink of death seared Culduin's nose. What devastation men and elves had learned to wreak upon each other.

More arrows flew. Black barbs shot back, and the elf beside Culduin spun with a grunt as a shaft caught the soldier in the ribs. He wobbled with his back to the gap between parapets, then tipped backward.

Culduin shot a hand out to catch his comrade by the collar. He hauled on the fabric. The elf in his grasp winced but thankfully slumped down with his back securely against stone rather than air. The shaft had sunken deep, and likely well into the wounded elf's left lung.

"Medic!" Culduin scanned the wall for the one type of personnel he knew to be in perilously short supply.

"Cannot . . . breathe . . ." the soldier heaved, more air than voice.

Crouching beside him, Culduin placed a palm on the soldier's forehead. "I know. Try to stay calm." Upon a closer look, the soldier's smooth face and willowy build rumored his youth. His green eyes radiated fear. "Just sit tight. The medics will get you off the wall and to a safe place to treat you."

Culduin prayed the soldier would not look too closely along

the length of the parapet and notice just how many of his brethren shared his state. He lifted his eyes to the leaden heavens. The wind gusted and turned raindrops to needles.

So many wounded, and so much battle still to turn in the allies' favor.

Clink.

The ring of metal upon stone made Culduin jump. Similar peals tolled to his left and right. Grapples.

Culduin swore under his breath. What kind of throwing arm did they train into Tebalese soldiers for them to be able to land a grapple fifty feet up? He peered over the edge and found enemy soldiers maneuvering harpoon launchers into place at the foot of the wall. They loaded grapples, fitted with long ropes, into the mechanisms.

"Cut the ropes," Culduin ordered. He rose, pulled his shield from his back, and held it to his right. He dashed along the wall, repeating the order. *A pox upon the chaos of war. Swat one fly to be stung by a swarm.*

"Durik, you coward, come out!" The voice of Vinyanel Ecleriast echoed over the battlefield, shaking the very air with the miraculous amplification provided by the power of Creo. "Face me if you have the spine to do it. Or else we will run down every one of these subjects of yours until you alone stand like the naked traitor you are."

The silver dragon passed overhead, flying straight over the enemy forces, and the dark army scrambled to swap grapples for harpoons. A phalanx of dragons in green, orange, blue, copper, and opal followed in Majestrin's wake, and a line of armored griffons and winged lions brought up the rear. Even the elves, who had lived most of their lives in the company of such formations working maneuvers over Delsinon, paused in awestruck wonder. The winged warriors and their riders shot into the distance. At their head, the black-armored High Lord bore the heavenly claymore aloft.

For a fleeting moment, a wave of embarrassment swelled in Culduin's middle. How presumptuous he had been in entertaining the notion that he possessed the might to wield a weapon so far beyond his spiritual mettle.

Culduin buried the thought in favor of urgency and ran the wall. He drew his longsword and severed as many ropes as remained taut along its length. He stayed his blow at the sixth rope, however, for an Elgadrim soldier, pale and bearing an ugly gash across his head, struggled up the line. Once the man had pulled within arm's reach, Culduin extended a hand to assist him the rest of the distance.

The Elgadrim footman spoke no word but nodded and smiled—a rather cold, uncomfortable smile, as Culduin saw it, but then, what man's emotions ran as expected in such a situation? The footman swung his leg over the wall's summit. He wrenched a knife free of his belt.

And slashed at Culduin.

A bruising stroke ripped through Culduin's tabard and across his torso from his shoulder to his hip but failed to pierce his mail. Culduin whipped his sword around, scarcely in time to catch the footman's next lunge. Thunder pealed.

"What in the—" Culduin bit off his astonishment as he shoved the man back. He dodged the next attack, flipped his longsword in his grip, and drove the point into the Elgadrim soldier's back—or at least he would have, if the blade did not skitter aside as though he had stabbed stone. The stroke at least threw his opponent off balance. He staggered forward.

"Sergeant, here!" A wounded elf threw his own sword to Culduin. "It is blessed."

Culduin caught the sword in his shield hand, just in time to block another slash from the traitorous man. Bewildered, he switched the blessed blade to his sword hand. He swept it across his attacker's torso. This time, it opened a gash, but the flesh merely oozed thickened, clumpy blood.

Horror mounted. What devilry plagued this man? Another block, this time with his shield, then Culduin plunged forward. His blade pierced the enemy, straight through the face. The man slumped, and in a noisome cloud of ochre and black, a plume of mist rose from the man's mouth to ride away on the wall-top wind.

45

The Storm Strikes

*C*ulduin bent and braced his palms on his knees, quelling a wave of nausea that gripped him. The Elgadrim body that lay at his feet had the look of a corpse hours dead, pale and beyond bleeding.

War left him no time for reflection as Tebalese soldiers reached the top of three ropes. He parried their attacks. Fought with renewed vigor. He kicked two enemies back off the heights to their doom. Did Queldurik's army yet rue the day they assented to assault Bilearne?

A shimmering cloud of tiny lights blanketed the parapet, and Culduin pushed wet hair from his eyes to glance skyward. *What do they throw at us now?* High over the battle-field, High Lord Ecleriast and his silver dragon shot toward the battle that boiled inside Bilearne's gates. Battle fires glinted from the dragon's polished scales and sent thousands of motes of light to speckle everything below. Between slashes and parries, Culduin took grim satisfaction that the fight on the ground likely took a hefty tip in the allies' favor.

The silver dragon heaved a long gust from his maw, a white storm, that splashed against the throng of enemies bulling their way through the gatehouse. With a sizzling crack and a cloud of vapor arising, the dragon's breath enveloped the tower, its inhabitants, and scores of enemies outside. The wyrm sped past and banked, leaving behind a glittering ice sculpture of that moment in the battle.

Elgadrim and elves on the inner wall lifted their voices in a chorus of cheers.

Between thrusting back ladders the enemy propped against the inner wall, Culduin noted other flyers in the fray—dragons of every hue lanced through the falling rain, wreaking havoc with claw, tail, bite, and breath. The last of the enemy's siege towers toppled when Ecleriast's dragon clubbed it with his tail.

But still the enemy fought on. Throughout the bailey, still too many slashed with swords and axes. Not just men, but the goblinoid horrors of the deepest woods and caverns, plus the cursed dragon-kin throwing spells and commands.

Lightning struck with a sizzling boom, too close to the outer wall. The wind buffeted the battlement, and Culduin grabbed the wall to keep his feet. Another grapple, another rope cut. Higher winds roared. Rain pelted. Soldiers to Culduin's right shouted and pointed into the clouds.

At first, he thought they all referred to the phalanx of Windriders as they flew in magnificent formation.

"The storm! What devilry?" a soldier nearby yelled.

And then he saw it. The dark clouds above swirled with the wind. Debris strafed those on the wall as it, too, kicked up in the tumult.

Flash! *Boom.*

Faster than nature could have ever devised, a funnel of cloud stabbed down from the heavens, directly in the Windriders' path. The maelstrom, crackling with purple energy, sucked in dragons, griffons, rocs, hippogriffs, and their riders, and flung them through the sky.

The spinning torrent grabbed the emerald dragon from the air and flung him straight for the inner wall. Culduin's detachment, transfixed before, dissolved into chaos. Before Culduin could so much as duck, the dragon crashed into the wall. Rock exploded. The battlement beneath Culduin's feet gave way. He tumbled, followed by an avalanche of collapsing stone.

46

The Heart of the Battle

*A*nother handful of bloodied soldiers jogged into the Underkeep, the stretchers they carried between them heavy laden with the grievously wounded. Danae dropped her bandage scrubbing in a bucket of water and dashed to them. She searched each face of the newcomers. Two of the stretchers bore elves. Neither of them did she know.

The day after Culduin had answered the call to arms crawled by with agonizing sluggishness. She shuffled back to her cleaning. Could the rumors be true that Queldurik's priests found a way to throw the Windriders from the sky? After the thunderstorm with its freakish lightning and stories of spinning clouds that destroyed all in their path, Danae wondered how much of the city above remained on its foundations.

She looked down the row of cots, over a half-dozen soldiers, to where Praesidio . . . remained. Helvia laid a clean, wet cloth on his sweaty forehead. Since his surgery with Culduin, Praesidio had not so much as fluttered open an eyelid. Nothing but pallor and sudden spikes in temperature where perspiration rolled down his temples.

For the moment, the steady stream of wounded flowing through the Underkeep gates seemed to have slowed. Helvia approached with yet another load of bloodied bindings. How many times could they reuse what they could glean from soldiers who had succumbed to their wounds before they risked infecting new patients? Risk or no, reuse was all that remained to them, or else see the new wounded bleed to death. Danae took Helvia's basket with sluggish arms.

"You seem deeply weary." Helvia stepped up beside Danae at the basin and began to scrub. "Body and spirit."

"No wearier than the next worker," Danae said. At least she had Helvia to talk to through all the chaos.

"That, my dear Danae, is nothing short of a bald lie."

Or maybe talking with Helvia was not so great an idea. Danae dumped the new load into the water. She squinted back through the dimness toward where Praesidio lay, fighting to make out if his chest still rose and fell, or if he, too, had fought the final battle.

"There's just no end to the work, and so little of it turns out well," Danae said.

Helvia regarded Danae with a long, discomfiting gaze. "Your avoidance of your fears will devour your soul, you know."

"My fears?" Danae clutched the edge of the basin. "How would *you* confront the fact that you've killed the only two people you know who ever tried to help you?"

Helvia clasped Danae's free hand.

"So quickly you choose despair. The one you know of still draws breath."

"But for how long? And the other? You've heard the reports. The magnitude of the destruction. They may never identify half the dead before they burn them to stave off plague. So many of the elves they bring in are from the Formenar legion. Each hour that passes . . ." Danae struggled against a rise of emotion. "I get surer any news that comes won't be good."

"If he did die," Helvia said, "he died well."

Danae sucked in a breath and choked on it. "But it isn't fair. There was more . . . more I needed to say. There wasn't time."

"You've forgiven him, then?"

Danae gaped. "What? Forgiven? What do you—"

"I have ears in places you don't yet understand." Helvia added more soap powder to the wash. "Despite what's happened to your friend, your heart will only heal if you truly release your claim to your wound. Are you ready to do that?"

Working a stained bandage in white knuckles, Danae spoke through a constricted throat. "I want to be."

"Why do you hold on to the fear of what might have happened and let it blacken all that actually did?"

Danae began a sentence but abandoned it just a few words in.

"Danae, does one bruised apple ruin the whole bushel?"

"If you leave it there too long," Danae whispered.

Helvia lifted one chocolate-brown brow. Somehow, the expression seemed oddly familiar. "Ask yourself who leaves it there, then. Embrace truth. Reject fear. Linger in gratefulness."

A quiet moment passed, where Danae gazed again upon Praesidio, then beyond him. "Well, Helvia, you're right, of course. How are you always right?"

"I've had an excellent teacher. And I've spent more time in *The Tree* than you've been alive." Helvia wrung out her bandage and hung it on the drying line. "I pray you should have the chance to amend affairs to your liking. After you forgive your friend, if things don't turn out how you'd hoped, I pray you'll extend that forgiveness to yourself next."

Helvia's words echoed in Danae's mind long after their conversation ended. How they rankled her spirit! Culduin's crazed intentions had not been his own that fearful day in the Elgadrim village. If he had been guilty of anything, it was merely weakness in resisting the Sword's overtures, and had not they both faltered under the weight of that test? The Sword spoke to his inner craving for power and significance. Was that any greater sin than the despair it stoked to irrationality in her?

If Danae were to be honest with herself, there was very little for her to forgive. What vicious brand of cruelty had she subjected Culduin to in sending him away after all he had sacrificed? He could have left her to freeze or drown or die of infection the afternoon he found her on the flooded banks of the Nuruhain. His generosity in the months since then had only grown.

The greater measure of forgiveness was hers to seek—was there any chance Culduin would not offer it?

"Mistress," a soldier rasped. "Can I get some water?"

Danae turned to the soldier, a blond man with a bandage around his head and ear. Her breath caught in her throat. "Maker's . . . Lucius! You're alive!"

He pried his swollen eyes open. His mouth turned up in a crooked smile. "I guess so. It's hard to tell at times." Aside from bruises and the edges of cuts his bandages did not cover, his skin seemed deathly pale.

Danae put a palm against her brow. "What happened after the fiend picked you up? How did you get here?"

Lucius shrugged. "So there really was a fiend? I did not trust my memory on the events of that day."

At the end of the row, Danae found the water bucket and the dipper. She drew a portion of water and brought it back to him. "Can you sit up at all?"

"No, I'm afraid not." He lifted a wad of rag in a bruised hand.

"They've just been wetting a cloth and trickling water into my mouth so far."

"Is there anything I can do for your wounds?"

Lucius sighed. "Only if you're a master healer. Apparently I have a broken piece of a blade in my skull, and the surgeons are mostly agreed I'm better with it in my head than out. That happened in the fiend battle, maybe?"

Danae soaked the cloth in water and trickled a small amount between Lucius's cracked lips. "Well, he did cut you across the head."

Lucius swallowed with difficulty but smiled once again. "I'm glad you came out all right. Lucky Ecleriast came along." His mouth twitched.

"It was a surreal business to be mixed up in, no matter what." Danae sat on the stool beside his cot. "I'm glad that part is over with." At least, it was easier to feign relief until some Elgadrim official declared her unworthy of Thaumaturgy training for her flagrant regifting of a holy relic. She drew and released a long breath, but failed to dismiss the sick flutter in her gut.

Lucius's expression sobered. "What will you do from here?"

Danae propped her chin on her hand. "Go home. Eventually. If the battle here is indeed over. What about you?"

"If my liege is willing, I will return to his service as a warrior while battles remain to fight," Lucius said. "But I suspect, until I am fully healed, I will return to the library as an archivist."

Danae brightened. "Archivist? The legendary library here is what convinced me to leave my home in the first place. Keeping track of all that must be a job for a veritable army."

"Never ending, that's for sure. We Elgadrim seem to have a chronic case of bibliophilia."

Danae snickered. "I know it's odd to say so, but it's good to see a familiar face down here. You should rest for now, but maybe I can come back later to talk."

"I'd like that," Lucius said.

---

*C*ulduin Caranedhel forced his eyelids to part, but at first, he beheld nothing but white haze. Beyond the shrill ringing in his ears, groans and cries rode a hissing wind. His own head shrieked with pain. Edges of broken stone bit into his sides, shoulder, and hip, and he was vaguely conscious of a stream of blood running from his nostrils and across his cheek.

The clang of weapon against weapon rang clarion in the distance. Goosebumps swarmed over his flesh. He knew the ring of that blade, the blade he had felt buzz in his grip as he fought for his own life in the gladiator ring. Had he been felled in a combat round of a tournament? Property of a spiteful mermaid?

No. His senses returned in full. The haze retreated from his vision, and he found himself sprawled on a pile of rubble that was, last he knew, Bilearne's inner wall. Beside the toppled stonework, a green dragon lay in a twisted pile. Soldiers all around him, both Elgadrim and elf, bled. Few moved at all.

Culduin sat up, battered, but surprisingly unscathed for having suffered the collision and maelstrom that faded back into memory. Only a light drizzle remained of the lashing thunderstorm. Some devilry of Queldurik's had leveled friend and foe in a twisted path around him; the fearful, whirling funnels of cloud had thrown the Windrider Battalion against walls, towers, and the ground, and had left staggering destruction in their wake.

Clang!

Swords rang again, oddly singular for a battlefield.

Amidst pain in every conceivable place, Culduin struggled to his feet and peered into the distance. One of the swaths of destruction led to a wide space, where Lord Vinyanel Ecleriast held Queldurik, false god and demon commander, in a bind, mace haft to hilt. In the farther distance, Ecleriast's silver dragon stretched on the ground, motionless. A griffon and its rider lay beside the dragon, as did a roc, whose rider Culduin did not see.

Ecleriast and Queldurik strove against one another, with Ecleriast's superiority in strength pushing his opponent to his knee.

"Legions, to me!" Queldurik roared.

From the eastern perimeter of the clearing, dark figures stirred among the stones. Fiends, taut skinned and leering, emerged like slithering scavengers. They pressed toward the melee.

Culduin broke into a limping jog toward Ecleriast. Even one of his legendary prowess could not stand long against both Queldurik and a detachment of underworld apparitions.

Ecleriast threw his offhand around in an arc, toward the approaching fiends, and a spray of golden shimmer flew across the field of contest.

"Creo turn you!" Ecleriast cried. "Return to the depths."

The fiends quailed, and a half dozen burst to ashes in the cast of the golden light. The larger, more gnarled, and vicious only hesitated, however, before resuming their approach. Before Ecleriast could clap his hand back onto his sword grip, Queldurik recovered a two-footed stance.

"I must be mad," Culduin muttered to himself. He drew his bow and fitted arrows to the string. He took aim and loosed the arrows at the frontmost fiends of those closing in on Ecleriast. At least he had the high ground—that was, until the fiends put wings into motion.

His arrows struck both targets, one in the eye, the other in the chest.

And bounced off.

"*Cha-thrath*," Culduin said. Mundane arrows would serve no

purpose against fiends, of course, except to draw their snarling attention. The leading fiend turned his path toward him and waved a companion to follow.

Culduin reached back and exchanged his bow for the sword a wounded comrade had offered him on the wall—a blessed weapon. Only this of all his arsenal had any might against the creations of Darkness.

The peal of steel on stone and a sharp blow to Culduin's shin jarred his attention. A glance down revealed an eight pointed-throwing star by his foot, though terrain and leather had thankfully spared him a gouging. No time to seek the thrower. Cover was his chief need. *I must have hit my head harder than I thought . . . shooting useless arrows in the open?*

New mounds of debris were in abundant supply, so Culduin dodged the next star that sailed in. Around the opposite side of the ruin he chose, he leapt atop a fallen column. Some cover, some advantage. It seemed the best he would do in the face of the two fiends barreling in. He weighed the unfamiliar sword in his hand and adjusted his grip.

Before Culduin could again mark their position, the two fiends wheeled around Culduin's cover from either side and came at him from both right and left. They raked with blood-stained claws. One assault Culduin deflected; the second slashed his chain shirt and opened a roaring wound on his ribs.

Curse the greater pain of wounds dealt by the damned.

Culduin spun with the blow and used the momentum to bring his blade around. The bright silver length of the sword slashed across the fiend's neck and shoulder and flung tarry ichor into the air. He caught the next swipe from his other opponent on his bracer.

Still, the crystalline ring of the Sword of the Patron under-scored Culduin's lesser fight. Grunts and shouts from Ecleriast's battle told him nothing of who held the advantage. Culduin kicked the wounded fiend back, slashed at the other, opened a superficial wound.

Ecleriast cannot fail. The Sword will not be lost to us again. Our only hope is in that contest!

One of Culduin's combatants dove in and clamped long, needling teeth onto his thigh, and the bite burned like boiling oil. All he could envision was the beast taking a meaty chunk out of his leg. He flipped his sword in his grip and drove it downward, into the base of the fiend's neck. Even as claws raked Culduin's face from one side, the fiend on the other slumped, released his leg, and collapsed into an ochre pile of stinking ash.

Culduin stumbled from the slash to his face, his own blood blinding his right eye. He barely parried the next flurry of claws from the remaining fiend. A great shape swooped toward him from his blind side—perfect, more fiends to make short work of his attempted heroics. He should have just lain in the rubble, waiting for healers.

A strong grip on the back of Culduin's tabard and chainmail wrenched him skyward. The fiend's final attack clipped his boot but made no rent. The flap of huge wings buffeted the air. He surged higher.

Culduin strained to cast his glance to his captor, who he could only assume was planning on amusing its fiendish self by dropping him from a height and watching his body break on the ruinous remains of Bilearne's noble architecture. The emerging sun glared in his one good eye. He slashed clumsily.

The beast caught the blade in a talon—a reptilian talon, not a twisted, black hand like the fiends had.

"Hey now, none of that. You're one of ours, aren't you?" The creature's voice was feminine. Young.

"Who . . . who are you?" Culduin asked, his voice coming out in a dry croak.

"Oh, now I see. You're not our battalion. No matter, Windrider or not, my master could use a hand."

Culduin wiped blood from his eye with his tabard's shoulder. Seeing clearer, he discovered his bearer was certainly no fiend, but a pearly-scaled dragon, probably a youth, judging by her size.

"Your master," he said. "You mean your rider? What can I do?"

The dragon laughed, oddly cheerful on the field of battle. "No, I don't have a rider. Vin won't allow it yet, the curmudgeon. I need you to help *him*."

"So we meet again, Iriscendra," Culduin said. "It's no blow to the head making me think I knew your voice."

She wheeled in the air, and Culduin once again caught sight of the conflict between Queldurik and Ecleriast. For every blow Ecleriast dealt Queldurik, he fended off three attacks from a swarm of fiends behind him. Piles of ash mounded around his feet. The Sword made short work of such minions. Those the Sword did not defeat faced bursts of magic from Ecleriast's shield hand.

Culduin chided himself. *In Ecleriast's hands*, the Sword made short work of such minions. The Lord of the Windriders wielded the supernatural claymore with a graceful speed Culduin could only attain in his wildest imaginings.

Even with the lithe quickness bought over five centuries of training, Ecleriast had taken a beating, and Queldurik continued to dish out brutality with his flail. The undying man, swathed in green, black, and gold, brought the weapon around with a mad cackle, and the spiked ball caught Ecleriast in the side of the leg. He staggered.

"Fool," Quedurik said, his voice augmented to an eerie echo. "You're nothing but a lame nag, past your time in the service of war, but too stupid to go to pasture."

"Great irony," Ecleriast shot back, "coming from a man who

only remains undying as long as his thralldom suits the Darkness's purpose." He cleft through two fiends in one stroke, but Queldurik deflected the blade with a nebulous orb of energy that surrounded his left forearm.

Culduin called above the wind of his flight. "Iriscendra, you saw me against only two fiends, who likely would have torn me to bits had you not come to my rescue. I will be shredded to a mist if I enter that melee."

"Don't be silly. I know that," Iriscendra said.

Culduin huffed. "No gentle lies from you, I see."

She laughed again. "Elves and their delicate feelings. But do you see that weird Curse Shield Queldurik has? We have to get rid of it."

"Again," Culduin said, "what use am I, if Ecleriast has not found a way?"

"He can't break it because somewhere around here, there's a priest of Darkness keeping the Curse going. Don't tell me you're no good at fighting priests."

They circled the battlefield, and Culduin alternately scanned the perimeter and kept stock of the fight. Those soldiers of the Allied army that remained after the blast appeared to be assembling inside the remains of the second wall. Far too few ranks and files.

"Still begging your pardon, but you're a dragon. Why do you need me?" Culduin asked.

"Vin made me promise no fighting. Still too young, he says. He almost didn't let me come at all. And the rest of the Windrider battalion, the ones Queldurik didn't mow down with those winds, are in the city driving out enemies who got inside."

Culduin bit his lip. Of course enemies would have plunged deeper into the city once the inner wall fell. But how far had they pressed? Had they reached the Underkeep?

The dragon circled closer to Queldurik and Ecleriast, and she took a long draught of air during the pass. "Ah, there it is."

She banked hard, and Culduin's stomach lurched. "There's what?"

"The Curse Path." She glided down until her claws met stone, and she released Culduin. "Whoever's making that shield is somewhere over this way. Follow me."

They circled wide of the position Iriscendra thought they would find the Curse Bearer aiding Queldurik. The battle around the field perimeter was regaining consciousness, one squadron at a time, as what men, elves, and monsters left battle worthy regrouped. A pang of guilt clutched at Culduin—did he even have a squadron to reassemble? Were greener soldiers panicking as commands shuffled and reassigned what fighters remained?

They darted from one mound of masonry to the next. The stuffy sound in Culduin's ears lifted further, and distant clatter of swords, shouts, and hooves added a chaotic underscore to his mission. The dragon led him to a three-walled, roofless shell, where Culduin leaned a palm against the wall to heave for breath. Each gulp sent shafts of pain through his side.

"Wait here," the dragon said. "I'll scout ahead."

Culduin nodded.

After waiting a short span in the wreckage of what had probably been a home, Culduin spotted the young dragon slinking back toward him through the rubble-strewn street. She peered through window frames and behind chunks of masonry. Culduin poked his head through a ragged opening in the wall of his hiding place and caught her eye.

"I found the Curse Bearer!" she whispered.

"That was fast. Faster than you seemed able to find me again."

"Everything looks the same type of wrecked around here. And you don't have magic spraying out of you all over the place to help me sniff you out."

Culduin furrowed his brow. So this young wyrm must have

an ability like Danae's—the sensor ability Praesidio had sought to train her to master.

Danae.

Had the battle found her by now?

"Master elf?" Iriscendra said.

Culduin shook off his wandering contemplation. "Sorry. I am apparently still rather jangled. The Curse Bearer?"

"A man, I think," Iriscendra answered. "But wearing a metal skull mask and red robes, so I couldn't be sure. Also, very spiky armor. He looks like an evil dragon fruit."

Culduin stifled a laugh. The battlefield took a different cast through the eyes of a nearly invincible reptilian youth. He cleared his throat. "An Inquisitor then."

"This way. We need to hurry."

Culduin forced his limbs back into motion. Stealing along after even a short respite reawakened the searing pain in his wounds. "You are certain you are forbidden to fight?"

Iriscendra pressed on through the rubble without offering a response. She slowed to a crawl, then pointed with her snout to a low building ahead, mostly intact, that faced the clearing where Ecleriast and Queldurik labored on in combat.

Through a chink torn from the wood door on the rear of the building, Culduin caught limited sight of the Inquisitor inside, whose back was to him. The red-robed priest of Queldurik held aloft a thick scroll that he unrolled a few lines at a time. As he read the arcane characters on the vellum, they glowed momentarily, then vanished from the surface. A length of blank, unrolled vellum piled on the priest's feet, yet the scroll had many more turns of the roll remaining.

Culduin eyed the flanged mace on the Inquisitor's belt, then surveyed the man's apparent lack of wounds. In Culduin's current state, he would enter a fight with this priest at an immediate disadvantage.

But to end the Curse, perhaps no attack was needed.

Culduin crouched and rummaged his pack as silently as haste would allow. He withdrew gauze and two flasks of lamp oil, along with twine. He wrapped two arrow tips with the gauze, secured them with the twine, and shoved them into a flask of lamp oil.

"We are going to need an extra measure of assurance," he whispered to Iriscendra. "I need you to splash my second flask of oil on the scroll."

"But I . . ." The dragon's protest shifted to a smirk. "Splashing isn't fighting. And I bet that Curse Bearer won't break his chant over a little splash."

"You have the idea. I will stay here, at the ready."

The dragon took Culduin's oil flask in her foretalon and slipped around the corner of the building, a sparkle of mischief in her blue eyes. Culduin lit his first arrow. *Do not dally, young one.*

His view through the chink in the door had its limits, but it offered enough for him to catch sight of a flurry, where the Inquisitor twisted, and the cadence of his Curse took on a perturbed note. Culduin nocked the lit arrow. Took aim. Released.

The arrow sailed through the chink and struck just below the rolled portion of the scroll. Culduin's arrow tip punched through the vellum and pinned it to the column the Inquisitor had been using for cover while keeping stock of the battlefield. Without waiting, Culduin grabbed his flint and steel to strike a spark for the second arrow.

The Inquisitor spun toward the back of his shelter. *"Hagran necturu!"* His voice echoed from behind the steel bones of his mask.

Culduin struck the flint again—of all times for the spark to take multiple strikes!

The Inquisitor yanked his mace from his belt. *"Dankerra stro-vuqe. Obcha."*

"So he is rankled. Not surprising," Culduin grumbled to himself. Finally, the flint sparked, the arrow lit.

May the Maker see the scroll destroyed. He kicked the ragged door in and took aim at the Inquisitor, who did not hesitate to charge.

The second flaming arrow caught the priest, mace high, in the shoulder, right at the joints of his banded mail. The neckline of his cloak kindled. He still brought his mace sailing for Culduin's head.

Culduin ducked. His tabard and mail yanked tight across his chest.

The Inquisitor's charge fanned the flames that licked over his cloak's collar. He yelped, skidded to a halt, and batted at the fire with a spiked gauntlet.

"Time to go!" Iriscendra said.

As Culduin once again rushed skyward, clutched in the talons of the little dragon, the sight of the writhing Inquisitor shrank from view. The flicker of firelight shone out the front window of the Inquisitor's hiding place.

"See, I knew I found the right elf!" Iriscendra said.

"Admit it, I was pretty much the only elf standing at that point."

"Well, there was that." She climbed higher, circling the battlefield.

Rolling drums rumbled from the south. Culduin strained his weary sight that way and found distant columns of soldiers on the wide road to Bilearne. They flew the gargoyle flag. No matter what he had accomplished, there was battle yet to fight. But Queldurik's next wave of recruits was not upon them yet.

Culduin's dragon rescuer banked, and he caught sight once again of Ecleriast and Queldurik. Flail met shield in a thunderous crack, but the two opponents faced off alone. All the fiends had fallen. Or fled? Culduin could not know. Both the remaining fighters' movements dragged, sluggish and exhausted.

The field of protection around Queldurik's forearm flickered and went out. Culduin grinned.

"Get him, Vinyanel!" Iriscendra squealed. They landed on the tiled roof of a building about five hundred paces from the battle.

A fey smile pulled Ecleriast's weary mouth crooked, and he flashed the Sword of the Patron around in an upward swing that blurred the blade with its speed. Queldurik gestured to block, but this time, to no avail. The glassy blade swept through Queldurik's forearm, then along his ribs, and through the joint of his shoulder. His green-plated arm flew free of his torso in pieces.

Culduin's eyes stretched wide. Could he possibly be bearing witness to the end of a cult that had wrought so much ruin over so many generations?

Queldurik stumbled back, equally wide-eyed. "Priests!" he cried.

Ecleriast swung the Sword again, its blade singing through the air in a chord of fell beauty. Queldurik's flail interposed, only long enough to deflect the stroke before Ecleriast cleft asunder the haft of his opponent's weapon.

Red-robed figures scrabbled from another toppled building to the left of the battlefield, and they encanted as one: *Echthu Imannirah!*

A green slash cut across the ground between Ecleriast and Queldurik. Searing light blazed up from the crack as it spread to encircle the one-armed commander.

A boom so loud that it plunged everything into deaf silence rocked the tiles beneath Culduin's feet. A pillar of emerald flame erupted from the circle where Queldurik stood, and the earth around it bucked. Ecleriast flew back. A giant wave roiled toward Culduin, a wave of stone, spreading outward from the roaring column of flame.

Chunks of Bilearnean architecture broke free and stormed toward Culduin and Iriscendra in a gale. Culduin spun, his only thought to bail from the roof. The tsunami of flying rubble struck. The force of the impact threw him skyward. From there, he knew no more.

47

Clinging

*D*anae lay in bed long after the morning rumbled into motion in the Underkeep, the third morning since they had heard news of the Windrider crash, but newer rumors spoke of the tide turning in the allies' favor. She kept her coarse woolen blanket over most of her face, leaving a scant pocket where she could suck in fresh air, but made sure no one might call her bluff of slumber and summon her to work. She simply had no heart for the tasks. What was the point of meandering through a day where she had no hope of making anything right?

She drifted back and forth over the river that separated wakefulness from fitful dreaming, the noises of the Elgadrim working around her wending their way into her subconscious.

"The enemy retreats . . . the last of the wounded should caravan in shortly . . . the elven Windriders, simply fantastic, there are no other words!" A silver dragon wove through her dreams, reawakening the heart-pounding terror she had felt in seeing it the first time. The voice

of Vinyanel Ecleriast chided her not to waste time. Culduin's prone form lay in a pool of deep-red blood in a cheerless, gray courtyard.

"Nay, to my wonder, I have weathered the storm . . ." Culduin's voice echoed over the image of his still body.

Danae's eyes fluttered open, and the tatters of Culduin's words pierced her.

"My thanks for your concern."

The lilting accent of those words was assuredly not Elgadrim. There were enough elves about, so it was no longer a surprise to hear the Delsin fluidity of speech.

"Have you seen a strawberry-haired Radromirian girl? Petite, pretty . . . an excellent chemist."

Danae thrust her body upright. She flung the blanket from her body and scanned the chamber. The cots remained; the familiar handful of workers moved from task to task. Soldiers passed through the room, bearing stretchers of wounded. The gates at the front of the Underkeep stood wide, and blinding sunlight streamed through.

Against the light, two figures approached, but in silhouette. The taller of the two sported the wide bulk of plate armor. The daylight edged the shorter figure's wavy hair in a copper gleam.

Danae bounded from bed, barefoot and fleeter than any reservations she once might have entertained. She shouldered her way through the soldiers, healers, and stragglers that stood between her and the entry to the chamber. Just as the figures in the light turned toward her, she grappled her arms around Culduin in a ferocious embrace.

Culduin's posture was stiff at first, but the rigidity in his muscles melted after a moment. He clasped Danae with strong arms. Here was an embrace that offered security, but not as a father holds a child. No, in the power of his arms, a force of wild potency swept through her. How would she let go?

Finally, after a long enough time that it became obvious all in the vicinity were staring, High Lord Ecleriast not excluded,

Danae lifted her head from Culduin's chest to gaze up at his battle-weary face. A layer of grime darkened his skin. Scratches crisscrossed his cheeks, the blood from them only perfunctorily wiped aside. Yet, as his eyes met hers, his weariness drained away to be replaced with relief and quiet joy.

"You're alive!" Danae whispered, somewhere between laughter and tears. "You're really alive!"

Culduin smiled. "Yes, against great odds, it appears as though I have been spared."

Their gazes locked. Culduin's eyelids grew heavy. A tingle, more captivating than any signature, roared through Danae's body as her breath shortened. She reveled in the obvious might of his battle-hardened muscles.

Culduin lowered his head and gently slid his hand under Danae's jaw to tilt her face up toward his own. His nose brushed along hers.

"Master Caranedhel!" a voice called. An elven surgeon, splattered in a fresh layer of blood over dried remnants, tugged at his arm.

Culduin turned his head, and Danae's knees weakened. She clutched his shoulder to steady herself.

"Thank Creo for another medic. High Lord Althoron of the Wardancers is beyond my aid!" The surgeon jabbed a pointing finger across the hall.

With a low growl, Culduin released the embrace. He stalked after the surgeon and out of sight.

Danae cupped a palm on her forehead. Her mind reeled, full of swirling giddiness and shock. A thin thread of frustration at a sweet moment lost wove through it all.

"Mistress," High Lord Ecleriast said, breaking Danae's crestfallen examination of Culduin's departure. "Where is your mentor? Master Caranedhel told me he did all that might be contrived for him, before he was called away to battle."

Danae swallowed. "You mean Praesidio?" she stammered,

her face suddenly aflame with heat. "Oh, he's here." She led the elven commander down the row of bunks to where Praesidio lay, unwaking for so many days, grayer, gaunter than ever.

Lord Ecleriast raked his tousled, platinum locks away from his face. "I am surprised he has clung to breath this long."

"It's long been held that he needed miracles," Danae said. "And I'm too new to the discipline to know what to ask, other than Creo spare him."

Lord Ecleriast smiled, softer than Danae had imagined him capable. Lines of wisdom and depth creased around his mouth, and his violet eyes lit with a subtle fire. "Then you have done your part. I suspect he would have long ago departed were it not for your earnest supplication." He knelt beside Praesidio's cot, lifted his chiseled face toward the Underkeep ceiling, and closed his eyes.

"*Creo mindheri se corpethe, doulenet is pa tumne altur.*" Lord Ecleriast murmured. His gauntleted hands glowed in a nimbus of azure light. The light grew and flared, and he placed them on Praesidio's crusted chest. The Virtus's signature burst across Danae's mind, heart, and flesh, its sensation joyous and somber all at once. The illumination surged blindingly before dissipating in shower of sparks.

When Danae's vision cleared, Praesidio drew in a deep breath and turned his head to her. She clapped her hands over her mouth.

He smiled weakly. "Thanks be to Creo for pulling me back from the threshold of the next life, for long I tarried there!" Praesidio looked to the warrior at his side. "High Lord Vinyanel Ecleriast." He clasped his fist over his chest, though he lifted his arm to do so with a sluggishness that betrayed lingering weakness. "You've changed little in two centuries."

Lord Ecleriast grinned and shook his head. "Two and a half, if I recall correctly. But what's fifty years between elder races? I bring you healing only as Creo gives, as a thanks for a kindness once done to me by one Master Aulus."

"Who's master Aulus?" Danae whispered.

"My father," Praesidio replied. "It's a long story."

Danae stared in wonderment. Oh, to have centuries to learn the art of being Creo's magnificent vessel. But being the simple girl she was, she would have to settle for whatever years he granted her and make the most of them.

---

*A*fter a full afternoon, overnight, and another day of surgery and healer's work, Culduin stomped through Bilearne's empty streets. Smoky darkness shrouded the thoroughfares. He took a well-aimed kick at whatever debris happened to stand in his path. His march carried him through the ruins of the city's northward gate.

He offered a nod to the haggard gatekeeper who stood with a polearm gripped in his one good hand. The other hung in the fetter of a sling.

Just beyond Bilearne's scorched walls sprawled a vast encampment of silvery tents, their gossamer sky-blue banners fluttering in the breeze. A few voices drifted on the same wind. His brethren sang low songs of valor and of homegoing. At the far side of the encampment, a huge pavilion sheltered the Windrider battalion mounts as they healed from their ordeals, Ecleriast's silver dragon included.

Culduin marched down the central alley between the tents, where Thalius stepped out to meet him.

"You return to us," Thalius said. He took a hard look into Culduin's face. "What is this? It did not go well. She was not pleased to see you."

"What have you to eat?" Culduin said.

Thalius smirked. "Have it your way. Come, I have half a pheasant I roasted and some spring onions."

They ducked into Thalius's tent, where a pewter plate of the food he promised sat upon a crate and two bedrolls stretched across the floor. Culduin plunked on the ground and shoveled a few bites of the fowl into his mouth. Even cold and prepared with Thalius's lack of skill, the savory meat exploded with gratifying flavor in his mouth. How long had it been since he had properly eaten?

"Are they not feeding those in the Underkeep?" Thalius laughed. "I am surprised you stopped short of swallowing that, bones and all. Now, has the food put you in better humor?"

"Slightly." Culduin regarded Thalius from beneath lowered brows. "And the provisions over in the Underkeep are short, so I did not avail myself of them. Not that I had time anyway, with all the wounded."

"They put you right to work, then."

Culduin swallowed a chunk of dark meat. His glance darted to the tent wall. "Essentially. How goes it with the allies?"

"The human forces report they continue to push the Tebalese back north, though companies of fiend-binders regroup upon occasion and hold the enemy's retreat from becoming a complete rout." Thalius sat on a cushion and leaned back on his elbows.

Silence ensued, punctuated only by Culduin's knife grating on his plate as he scooped up the last mouthful of the onions.

"And Durik?"

"Since the priests opened the portal around him," Thalius said, "he has not been seen. Ecleriast has vowed to chase him across every plane and dimension, if need be."

"The coward." Culduin snorted. "Suddenly short an arm, Durik thought better of his haughty presence on the field."

"I might be haughty too if I could overturn a square league

of earth, even in retreat." Thalius rolled his eyes. "But you stall. Out with it, little brother. Did you see her or did you not?"

Culduin dropped the plate with a noisy clang on the crate. "Only for a moment."

"And?" Thalius held out a beseeching hand.

"Must you pry from me my failures?"

"If you would rather just stew about it, be my guest."

Culduin blew a huff. "Very well. I got to the complex, and scarcely after I had passed the gate, Danae barreled into me, barefoot and clad in a dressing gown. She gripped me with a fierceness I had not dreamed probable."

"I suppose things go downhill somewhere from here, because at the moment, this story has promise." Thalius sat up and propped his forearms on his knees.

"I drew her to me, we exchanged a few 'oh, good, you lived' sort of obligatories, and there I was, right on the cusp. I had her! I could feel her tremble against me. She flushed and her breath was short. And just in the moment before signet met seal, did not another medic fairly drag me from her?"

Thalius opened palms to the sky. "Ah! Could it have been so urgent?"

"And so Commander Althoron's sucking chest wound stole the moment, and I despair of ever having the convergence of circumstances again."

"You should have laid the medic low and gone back for what you were after."

Culduin scoffed. "That would have set just the mood."

"You would be surprised, brother. Determination goes a long way in a woman's eyes."

"You shall have to forgive my lack of assertiveness in this arena, then." Culduin rubbed his eyes with the heels of his hands. "For my hesitancy and my blundering, I now have the moment seared into my memory, kindling a fire I have no means of quenching."

"You need to kiss more girls." Thalius leaned back on his hands. "What a shame for one missed kiss to plague you so."

"Thank you, no," Culduin said. "I have no desire to rival your record in heartbreaking."

Thalius pressed his fingertips to his chest in a melodramatic performance of wounding. "Woe unto me for how many young lives I have ruined. You weigh it all too heavily, Culduin."

"*You* weigh it short. It matters, Thalius. More than anything I have faced in life thus far. Mock me if you will, but you do so only because you have found no mate so worth pursuit so as to understand."

Any rebuttal Thalius might have offered broke and fell from his lips. The spark in his eye mellowed. "You may be right, little brother. It may be as you say." He draped an arm across Culduin's shoulders. "The time will come. Did you not seek her after the work was finished?"

Culduin sighed. "She had been situated in better quarters, and an Elgadrim woman named Helvia informed me Danae had just dropped off to a well-earned sleep. I do intend to find the location of these quarters in the morning."

Thalius nodded. "That is good. For now, however, I suppose you are just left to kicking things and dreaming."

Culduin rolled his eyes. "Familiar comrades in my position." He forced himself to his feet, though his legs shouted their protest since he had allowed them enough respite to recall their deep fatigue. He groaned and stretched. "Before I manage to get comfortable, I suppose I had better get back to work."

"You have assignments here?"

"Nay, brother. Our medics have those here well in hand. I have arranged for an extension of my furlough, that I may remain where I belong, even after our battalion moves out."

Thalius cast Culduin a knowing smirk. "Among the humans."

Culduin nodded. "Among them, and beside one in particular."

"Who am I to begrudge you this facet of your calling?" Thalius clasped his brother's shoulder. "You'll stay in touch, when you can, of course."

"Of course," Culduin replied. "Thank you for understanding. Make my case with Luidriana, will you not?"

Thalius saw Culduin to the edge of the encampment. They exchanged a tight embrace, then turned and lost sight of one another in the post-battle gloom.

48

A Deadlier Objective

*B*a-al Hilekar tapped the vial of powdered skulls with a clawed finger while he circled it over the basin of bile and cursed water.

"*Echthu, monnimet al dunask,*" he murmured. "*Echthu, Ba-al Zechmaat, dag legrash.*"

Tiny bubbles wriggled up the sides of the basin to burst on the water's surface, increasing in number until the liquid sizzled under a fine foam. He stared at the green roil until it parted in the center and drew back, to reveal the shimmering visage of his liege. Ba-al Zechmaat glowered behind a bare stone altar, his banded arms crossed over his chest.

"Who dares interrupt—oh, it's you, Hilekar. What took you so long?" Ba-al Zechmaat said, his voice echoing in Hilekar's mind.

Hilekar clutched the basin's sides. "Human troops are slow to settle in."

"Settle?" Dark creases scored Zechmaat's frown. "What need is there to settle in, when I am sure they plunder and revel?"

"You have had no word from His Dark Highness?" Hilekar swallowed.

Zechmaat paused. His eyes narrowed, though their glow intensified. "Lord Queldurik has not seen fit to bring me revelation."

Amidst a grumbled string of epithets, Hilekar contemplated tipping the basin and disrupting the channel between himself and his superior. Queldurik's loss of his right arm and subsequent unraveling of the Tebalese strategy was his own doing. Why should Hilekar incur Zechmaat's wrath as the bearer of ill news? But if he said nothing now that the topic was afoot, Zechmaat would deem him craven and strip him of title. Or worse.

"My Great Ba-al, the men are wary and unsettled, as we are in retreat."

"Retreat." Zechmaat grimaced as though stricken with reflux. "You had Mystrin's sword in hand and Queldurik himself in your midst. How is retreat even possible?"

"About Mystrin's sword . . ."

Zechmaat slammed his hands on the surface of the altar, and flames erupted from his palms to lick over the stone. "I extended you more mercy than you deserved when you lost the girl at the tournaments of Scraga." He quieted. "I will not ask this more than once: Where is the Sword?"

"The . . . Delsin have it, Your Eminence." Hilekar delivered the response with as flat a tone as he could muster, despite his visions of every manner of painful punishment. "They sent their infernal Windriders to aid the Elgadrim."

"Windriders. Just perfect. And do any of our allies know of this, other than you and me?"

"Word is spreading."

Zechmaat spun and marched away from the altar, out of the range of Hilekar's scrying basin. Before Hilekar had the chance to resolve himself fortunate and break the Curse of the scrying basin, Zechmaat stomped back into view.

"And what of our secondary objective in the Bilearnian siege?"

Hilekar drew a breath. "The infidels pushed our forces from the city before we reached the library square. However, I have a plan to access the library after the Elgadrim's vigilance turns to thoughts of rebuilding."

"It had better be good. A twofold failure will seal your eternal torture, Hilekar."

"My only inclination is to serve." Hilekar cast his glance to the ground. Seething heat coursed through his veins.

"I understand that most of the lesser fiends returned to the spiritual realm during the battle anyway. You are stripped of your command."

Hilekar winced. "You are merciful, my liege."

"With your newfound free time, you will devise the cunning to accomplish the secondary objective." Zechmaat jabbed a finger toward him. "Fail me in this, and the whole of our long-crafted campaign will be for naught."

Ba-al Hilekar bowed. "That will not be the case, my liege. Our necromancers' means of deception is, so far, working quite well. I assure you, I will deliver to you the key to opening the Algondolith Portal."

"I hope your confidence is not misplaced." Zechmaat leaned in so the scrying basin framed the glow of his narrowed eyes. "Drex tells me the augmenter we need is nearly ready for binding."

Hilekar licked his lips. Oh, to be an indispensable part of the plot that would finally bring Creo's pathetic following to ruin.

"Oh, and one final thing, Hilekar," Zechmaat said. "That girl. The augmenter's daughter? She's pissed in my potions one too many times. The sooner you split her on an altar, the better."

ABOUT THE AUTHOR

Rebecca P. Minor is an author, artist, and nerd herder who constantly perpetrates her hare-brained schemes on her long-suffering three sons, husband Scott, two cats, and various fancy rats. Her ideal life involves writing and selling books from a vardo, but for now, she'll settle for planning the next adventure from her suburban home outside Philadelphia.

ALSO BY REBECCA P. MINOR

NOVELS

Curse Bearer , The Risen Age Archive, Book 1

Divine Summons, The Windrider Saga, Book 1

A Greater Strength, The Windrider Saga, Book 2

Valor's Worth, The Windrider Saga, Book 3

SHORT STORIES

Beyond Price

Wish Wary